Deadline

JUDY MCDONOUGH

Judy McDonough

Cover Design and Interior format by The Killion Group
http://thekilliongroupinc.com

ACKNOWLEDGEMENTS

Jennifer Bray-Weber. My amazing editor and friend for being honest with me and teaching me so much in the process. Thank you for handling my meltdowns with gentle compassion and for understanding my frustration. . .all of my frustration. I could not have done this without you. You are a true rockstar.

Nina Cordoba. AKA, the Query Fairy. Thank you for working your magic with my blurb. It's difficult to summarize a story that has already been summarized by someone else, but you managed to make it sound even better. For that I sing your praises and wonder what it must feel like to be so gifted.

F. Anthony Musgrave, PLLC. Thank you for being readily available to help me escape the claws trying to drag me down.

My Street Team. Jenny, Noel, Jenine, Noelle, Harriet, Jayne, Krystal, Jenn, Gail, Kama, Kristin, Dana, Michelle, Wanda, Tria, and Jennifer. Thank you for pimping me out. Your support and enthusiasm means the world to me and keeps me going.

Momma. Without you I would never have finished the legwork of this long and frustrating process. You spent hours on the phone listening and offering suggestions, told me what was good and what wasn't, encouraged and bragged to everyone you know. Thank you, Momma. You're my biggest fan, and I love you with all my heart.

David Rojas, JD. Thanks for sharing your legal ninja skills without hesitation or fees to a chick you hardly knew. Sorry I bombarded you with questions so soon after meeting you.

The Northwest Houston RWA chapter. Thank you for holding my hand and guiding me through the dark when I was clueless about my next step. Jenn, Stacey, Rhonda, Jan, Will, Robin, and Raven. I owe you so much.

My former publisher. Thanks for getting me started in what I hope will become a flourishing career.

Sue Quiroz, Regina Carpinelli, and Heather Graham. You guys have given me my first taste of opportunity and enjoyment in this public career and I can't thank you enough for your guidance, attention, and friendship.

DEDICATION

For my boys—the big one and the little ones.

Thank you, Mike, Riley, Reece, and Rowen for sacrificing home cooked meals, play time, cuddle time and anything else that may have suffered so I could finish this story. Most of all, thank you for your patience, encouragement, and pushing me to write, for not letting me quit, and for telling everyone you know about my books.

I love you.

ONE

The oyster shell gravel crunched beneath the worn tires of Caroline's Jeep Cherokee as she pulled into the long driveway of the huge plantation home. She squinted through the torrential downpour to compare the address on her map to the golden numbers strategically placed between the majestic columns. Caroline had never seen rain like this. She'd grown up in Arkansas, only one state away, but the raindrops here were different. They were gargantuan and the intensity had strengthened since she'd stopped. *Great.*

Her heart still pounded from the almost-accident she narrowly avoided just after crossing into the tiny town of Golden Meadow, Louisiana. That would've been a fun one to explain. *"Honest officer, I swerved so I wouldn't hit the person standing in the road. . .in the pouring rain and darkness. . .in the middle of nowhere."* Unbelievable.

She still had no clue who it was or why he or she was there, but when she'd stopped screaming and looked out her back window, whoever she'd nearly creamed had vanished. Yet another creepy incident to add to her list of unexplainable episodes. Caroline couldn't ignore the hairs standing at attention on her arms. This spooky bayou was already getting to her and she hadn't even stepped out of the car yet. She had to pull herself together. No time for crazy right now. As much as she dreaded it, she had a mission to accomplish. She was about to rock Eddie Fontenot's world.

It was nearly impossible to see the house number for the giant raindrops slapping her window like water balloons, but she finally confirmed she was at the right place and groaned. She instantly wished she'd stayed at her mother's house in Arkansas. *Damn Trevor for making me do this! Damn him!*

After two years together, you would think she'd be used to the spontaneous, sometimes moody architect's crazy ideas, but since she'd accepted the two-something carat rock weighing her finger down, she had to admit Trevor had been a different person. Caroline stared at her ring finger and wiggled it so the diamond caught the light from the nearby gas lamp. It was fabulous. Not quite square, more rectangular and it sparkled like the stars on a moonless night.

Caroline remembered something her best friend said in an argument over three months ago. Kristy's words still stung as if she'd just said them.

"Perhaps you should look up a more accurate definition of gentleman. He most certainly does manipulate you. You're just too blinded by the rock to see it."

Was she blinded by the rock? No, she didn't care about material things. Maybe Kristy was right, maybe Trevor did manipulate her sometimes, but Caroline loved him. She'd been with him long enough to know she was *in* love with him. She and Trevor had a great relationship.

He had talked her off the ledge every time she thought she'd had enough of college. His patience while pulling all the late nighters tutoring her in advanced math, the romantic dates and high-end concerts of her favorite bands, and his ability to keep her focus on the goal. He'd pulled some strings through his friends who now worked at the University to

2

help her get the professors she really wanted. Also, the never ending physical attention and awareness she absorbed every second they were together. They trusted each other, rarely fought, and she loved him. Every defined inch of the naturally bronze skin he'd inherited from his Native American ancestors.

Her body tingled remembering their last date before she left when he described the deliciously erotic ways he would rock her world on their wedding night. He could hardly keep his hands off her when they were together. Her heart thrummed with anticipation, and nerves, of their wedding night, but she had no doubt Trevor could handle her with care. "This ain't my first rodeo" were his exact words. She forced herself not to think about the number of rodeos that helped him perfect his ride.

Just to be cautious, and to prevent her discussion with Eddie from focusing on her new bling, Caroline slipped the ring off her finger and tucked it safely in the inside zipper pocket of her purse. She wanted the focus of this meeting to be why Eddie left, not Trevor's money or the assumption she was shallow and blinded by lavish gifts. Trevor loved Caroline and wanted to spend the rest of his life with her; it just so happened he came from money and had a great career. Sparkly rings and wealth weren't important to Caroline, and clearly not why she agreed to marry him.

However, Trevor's temper had reared its ugly head more since she accepted the lovely token than it had the whole two years they'd been together. Curt texts and voicemails when he couldn't get hold of her, she'd overheard an unsettling phone conversation between him and his dad, and worst of all, he'd booked a church and reception hall without even talking with her—the bride, about it!

Caroline sighed, fogging her windows a little. Perhaps he's been this way the whole time and she only noticed now since she'd promised to be with him forever. She wondered about the real motivation behind him sending her down here. Trevor explained it as wanting her to make amends with her estranged father before they got married so there would be no surprises in the future. No skeletons in the closet or unfinished business. Whatever. Caroline shook her head and rubbed the twitching muscle in her eyebrow. She could respect that, but had a feeling his reasoning stemmed from the contents in his boxers.

She stared at the beautiful home she never had a chance to enjoy—or even visit! Her heart raced with anxiety as she clenched her jaw. She loved her fiancé, but this was ridiculous. Love doesn't have conditions, right? Why did Trevor care if her father was included in their lives anyway? He hadn't been in her life in twenty-three years, why should it matter now? Why was she sitting in Eddie's driveway having this crazy internal battle?

She knew why. Her uncontrollable curiosity. She wanted to meet him. She needed an explanation. Answers. She needed to know why he never felt the desire to know about her or how she was doing. She needed closure.

Time to finally hear his side of the story. Her mother said he offered her money, but she wouldn't take it. Emily hadn't wanted a pity-driven severance package, and her mother, Caroline's grandmother, was ill, so she moved back to Arkansas to be closer to her parents. That was Emily's side of the story. Caroline wondered if her mom's version of the story was, in fact, influenced by her role as the woman scorned. She assured Caroline her father wasn't the coward she'd made him out to be. That he was a good man easily influenced by his pushy family.

Apparently Eddie was fine with Caroline not being in his life, and now she expected him to what? Open his arms and accept her into his home for an extended period of time? She at least wanted to know why he hadn't pressed for joint custody rather than moving on with his posh lifestyle pretending she never existed.

She had the whole summer to work things out with him, but hoped all would be resolved in less than a week. Maybe that's all it would take and Caroline could get on with her life. Maybe even as quick as the weekend.

Her mom's encouragement to form her own opinion of her dad and his family was understandable, but Trevor's suggestion to stay the whole three months and come back just before the fall semester was insane! She already missed him and his comforting embrace. Besides, what could she possibly have to talk about with the man who abandoned her, obviously still doesn't care about her existence, and lives in a gigantic house full of people she doesn't know? At least, she assumed it was full. It's awfully big for him to live there alone.

She swallowed the stinging ball of nerves at the realization of not knowing if she had a step family. That part had her almost as nervous as confronting the man she never cared to meet at all. Almost. She would just play it by ear and gauge his reaction to her presence.

Caroline admired her father's home and wondered how long it had been there. Had to be at least a century. It reminded her of the recurring dreams she'd had, like a scene from *Gone with the Wind*. She sighed. Maybe Trevor was on to something. Caroline could understand where he came from in one sense. It's best to clear the air and start with a fresh, clean slate. No sullen, bitter past haunting them. Trevor had a good relationship with both of his parents, from what she could tell by the two or three occasions she had seen them. In the long run, when she and Trevor had kids, it would be nice for them to have both sets of grandparents. Okay, enough stalling.

As she opened her car door, the stinging rain battered her exposed skin. She tried to open the faulty umbrella, but it wouldn't latch to stay open. She grumbled under her breath and opted to run to the porch. So much for making a good first impression. She'd look like a drowned rat by the time she reached the front door. On her third step off the crushed shell surface of the driveway, her boot sank in about three inches of mud.

"Gah! Great. Fan-freakin-tastic!" She held the broken umbrella over her head to protect as much of her hair as possible, but it was no use. Nothing was going her way. She glanced up at movement from the corner of her eye and squinted through the rain. Someone observed her, completely motionless, from a dark third-story window. *Terrific. So much for no one witnessing my embarrassing moment. Oh well, might as well go all in and finish the humiliation.* Caroline slung the mud from her boot the best she could as she limped her way toward the house.

She approached the broad, extravagant front porch, and studied the old mansion. It reminded Caroline of her latest dream of the auburn-haired girl dressed in a flowing white nightdress who wept uncontrollably while frantically scribbling in a journal. The details of the one she'd had a few nights ago stuck with Caroline despite the blinding headache that always accompanied these particular dreams. She had admired the mahogany canopy bed and the sheer white material cascading from the beams. A perfect complement to the exquisite matching dressing table and mirror. The immaculate fixtures and decor were stunning and very elegant.

Before the girl busted into the room, Caroline had peeked out the bedroom window to the male voices she'd heard below outside. Men stood in the yard smoking cigars and wore skinny bow ties, and a couple had on bowler-style hats. Like in her previous dreams, the characters were dressed in fashion reminiscent of the mid 1800s.

Caroline peered through the darkness to see if the yard looked the same, but the much-too-brief slack in the rain prohibited her from seeing much past the porch. Unable to shake the niggling déjà vu feeling, she faced the house again and soaked in the ambience of the historical home. The flickering gas lamps flanking the front door lit the area enough for her to see that the black paint covering the wooden shutters couldn't hide the scars from years of abuse provided by Mother Nature. Though somewhat battered, they reflected the care and hard work it took to preserve the brilliance and luster of the historical structure. Caroline brushed her fingertips across the clean, white paint that covered the regal columns and admired the matching white rocking chairs.

Amazed by the grace and beauty of the home, Caroline peeled the tail of her soaked shirt from her skin to ring out the saturated fabric, and knocked the remaining mud from her boot. She flipped her head over and fluffed her wet hair, tossing it back again to smooth it while she silently stoked her courage. Procrastinating, her eyes scanned the structure one last time. The house had obviously been built to last. Man, Trevor would die over this incredible architecture. If the gorgeous outside provided any indication of how prestigious the inside would be, Caroline was way out of her league. And she was about to find out.

With a deep breath and a silent prayer, Caroline blindly wiped beneath her eyes to remove any possibly smudged mascara and murmured, "Here goes nothing."

Another deep breath, she finally knocked. After a few moments, the beautiful solid wood door slowly opened. A small-framed woman in her mid-forties stood at the threshold. Her deep blue dress matched her vibrant eyes and contrasting pale skin. Her hair was swept up in a French twist, but the shiny, dark spiral curls that framed her petite features didn't hide her unmitigated surprise. She stared at Caroline for a long moment as if she recognized her. The tiny woman's eyes never left Caroline's face, and she shook her head like a child shaking an etch-a-sketch toy.

"Um, hi there. I'm looking for Eddie Fontenot." Caroline tried to force herself to smile, but the nerves made it difficult.

The woman stared blankly. "Certainly, wh-who may I tell him is calling?"

"Um, you may tell him his daughter is here."

The lady, with her mouth still hanging open, hesitated. "Uh, sure, one moment please."

As the woman turned to go get him, Caroline heard a man's voice. "Who is it Delia?" The door still open, she could see him coming down the stairs. Suddenly, she couldn't breathe. When the woman didn't answer him, he asked her again, "Delia, who's at the door?"

Delia said nothing and turned to look at her through the open door. Caroline's heart threatened to burst from her chest. His eyes followed Delia's and he stopped cold when he saw her.

Delia choked out a whisper, "She says she's your daughter, sir."

TWO

Time moved in slow motion for the next few minutes. He glided over to the door wearing a shocked, deer-in-the-headlights expression. He stood in front of Caroline, his mouth slightly open as he sucked in a breath. She exercised every ounce of control not to cry, scream, look away—move. This was her father. A male reflection of her own face. She stared back into his eyes as they had a miniature standoff to see who would make the first move. . .or blink.

Eddie's voice came out as a whisper. "Caroline?"

She couldn't move or speak. Thankfully, he continued.

"I can't believe my eyes. Is it really you?"

She swallowed the lump in her throat, "Hi."

His face transformed from cautious to elated as he bounded forward to hug her. "Tell me you're not a hallucination that could disappear at any moment."

He hugged her tightly, held her back at arm's length to take her in, and squeezed her rigid frame again. Caroline, slightly uncomfortable with the sudden contact, let out an awkward, involuntary sound causing him to step back abruptly.

"Oh my goodness, I'm so sorry! Please, come in out of the rain! Can I get you anything? Water, sweet tea, Coke." Eddie observed her wet clothes. "Maybe a towel? Delia, go get her a glass of tea and a fresh towel to dry off with, please?"

Caroline set her dysfunctional umbrella on the porch and stepped inside. She slipped off her wet boots, careful not to smear mud all over, and looked everywhere but at her father. Maybe if she avoided eye contact she could gather her thoughts and wouldn't embarrass herself by saying something stupid. She finally looked at him and her freshly stoked courage dwindled. The admiration on his face caused the lump in her throat to feel like a softball, so she smiled awkwardly and tucked a lock of hair behind her ear as she bent to move her boots out of the way. When she looked up again, Delia rounded the corner with a giant, sparkling glass of iced tea and a fluffy hand towel.

"It's sweet, I hope that's okay."

"Perfect, thank you." Parched, Caroline quickly drained the glass until there was nothing left but ice. Their eyebrows raised in surprise and Delia took the glass from her.

"I-I'll go get you a refill."

Eddie hadn't stopped looking at her since she made eye contact with him. She averted her gaze while drinking her tea, and now tried to find the courage to look back up at him. Incredibly nervous, everything about the situation was awkward and uncomfortable, and try as she might, she couldn't face him yet. She chickened out and continued dabbing her face and hair with the towel. She pretended to study the elegant hardwood floors, trying to remember her mother's pep talk and what all she'd planned to say.

He spoke first. "Caroline? Are you alright?"

The gentleness in his voice shocked her. Her mother's favorable description of him flitted through her mind. She instantly found the courage to look at his face, pulling her shoulders back confidently. "Yes, I'm fine. Thank you."

Delia proudly chimed in as she rounded the corner with a fresh glass of tea. "She looks just like you, Mr. Fontenot. I was completely shocked when I opened the door. She's just. . .stunning!"

Without removing his gaze, he spoke in disbelief. "I can't believe you're really here." His voice barely audible. He was trying not to cry. He cleared his throat a few times and rubbed his palms together.

Aww, man. Please don't cry. . .don't cry. My walls are already shaky. I can't handle seeing a grown man cry.

He slowly reached out to caress her face, and Caroline had to force herself not to flinch away from his touch. She didn't want to offend him, and the gesture seemed innocent enough. Besides, his palms were clammy. At least she wasn't the only one sweating bullets. She needed to move this along before the awkwardness took over and she ended up dashing back to her car and peeling out.

"Eddie?" She saw him flinch so she quickly recovered. "Oh. W-would you rather me call you Edward, or Mr. Fontenot? I thought my mom said you preferred Eddie."

His expression turned worrisome. "No, Eddie is correct. Or, if-if you want to, if you're comfortable with it, you can call me Dad."

Not yet, slick. That's got to be earned. Her mom was right. She did look just like him. They had the same hair color, eyes, face shape, nose, cheek bones. . .the same face! His salt-and-pepper hair was handsome, very debonair, and he was taller than she expected, probably just under six feet. She wasn't quite ready to call him Dad, though. That had been a foreign term her entire life.

"I am still trying to convince myself I'm not dreaming, and you're really standing in my house right now. You are so beautiful. You've grown into such a lovely young woman."

Slightly uncomfortable, she studied the antique bench near the door. She smiled and nervously tucked her hair behind her ear again.

"Thanks."

"Goodness, where are my manners? Please, won't you come in and have a seat?" She followed him into the formal living area and sank into a big oversized chair. She knew, like her, he must have hundreds of questions for why she suddenly showed up on his doorstep, but for the moment they just sat in silence observing each other. He didn't look like the evil villain she'd always imagined capable of abandoning his family. He seemed very welcoming and friendly, and Delia's presence helped relieve the tension. However, she had disappeared and now the silence had become an issue. Caroline finally broke the trend.

"So, you're probably wondering why I'm here, huh?"

He smiled. "Yes, I am. But, honestly, as long as it's not serious and you and you're mother are okay, I don't care about any other reason. I'm happy you're here." That was refreshing. . .and annoying. She was glad things were going smoothly, her unannounced visit hadn't angered him, but a small part of her wanted him to be angry. He was much too happy and polite for an estranged father meeting the child he disowned and ignored her whole life, and how dare he pretend to care how her mom was doing. She could tell he knew she had another shoe ready to drop, and he appeared to mentally brace himself for it.

"Well, first, I need to apologize for not giving you a heads up that I was coming. That was rude of me, but I honestly didn't know what to say if I called. I just. . .came."

12

He nodded, still cautious. "Certainly. No apology necessary. We have—"

"There's more." She hated interrupting anyone, but if she was going to get this out she needed to get to it.

His mouth snapped closed and he straightened up with a more serious expression. "Of course. Please, continue."

"You should know it wasn't my idea to come down here." His shoulders sagged a little so she quickly continued. "I'm engaged, and my fiancé wanted me to meet you and give you the opportunity to come to our wedding. He thought it would be a good idea to start our lives with no underlying issues that may rear their ugly heads in the future."

He nodded. "That's very mature and responsible."

What does he know about responsibility? Responsible people don't run out on their families.

"Yes, well, you should also know I wasn't thrilled with the idea. I haven't exactly been your biggest fan."

Eddie closed his eyes for a moment and Caroline felt the pain her words had caused. When his eyes opened, his green irises glistened like polished emeralds. "I understand. I gave you no reason to be."

Just when things were getting good, Caroline's stomach growled. Snarled was more like it, considering she hadn't eaten anything since she left her mom's house.

"Are you hungry? Delphine is probably finished with dinner by now. I would love for you to join us."

"Famished. Thank you."

"Great. How long will you be staying with us?" Caroline's heart twitched. Had he already assumed she would stay in his house? And who, exactly, was us? "That is, if. . .if you'd like to stay here? Did you have plans to stay elsewhere?"

"I haven't made reservations anywhere. Like I said, I just came. I assumed there would be vacancy at a nearby hotel, but if you have the room and don't mind, I could stay here. Clearly we have a lot of ground to cover, much to discuss, and it would probably be quicker and easier to get to know each other if we weren't separated by miles to the nearest hotel. That's completely up to you, though. I don't want to impose."

His relief answered her before he ever opened his mouth, and he smiled as he stood. "Of course, sweetheart. We have more than enough room. How long will we be allowed to enjoy your company?"

"Let's start with the weekend, and go from there. I have nothing I have to be back for until September, but I don't want to overstay my welcome. Once I fulfill my purpose for coming down here, I'll get back to my life and let you continue with yours. Hopefully we'll both be one friendship richer."

"I understand your reluctance to stay as I'm sure this is very difficult for you, but I hope to be more than your friend when you leave here. We haven't. . .I mean, I hoped. . ." Eddie sighed and ran his hand through his hair. "Look, I realize I haven't earned much right to. . .be your father or claim your time, but I selfishly want to invite you to stay longer. You will not wear out your welcome and. . .I-I really want you to stay."

She hesitated and glanced at the door, "I don't—"

He stepped closer, commanding her full attention and weakening her nerve. "Please. Please give me the opportunity to redeem myself." He rubbed his forehead, clearly torn with her hesitation of him. "I know you owe me nothing, but you're here. It's an answer to my prayers that you're standing in front of me right now. I'm asking for a second chance. Please, say you'll stay at least a week."

Eddie was persistent, she had to give him that, and she did want to learn more about him. "We can discuss it over dinner."

His charming smile pushed against the walls surrounding her heart. He clearly wanted her to stay, and the joy he expressed just because she didn't flat out reject him was sweet. Her emotions were all over the chart, but she still needed some answers. An explanation. What has he been doing all these years? Obviously something more important than her. Caroline wondered what excuses he would give for his irresponsibility. They'd have to be really good for her to want to stay any longer. He'd better be creative because she already had one foot out the door ready to bolt.

Delia met them in the dining area with two fresh glasses of iced tea. The mouthwatering aroma that filled Caroline's nose prompted another growl from her impatient stomach.

"You hungry, beb?" Delia chuckled and winked.

"Starving." Caroline smiled, amazed how at ease she felt around this woman.

"Well, you're in for a treat tonight. Delphine's got some blackened tilapia and rice pilaf fuh ya. You like fish?"

Caroline nodded, not quite sure who Delphine was, and admired the beautifully set table with burgundy placemats, matching napkins, and fleur de lis napkin rings. Delia, who had discretely slipped from the room again, must have used the fine china because Caroline had never seen dishes this exquisite. A long rectangular table with enough seats for ten people filled the room, but tonight it was just her and Eddie eating. Delia and Delphine both ate in the kitchen.

"Do they always eat in there, or is it just because I'm here?"

"No, they usually sit at the kitchen table together."

"So, you would have been sitting at this big table all by yourself tonight if I hadn't shown up?" He stared at his salad for a moment as he knocked a crouton around with his fork.

"No, I don't usually eat a formal dinner, I mostly snack here and there. Sometimes I'll take a plate up to my office." He obviously didn't want to talk about his eating habits and changed the subject.

"So, you mentioned a wedding."

Caroline nodded, trying to read his expression. Was that sadness? Shame? Perhaps for not being around to approve any guys she dated or married. Who knew?

"Congratulations. What's his name?"

"Trevor Callahan."

"Where's he from?"

"Chicago."

"Chicago?" His eyebrows shot up. "I thought you and your mom were living in Arkansas?" Caroline bristled from his ignorance.

"If you'd kept in touch you might have known I received a scholarship to the University of Chicago where I've been for the past four years." Eddie paused for a moment, his fork halfway to his mouth. Caroline immediately felt bad for her outburst, surprised how easily her temper influenced her response. Her eyes fell to her lap as she fingered her napkin, but she refused to apologize. "This fall is my last semester and I'm due to graduate in December."

Eddie remained silent until she looked up again. Sadness seeped through his mask as he studied her face. Her mother was right. He beat himself up for not being more involved in Caroline's life. However, he didn't address her snide remark.

"What's your major?"

"Nursing."

16

He nodded with approval. "That's a good major." She didn't necessarily agree with him and he could tell. "Nurses are needed everywhere." Caroline didn't respond. "You don't like nursing?"

"Not particularly, no."

"Why'd you choose it?"

She shrugged, "I like it all right, I guess. It's not exactly my passion, but it will pay the bills. I want to help people, but I think I lack the special untaught skills it takes to be a good nurse. Don't get me wrong, I'm excelling in my courses and completely respect the profession, but. . ." She picked her glass up and brought it to her lips as she mumbled, "It takes a special kind of person to be a nurse. A good one, anyway." The sweet tea was ice cold and soothed her parched throat. Delicious. She forced herself not to smack her lips in satisfaction and added, "I turn green with catheters and I don't do vomit. Can't clean it up without adding to it."

She smiled and shook her head. "My mom tried to warn me that I wasn't cut out for the profession, but I didn't listen." Caroline held his gaze. "She's usually right about those things. . .and people." Eddie shifted in his seat and wiped his mouth, still avoiding her attempt at confrontation and nodded slightly.

"Emily was always very intuitive." A reminiscent smile curved the corner of his mouth.

Why is he smirking? What's that about? The twinge of an unfamiliar emotion coursed through her. Uncertainty? Anger? Hope? Hope? For what? No, certainly not hope. An unexpected wave of chilled air cloaked her skin with goosebumps. She casually dabbed her bare arms with the towel Delia had given her as if she was still damp so Eddie wouldn't notice her discomfort. Despite the incredible aroma sneaking from the kitchen, Caroline felt strange. Like the air around them was electrically charged.

"But you must be doing alright to be so close to graduating?"

She sighed and took a drink, chalking up the indescribable feeling to nerves. "It's too late to change my mind now anyway."

"Life's too short to be stuck in a career you don't enjoy, Caroline. Believe me. I've seen some talented people waste their lives working in the wrong profession."

Delia refilled their tea glasses and winked as she served the main course. Caroline was thankful for the distraction. A welcome break from attempting to forge a relationship that had never existed and trying to pinpoint the cause of her weird sensations. Plus, it kept her from spouting more sarcasm coming across as a bratty teenager. Eddie's avoidance of her questions unnerved her. Why couldn't he at least acknowledge his dereliction as a father? She struggled to think of a way to bring up the huge elephant in the room. How to ask him why he left. The painful growl from her midsection demanded priority so she dove into the plate of delectable food, taking no prisoners.

She savored the first bite of the blackened tilapia. Her tastebuds rejoiced as the Cajun spices danced on her tongue. She'd never tasted anything so delicious, and she made a point to chew slowly to enjoy every flavor of that first bite. However, she inhaled every bite after that. Her gluttonous thoughts were interrupted with a surprising question.

"So, apart from college and a fiancé, what all have you done with your life?"

Her golden opportunity. Now, to decide the best way to answer such a loaded question. This was her chance to demand answers to the questions that consumed her for so many years. Caroline slowly leaned back in her

18

chair and took a drink to wash down her most recent bite. Then, she wiped her mouth and took a slow, calculated breath. Time to unleash hell.

THREE

"My life. You want to know what I've done with my life?" She folded her hands in her lap and conjured the courage from deep within.

"Well, let's see. After my father abandoned my mother and me, I was pretty much raised by my grandparents, so my mom could work two jobs to support us. Then, I would have grown up never learning the basics of sports, cars, hunting, fishing, or guys, but thank goodness my grandpa was around to teach me." Eddie watched with no expression, no surprise, as she continued describing her life without him.

"I went to church with my mom and grandparents every time the doors were open. Two days after my thirteenth birthday, I watched my grandpa shatter into a million pieces when my grandma died because they had the kind of love people only dream about. I witnessed just how strong my mother was as she picked up the pieces of her grieving father and took care of him, two jobs, her teenage daughter, and herself without once complaining." Caroline couldn't be sure, but she thought she caught a brief glimpse of despondency in Eddie's expression. She wondered how well he'd known her grandfather.

"I attended church camp that summer where I met my best friend, Kristy. Unlike my mother, I'm introverted and shy, so I didn't have much of a social life outside of my friendship with Kristy. She lived in Tennessee, but we kept in touch through the years. I worked my tail off to maintain a 3.9 grade point average so I could apply for a scholarship to the same college she chose. That's where I met Trevor. He's handsome, charming, and successful, and managed to fill the black hole left in my life by my estranged father so long ago. Plus, my mom adores him."

They had a short standoff as Caroline waited for some sort of reaction from him. Nothing. No anger, sadness, happiness. . .nothing. His apathy drove her crazy. Even more nervous now, she swallowed the remaining moisture in her mouth to soothe her burning throat. Emotion boiled her insides, and she knew if she didn't calm down she would lose it and start crying. But why wouldn't he say something? Address her allegations? Explain or at least defend himself!

"How is your mother?"

Caroline nearly choked on the tiny bit of saliva she'd conjured up and coughed in shock. He watched, intrigued, as she took another drink. "Seriously?" She dabbed her napkin against her watery eyes, the traitorous tears threatening to overflow, and mumbled, "Like you care."

Eddie's eyes narrowed slightly and he opened his mouth to speak, but Caroline's temper got the best of her again. She swallowed back the lump in her throat and stubbornly tilted her chin. "She's great. More than great, no thanks to you. Do you even know when my birthday is?"

His brow raised and shoulders squared. "Of course. You were born May thirteenth at eight-oh-four in the evening after your mother endured twenty-one hours of exhausting labor."

Speechless, Caroline honestly didn't know what to say. Her pounding heart was desperately trying to escape from her chest.

"So tell me about your fiancé. What does he do in Chicago?"

Whoa, talk about changing the subject. Caroline cleared her throat, hoping she didn't appear as flustered as she felt. "Um, he's an architect. He mostly does restoration designs for historical buildings so they don't lose their value and beauty, but still have all the modern conveniences."

Eddie nodded. "How does he feel about your major?"

What? We're back on that again? "He's fine with it. Trevor is very encouraging and supportive."

"Good. You deserve nothing less. Tell me, if nursing isn't really your passion, what is?" She cocked an eyebrow and shrugged hoping that would suffice, but he continued. "I'm simply curious. Trying to understand how someone so intelligent and beautiful could allow herself to be unhappy doing something she doesn't love."

"I'm good at it."

"I'm sure you are, but if you don't love it, you'll never be happy."

My happiness hasn't concerned him before, why does he care now? She pursed her lips and tried to think of a logical answer rather than what she really wanted to say.

"Happy. Hmm. Okay, well, I enjoy the more. . .artistic kinds of things. You know, like music, painting, movies—that kind of stuff. Unfortunately, I didn't realize it until my junior year, and by that point I had changed my major once already from marketing."

"You didn't want to change it again?"

"No way." She shook her head unsure if this was small talk or an inquisition. She should be the one asking the questions, right? Only, she couldn't think of what all she wanted to ask because he took over with the interrogation. "All my friends were already graduating a semester ahead of me. I didn't want to be stuck there a full year without them."

"You would still have Trevor." Caroline's annoyance had reached its peak. Why wouldn't he just drop it? "How long have y'all been together?"

"Two years. But we just got engaged in March."

"That's a fair amount of time to consider marriage. I'm thankful he made you come down here. You two happy?"

"Trevor didn't make me do anything. He asked me to do this, but it was my choice to follow through with it." *Though I'm doubting that decision now.* "We are very happy. Why would you ask that?"

He grinned and took a drink of his tea. Without looking at her he said, "Just wondering. Marriage is a pretty serious step. Both parties have to be fully committed and ready for the plunge."

Caroline felt her eyebrows twitch and knew her temper had its toes on the ledge. The stubborn bull within her had its nose in the crack ready to burst through the gate and unleash hell. "We are perfectly happy and committed, thank you very much. And I'm quite capable of making a decision of this caliber without unwarranted advice from someone who gave up his right to approve my boyfriends before I ever said my first word."

Without acknowledging her jab yet again, Eddie raised his glass to his lips. "Yes, quite. Where's your engagement ring?"

She glanced quickly at her left hand, moving it under the table once she realized she wasn't wearing it. She immediately regretted slipping it off in the car before she came in as it would come in very handy at this particular moment. While she subconsciously rubbed her naked ring finger beneath the table, a twinge of panic, or anger, settled in her gut causing her dinner to churn. She fidgeted, trying to appear calm and collected. Sure and unaffected by his challenging tone. Eddie was obviously more comfortable with this unscheduled get-together than she. "I have a ring. It's uh. . .it's in my purse. I didn't wear it while I was driving because my, um, my fingers swell and it gets. . .too tight." Stuttering. Wonderful. How convincing she must sound stumbling over her words.

Eddie replied without looking as he took another bite. "I believe you."

That was it. She'd had enough of this. She let out a frustrated huff and forcibly placed her palms on the table. "You know, I don't have to explain myself to you. You haven't bothered to be included in my life for twenty-three years, and clearly, judging by your apathy and unwillingness to explain yourself, you have no problem with your decision. Frankly, I don't appreciate your attitude and especially don't need your advice about my love life considering the source. You are hardly the example I wish to follow." She threw her napkin on the table and stood, fighting back the emotion with deep breaths and avoiding eye contact. She refused to cry in front of this man. "This was a huge mistake. I agreed to come meet you, I have, and now I'm leaving. Have a nice life, Eddie." She spun on her heel headed for the door.

He chased after her. "Sweetheart, wait. I'm still your dad."

She twirled around to face him, eyes blazing, tears welling, and finger pointing. "Don't you dare call me that. And you are not my dad. That is a position to be earned, not an entitlement simply because you knocked someone up during a teenage fling." Her quivering voice betrayed her control.

His jaw dropped, and he whispered, "That's what you think happened?"

Caroline tilted her head away from him, chest heaving and willing herself not to cry. She was so angry and still hadn't gotten any answers. She took a deep breath to gather her emotions before facing him head-on with her inquiry. She cleared her throat in a failed attempt to speak clearly as she choked out her questions and demanded answers.

"Why did you leave us? How could you abandon my mother when she needed you most? You left your wife, the woman you vowed to love, honor, and cherish, to fend for herself, working two jobs and living with her parents until she could afford to support the baby you helped create! How 'bout that commitment, Eddie?"

"Caroline—"

"Why did you never attempt to contact me, or at least check on us? Were you never curious about me? About how I was doing? What I looked like? Didn't you miss us at all?" Rogue tears slipped down her cheeks and she angrily brushed them away. "Didn't you ever worry about how my mom was able to afford to live while supporting herself and a baby without your assistance?"

The spicy fish she'd consumed rebelled in her stomach. She felt sick. And Eddie, calm and collected, simply stared at her without uttering a single explanation. She let out a resigned sigh and swept a hand through her hair, certain she looked as awful as she felt. Eddie took a step toward her and extended his hand, but she stepped back just out of his reach, rejecting his affection. It was incredibly difficult to stay angry with him when he refused to fight back. He gave her no fuel to stoke the embers of her fury. She had to pull herself together or her defenses would crumble like they always did when she fought with Trevor. She never could stay mad at him.

"Caroline—"

"My mom said you saw me when I was two." His hand slowly dropped back to his side, his wounded expression twisting the knife in her heart. Like the coward she was, she broke eye contact and fidgeted with her key ring, gathering her thoughts and speaking slowly and calmly.

"I need to know if you ever thought of me after that, just once. Did I ever cross your mind? Did the desire to take responsibility for your actions ever occur to you in the past twenty-one years?"

"Are you finished?"

Caroline glanced up quickly, anger emanating from her. She ground her teeth as her eyes narrowed, ready to end this and be on her way. Eddie wasn't the monster she expected—he was worse. She was almost fooled by his persistence and genuine desire to know her, but when she cut to the chase and demanded answers, he couldn't hide his blatant detachment. Caroline saw right through his little act and she'd seen enough.

"Who do you think you are?"

"With your food, I mean. Are you finished eating?" His green eyes filled with concern and sincerity. She'd misunderstood, but that didn't change her desire to leave. Trevor could have his stupid ring back. She refused to suffer through any more of this nonsensical torture.

"Oh. Yes, I've had plenty. Thank you for dinner. It was delicious." She briskly walked to the front door and slipped her feet into her boots.

"Please, don't leave. I've been waiting for this moment for over twenty years, but I still wasn't prepared."

She finished with the lacing and faced him. Though he stood a good eight or ten inches taller than she, it didn't hinder her resolve.

"No preparations necessary. I've seen all I needed to see. Goodbye, Eddie." Caroline left her broken umbrella on the porch alongside her now broken, rather than nonexistent, relationship with her father, and, after her first step off the porch, she paused in shock—or fear, of the menacing darkness.

Had it been this dark out here when I arrived?

Not a sliver of moonlight to be found, and the once-flickering gas lamps seemed dim with sadness. She shuddered and sprinted through the rain to her Jeep. She slipped behind the wheel, slammed the door, and pounded the steering wheel. Tears streamed down her cheeks as she started the car, and her head throbbed in the center of her forehead. Ironically, the same place her head ached in the series of cryptic dreams she'd had leading up to this trip. This disaster.

The throbbing intensified like someone had whacked her with a heavy, wooden baseball bat. She turned the radio off and the air conditioning full blast to provide, though minuscule, a bit of relief while she wept in the sticky humidity.

Her curiosity had finally gotten the best of her, and, after only a couple of hours with the man she never thought she would face, she blew it. She resented Trevor now more than ever for making her do this. Was Eddie right? Had Trevor made her come down here? She shook her head. No, she could've easily said no. Right? Caroline groaned. She should've said no.

Her emotions were scattered all over the place, and she didn't know what to think or how to feel now. Caroline had imagined fifteen different possible outcomes of this task and strategized how she would handle his reaction. What she didn't take into account was her own reaction. She hadn't handled it well at all. She wanted so badly to leave this place with answers, a stronger-than-ever bond with her father, and great news to tell Trevor. Instead, she was leaving ready to shove Trevor's ring down his throat. Caroline feared she would arrive back in Chicago with neither a father nor a fiancé.

"Screw it. I'm getting as far away from this mistake as possible." She jerked the gearshift into reverse and floored it. But through the mixture of pitch darkness, rain, tears, blinding headache, and unfamiliar curvy driveway, she managed to veer off the solid path and sank both rear wheels into the soft ground. Frustrated, she continued pressing the accelerator begging the Jeep to regain traction, and cursing herself for not upgrading to the four-wheel drive model. Unfortunately, her spinning tires sank deeper and she was officially stuck.

Banging on the steering wheel again didn't relieve her extreme frustration, and when she looked up, Eddie stood in the rain illuminated by the high beams of her headlights. Caroline dropped her face into her hands and cried when the soft knocking on her window startled her.

"Go away!"

"Caroline, please come inside," he yelled, his voice muted through the closed window.

"No! I'll sleep in my car until a tow truck can come first thing in the morning and get me out of here."

"Please. I need to talk to you. You deserve answers, and I want you to stay. Please come inside."

She really didn't want to sleep in her car, and she did deserve some answers. And honestly, she wanted to like him. She didn't want this trip to be in vain. She'd come all this way and perhaps overreacted a little. She certainly hadn't been the example of the classy, respectful young woman her mother wanted Eddie to see. Nothing had gone the way she'd planned since she arrived. It all started when she stepped in the mud walking up to the door, and now here she was in the mud again. Realizing fate was against her, Caroline finally released her pride and killed the engine as Eddie tucked her under his umbrella and helped her to the house.

"I'll get your car out for you first thing tomorrow. I promise."

Promise. Caroline glanced back up at the dark, third story window where she'd seen her observer before, but this time it was empty. Much like her heart. She pressed her eyes closed for a moment and prayed for the strength to see this through. For the strength to forgive. When she opened them again, the rain had stopped and the darkness seemed lighter.

FOUR

The seconds crept across the silence like hours amplifying her discomfort. An exhausted and somewhat dazed Caroline removed her boots again while Eddie waited patiently. She was tired, weak, and completely deflated after this evening's emotional roller coaster.

Before stepping completely into the foyer, she glanced longingly one more time at her half-buried car and wished she could disappear. Why could things never go her way? Confrontations were not a strength of hers, but swallowing her pride was even harder. Caroline did her best to hold her head high and blankly stared at the wall as Delia handed Eddie two bottles of water and disappeared again.

"Come upstairs with me for a minute."

Caroline followed Eddie up the stairs to what she guessed was his office. He motioned for her to sit on the brown leather sofa. He closed the door and pulled up a matching brown leather chair directly in front of her so they were sitting face-to-face. He reached for her hands and her first instinct was to withdraw, but she didn't. She was still angry, but stuck with nowhere else to go, and her perseverance was defeated.

Deep down she wanted to like him, and he was making it really hard not to with his compassionate regard. She didn't want her efforts to be a total waste. After all, she had driven ten hours to get here, and there was still Trevor's condition to fulfill. She talked big, but she loved Trevor and didn't want anything to stand in their way of happiness. Besides, despite her anger with his arrogant line of questioning, she desperately wanted to hear what her dad had to say. Eddie held her hands and spoke gently, looking her in the eyes the entire time.

"I'm really sorry for my behavior earlier. I never meant to offend you. The last thing I want to do is push you away with unwelcome interrogation. I owe you an explanation, and I appreciate you offering your time to allow me that luxury."

Caroline scoffed. It wasn't like she had much of a choice. Her car was axle deep in swampy mud and she had no idea where the nearest hotel was. Eddie noticed her reaction and added, "I realize your choices were limited, but I believe fate brought you here. That there was a reason you weren't able to leave. This is my second chance and I really want to make things right." He waited until she looked up to permit him to continue.

"I wish I had a legitimate and logical explanation for why I left you and your mother. I would love to be able to blame it on my job, or my family, or some other completely understandable reason for leaving the two most important people in my life—but I can't. I honestly have no good or decent explanation for you. I was young, stupid, scared, inexperienced, selfish, you name it. I was wrong. I shouldn't have left, and if I could go back and change any part of it I would. But I can't." His voice shook.

"Your grandmother had been diagnosed with breast cancer right after we filed for divorce, so I knew your mother would want to go back to Arkansas to be with her. My father was preparing me to take over our

31

family business, so even if we hadn't divorced, there was no way I could go with your mother. I didn't fight for joint custody, not because I didn't want you, but because I didn't want to make you suffer by stretching you between two families, two states—being torn between who you spent time with.

"I promise you not one single day of my life passed without me thinking about you. Not a moment when I didn't regret not staying with your mom, or at least trying to work out some sort of joint custody. I knew Emily was fully capable of taking care of you, so I just. . .let you go. I offered to give her money, but she told me she didn't want or need anything from me. I sent her some anyway in the mail, but the letters would come back unopened. She knew me well enough to know what was in the envelope, I suppose."

Eddie stared at their hands and Caroline practically saw the painful memories flashing across his face. "Leaving you was the hardest and dumbest thing I've ever done. I had a birthday card for you stamped and ready to send every year for ten years, but I never sent them. I thought it would be easier on you if I never existed. I assumed your mother would move on and remarry, and if I never intruded then you wouldn't know me enough to miss me. I will never forgive myself for all the precious memories I missed out on and will never be able to get back."

Caroline intended to be tough on him, hard and not easily swayed, but he made it difficult with his tenderness and sincerity. "Why did you and my mom not work out? Was I the reason you left? Was I the reason you couldn't get along?" Caroline felt her throat tighten and cursed herself for being so sensitive. She didn't want to let him off the hook quite so easily, but she really wanted to believe him, and her unshed tears were weakening her resolve.

32

"Caroline, honey, absolutely not! We were both very young and immature. Honestly, she grew up like she was supposed to, and I didn't. I am so terribly sorry I left you. It's the biggest mistake I've ever made, and the fact that you are sitting in my house this very moment is an answer to my prayers. Please forgive me. Please, please forgive me. . .for not being a father, a role model, a friend, or a parent. So many times I've thought about what I should say in this moment—trying to prepare for this day I knew would eventually come. Rehearsing in a mirror didn't make it any easier for me to look into your beautiful face and justify why I was a deadbeat dad. Please, Caroline. Please say you'll forgive me."

Her brow furrowed. "If you've rehearsed all these years what you would say to me in this moment you knew would come, why did you wait for me to come to you? Why didn't you come to me? My eighteenth birthday, when I was officially an adult, would have been the perfect opportunity for a reunion like that." Anger coursed through her softened veins, strengthening her courage. She stood to pace around the couch and put some space between them as she spoke animatedly with her hands.

"You could have surprised me for my high school graduation. You've had ample opportunity to make up for lost time, but you chose not to. I've hated you for so long. Until Trevor, I resisted every guy that ever wanted to date me because I was afraid to get close to anyone for fear they would leave. You chose to continue living your life as if I never existed. Why? Why, Eddie. I get that you didn't want to confuse me or make it harder on me when I was young, but what about after I was old enough to understand? Huh? What about then? You'd rather your own daughter continue her life not knowing you? Hating the phantom father figure she dreamed about at night? Wondering what was so bad about her that her own flesh and blood didn't even want to meet her, much less take care of her?"

He intercepted her pacing by putting a hand on each of her shoulders. She tried to push him away, but he forcefully pulled her into a tight hug. She struggled, but he resisted, keeping a firm grasp around her as she wailed, beating her fists against his back and ribs. The tears flowed as she yelled for him to let her go.

He spoke softly into her hair as he swayed gently from side to side trying to counteract her resistance. "I can't, sweetheart. I can't let you go again. I made that mistake once, I'll never make it again. I love you, Caroline. I've loved you from the moment I saw your beautiful, red, screaming newborn face, and even though I wasn't in your life for the first twenty-three years, I want to be in it from now on."

Caroline stopped fighting him and sagged in his embrace continuing with her emotional crash. His words penetrated her soul, breaking and mending her heart at the same time. She'd wished so many nights in her childhood to hear those words from this man, and now she finally heard them without having to ask. Caroline's body convulsed with sobs as she soaked the front of his designer shirt with her tears. Eddie's voice was thick with emotion as he continued shredding the scar tissue from around her heart.

"I'm sorry for everything. I'm sorry for the pain and struggles I caused you growing up. For skewing your view of relationships. But if you'll let me, I'll spend the rest of my life making it up to you. I love you, sweetheart. So much."

This moment topped everything Caroline had shared with any man ever involved in her life. She could not imagine how difficult it was for him to pour his heart out while she continuously resisted and fought his efforts, especially within the first hour of seeing her since her toddler years.

34

She whispered, "I do forgive you. That's why I'm here." The never ending tears continued to roll down her cheeks. Caroline suddenly realized she hadn't come only because Trevor insisted. Her final decision to come here was due to curiosity and the need to forgive. Her whole life, she'd fiercely resented her dad, and something inside her wanted to give him the opportunity to change those feelings in her heart. She was so glad she came.

"I mean, that's not the only reason I'm here. I told you, I didn't want to come at first, but Trevor asked me to drive down here and reconcile with you before we started our lives together."

Eddie pursed his lips and nodded appreciatively. "He sounds like a good man."

"He is. It's funny, I was very angry with him about it. He made it a condition to our engagement." Caroline picked at her nails. "I wasn't going to do it, but I, uh, I talked to Mom about it and she encouraged me to come."

Eddie's eyebrows shot up and his chin dropped to his chest in disbelief. "Really? Now that is surprising. I assumed your mother's opinion of me consisted of hot coals, horns and a pitchfork."

Caroline smirked. "Normally it does, but this time she said I should come and speak to you in person. Get to know you myself rather than just believe what she told me about you. . .to hear your side of the story and make up my own mind."

He snorted with approval. "You are the best gift she ever gave me, and I threw you both away. Yet, here you stand. Your mother is an incredible woman and I can see the apple doesn't fall far from the tree." Caroline looked up from her jagged cuticles to see his eyes welled up with tears. He blinked and they streamed down his face matching her own. They were both a big sappy mess.

35

They hugged tightly, neither one wanting to let go first. With the summit of this mountain attained, the levy breached, the battle conquered, they cried. They laughed. They got to know each other on a new level that neither one had the opportunity to before. Eddie held her face in his hands brushing a wild strand of hair from her eyes. Eyes she knew must be red and swollen, but seeing the admiration and gratitude beaming from his face left her without a care about her appearance.

"There's no way I could ever deny you, that's for sure." The pride bled through in his voice causing her to blush from his intense focus. If he looked hard enough, he would notice every imperfection she wasn't quite ready to reveal yet.

"I suppose I should get my stuff and bring it up to a room. Which one should I stay in?"

"You are welcome to take a look around and see which room you like the best. All the rooms on the left side of the staircase are vacant, so take your pick." She followed him into the hall to the staircase.

"Wow, you mean I could have my own wing of the house? Awesome." A bit confused, she was sure she'd seen someone watching her from a window on this side of the house. Eddie paused on the first step and smiled, clearly relieved they'd talked.

"Hey, are we the only ones here right now? You, me, the two ladies downstairs?" she asked.

"Yes, why?"

Caroline shivered from the chill creeping up her spine. "Do they come up here a lot?"

"Not really. They only come up to the third floor when they're cleaning or changing the sheets. Their bedrooms are downstairs. Why, what's wrong?" His concern deepened.

"Nothing. I just thought I saw someone looking out a third floor window earlier. Probably just a reflection or something."

He shrugged. "Probably. I'm going to call a friend real quick about getting your car out of the mud in the morning. Feel free to explore wherever you want. You won't disturb anyone."

Caroline walked through the hall of the West Wing, peeking her head into each room to see which one she liked best. She was completely baffled why no one wanted to live on this side of the house, but wasn't complaining about having her own space and privacy. The home was exquisite. A girl could get used to this, considering most of the bedrooms were nearly as large as her entire apartment.

Her body tingled strangely as she peeked her head into the third room she'd approached. A crippling sense of déjà vu encompassed her and something in her head screamed that this room was the one. She had been here before. But when? How? The hairs on her arms and the back of her neck stood up as memories from her latest dream flashed through her head. The canopy bed was exactly like the one she'd awoken in wearing someone else's clothes.

Caroline stepped farther into the room and the tingling increased. She shivered and briskly rubbed her arms. Getting soaked earlier combined with her emotional breakdown and this strange coincidence had her chilled to the bone. She couldn't believe the similarities this room had to the one from her dreams. Caroline slipped her hands through the silky canopy cloaking the bed as she remembered the last time she'd seen this place. The young red head was staring out the—Oh! The window—it was in the same place! Caroline paused, a bit of fear bubbling deep in her belly. Had she had a premonition?

As she stared out the same window, Caroline inhaled imagining she could smell the cigar smoke the nineteenth century gentlemen smoked in the yard next to a pond. She squinted her eyes through the darkness and rain for the landscape, but could only make out dim lights strategically placed in what she assumed was flowerbeds. She turned to view the room inside from a different angle.

Caroline belonged in this room. She felt in her core. As if the ghosts of the past were calling her to choose it. Only, she didn't believe in ghosts. Not completely anyway. Though the hallucination that caused her near crash tonight, the mysterious charge in the frigid air, and the creepy, unexplainable things that had happened to her over the past few months now had her questioning that ridiculous theory. This room, however, was merely a coincidence.

"Just a coincidence," Caroline muttered to reassure herself.

She gently smoothed her hand across the exquisite carving of the antique dressing table. It was very similar, if not exactly like the one the girl sat while writing in her journal. So creepy. Caroline winced as she caught sight of her reflection in the attached mirror.

"Ugh, geez. I look like death warmed over." She fluffed her hair and bent forward to get a closer look as she licked her fingers to wipe away the smudged mascara that had streaked down her cheeks with the waterfall of tears. Once she was presentable she straightened up and smoothed her clothes.

Caroline caught a whiff of a feminine fragrance. Strong, as if the person who wore it stood right behind her. She noticed an antique perfume bottle placed near the base of the mirror. She shook her head, ignoring the goosebumps that now covered her skin, and picked up the delicate glass bottle, turning it in her hands to inspect the intricate design. This must have once been a very expensive perfume, she thought.

"Just a coincidence," Caroline reminded herself.

She sniffed the bottle, but couldn't smell anything. Caroline's brow creased. Certain she'd smelled women's perfume, now she knew she was losing her mind. She sniffed it again to confirm.

"Hmm. It must be too old to have a smell anymore. How strange."

She carefully put it back where she'd gotten it and set her purse on the antique dressing table next to a large, ornate jewelry box that looked as old as the rest of the furniture in this room. Caroline wondered who it had once belonged to, but honestly didn't care. She'd chosen it strictly out of curiosity if nothing else. It was beautiful, and she couldn't wait to wake up in that canopy bed. It was every little girl's fantasy to have a bed like that. Hers included.

She hesitantly left her chosen quarters to head down the stairs. The connection she felt to a room in a house she'd never stepped foot in until today was surreal. She couldn't help but feel the recurring young woman from her dreams needed her somehow. She wanted to find out everything she could about this place and her family heritage, and that room had enough character to practically speak for itself.

Caroline suspected there was a reason she'd been having these dreams. She didn't know why, but her gut told her they were more than just dreams. A message of some sort. She wished she could find the journal she'd stumbled upon in one of them. It had made an appearance multiple times, so it had to be a key player if, in fact, these dreams meant anything at all. She may decide to stay longer than just the weekend to play detective for a while. It might be fun.

She'd made great progress with her father tonight, and believed they would someday have a strong relationship. For now, though, until she felt more comfortable with the whole situation, she would stick to the original plan to stay for just the weekend. She really wanted to explore the house to see if anything else familiar popped up, but she needed to pace herself.

First, she needed to unload her car despite the rain and mud. She stopped short, taken aback when she saw all her bags neatly placed at the foot of the stairs. Eddie, Dad, had brought them all inside and was headed up the stairs with a couple as she came down. She hadn't intended to bring all of them in considering she'd only planned to stay a few days, but she didn't want to burst his bubble by telling him that now after he'd braved the downpour to fetch them. "Thanks, you didn't have to do that. I could have gotten them."

"Don't be ridiculous, it's raining out, and I've no intentions of making you do any manual labor in this house."

"Aww, come on now, you're gonna spoil me." She didn't object, though. She was dead on her feet after this long day and desperately wanted to wash up and sink into that fluffy bed. Caroline smiled as she carried her small toiletries bag up to the room. . .her room.

FIVE

Sunlight beamed through the window, shining brightly across the bed. Caroline looked for a clock, but there wasn't one. She patted around the nightstand until she found her cell phone. 6:04. Ugh! She tossed her phone down on the soft, fluffy bedspread. Her eyes popped open when she remembered where she was.

Oh my goodness! I'm in Louisiana! I made it. Last night wasn't a dream.

After the long drive and the nerves, everything seemed foggy. She rubbed her dry, aching eyes, a result of the crying last night. As she lay there replaying everything that happened, her thoughts were interrupted by someone singing outside directly beneath her window.

She rolled out of bed, nearly falling flat on her face. Apparently the fatigue had officially caught up with her. Freezing, she put on her robe and shuffled her stiff legs to the window. This was definitely the same window in her dreams. Were they premonitions? No, premonitions predicted the future. Her dreams were of something that happened a long, long time ago.

She peered outside and spotted a very muscular, tan body clad in a white tank top and cut off jeans. Between Trevor's naturally bronze skin, Eddie's sun-kissed hue, and this guy's tan, Caroline felt like a vampire. Even pale Delia had more color than Caroline. If everyone in the bayou was as tan as the folks she'd seen so far, her milky skin would shine like a new penny around here. He pushed a wheel barrow overflowing with dirt to a space just beneath the window. She couldn't see his face for the ball cap he was wearing. He came too close to the house for her to see him anymore.

Clearly not thinking, she leaned forward quickly and slammed her face into the glass of the closed window. She rubbed her aching forehead, thankful no one had witnessed her smacking her face like an idiot.

Great going, dummy. You're starting the day out gracefully.

She waited for him to come back out, but he must have been planting. She could only hear him now. He was singing a song she'd never heard before. It was smooth and bluesy, but it also had an edge to it similar to Jon Bon Jovi. Definitely a sexy voice.

She smelled coffee and some sort of bread baking. Blueberry muffins? Whatever it was smelled heavenly. . .especially the coffee. She hurried to the bathroom down the hall to take a shower before anyone could see her looking like death warmed over. After her strenuous, anxiety-filled evening, her muscles rebelled by knotting into baseball-sized clumps. While the scalding water worked to relax her tension, Caroline's mind raced.

Exactly how many rooms does this mansion have? How many people live here? Are there antique treasures hidden in nooks and crannies all over the place like in some of the movies I've seen?

She couldn't wait to explore her family's historical home. She appreciated the updated showers and wondered when the bathrooms had been restored. She bet Trevor would love to get hold of this place. This was right up his alley. Next to the shower was an antiquated porcelain claw foot bathtub that looked like it had been there for a very long time. Still in great condition, though. The home had been very well maintained over time.

An image of the guy who had attacked her in the first terrifying dream invaded her thoughts. His black, stringy, chin length hair, sinister laugh, and the ice cold blue eyes continued to haunt her. She wondered about his significance in this mystery. Her stomach twisted with the possibility that these people might have once really existed and possibly lived in this area. . .if not in this house!

This new anxiety quickly undid some of what the hot water had accomplished relaxing her tightly wound body so she shut off the water and the negative thoughts. She quickly dressed for the day before any more crazy thoughts crept into her mind.

Caroline towel-dried and whipped her hair into a loose ponytail at the base of her neck and scurried down the stairs. The little bounce in her step surprised her after the dread she had felt before—and shortly after– her arrival. Strangely enough, after unloading on her dad and releasing all the pent up emotion, she was comfortable here. So far.

Her eyes scanned the open areas around the spacious floor plan and saw no signs of life on her way to the only space she was sure about from her brief observation last night. The kitchen. Apart from the two women, Delia and the other woman with a D name, she appeared to be the only one awake. She surprised them when she walked through the kitchen doors. They had been laughing about something and instantly stopped when they saw her.

"Oh, good morning, Miss Caroline, would you care for some breakfast?"

She adored their southern hospitality. Something she'd missed in Chicago. "Yes, ma'am, please. It smells wonderful!"

The other woman introduced herself since Caroline hadn't formally met her last night. "G'mohnin' bebé, the name's Delphine and I do the cookin' 'round here. You eva need anythin' you just holla, boo, ya heard?" Delphine, that was her name. The accent intrigued Caroline and she wanted to hear more.

"Yes, ma'am, I'll be sure to do that. Supper was delicious. Thank you so much."

"Oh, you welcome, bebé."

She enjoyed a delicious cup of a New Orleans Blend coffee with a bit of flavored creamer. Kristy always teased her about her sissy creamers, but she didn't care. She liked coffee, but not without sugar and at least milk. The brew was so delicious she went back for a second cup.

"This coffee is incredible. Why does it taste so much better than the other brands?"

"It's the chicory, beb. Gives it that extra lil' kick." Delia laughed, "My daddy always said it'd put hair on your chest."

"So dat's what caused it. I knew it wudn't dem hormones. Call my doctah. I need my money back." Delphine winked and cackled as she flipped a pancake.

Caroline laughed with them as she soaked in her surroundings. The coffee really was amazing. The bitter chicory contrasted perfectly to make it rich and robust. Strong but smooth, it was delicious. She enjoyed listening to Delia and Delphine's verbal sparring as they joked and laughed after nearly every sentence. Their happiness was infectious.

The accent down here wasn't like the twangy southern accents portrayed in the movies, it was like nothing she'd ever heard. The dialect was interesting and unique. Similar but different to the stereotypical New York accent, yet perfectly fitting for the exotic and mysterious bayou region. The inflection and cadence as they delivered each sentence had a French infused melodic flow which caused it to almost sound like another language, but Caroline understood them. Mostly. She wanted to sit there and listen to them longer, but they had come to a lull in their conversation.

"Delia, who was the guy singing loudly beneath my window this morning?"

She and Delphine giggled, "Oh, that's Beau. Don't mind him, boo, he's the gardener. He loves to sing for us and we love lookin' at him—I mean, listening to him." She winked and they all laughed. Now Caroline really wished she had seen his face. Sure, she'd already promised her heart to someone else, but it wouldn't hurt to look.

Eddie sauntered into the kitchen. "Good morning, ladies. What's all the giggling about? Hmm? Checking out the gardener again, Delia?"

Delia scurried around collecting the dirty dishes as she quickly said, "Oh, no sir, we was just filling Miss Caroline in on who woke her up this morning."

He looked at Caroline and frowned, "Did he wake you? He usually starts early so he can be done before it gets too hot. I can ask him to wait a bit before he starts."

"No, no it's fine, really. Honestly, the sun woke me up first. The singing was just what got me out of bed. Curiosity, I suppose." She sheepishly grinned and he smirked, triggering her defenses. "What?"

"Oh, nothing. What would your fiancé think about your curiosity?" he teased playfully.

"Oh, come on, I'm engaged, not dead! I like a little eye candy every now and then, too."

"Eye candy? Is that what the kids are calling it these days?"

She sipped her coffee, "More like ten years ago, but yeah."

He smiled admiringly. She could tell he was grateful she was there. "Good morning, Caroline. I can't tell you how lovely it is to see your smiling face in my kitchen. . .after all these years."

She couldn't explain why, but things felt right. Like the missing link in her life had been restored. "Good morning, Daddy." She kissed his cheek and swore his chest puffed with pride. Who knew one little word could make such a difference in someone's life. She headed toward the stairs to finish unpacking.

"Uh, Caroline. Do you have a minute?"

She stopped quickly after only two stairs up and turned. "Sure, what's up?"

"Last night, in my desperate attempt to convince you to stay, I forgot to disclose a very important detail. I did get to see you when you were two-years-old."

"Yes, my mom told me that. She never told me why, but she did tell me you hadn't seen me since I was two."

He hesitantly continued, his face serious. "I mentioned last night that I'd left when you were only six-months-old, but when you were two, I remarried and requested you guys come down here for the wedding." He cautiously studied her face for a reaction.

"That's great. I'm glad you were able to find someone who made you happy. Where is she? What's her name? Why wasn't she here last night for dinner?"

He grinned, amused with her interrogation. "Her name was Elizabeth and she passed away a long time ago."

"Oh. How sad! I'm so sorry for your loss."

Eddie's head tilted slightly and his eyes brimmed with emotion. "Thank you. That's very sweet. It was a real tough time."

He paused and Caroline held her breath wondering what else he had neglected to tell her. "It wasn't too long before I met my current wife, April. And, um, well. . ." He didn't look away, focusing intently on her reaction. "You have a brother and a sister, Caroline." Her stomach churned preventing her brain from forming a proper response, so she simply stared at him. "Unfortunately, they spent last night with friends and April went to New Orleans this weekend. They'll all be back today so you'll be able to meet them."

Caroline didn't know how to react. "Oh. Okay." She needed time to digest this new information, so rather than blurt something embarrassing, she slowly started up the stairs. He hadn't told her this information last night probably for fear she would storm out of his life without looking back. And he would have been correct. He waited until things were okay between them to drop this bomb. Smart, Eddie.

She'd always wanted siblings, but her mother never remarried. Now she had two, plus a stepmother. Excitement rather than resentment bubbled in the pit of her stomach regarding her family in-a-box. Halfway up the staircase she turned to find Eddie looking pensive and worried. "You know, I'm really glad I came down here. I am. I'm not resentful anymore. Now I'm really eager to learn more about you and your family. . .my family." His shoulders sagged with relief as she made her way to her room.

Back at her window, Caroline looked out hopefully, but Beau must have finished. She frowned, disappointed she missed her chance to see what Delia and Delphine were talking about. Caroline couldn't imagine anyone more beautiful than Trevor. He was by far the most handsome specimen of a man she had ever seen.

She took in the furnishings of her new room in the fresh light of the morning sun. Could it all be the original furniture and fixtures from when the house was built? They were in pristine condition. And what was the significance of the window? Caroline noticed something on the left side of the glass, just above the middle window pane. An etching. She rubbed her fingertip across the raised edges of the perfect script as she made out the letters, shocked when she recognized her own initials. Her heart raced as she brushed the pads of her fingers repeatedly across the peculiar find.

R. C. F.

No way. Coincidence? Fate? How is this possible? As she scraped her fingernail across the ridges of the scratched glass, the hairs on her neck prickled. Caroline couldn't imagine why her initials were branded in a window she'd never seen before. In real life, at least. Did they belong to the girl from her dream? Who was she, anyway? Was the poor woman enslaved in her own home? Perhaps leaving her mark like a prisoner in a cell?

Caroline's mind effectively blown, she finished her coffee and unpacked her things as she resolved to learn more about this mystery. If it was indeed a premonition she'd had, fate clearly sent her a message, but what? It was Trevor's idea for her to come here, maybe the message regarded him? Maybe God knew deep down she needed her father in her life. She didn't know or understand how, but Trevor's silly condition had some significance to it, and now she was determined to find out what.

Portions of her dreams had literally come to life in this antebellum home, and the puzzling ginger-haired woman who, if she really existed, possibly left clues all around for someone to find. That, combined with the packaged family and all the interesting people Caroline had met thus far, successfully piqued her raging curiosity.

Miss Scarlet in the conservatory with the sexy gardener's shovel. Caroline snickered to herself as she hung her clothes in the closet. She loved a good mystery and had a feeling she'd be staying the whole three months.

After calling Trevor and her mom to say good morning and let them know she arrived safely, she left a voicemail for Kristy letting her know she'd made it, and slipped away unnoticed to explore the house. Three stories of open hallways crowning a beautiful winding staircase. Caroline recognized the immaculate hand carved woodworking of the scrolled stair rails from spending quality time with her grandfather in his workshop.

As she descended the ruby-carpeted steps, she slid her hand over the smooth mahogany railing, inspecting its brilliance. This type of precision and detail could only be crafted by someone who took pride in his talent and poured his time, sweat, and heart into his work. The quality a reflection on his good name.

The first floor consisted mostly of the extravagant entertaining rooms. The formal and informal living areas, formal dining, parlor, kitchen and breakfast nook, though this particular breakfast nook was much larger than any she'd ever seen. The second floor housed bedrooms of all types and sizes, several of which were occupied, further piquing her curiosity. Also, a huge bathroom with another antique claw foot tub, and a lovely library stocked with enough books to rival any bookstore.

The third floor, where her chosen room was located, also had bedrooms and a solitary but elegant bathroom, as well as a large space that had been renovated into a theater room with stadium seating and surround sound. Eddie's centrally located office sat just to the right of the stairway preceding a hallway of several locked doors. Caroline wondered what kind of secrets or treasures needed locking up, but opted not to snoop. . .yet.

Satisfied with her brief exploration of her temporary new digs, she enjoyed lunch with Delia and Delphine before finally stretching across her comfy bed for an afternoon power nap. She hadn't quite fallen asleep when she heard the front door open. She stayed in her room to allow Eddie the chance to explain to April what was happening. That is, if it was April who came through the door.

Caroline heard a very adolescent-sounding voice. She peeked from her room and saw a young boy with shaggy brown hair wearing headphones. He flipped through his iPod while pacing around downstairs. Eddie strode into the foyer, handed him something, and tugged the headphones out of his ears to talk to him.

"Listen, I don't want you over there all day, understand? I have someone I want you to meet, but she's unavailable right now, so make sure you're home for dinner. Be here by six o'clock and no later, got it?"

"Yeah, Dad. I got it."

Her brother. This was crazy. She considered going down to meet them right now since she was awake, but chickened out. She didn't know what to say and wasn't quite ready yet.

Just as this reality was sinking in, a teenage girl with long blonde hair came prancing from the kitchen. "Can I have some money to go shopping with Lindsey? She said we're going out to eat for lunch, too, and I don't want to be the only one there with no money."

"How much do you need? Will forty bucks cover it?"

She smiled, but it wasn't the same as Eddie's. She must take after her mom. "Thanks, Daddy!" The blonde girl looked at the boy and her smile faded. "Come on, Remy, it's time to go." Remy didn't budge. He was still playing with his iPod. She yanked the headphones from his ears, nowhere near as gently as Eddie had.

"Hey! Stop it!"

"Come on! Lindsey is waiting and I still have to drive you to your little troll's house! Let's go!"

"Hey, you two will get along or neither of you will be going anywhere this week. Is that clear? Claire, make sure you pick him up and get back here by six o'clock, do you understand? I have a special surprise for everyone tonight and I want you all here. Got it?"

She rolled her eyes, "Got it. We'll be here." They walked out the door and there Caroline stood. . .utterly astonished.

I have a brother and sister. Claire and Remy. I love their names.

Only her second day and she already discovered an entire family she'd never known. She still had to meet them, and frankly that terrified her. Nervous excitement laced with uncertainty rumbled through her chest, so she focused on her reason for coming down here. A simple task to find closure had bloomed into a potentially loving relationship with the big family she'd always wished she had. And, of course, the bonus hot gardener, Beau. Wow, this was a lot to absorb all at one time. She wondered how they would react to her. Guess she'd find out soon enough.

While unpacking her things, Caroline pulled her engagement ring from the inside zipper pocket of her purse and quickly slipped it on before her stroll around the grounds. She told Eddie her plans, and he offered to give her a tour of the grounds, but she told him she'd rather explore on her own for now. She needed time to think and absorb everything that's happened, and a solitary walk through nature was the perfect way to do that. She sensed his disappointment and appreciated his desire to spend time with her, but she really needed some alone time to reflect and explore this new spectrum of her life.

Eddie drew a small map of the outbuildings and trails so she wouldn't get lost. Lost? Was the property that big? She hoped she wouldn't regret her decision to go alone as she changed from flip flops into a pair of sneakers, and grabbed a bottle of water just in case she wound up walking several miles. From the sound of it, there would be plenty of exercise involved.

As she stepped out, her dad offered her a warning. "Watch out for alligators."

Caroline froze. "Seriously? There are alligators on the property?"

He chuckled. "This ain't Chicago, honey, you're in the Bayou now. There's always a possibility of gators in the woods. . .and snakes, too."

Now she was officially a little freaked out. She glanced at the hand-drawn map and randomly chose a trail to start her journey. The grounds were fairly clear with nothing special to see except the wild dogwoods woven throughout majestic oak trees. The path was sparsely lined with a mixture of cypress and super tall pine trees with squirrels jumping from branch to branch overhead.

The day was already hot and the skies clear, but after the storm last night, the humid air was stifling and burned her lungs as she felt the need to gasp for breath. However, she enjoyed the freedom of being outdoors. The soothing sounds of birds chirping, and the winds whispering through the leaves were calming, like a lullaby. Scents of pine and earth rooted her to the natural world around her.

After traveling that lovely but monotonous path, Caroline needed a change of scenery, and studied her map. If she cut through to the left she would intersect a different, more curvy trail. Caroline paused to take in the scenery. Incredibly beautiful oak trees dripping with Spanish moss stood like quiet sentinels towering protectively over fragrant, blooming magnolia trees. The landscape surrounding her was like a painting come to life. This was exactly what she expected, only she imagined it a little more swampy and less woodsy. It was gorgeous. Maybe this trail would lead to more interesting things.

Honestly, she knew exactly what she was searching for. After the room that was so much like the one in her dream, she knew she was looking for the trail she'd been on when she overheard the argument in her most recent dream. She cut through the brush to make her way across another trail.

She snapped twigs and crushed pine cones with each step, just like in the dream, searching for that lone, citrus tree under which she discovered the journal. She reached the other trail without finding the specific setting or the tree she needed. Caroline wished her conscience, or sixth sense, or whatever it was stalking her for the past few months, would give her a little insight and lead her in the right direction. Oh well, maybe next time.

She shook her head at the ridiculous thought. Looking for landmarks as if her dreams were literally coming true. Wishing for some otherworldly power to lead her to a fictional dream-inspired citrus tree to find a journal that probably never existed. Stupid. All just a coincidence with the room, canopy bed, and window. . .in the perfect place. . .with the same view and antique dressing table nearby, and her initials engraved in the window pane. Coincidence. Right.

Caroline followed that trail for another ten minutes with no idea how far from the house she was, or if even still on Eddie's property, and wiped the sweat dripping from her hairline. Thankful she hadn't stumbled on any alligators, she chugged her water, mentally complaining about the miserable heat and humidity. She wished she had a cool place to rest before heading back to her dad's house. Caroline had grown accustomed to Chicago weather, so her body wasn't used to this climate. She fluffed her shirt to cool her overheated body when she heard a voice in the distance. She tried to decipher which direction it was coming from, but it bounced off the trees. She couldn't tell where the sound originated.

She checked her map to see if she could pinpoint any of the outbuildings her dad had drawn, but she wasn't exactly sure which trail she was on now. If she guessed correctly, there should be a small one on this path around two more curves. She saw a roof as she rounded the second curve. Caroline stopped walking to listen for the voice again, but heard nothing.

She walked closer to a small log cabin, careful not to surprise anyone. Over the dull hum of the A/C unit, she heard music coming from inside. Caroline looked around and spotted a big log near the corner of the cabin and rolled it beneath the window. Using her makeshift step stool, she peeked inside.

The small kitchenette held a bistro-style table and two chairs. To the left, close to the front door, a sofa and a recliner faced a flat screen television mounted on the wall. Apparently somebody lived here, but didn't seem to be home. It could be a guest house, but not likely with the air conditioner running. Caroline hopped off her perch and checked the front door, hoping to ask the tenant for five minutes of relief. She knocked, and no one answered, but the door wasn't latched well and opened slightly.

A gust of cold air caressed her face luring her inside for a more thorough helping. Caroline breathed deeply and sighed, longing for more and gave in to her powerful desire to have a bigger dose of the refreshing air conditioning. Unsure why, insanity, she supposed, she stepped inside and hoped whoever lived here wasn't home. Jazz music blasted from the back room, probably a bedroom, but she didn't care. She only needed a moment to cool off before her long trek back and then she'd be on her way. She took a good look at the cozy little cabin, drawn to its appeal and hummed along with a song she recognized.

"Hello? Is anyone home?" At least the occupant has good taste in music.

As if someone else controlled her limbs, she inched farther into the space noting the remarkable order and cleanliness. The rejuvenating frigid air cooled her sweaty skin and she could finally breathe normally again. The tiny cabin should've seemed cramped, but it wasn't. There was a place for everything and everything was in its place.

Insanity. That had to be it. She had to be insane wandering into this house, but she couldn't stop herself. At least that might work in court when she was arrested for trespassing.

She walked into the comfortable living area clutching her water bottle and nervously looked around. *Why am I doing this? Turn around and walk out. Now. Don't be stupid, even if nobody's here, this is someone's home.*

Caroline should've listened to her conscience, turned around and left as if she'd never been there. But something kept her walking. A powerful force pulled her down a short hallway, past a closed door she assumed was the bathroom, until she had stopped outside the source of the music. The bedroom. The door was only open a few inches. If someone was in there, she at least wanted to apologize for trespassing and thank them for letting her share their air conditioning. She gently knocked and slowly pushed it open to take a peek. The room was empty. Strange that someone would leave with the music blaring.

A neatly spread Queen size bed centered the room banked by a chest of drawers with two picture frames on top. A gun rack with four rifles hung on the wall. She stared at the weapons for a moment. Specifically the bottom rifle. It was more of an assault weapon rather than a hunting rifle.

She didn't know who lived in this cabin or how close she was to the plantation house. But she desperately wanted to see what the occupant looked like and then get out of there. She stepped into the bedroom to look at the pictures in the frames when she heard the unmistakable pop of the shower shutting off. Oh, crap! There is someone here!

Caroline's heart leaped into her throat and she quietly, but quickly headed back down the hall toward the front door. Just as she reached the closed door she'd assumed was the bathroom, it flung open and a wet, very muscular, very naked, male body emerged. Wearing a towel draped over his head, and humming to the music, he slammed into Caroline, nearly knocking them both down. She fell to one knee and dropped her water bottle as she reached out to catch her balance. It was then she realized both of her hands were gripping his bare, wet hips.

Caroline screamed. He gasped and grabbed at the towel with one hand and her arm with the other hand, but his hands were wet. She slipped from his grasp and ran past him, sprinting toward the door to get out of the house before he could attack her. She hadn't seen his face and the moment she realized he was naked, she closed her eyes, but not without first getting an eyeful of everything else. Using her wet hands like blinders on a race horse, she only opened her eyes to see the floor while running for the door. Exiting his house, she yelled, "I'm so sorry!"

She did not look back as she ran full speed to the plantation house in panic and complete humiliation. She faintly heard someone yelling after her, but dared not slow down or turn around. She had an advantage since he was naked. Oh, boy was he naked.

SIX

Trevor's hands aggressively roamed the contours of her voluptuous curves igniting their passion with every inch of progression.

"So sexy." His whisper, combined with a gentle nip to her ear lobe prompted a sensual moan from her sending arousing tingles shooting through his body. "I want you, baby. I want you bad."

The entire atmosphere in the room had changed, his heartbeat pounded in his ears. He was much more skilled with foreplay than she was, but he couldn't wait to teach her how he liked to be pleased. Her receptive moans were satisfying enough. For now. Her eyes closed, and he knew she'd been holding her breath while he kissed down her neck, his hands simultaneously roaming her body and pulling her close. He pressed Caroline's body against his to show her how she affected him. Judging by her reaction, he'd successfully sent shockwaves of desire all the way to her toes.

He continued his traveling kisses, working his way back up to her wanting lips. He grasped her hair at the nape and tilted her head back to expose the sensitive skin of her neck, nipping gently with his teeth. Her chest heaved as she panted for air.

Her irresistible eyes blazed, causing a deep groan to rumble from his chest.

"Trevor. . ." she begged.

The invitation in her tone was all he needed to take control. She dropped the bouquet he'd brought as he scooped her into his arms. She wrapped her legs around his waist, and he carried her to the couch, never removing his mouth from hers.

Her hungry tongue and faint taste of cinnamon induced a high he hadn't felt in a long time. Lost in the moment, he nearly exploded when she tangled her fingers into his hair and bit his bottom lip. He stiffened all over, his grip tightening around her thighs as he pressed into her harder. A sly grin stretched across her face, her jungle cat eyes sparkling.

Trevor always loved her bashful, blushing responses when she witnessed what her touch did to him physically, but this look was different. She seemed to thrive on his reaction, thirst for it. If she only knew how hard he was struggling to control himself with her looking at him that way. When she touched him like that. He was up for the challenge as long as he was allowed to enjoy the fruits of his labor someday. The sooner the better. He would show her what pleasure felt like and unleash that feral beast he knew existed beneath her innocent, untainted exterior.

The sensuality and warmth from the soft curves of her body was intoxicating. He shed his stiffly pressed blue dress shirt. Hunger filled her eyes, her tongue slipped across her lips. This was a side of Caroline he'd never seen before. Trevor wanted to throw their abstinence agreement out the window and ravage her like a starved lion.

"Mmmm, you taste and smell so good. I can't get enough." He ran his smooth hands over her tight yoga pants, clawing at the stretchy material, his desire reflected in his heavy-lidded gaze. "I want you so badly. All of you."

She pressed her eyes tightly closed. "Restrain yourself, Mr. Callahan. You wouldn't want your blushing bride to be used goods, would you?"

Damn. "Does it count if my blushing bride was used by me?" He tilted his lips into a sly grin and nuzzled her neck.

"Mmmm," she purred. "I won't tell if you won't."

His head snapped up and passion flamed from his pores. Her focused smile confirmed what he'd just heard. She'd never said anything like that before, but she didn't have to tell him twice. He ripped her clothes from her body, relishing the sight of her pale satin skin pressed against his, quickly moving his kisses into unchartered territory. She squirmed beneath him and he took his time to fully appreciate this rare allowance. He closed his eyes and savored her sensual cries as he pushed her over the edge.

Now it was his turn. He'd waited two years for this moment. He quickly disrobed and made his move, prowling over her like a possessive predator when she placed both hands on his chest to stop him. He paused, confused and beyond controlling his raging hormones, when a loud knocking interrupted his pre-coitus bliss.

What the hell? "Ignore it. Let me make love to you, Caroline."

"No, wait. Stop."

"What? Why?" His frustration melted his control.

The door banging grew louder, shaking the pictures off their hooks.

"Get the hell outta here! I'm busy!" Trevor was livid, at war with himself while trying to control his anger around Caroline. He was used to her stopping him in the heat of the moment, but she'd never let him get this far. And he was way past the point of no return. The inner gentleman who loved her, wanted to respect her and settle for cuddling, but the man in him who craved her wanted to bend her over and show her the repercussions of pushing him too far. Trevor resisted his urge to punish the one woman who could cripple his defenses and sat back on his heels, breathing deeply. What had gotten into him?

This time the door flew open and slammed against the wall, embedding the door knob into the sheetrock. Trevor jumped up, ready to protect his woman and pound the fool bold enough to bust in.

"Dad, what the—" Trevor stood in the center of the apartment, naked and confused.

His father barged in, his obnoxious laughter filled the room. Caroline, fully clothed, seductively approached Kenneth Callahan and looped her arm through his. She wickedly cut her eyes at Trevor and grinned as she allowed his father to escort her out of his life. Certain his heart had been ripped from his bare chest and crushed before his eyes, Trevor stood frozen, stunned beyond words as the woman he loved, and his father, his own flesh and blood, betrayed him. An agonizing howl echoed through the halls as Trevor dropped to his knees and screamed for mercy.

Trevor sat up screaming in his bed, chest heaving and heart pounding. A nightmare. Trevor's eyes shifted around the room checking for signs of Caroline or his father. There were no shredded clothes on the couch, no bouquet of flowers scattered on the floor, no smashed sheetrock, and no Caroline.

Trevor brusquely rubbed his face as a string of expletives that would make a sailor blush slipped past his lips. None of that hell happened because Caroline was in Louisiana. So why would he dream about such a horrible, and highly unlikely, experience? He wondered what the underlying message or symbolism could mean. He'd had erotic dreams of Caroline before, but none where she left with his dad, of all people.

61

The bitter taste left in his mouth from the memory of Caroline's wicked grin as she left with his laughing father made Trevor want to hurl. He brushed his teeth twice, and let the scalding water from the shower pound on his aching shoulders for half an hour. When he finally shut the water off, his muscles still twitched from the residual stress.

He towel-dried and collapsed naked across his bed. The fan whipped in a speedy rhythm sending swirls of cool air that prickled the hair follicles on his bare skin. It was refreshing and reminded him he was awake. That all-too-real dream had freaked him out beyond measure.

He could still feel Caroline's silky skin beneath him. Her scent taunting him from the depths of his memory. And his dad—oh, his dad was lucky that was just a dream. The rage that brewed within from the subconscious betrayal provoked violent tendencies toward his father. Violence he hadn't known existed and never imagined he could possess. Sure, Kenneth was pushy and abrasive, and Trevor had seen firsthand when his mother suffered from the Callahan temper. But the constant nagging about Trevor's relationship with Caroline had nearly pushed him over the edge. That had to stop.

He should've known he was dreaming when Caroline gave him the green light to make love. He knew she wanted to wait until marriage, that's why he'd waited two years and existed as a walking boner on a constant basis. She was worth the wait, and he desperately hoped sending her down to Louisiana to repair her nonexistent relationship with her father would sway her opinion and reluctance to get married. The sooner they said their vows, the sooner he could relieve his misery and finally have a sexually active and completely sated relationship with the woman he loved.

The past six months have been terrible as he was constantly on edge about every damn thing. He nearly bit his secretary's head off the other day because she told him she was headed out for some food and asked if he wanted some. Hell yes he wanted some, just not from her. Though the thought to dabble on the side just to relieve his stress had crossed his mind, he never acted on it. He wanted to be faithful to Caroline so their relationship would be unscarred. Plus, if she ever found out he'd cheated on her, she'd never forgive him.

The confusing piece to this whole puzzle was his dad. Why was he so worried about Trevor's relationship with Caroline or her relationship with her dad? When he'd suggested sending her down there implying her reluctance toward marriage had something to do with the lack of a father figure in her life, Trevor couldn't see any argument with it. His dad had a point and at this phase in his life, Trevor was willing to try just about anything to speed up the process. With twenty-nine looming around the corner, he wasn't getting any younger.

His cell phone vibrated, jolting him from his thoughts and reminding him he was naked.

"Callahan."

"Hey, son."

"Dad." Trevor bit his tongue to keep the unsolicited anger from seeping through. After all, his dad knew nothing of his nightmare.

The confines of the small sports car were suffocating Trevor. He muttered a curse causing his dad to look his way. Trevor shook his head to avoid discussing his frustrating nightmare. What was his deal? It was just a dream. Clearly, because there was no chance in hell Caroline would have sex with him before they were married. Lord knows he'd tried enough times already and surprisingly gotten farther than he'd ever expected, but never as far as his subconscious had last night.

He couldn't remember the proper terms of bases, but at least he wasn't sitting the bench. Caroline had a great body and he was thankful she'd at least allowed him to intimately touch her, but he wanted more. Soon.

"Who pissed in your cereal this morning?"

Kenneth Callahan's gruff voice could cause a worm to shrivel under the pressure. Trevor respected his dad for how hard he'd worked to succeed in business, but he didn't appreciate him meddling in his personal life. It's bad enough his dad pushes him in reality, but now he was invading Trevor's dreams.

"No one. What do you need my help with that was so important you had to wake me up at the butt-crack of dawn?" He hadn't woken Trevor up, not physically, anyway, but Kenneth didn't need to know that.

Kenneth laughed loudly, effectively causing Trevor's already pounding head to throb even worse. "Testy, aren't we? What's the matter, you couldn't find someone to handle your morning boner while the girlfriend's away?"

"Dad, she's my fiancée now, and I've never cheated on her, and don't plan to start. So if you want my help with anything, I strongly suggest you back off. I've been nice so far. Don't push me."

"Easy, killer." His dad smirked. "Just a few designs I need you to approve and sign. The buyer needs them by ten today, but I have a few questions for you about a future project I'm working on."

Trevor nodded. Kenneth's phone rang and Trevor noticed his hesitancy to answer it. His clipped one word answers added to the mystery of the caller, further piquing Trevor's curiosity. It was unlike his dad not to control any conversation. When he hung up, Trevor considered asking who it was, but opted against it. He wished he had when his dad continued pressing about his sour mood.

"So what's the problem?"

Trevor gave him a warning look and shook his head. "How long is this going to take?"

"We'll be done by lunch. Maybe you can go get laid so you'll be in a better mood. I can send a couple girls your way if you need me to. Your fiancée will never know." He laughed boisterously again and Trevor ground his teeth. There would probably have been a time he would've joked with his dad and maybe taken him up on his offer, but not now. Caroline was different. She was special. And she was his.

Trevor squirmed as an unpleasant memory of a time he almost blew it with Caroline crept into his mind. He'd had way too much to drink and tried to force himself on Caroline after Kristy's party. The terrified look in her eyes when he got so angry with her for stopping him still haunted him. He didn't remember being that aggressive, but his intoxicated memory was cloudy.

Even still, it was a close call and he didn't like losing control like that. Suggesting she spend the summer in Louisiana was difficult, but it would ease some of his temptation to push her sexually. Trevor wanted her to build a relationship with her father, which can't be done in a short amount of time. Plus, he was ready to marry her and if this summer excursion helped speed that up, even better.

His relationship with Kenneth Callahan wasn't the textbook father/son bondfest, but Trevor loved his dad. If he ever needed anything, he could expect his father to deliver. He had been fortunate to share a strong relationship with both of his grandfathers and wished for his child to have the same possibility someday. Especially if it was a boy. He wanted Caroline to know what it was like to have a father so she might be more inclined to include Kenneth and Eddie both in their lives. That's assuming his latest dream doesn't come true and he gets screwed in the end.

SEVEN

Back in the safety of her own room, she kicked herself for going inside that house. *What was I thinking?* She closed her eyes and had an instant snapshot engrained in her memory of what she *did* see. Caroline didn't know of any other time in her life when she felt more ashamed, mortified. She desperately hoped he did not get a look at her trespassing mug. Maybe she could pretend nothing ever happened. She thought about asking Eddie who lived in the log cabin, but decided she didn't want anyone to know she had been anywhere near that place.

Regaining her composure, she prepared to emerge from her sanctuary. When she'd approached the plantation house earlier, she noticed her Jeep parked on the driveway again, nice and clean. Eddie must have washed it for her after he had it towed out of the mud. She would thank him later, once she could look at another human being with a straight face.

If she planned to successfully come across like nothing ever happened she needed to act normal, not hide, and, most importantly, be as graceful as possible. Strangely enough, that last part had become a challenge the second she crossed the bridge into the bayou, starting with her near-wreck avoiding an apparition—if such things even existed. Caroline had stuttered, stumbled, and made the dumbest decisions of her life since she got here. Who was she kidding? She was a bumbling idiot.

Caroline sighed and laughed hysterically at herself. She thought about what that experience must have been like for him. Whoever he was, he just got caught in his birthday suit, every beautiful rippling muscle of it, by a strange woman who had encroached his private space, in more ways than one. He would probably try to pretend nothing ever happened, either. Caroline was sure she had nothing to worry about. At least that's what she told herself.

Before she could face the rest of the world, Caroline called Kristy. She knew Kristy was the one person she could confess her sins to who wouldn't judge her for stupidity.

"Hey girl! Got your message. How's Cajun country?"

"Oh my gosh, Kristy. You're not going to believe what I just did."

"What happened? Are you okay? Was your dad pissed?"

Caroline forgot she hadn't told her how things went. "Oh, no, things are great with my dad. We talked everything out and we're cool. I'm talking about something totally different and much worse."

"Oooh, do tell. This sounds good."

Caroline could hear the smile in Kristy's voice. "Well, I was exploring the property, you know, to get away and clear my head. The humidity is unreal down here. So, I saw this cute log cabin and it was so hot and humid out I could barely breathe, so I knocked to see if whoever lived there would let me crash for a few minutes to cool off."

"Mmm-hmm. Oh boy. What did you do?"

"Well, no one answered, but the door wasn't locked or even closed securely, and when I knocked it opened."

"Oh, geez. Tell me you didn't go in."

"I went in. It was fine until I literally ran into a hot naked guy just out of the shower."

"Whoa, whoa, whoa. . .hold up. What? All I heard was hot naked guy and shower. Say that again?"

Kristy was hanging on her every word, so she spoke slowly and clearly. "Kris, my body collided with a very muscular, naked body that had just gotten out of the shower. I fell to my knees from the impact and didn't realize what had just happened until I looked up to find my hands grasping his hips, and I was eye level to. . .well, to his. . ."

"Oh. My. Gosh! Caroline! That is hysterical! And so freakin' awesome!" Kristy's laughter howled through the speaker. "Did you see his goods? Did he see you? What did he say?"

"Well, I panicked and didn't exactly stick around to chitchat. He had a towel over his head so I don't think he saw me. Thank goodness!"

"But you sure saw him, didn't you? Aaack! I can't believe it, you little criminal! I'm so proud." Kristy squealed through the phone, and Caroline smiled at her reaction. She knew Kristy would enjoy her humiliation.

"Well, I didn't see his face."

"That's okay, honey. You saw the best part."

She smiled. Kristy's experience and finesse with guys outweighed hers by miles. Caroline was shy and tended to be quite awkward and naïve. Kristy probably would have confidently walked away from that embarrassing situation with a date. "So, I learned I have a step mom and a younger brother and sister, but I haven't met them yet."

"Oh, that's great, C! That's almost cooler than hot, naked, wet guy. Well, okay, maybe not, but it's still awesome. How was your dad?"

"He was great. I'm really glad I came. As mad as I was at Trevor for pushing me to do this, I'm glad I did."

"Yeah, well, Trevor still could've presented the idea to you in a much better fashion rather than making it a damn condition to your engagement. Then booking a church without telling you in a desperate attempt to push up the date. . .I mean, really, who does crap like that?"

"Well, I made him cancel that reservation. I'm not Catholic so they wouldn't perform the ceremony anyway. Besides, I'm sure his impatience has a lot to do with his eagerness to get me in his bed."

"Of course he's eager. Honey, he's been trying to get in your panties since he laid eyes on you. It'll do him good to wait a little longer. For someone who probably had his booty calls on speed dial, I'm shocked he's been good for this long. He obviously knows he's lucky to have you, so don't let him push you around."

"He's not pushing me around. Yes, I knew about his reputation before we got together. Think about it, Kris. He was used to getting some whenever he felt the urge. I've been with him for over two years and sexually we've never done anything more than heavy petting. I'm sure he's frustrated."

"Who cares. That doesn't give him the right to force you into something you're not ready for. I mean, y'all just got engaged. Enjoy being a fiancée for a while before you have to worry about being a wife. Take your time, relax and enjoy your new family. Don't worry about planning a wedding yet. This isn't a research paper, there's no deadline. Trevor's sexual needs can wait. Lord knows he's had enough nookie to last a lifetime."

Ready to end the attack on Trevor, Caroline lied about needing to get off the phone and promised to call Kristy later. She flopped back on the bed and closed her eyes as she remembered her last date with Trevor before she came down here.

"Trevor, I need to ask you something. It may make you somewhat. . .uncomfortable."

"Hit me with your best shot."

She breathed deeply, desperately trying to figure out how she should word this difficult inquiry. She knew he'd slept around, but, since they hadn't slept together, she never felt justified in asking how much. "How many. . .well, have you kept track. . .um—" She suddenly realized a burn crept up her neck.

Trevor chuckled. "Who was this supposed to make uncomfortable?"

She playfully smacked his arm. "Just let me get it out, okay. How many women have you slept with? There. I said it, now stop teasing me and just answer the question."

He stopped laughing, but still wore the crooked smile she so adored. He sat thoughtfully for a moment. "I went through a phase my Freshman and Sophomore years at the university, and I'm not proud of it. But, Caroline, if you're concerned about STD's or anything, I don't think you need to worry bec—"

Her hand flew up to quickly interrupt him. "No, no please stop! I don't want details. Just a number will do."

"Does it really matter how many? The fact is I have been with other women, and I was careful. Do you really want a number?"

"Yes, I would like a number. I'm curious and I'd like to know."

He cautioned, "You should be careful what kind of questions you ask because you may not like the answers you get."

"Just tell me already, I can handle it."

He fidgeted, flicking the metal tab on the top of his Dr. Pepper can. "The truth is, well, I went to a bunch of parties and drank a lot of alcohol. So I really can't be sure."

It took everything she had to keep her eyes in her head, so she closed them and tried to remember to breathe. How can he not be sure of how many?

"I think between the girls I actually dated, and the possible one night stands from the parties. . .I think I'm somewhere around twenty-five. But like I said, there was a lot of alcohol involved so I can't be sure."

"You've had sex with twenty-five women?" She spoke as calmly as she could manage.

Now worried, he rose up on his knees. Quite the contrast to the relaxed position on his side.

"You see, this is why I warned you that you may not like what you hear. I didn't want to tell you how many because I knew you would react like this."

"I was expecting you to say something like, eight or ten. Not twenty-five! Good grief, Trevor! I don't think I even know twenty-five people." She wondered how badly he cushioned that number, and what the real number was? The one he gave her was bad enough, though. He sat with his head down in shame. The silence was deafening.

"Sweetheart, I've made mistakes in the past, but please don't let that dissuade how you feel about me now. I know plenty of guys who make me look like a saint. One of my frat brothers used to brag that he was up to eighty-five women with a goal of triple digits before the end of the year. Believe me, I promise you'll reap the benefits from all my. . .practice." He smiled. Smiled!

"Eighty-five wom—what! Are you kidding me? Practice. Is that what you call it? Well, that's reassuring. In that case, I'm gonna be the worst lover you've ever had, considering I've only been to third base twice in my whole life!"

He frowned, "Who did you make it to third base with besides me? I'll kill 'em." She smacked his arm and he flashed his magnificent smile. "I'm kidding. That's perfectly okay, baby. I'll make sure you get plenty of practice."

Practice. Maybe that's what she needed, more practice. Just the memory of what happened after that conversation had her heating up. She'd practiced some on her own, not that she knew a whole lot about what she was doing, but the way Trevor could make her feel with a simple promise, she knew her meager touch was nothing like the real thing. Trevor had given her a little taste of what she had to look forward to, and it was hot, she only wished he hadn't practiced with so many different people.

EIGHT

Walking down the stairs, she heard the grandfather clock chime four times. Dinner in two hours. Two hours until she met the rest of the Fontenot family. She strolled into the kitchen to see what Delia and Delphine were up to. Delphine was preparing the food. She peeled and deveined jumbo shrimp while humming an upbeat tune. Caroline asked if there was anything she could do to help and Delphine laughed. Delia came bustling into the kitchen just as Caroline was about to ask what was funny, and she answered the question for her.

"No, Miss Caroline, Mr. Fontenot would have our heads if he knew we put you to work."

"Even if I wanted to help?"

"Yes, ma'am, even then. He's so enchanted that you're back in his life, he wouldn't think very kindly if he found out you were helping the help." They chuckled.

"Well, okay then. Do y'all mind if I hang out in here and watch? I love to cook, so I am always interested in learning new things."

"I s'pose there's no harm in watching. What do you think, Delphine?"

"Won't botha me none. 'Sides, she a dahlin' lil thang, maybe she can teach us somethin', huh, Delia?" Delphine cackled.

Caroline enjoyed their company. They made her laugh and feel welcome, like a part of the family.

"Which room you chose, boo?" Delphine asked.

"I chose the one with the white canopy bed and the window facing the duck pond."

Delia chimed in. "Ahhh, yes, that's the best room in the house."

"Really? Why is it the best?"

"That was Miss Rachel's room. . .and only her room."

"Who was Miss Rachel?"

"She was the first lady of the Fontenot plantation. This house was built for Mr. Fontenot and Miss Rachel as a wedding gift from Mr. Fontenot's wealthy family. They lived here before this town was ever called Golden Meadow. Anyway, she's the only one who ever stayed in that room."

"Ever?" The puzzle kept gaining pieces. "Why hasn't anyone else ever stayed in that room? It's beautiful! If you say it's the best room in the house, I would think everyone would want it." Caroline remembered the letters etched in the window. "I noticed the initials R. C. F. etched into the glass of the window. Were those hers?"

Delia nodded, "Back then, when a man gave a woman a diamond for their engagement, it was customary for her to see if the diamond was real by etching her initials in glass. If the diamond scratched the glass, it was real. If it didn't, then they knew it was a fake."

"What was her middle name?"

Delia and Delphine both shrugged. "Not sure, boo. I only ever heard her referred to as Miss Rachel."

Bummer. Caroline was curious if they shared the same names like their initials. Everything else was screaming coincidence, why not that, too? "So why is Rachel the only one who ever stayed in that room? I guess I don't understand the problem. I mean, it's just a room, right?"

Delia and Delphine looked at each other and Delphine nodded her head. "Well, there was an incident that happened in that room, but we don't want to spoil your opinion of it because it really is the best. It's the biggest room and it has the best view."

"No, please, go on. I love it, so I doubt you'll say anything that will cause me to move out of it." Caroline casually rubbed her arms in a poor attempt to disguise her chills. She couldn't imagine what they would tell her, but after everything she's seen in relation to her dreams, she needed to know. As much as it freaked her out, she was hooked on the mystery this story provided.

Delia continued slowly, choosing her words carefully. "They say she killed herself by jumping out the window. She hit her head on a stone garden statue below her room."

Delphine chimed in, her Cajun accent heavy, "The story also claims if she'd hit huh head anywheah 'sides right between da eyes, she mighta lived through the jump."

Chills skittered along her skin. Every one of her dreams was accompanied by a throbbing pain between her eyes. She had goose bumps from head to toe, and a shiver crept up her spine. Was this the reason for the recurring dream? Was the young woman in her dreams Rachel Fontenot? If it was, who raped her and threatened to kill her if she told anyone?

Now completely obsessed with learning more about Rachel's story, Caroline was determined to find out the truth.

"So, the room you're staying in has never been occupied after Rachel," Delia said. "People are a little spooked about staying in a room where someone killed herself. I guess they're afraid it might be haunted by her ghost. If her committing suicide is what you believe truly happened."

"You don't?"

Delia's face crinkled up causing the crease between her brows to deepen. "I can't be sure, boo. It was way before my time."

Caroline believed there was more to the story, but didn't push her luck. She thanked them for the interesting history and for letting her hang out with them before she excused herself to freshen up for dinner. Now that she knew more about what happened so long ago, maybe her dreams would make more sense. If she had another dream. She wished she could know when to expect one.

She wore one of her nicer outfits for dinner since she would meet the rest of the family for the first time. She freshened up until she felt presentable enough to make a successful first impression.

The grandfather clock chimed six times. *It's Judgment Day.* Caroline spritzed perfume in the air and walked through it before she made her way down the stairs to meet her new family. Her dad walked in the front door just as she was halfway down the stairs. His face lit up like the Christmas tree in Rockefeller Center.

"I gotta say, you are a sight for sore eyes."

She smiled. "Hi, Daddy."

He hugged her tightly and kissed her cheek. "Hello, beautiful." A hug and a kiss on the cheek seemed to be the normal greeting from everyone down here.

In the midst of their embrace, the front door opened and a tall, beautiful, extremely skinny blonde woman walked in. Had to be her step mother, April, though she didn't look like she could be any older than thirty-five years old. She stopped dead in her tracks and stared in horror at her husband with his arms wrapped around Caroline. She looked ready to kill someone. Eddie quickly held Caroline's hand and led her over to April with exaggerated enthusiasm.

"April, I'd like you to meet Caroline."

She peered at Caroline much like a snake eyeing a mouse.

"She's my daughter with my ex-wife, Emily."

It still didn't seem to reassure April, knowing that Caroline was Eddie's daughter instead of someone trying to steal her husband. But after she finished glaring at Eddie, she at least managed to fake a smile as she looked at Caroline.

"Hello, Caroline. I vaguely remember my husband mentioning a daughter from a previous marriage. What a surprise to meet you now." She cut her eyes back to Eddie. "So unexpected. A call would have been nice."

"My apologies, April. I should've given you a heads up, but I honestly didn't know how to tell you. Besides, I didn't think it would be a problem."

April plastered her fake smile back to her emaciated face and looked at Caroline again. Strange, the daggers shooting from her frosty eyes contrasted greatly with the smile on her lips.

"No problem, darling. Caroline, it's a pleasure to meet you."

Caroline didn't realize it was possible to use the word "pleasure" while displaying such a nasty expression. She gave the sweetest smile she could manage. "The pleasure is mine. It appears I have gained another mother." Never mind that she could pass as a wicked step mother.

April wasn't extremely thrilled with that comment either, it seemed. "Yes, and it seems I have inherited another child. If you'll excuse me, I need to. . .freshen up before dinner."

Caroline could see why her dad skipped formal dinners so often. Was April always like that, or did she just not like Caroline for some reason?

After she walked away, Eddie put his hands on Caroline's shoulders and spoke barely above a whisper. "I'm very sorry, Caroline. She usually isn't like this. She must be tired from the drive. She'll warm up to you, I am sure of it." Caroline certainly hoped so. She didn't think it was possible for April to like her less.

"Maybe she's hungry. She looks like she needs to eat."

Eddie chuckled. "Yeah, she's always watching her diet and obsessing over her weight."

Caroline's eyes grew big with disbelief. "Really? She's so thin! As it is, I'm sure she has to jump around in the shower just to get wet!"

Eddie released a bellowing laugh. "That's really funny, Caroline. I'll have to remember that one."

The door opened and in walked her new siblings. They stared at Caroline for a moment and looked at Eddie with apparent curiosity.

"Claire, Jeremy, I'd like you to meet Caroline. She's your sister."

They both smiled, clearly wanting an explanation, but not pressing the issue at the moment. Remy was the first one to move and gave her a big hug and a kiss on the cheek while Claire gave her dad a wide eyed stare. Remy, nearly Caroline's height, didn't have to stretch very far to reach her face. "Awesome, I have a hot sister!" Claire quickly smacked him upside the head.

Claire grinned. "Dad! You little player! You have some explaining to do. Why didn't you ever tell us?" She focused on Caroline who was holding back a smirk. "I can't believe I have a sister. An older sister. This is crazy! And wonderful!" Claire squealed and reached out with both hands to hug her neck.

Caroline glanced at her glowing father. She could tell he hadn't been this happy in a very long time.

Delia announced dinner was ready. Eddie shooed Claire and Remy to put their belongings away and wash up, assuring them they'd have time to ask questions later. They sprinted up the stairs, and Caroline turned to her dad. "How old are they?"

"Claire is sixteen and Remy will be fourteen next month."

"They're great, really. I'm totally psyched to have siblings. I always hated being an only child." Caroline caught a glimpse of pain briefly cross his features. She immediately regretted her words. It wasn't her intention to rub it in.

They ate at the large rectangular dining table for dinner. Eddie was at the head of the table, April and Claire on one side, Remy and Caroline on the other. Awkward at first, but thankfully no one used dinner time as a twenty questions session. Caroline mostly stayed quiet, but not as quiet as April. She didn't utter a word during dinner. She sat directly across from Caroline and made a very strong point not to make eye contact.

After dinner, April excused herself with a headache. Caroline was relieved. Without a word, the woman made her feel very uncomfortable. Embarrassed by his wife's behavior, Eddie followed her upstairs, no doubt to discuss Caroline. The uneasy feeling in her stomach threatened a rough, digestive night.

But she had a great conversation with Claire and Remy, until Claire's cell phone rang.

Remy rolled his eyes, "Well, so much for talking to her. She'll be on the phone for hours now with her best friend Lindsey. Wanna go play the X-box?"

Caroline smiled, "Thanks, but I am no good at video games. You'd kill me."

He smirked. "I'd probably kill you even if you were good. I kick butt at video games. It's kind of my thing, you know?"

"In that case, I think I'll head upstairs to my room and chill. I'm still trying to catch up on rest from my drive yesterday."

"No prob. Hey, welcome to the family. I think you're pretty cool."

"Thanks, Remy, that means a lot." He gave her a fist bump and went to his room to play. Having a little brother was fun.

Lying beneath the bed's white canopy, Caroline couldn't help but think about the story of Rachel Fontenot. She really hoped she was able to dream about her again, to possibly learn more truth about what happened. Clearly the reason she came down here extended beyond Trevor's insistence.

The cryptic dream saga that had plagued her for months was more than just dreams. They were clues to a mystery. Unsure how or why she was chosen to unravel these clues, she was too involved to turn away. Unwilling to fully accept the whole ghost concept, perhaps something else permitted the dead to speak from their graves. She obviously never knew her, but Caroline's gut told her Rachel didn't kill herself.

She took her engagement ring off and admired it before she placed it on the nightstand. Tired from her busy day, Caroline could hardly keep her eyes open. She noticed two missed calls from Trevor, and considered calling him back, but it was pretty late, so she decided against it. Instead she sent him a quick text to tell him goodnight and that she would talk to him tomorrow.

Thankfully she brought her satin eye mask to keep the morning sun at bay. Unless Beau decided to serenade her again in the morning, she should get plenty of rest. It didn't take her long to fall asleep, and like magic. . .the dream began.

NINE

Caroline found herself in the woods again. She slowly twirled around, taking in the sunlight-dappled surroundings. The trees, full and green, told of the summer season. Her hair and clothes stuck to her skin from the steamy heat. At least this time she wasn't running.

She walked along the trail, not really knowing where she should go, waiting for a sign or a sound to catch her attention.

So far this dream was miserably boring. The middle of nowhere, by herself, in the sweltering heat.

Caroline spied an outbuilding and finally heard something. Soft crying or, maybe, whimpering. She ran to the side of the building to get a closer look only to stumble upon a young woman crouched beside the wood pile. The same girl from her previous dreams. Caroline assumed this was Rachel.

She wasn't sure what she should do. Doubtful if the girl could see her, Caroline approached her. Rachel jerked her head up, her bloodshot eyes terrified.

"Get down! He'll see!" she whispered frantically.

Caroline pointed at herself, confused. She squatted down next to Rachel, careful not to touch her. Her white nightgown covered in blood, Rachel hugged her knees, rocking back and forth, muttering hysterically.

"I cut him. I cut him. I had a shard of metal and I cut him."

"Who?" Caroline asked. "Rachel, who did you cut?"

"He was trying to hurt me and I cut him. Oh, but that only angered him more. But I cut him. His hand will need a doctor's care for certain. I cut him."

"Which hand? Whose hand? You have to give me a name."

"They have to know. They must know the truth."

"Rachel, I can't help you unless you tell me who hurt you."

She gasped, "Oh no, he's coming! He's coming back for me!"

Caroline stood and turned around, but saw no one. She heard a twig snap right behind her and felt the warm breath on the back of her head. She stood between Rachel and whoever or whatever was chasing her. Not positively sure they could even see or hear her, Caroline closed her eyes, gulped and started to turn around.

BAM! Caroline nearly jumped out of her skin. Something from outside slammed into her window. Something large enough and loud enough to cause her to jolt from her dream. Notably freaked out about whoever had stood behind her, about to do who knows what, Caroline was thankful she woke.

She rushed to the window seeing only the moonless, pitch black night. Nothing. She checked her phone for the time. Four in the morning. She couldn't imagine a bird flying into the window that early. It was still dark. Eew, I hope it wasn't a bat. Not sure she would be able to go back to sleep, she turned on her laptop and attempted to do some research about Rachel Fontenot.

83

Unfortunately she came up empty. With it being so long ago, there wasn't much about her but her birthday, which, oddly enough, was the same as Caroline's. Rachel was born May 13,1868. Same day over one hundred years before her. The only other information she found on Rachel was how she died. August 3, 1886, falling from a window and hitting her head, instantly killing her.

Again, the freakish coincidences were piling up. And so were her goose bumps. Though her mom always loved the name Caroline, her full name was Rachel Caroline. Emily had once mentioned Eddie had been the one to name Caroline. Guess now she knew why. It was a long time family name.

Rachel's middle name surely wasn't also Caroline. She'd have to go to the public library in the morning to look in old newspapers. Maybe knowing her birthday would help in her research.

Yawning, she put away her laptop and fell asleep. This time she had no dreams.

Caroline pulled the eye mask from her face at the sound of voices downstairs. Daylight filled the room and she reached for her cell phone from the nightstand, but it wasn't there. Sure she'd left it there, Caroline figured she took it with her to the window when she got up in the middle of the night. She retraced her steps, and found her phone on the edge of the dressing table. She couldn't believe what time it was. She'd slept until ten-thirty. Frustration pulsed through her. She wanted to get an early start at the library.

Caroline gathered her things for a quick shower and got dressed for the day. She didn't want to take the time to blow dry her hair, so she twisted it into a sloppy bun and dabbed on a little make-up to look presentable. She reached for her engagement ring and panicked. It wasn't on the nightstand where she'd left it. And she specifically left it there so she would know where to find it. Searching the floor on her hands and knees, thinking she must have knocked it off at some point during the night, Caroline could only think the worst. She couldn't find it. Her heart raced and she frantically searched the rest of the room, even stripping the bed. No luck.

Where was it? It had to be there somewhere. She probably flung it across the room when she jumped out of her skin last night, but it was nowhere to be found now. She'd have to find it later. Right now, she needed to get going in case the library closed at noon. If she had flung it across the room, it wasn't going anywhere, so it should be okay until she got home. She'd make a point to look for it when she got back from the library.

Down in the kitchen, she scarfed down a quick breakfast Delia had set aside for her while she and Delphine finished cleaning up.

After Caroline inhaled her food, and asked them where the nearest library was. Delia smiled. "The library is downtown on Maple Street."

"Right, small town. I remember. Can you give me directions?"

"Sure, love. I'll write them down for you."

"Can I ask y'all a crazy question? What is today?" Caroline had completely lost track of time and her cell phone with the calendar was still upstairs in her purse.

Delia smiled sweetly, "Today is Thursday, June second."

"Thanks. I guess I've been distracted lately."

"You have good reason, boo. You've been through a lot in the last couple of days. Stress like that can wear on a girl. That's what gives you gray hair, right Delphine?"

Delphine snorted. "Speak fuh yuhself, beb. Me and Miss Clairol have a great relationship."

The two of them cackled with laughter as Caroline thanked them and slipped out. She ran upstairs to get her phone and do another sweep around the room for her ring before heading out. She still couldn't find it. Pain shot through her gut. Not sadness from the inability to find it, but because of what Trevor would do if he knew she'd lost it. Though completely possible, she didn't want to consider the possibility of anyone taking it. Not her new family. The best way to ruin everything she'd rebuilt with her dad would be to blindly accuse someone in his house of theft. Caroline assured herself she would find her ring when she got back. She would. Hopefully.

Delia's directions to the library were straightforward and accurate. Amazed at how easy it was to find with only needing to make three left turns. Caroline walked into the library and went straight for the front desk. The decent-sized library for such a small town impressed her as she studied the rows of shelves and equipment.

No one monitored the front desk. Standing with her back to the counter she scanned the open space of the library for help.

"Hi there, how can I help you?"

Startled, she jumped and turned around.

A painfully attractive man with golden brown hair and matching eyes flashed an amused, magnificent smile causing Caroline's knees to grow weak. "Sorry, I didn't mean to scare you."

"No, it's okay, it's just. . .two-seconds ago no one was here. I turned for just a second and then. . .there you are. . .out of nowhere. I'm rambling. Sorry." Her face grew hot. *Great. I'm blushing! Why am I blushing? Why am I rambling?*

He squinted. "Hey, have we met? You seem. . .familiar."

"I doubt it." He was gorgeous, but Caroline couldn't help mentally rolling her eyes at his corny attempt to flirt. Next he'd probably ask for her sign. Good thing she was a stubborn, bullheaded Taurus.

He studied her face, her hair. "No, I'm good with faces, especially beautiful ones." He flashed a panty-busting smile and winked. "I swear I've seen you around."

Caroline shrugged, flattered and heating beneath his inspection. She had to give him props for trying. "Sorry. I don't think so. I'm not from around here." Severely handicapped in the flirting department, Caroline usually made a fool of herself, but this guy seemed to be a pro. "I'm sure you're mistaking me with someone else."

Still unsure, he shook it off and smiled again, appreciatively running his eyes up and down her body. "Yeah, you're probably right." He leaned forward resting his elbows on the desk, his deliciously masculine scent inflicting an acute bout of dizziness. "So tell me, beautiful stranger, what can I do for you today?"

He stood patiently watching her blush as she gathered her scattered thoughts. She couldn't understand why this random guy had such an effect on her. She'd spoken with hot guys before, she was engaged to one, so why did this one have her all flustered? "I, uh, I'm looking for old newspapers from the mid-1800s. How do I go about finding those here?"

He raised his eyebrows. "Wow, that's a long time ago. Those would probably be on microfilm."

"Micro-what?"

He flashed that alluring smile again. "Microfilm. Follow me and I'll show you where they are." He spoke over his shoulder as they walked to the back of the library. "You've never heard of microfilm? Where have you been?"

"Google." Caroline hadn't been in a library since high school, thanks to the internet.

He chuckled. "So I take it you've never seen one of these babies?" He patted a monster-sized ancient device. "Allow me to show you how it works. What month and year specifically are you looking for?"

"May 13, 1868."

"Okay, these are all the files from that era. They are obviously in chronological order, so here are the 1800s." He scanned the files with his finger until he found the 1860s. Next, he pulled out a long narrow box filled with spools of ribbon, only instead of ribbon it was printed plastic. "May thirteenth, you said?"

"Yes, 1868."

He pulled out a spool and booted up the machine. Caroline couldn't help but notice the mounds of muscle hidden beneath his semi-tight shirt. He was obviously fit. With golden skin and beautiful amber eyes that closely matched those caramel locks, he was dazzling. Not too tall, but not short either. Probably around six feet. Of course, to her just about everyone was tall. Her gaze dipped to his backside, perfectly rounded under his khakis.

He shifted and she looked up. A smirk spread on his lips. Caught! She had been caught checking him out. She was mortified. Her face burned and she was positive she turned three different shades of red.

He smiled, "Did you hear me?"

She'd been too busy drooling to hear him. *Oh, fantastic. Great job, Caroline. Real classy.* "What? No, I'm sorry. What'd you say?"

"I asked you if you saw how I loaded the spool onto the machine, and if you think you can do it yourself?"

"Oh yes, I saw. I'm sure I can remember. . .if I need to." Caroline wanted to crawl under the table.

"Are you sure? I could unload it and do it again for you if you'd like. Sometimes it's tricky to get it lined up just right."

"Yes, if you don't mind. Do it again for me, please?"

He paused for a moment, grinning, studying her face before he unloaded the film. Goodness, he was indeed handsome. He had a ruggedness about him that she'd never seen before. So hot.

For the second time, he loaded the spool onto the peg, threaded the plastic under the microscope-like piece, and hit a button. It made a loud noise as it loaded the machine, and suddenly she could see the newspaper on the big screen. It was so cool.

"Awesome! Thank you so much. I think I've got it now."

He stared for a moment. "Do you need help with anything else? I mean. . .while you've got my attention?"

Was he blushing?

"Um, I do have one question. Have you lived here your whole life?"

He smiled and said, "Born and raised."

Hmmm. A pure bred southern boy. Nice. Focus Caroline. "Well, I'm looking into some of my family history, and I don't know much about this area. Honestly, I don't know much about Louisiana. If you're not busy, I could use some help with the areas involved?"

His smile lit up that handsome face. "My shift's about to end. I'll be back in ten minutes."

"Great, thanks." Caroline really didn't need help. Not entirely sure why she asked him to stay, Caroline thought it acceptable to make a friend. To her good fortune, he just happened to be gorgeous.

She scrolled through the microfilm looking for May 13, 1868. The spool he chose started with April. They must be filed quarterly with this one being April-June. Caroline zoomed through April and tried to slow it down when it got to May, but not knowing how to use the machine was a hinderance. She didn't know how to stop it once it was going so fast. And then the slapping of the film echoed as it slid out of the machine and spun around on the unloaded spool. Great. Genius. How did he load this thing again? She mumbled under her breath. "Way to go, Caroline. Real smooth."

"Caroline? So that's your name?" She whirled around in surprise to see her handsome helper standing right behind her, smiling and clearly intrigued.

"Yes, my name is Caroline."

"That's a pretty name. I'm Cade."

"You have a pretty name, too. Well, not pretty, you're a guy, obviously." Good Lord, I sound like a ditz. "It's um. . .nice." A subject change would be great about now. "Short for Caden?"

"Yep, Caden Luke. It's what my momma calls me, but only when I'm in trouble." He chuckled.

"You either must not get into trouble very often, or you get into trouble all the time."

He frowned. "Why would you think that?"

"Your amusement when you said it gave it away."

He grinned again. "Nah, my mom usually lets me do whatever I want, considering I haven't lived at home with my parents in years. I'm a good boy—most of the time." He winked, his playfulness alluring. The adorable dimple in his chin didn't hurt his case either.

She turned to look at the mess she made with the microfilm machine and his eyes followed.

"Man, I leave you alone for a few minutes and you tear everything up?" He laughed when he said it, but she was still embarrassed.

"I'm sorry. I couldn't figure out how to slow it down before the spool ran out of film. Is there a trick to the controls or something?"

He leaned down over her right shoulder and readjusted the spool. She caught a whiff of his clean fragrance. He smelled like soap and body spray. Incredible and strangely familiar. Did Trevor use the same soap? She didn't think so, but she had smelled it before.

The heat from his body radiated his scent. It was positively intoxicating. He fixed the spool back to where he had it first, and scrolled slowly through May. He stopped it on May 13, 1868.

"Here's the date you were looking for. Is there a particular section you needed?"

"I need the birth announcements." He looked at her for a moment as if she was crazy.

"What?"

"Do you really think they put birth announcements in the newspaper back in the 1800s?"

"I don't know, it was a little before my time." She pushed the sarcasm.

"I think you need to find the hospital records to get that information."

"Well, where would I find those?"

"If the baby was born in a hospital and not at home, you may be able to get a copy from the courthouse."

"Great. Where is the courthouse?"

He smiled. "I can take you there if you'd like?"

"Thanks, but I have my car here. I can drive if you'll just tell me where it is."

"Tell you what, if you'll have lunch with me today, I'll drive you to the courthouse and then bring you back to your car?" Oh, he was good. Smooth, real smooth.

"Um, I should tell you I have a. . .well, I'm engaged." That didn't faze him as he stood patiently waiting for her answer. She added, "I guess so, but I really need to get those copies today, okay?"

"Sure thing, I'll take good care of you." He put the microfilm away as Caroline gathered her belongings. He let her walk in front of him as they exited the library. His charm melted Caroline's bones when she paused to let him go through the doorway first, but he refused with a crooked grin. He held it open and motioned ahead. "Ladies first."

TEN

Cade pulled his truck into the parking lot of a hole-in-the-wall restaurant. Caroline studied the dumpy exterior and couldn't understand how it was legally allowed to fully operate. She shot him a questionable look.

"Trust me. This place isn't much to look at, but they have the best food in town." She reluctantly stepped inside as he held the door open again. His hand rested on her lower back as she passed, allowing him to lead her to a table. He pulled her chair out and waited for her to get settled before he sat in his own chair next to hers. That interested her, considering Trevor normally sat across from her at a square table rather than beside her.

"What do you recommend?"

He answered without missing a beat. "Seafood gumbo."

She studied the lunch menu as the waitress came with two glasses of water. "Hey, Beau, how's it going?" She honed in on him like Caroline wasn't there.

He looked up and smiled. "It's good, things are good."

She continued with a lingering stare, obviously crushing on him. "You want your usual appetizer?"

He nodded. "Thanks, that'd be great."

Beau? Had she been asked out to lunch by the hot gardener? "I thought you said your name was Cade?" He looked up from his menu like he didn't understand what she meant. "That girl just called you Beau."

"That's what most people call me. Shortened from my surname."

"Oh. Okay, I'll bite. What is your surname?"

"Beauregard."

"Like the Confederate General?"

"Yep. I'm a descendant. General P. G. T. Beauregard was born in New Orleans. He was my G4 grandfather."

"G4?"

"Great to the fourth power," he said, grinning. "It's easier to say."

Caroline liked him. He made her smile. The strange comfort she felt with him though she just met him was confusing, but relieving. She needed a friend and awkwardness would complicate things.

"So tell me, sweet Caroline, if you know nothing about Louisiana or the history of your family, what exactly are you doing down here?"

"I came down here to visit my dad." Caroline didn't want to go into too much boring detail and ruin what was turning out to be a pleasant lunch.

"Your dad lives here? In Golden Meadow? I'm guessing since you're just visiting that you don't live close by?"

"No, I live in Chicago, actually." He leaned back in his chair with his hands clasped behind his head, and she saw the outline of his rippled abs. Trevor had an alluring body, but his wasn't as defined as Cade's appeared to be. Cade's body was sculpted and strong. . .enticing. She found it easy to imagine his arms wrapped around her providing a shield of security and a sense of intimacy at the same time. Too easy.

"So that was your jeep with the Yankee tags." He smiled and winked.

"You know, that must be a guy thing to notice license plates of random cars in the parking lot. My boyfriend does that too and it drives me crazy!"

Now more captivated, he leaned toward her. "So let me get this straight. You're engaged *and* you have a boyfriend? Man, you really get around, don't you?" He shook with laughter.

Caroline realized what she said and felt the burn of embarrassment. . .again. "I meant to say my fiancé."

"Ah. . .but you didn't." His matter-of-fact tone would normally anger Caroline, but she couldn't think of anything but her embarrassment. What had gotten into her?

"We haven't been engaged very long, only a couple of months, so I'm still getting used to the whole. . .idea."

He observed her discomfort with the subject. "I understand, I guess." However, his generosity didn't last long. He added, "I mean, it's a life-altering decision, so I could see how it would be easy to forget." She threw an ice cube at his head causing him to burst out in laughter again.

"I am engaged and I'm very happy about that fact. Trevor treats me like a princess."

He leaned in really close to her face, his whisper a feather brushing her skin. "Yes, I hear you. . .but I don't believe you."

He had some nerve! She wanted to box him in right in that sexy mouth of his. "You just met me! You know nothing about me, so why should I care if you believe me?"

He smiled, amused with her flaring temper. "Okay, *princess*, if you're so happy to be engaged, where is your engagement ring? Isn't that supposed to be his token of undying affection that you're to wear proudly displaying your love for each other, or something like that?"

The waitress brought their drinks and a plate of something she didn't recognize to their table and took their order. Caroline appreciated the distraction as Cade motioned for her to order first.

"I'll have the seafood gumbo, please."

The waitress wrote in her little note pad without acknowledging Caroline. She looked at Cade. "And for you, sexy?"

He smiled back at her and then looked directly at Caroline. "I'll have the same."

She took their menus and walked away as Caroline glared at him.

"Oh, come on, I was just giving you a hard time. It shouldn't bother you unless you have reservations about your relationship or decision to get married, should it?"

He made a good point. She shouldn't care what anyone else thought as long as she and Trevor were happy together. *We are happy together, right?* She hadn't really thought about it from that perspective.

"You never know though, someone might just come along and treat you like a queen instead of a princess."

She ignored him. She had to. She could easily get lost in him with a line like that. "So how 'bout you, Beau? Are you dating or engaged? Married?"

He took a long drink of water and smiled. "Nope. I guess I haven't come across the one for me—yet." He winked.

Was he serious? This guy was excessively confident, but rather than annoying her, she was intrigued. She liked the attention. Caroline looked down at the dish their waitress had brought to the table. "What is that?"

"Blackened alligator. It's delicious." He stabbed a piece with his fork and dipped it into a creamy yellow sauce.

"I've never had alligator before. What's it taste like?"

He smiled while chewing. "Tastes like chicken. Come on, just try it. You'll like it, I promise."

She stabbed a piece just as he had, dipped it and ate it. It was amazing!

A wide smile stretched across his handsome face in response to her enjoyment. "Yeah? See, I told you."

She nodded her approval, "It's magnificent!"

"So, who is it that you're doing research about from the 1800s?"

"My G3 grandmother." She smiled. He chuckled in appreciation. "At least I think that's how many greats it is. I'm not completely sure. It's a guess. All I really know is her name and how she died."

The owner of the restaurant made his way to the table with their gumbo. He smiled at Cade, set the bowls on the table, and patted him on the back.

"Can I reserve you this weekend for Saturday night from seven to midnight?"

Cade glanced at Caroline and looked back up at him. "Why, what's goin' on?"

"Jeff's band had to cancel, because Toby had to go to Lafayette for his grandma's funeral."

Cade's eyes genuinely saddened with the bad news. "Yeah, we can hook you up. We'll be here at six-thirty to prep, that okay?"

"Yeah man, thanks a heap. I owe ya one."

"You're in a band?" This guy gets more fascinating by the minute.

He nodded humbly. "My boys and I get together and play sometimes. It's no big deal."

"I'd like to see that sometime."

His head snapped up. "Come this Saturday night, then."

Caroline had no idea what her dad had planned for the weekend, if anything. But she desperately wanted to hear him sing again. "I'll have to check with my dad first, since I'm staying with him. I just got here a couple of days ago and I'm not sure if he has anything planned for me."

Cade nodded.

"So, you work at the library, moonlight in a band. . .what else do you do, Mr. Beauregard?"

He sat silently for a minute. "You can call me Cade. I like the way you say it."

Caroline's cheeks grew hot.

"I like that too," he said with a big smile.

She tried her best to play it off. "I don't know what you're talking about."

He laughed aloud. "Oh, come on. Whenever I compliment you, your face turns five different shades of red. It's adorable."

She looked down, almost dizzy with embarrassment. "You noticed that, huh?"

He reached over to put his hand under her chin, and lifted her face back up to look at him. "You don't need to hide any part of this beautiful face from me. You have nothing to be embarrassed about." Her entire upper body was on fire. She wasn't sure if it was from embarrassment or the burning attraction she felt toward him.

"Is it hot in here? I'm burning up. Can you ask him to turn the air down a little?"

He chuckled. "I'm not hot, it's just you."

She reached back and fanned her neck, thankful she'd twisted her hair in a bun. He stared with a strange expression before he slowly took a bite of his gumbo and then a drink of water.

"I'm a landscaper."

She had forgotten she asked what else he did.

"I work at a couple of places around town, mostly large properties, maintaining the landscaping. I only do two properties once a week. So where are you staying? Who is your dad?"

"Until day before yesterday, I hadn't seen my dad since I was a toddler," she said. "He and my mom divorced when I was just a baby, and my fiancé thought it would be a good idea for me to reconcile with my dad before we got married. Honestly, I didn't want to come. But deep down I was curious about my dad, so I came."

"I'll be sure to thank your fiancé if I ever meet him," he said sincerely. "So who's your dad?"

"Eddie Fontenot."

Recognition invaded his golden eyes. "Ahh, okay. That was your car I pulled out of the mud. You really had that thing buried. I should've caught that today, but I didn't recognize it all cleaned up. That's one of the places I do landscaping—the Fontenot plantation."

She nodded and smiled. "I know."

His head tilted, amused. "How?"

"Well, a couple of the ladies that work at the house were talking about the gardener and were calling him—you, Beau. I hadn't made the connection until the waitress called you by that name."

He smiled. "They were talking about me?"

"Yes, very highly, I might add."

His smile broadened and his brilliant eyes fixated on hers, melting her insides. "What about you? Did you talk about me?"

She shook her head, thankful she could answer innocently. "No, I didn't see you. I only heard you singing beneath my window Tuesday morning."

He frowned. "I'm sorry, I didn't think anyone was staying on that side of the house. If I had known you were up there sleeping, I would've been quieter."

She smiled again and took a drink. "It's okay. It was refreshing to wake up to such a se—pleasant voice."

He perked up. "You almost said sexy voice, didn't you?"

"No! I-I was going to say. . .um. . .soothing."

Clearly he didn't believe her for a second. "Right. Soothing. It's okay, I kinda like that you think I'm sexy. Well, my voice anyway." An amber fire smoldered in his eyes behind his long, black lashes. Caroline squirmed, exposed and vulnerable to his incredible charm.

She quickly looked down and ate another spoonful of gumbo. "You were right, this gumbo is delicious." He smirked at her pitiful attempt to change the subject. "So now you know where I'm staying. You said you haven't lived at home in years. Where do you live?" She raised her glass to her lips and cocked her eyebrow, challenging him.

"Well, I left home at eighteen for, um, work, then I came back after several years to live with my parents until I finished college. I've had my own place for a few years now. It's funny you should ask. We're kind of neighbors. I live in what used to be an outbuilding, but is now a renovated log cabin on the Fontenot plantation."

Swallowing her drink before she spewed it across the table on him, Caroline suddenly felt sick. The blood drained from her face as she realized his was the house she had trespassed in, and she had literally run into and touched his wet, naked body. She closed her eyes to make the panic go away. It didn't work.

ELEVEN

"Hey, are you okay? You just got really pale."

She looked up at him with indescribable mortification. Just as quickly as the blood drained from her face, it came back and she blushed so badly she had to be purple. Caroline abruptly stood up, hitting the table with her legs and sloshing her soup. "Excuse me, I think I need to go to the bathroom and die. I mean, I need to. . .um. . .I have to go. Now."

His brow pulled together, baffled but amused by her unusual and sudden act of hysteria. Then, as if someone turned the light on, understanding washed over him. He knew. He put the puzzle pieces together in his mind and knew exactly what caused her lunacy.

He grabbed her hand before she could run away, stood and put a hand on each of her shoulders to steady her, and looked into her eyes. Caroline stopped fidgeting, but she was positive her heart would explode if she didn't lie down. She stared at the hands she twisted into knots and focused on not fainting.

He spoke slowly and softly to calm her. "Caroline. . .breathe." She breathed deeply through her nose. It didn't help. "Again, slowly." Hyperventilation was inevitable, but his repose was quite effective. He did a great job calming her down though she couldn't know how or understand why. She had trespassed in his house! She caught him by surprise—naked! He should be furious, not helpful.

Thankfully, no one else had decided to eat lunch this early so the restaurant was fairly empty. She couldn't handle an audience right now. The employees witnessing her breakdown was bad enough, much worse, the impossibly beautiful object of her total disgrace standing in front of and reassuring her.

"Better?" He asked.

She nodded quickly, not taking her eyes from her wringing hands. She'd never wanted to disappear so badly in her life.

"Now, look at me."

She shook her head squeezing her eyes closed in shame.

"Caroline, please. Look at me."

Slowly, she trailed her tear-filled gaze up to his and he smiled. "It's okay. I know what you're upset about and I'm telling you, it's okay."

She breathed in another deep breath and nodded again. Caroline tried to speak but swallowed her words. His knowing eyes said way more than his voice, and Caroline felt serene beneath his intense stare.

"Don't try to speak until you calm down and listen to what I have to say." Cade had complete control of the situation for which she was thankful because she certainly did not. "You've been to my house."

She closed her eyes and dropped her face into her hands.

"Caroline, please. Look at me."

Forcing herself to look up again, she wiped the tears from her cheeks.

"It's obvious that what happened upset you. Or maybe you're a little embarrassed?"

She huffed. A little embarrassed was a colossal understatement.

He smiled at her reaction and gently pulled her with him to sit back down. "I need you to know that I'm not angry or upset. I am curious, though. . ."

Oh good Lord! Here it comes.

"Why were you in my house?"

Caroline took a deep, solid breath and then a drink of water to try to regain her composure. "I was taking a walk in the woods to explore the grounds. I'm used to this weather, and I was so hot and needed a break before I made my way back to Eddie's house. I-I. . .stumbled upon an outbuilding that looked like a log cabin—your log cabin. I had no idea whose it was, but I was insanely curious, and only needed a minute or two."

She closed her eyes and rubbed the stress lines between her brows. Getting this next part out would be difficult. How does one explain her stupidity and lack of respect for someone's privacy? "I tried to peek in the windows but saw nothing, so I knocked lightly, planning to ask for a few moments of cool air. When no one answered, I knocked harder and the door opened. I mustn't have been latched well. Anyway, I foolishly entered. . ." Caroline stared at his collarbone, too ashamed to look at his face. "I'm really sorry."

The corner of his mouth curved into a one sided grin.

Her tone shifted a little harsher than she intended, probably a result of her embarrassment. "You know, if you're going to walk around your house naked you should probably lock the front door."

He smiled, his gaze not faltering. "Forgive me, sweet Caroline. I had no idea a beautiful woman would wander into my house, and be coming from my bedroom, as I emerged naked from my shower."

She dropped her head again as she remembered that moment, remembered what she saw. She swore, as incredible as it was, the image had burned into the back of her eyelids.

"So, Miss Fontenot, since you've seen me in all my glory, there mustn't be much left that you're curious about. Unless. . .unless you didn't see as much as I thought you might have?"

Caroline closed her eyes in preparation for his next question.

"Of course, I didn't see your face because of my towel-covered head, and it all happened so fast. I'm curious, what exactly did you see?"

I knew he was going to ask that. She could only manage a whisper. "Everything."

His loud burst of laughter filled the near-empty restaurant. "Well, in that case, would you care to join me for dinner Friday night?"

She was furious. "You're enjoying this, aren't you? Do you not see how incredibly embarrassed I am?"

His eyebrows raised. "How incredibly embarrassed you are? I'm the one who was naked, remember?"

She flinched. "Of course. How can I forget?" By this point the constant fire in her cheeks was standard around Cade, so fighting it was useless.

"Well, on the bright side, at least you did apologize as you sprinted out of my house after attacking my vulnerable naked condition. By the way, you left your water bottle."

He smirked. Nice to know one of them enjoyed the embarrassment.

"I really am sorry. If I had known you lived there—especially if I'd known you were in a steamy shower, I wouldn't have invaded your privacy."

"Steamy?" Playful now, he pondered her choice of adjectives.

"Whatever." Defeated, she sighed and smiled back. "Can we go to the courthouse now so I can find out where I came from?"

"Yes, ma'am. You know what, sweet Caroline? I'm kinda crushin' on you."

"Well, control yourself, Mr. Beauregard. I'm taken."

He smiled as he ushered her toward the parking lot and mumbled, "Not if I have anything to say about it."

The courthouse, with marble steps leading up to a colonnade, sat majestically in the center of a square block. It didn't really fit in the quaint little town, but was beautiful just the same. Caroline asked the clerk at the front desk where she could find birth records from the mid 1800s. The attractive young woman asked for the birth date and name.

"All I know is her birthday and her married name, can you find it from that?"

Maybe a couple of years older than Caroline, she tried, rather unsuccessfully, not to gawk at Cade.

Her attention briefly flitted back to Caroline. "We'll find out. I'll try it and see what the computer gives me."

"Thanks. Her name was Rachel C. Fontenot and her birthday was May 13, 1868."

"I think I found it. Rachel Caroline Beauregard at birth and Fontenot at death."

Cade stiffened. "I'm sorry, did you say her maiden name was Beauregard?"

A smile stretched across her face obviously thrilled he spoke to her. "Yes."

He cursed under his breath. "Caroline, I'll meet you outside. I need some air."

105

Too distracted to realize why he was so upset, Caroline couldn't believe she shared the same exact name and birthday with this woman. Not to mention that apparently her ghost was trying to tell her something through her dreams! This was all just too strange. "Is there a way you can print everything you have on her for me? What do y'all keep here besides birth records?"

Noticeably upset at the exit of her eye candy, she sighed, perturbed with answering Caroline's questions now. "We hold birth, death, divorce and marriage records. I can print all those out for five dollars."

"Thank you, I appreciate your help." After a few moments, the young woman smugly handed Caroline the papers.

Cade paced in front of his large Chevy Z71 pickup truck.

"Hey, you okay?"

"Fine. Did you get what you needed?" She nodded and he opened the door for her to get in.

She skimmed the paperwork and finally asked Cade what had him so upset.

"It sounds like we might be related somewhere down the line."

Related? Surely not. It shouldn't bother her since there was no chance of having any kind of relationship with him. But it did.

"Did her birth records have the names of her parents?" He stared at the road, but didn't seem very focused on driving.

Unsure, she checked again. "Yes, why?"

"I'm just curious how we could be related."

"This says her biological parents were Ralph and Elizabeth Beauregard. Those names ring any bells?"

Cade seemed to relax a little, but not enough to please him. "Nah, I'll find out though." He didn't bring it up again.

Caroline slipped into a comfortable ease on the drive back to the library. She felt like she had known Cade for years instead of hours. It was a strange chemistry they shared. With Trevor, it took her months to feel this comfortable.

He parked next to Caroline's car. She hastily gathered her things, but when she reached for the handle, it opened. Cade had made it around to her side quickly to open the door, only he didn't let her out yet. As she swung her legs around in preparation to stand up, he stood between her and the ground blocking her from getting out. It was almost uncomfortably close. Almost.

Placing both hands on her knees, effectively causing her skin to tingle from the contact, he smiled, but not his usually charming expression. He seemed perplexed. Trying to think of what he wanted to say. "I'm really glad I ran into you, well, met you. . .officially. . .today." He nervously laughed. "I suppose we already ran into each other a few days ago."

Fighting back the blush that crept up her neck again from the mention of her most embarrassing moment, Caroline surveyed where his hands rested on her bare skin. Certain there should be palm-shaped burns from the searing heat. She wished she'd worn jeans, but doubted it would've made a difference. Her body responded to this man like it never had with anyone before, not even Trevor, and that concerned her.

He gathered her hands in his. She took the opportunity to study his face while he stared at their adjoining palms. His bone structure was classic, handsome, and she would describe him as a pretty boy. But there was a certain ruggedness about him that counteracted the refinement. His hazel eyes were intelligent, knowing, and she could see the potential seriousness, but the twinkle in them perfectly showed his playful nature. Like a moth to a flame, he drew her in like no one else. Ever. His strong rough hands were surprisingly gentle. He lifted the top of her hand to his soft lips and kissed it.

"It was such a pleasure spending the afternoon with you, sweet Caroline." Her cheeks tingled again. With the hand he kissed, he helped her out of the truck.

She hugged him in thanks and he returned her affection with a kiss on her cheek. He smelled amazing. She stepped back before she was lost in the sensual man-fog of Cade. "Thank you for inviting me to lunch and toting me around town. I really enjoyed myself. Again, I'm really very sorry I caught you—well, that I trespassed in your house."

He hugged her again tightly this time and whispered. "I'm not. I only wish you hadn't rushed out so fast. Then I would have already had two days with the pleasure of knowing you." He released his hug and waited for her to unlock her Jeep so he could open the door for her.

As she slid behind the wheel, he took her left hand and kissed it again. Exceptionally charming, he leaned on her door. "You never answered my question. Will you have dinner with me Friday night?"

"I suppose so, since you asked so nicely."

He smiled. "Great! Meet me at my place at six."

"Your place?"

Still smiling, and that twinkle back in his eyes, "Yes, my place. I believe you know where it is." He winked.

Heart pounding, she rolled her eyes and fastened her seatbelt as he closed the door.

It was four o'clock when she arrived home and no one was about. She took the stairs two at a time to her room and immediately got on her computer. She searched for genealogy of Beauregard in Louisiana and found a few potential results.

The best she could tell, she and Cade were not directly related. Not knowledgeable with proper terminology regarding extended family, she found Rachel Fontenot was General Beauregard's second cousin, or first cousin once removed, however it's supposed to be stated.

By the time they made it through all the greats in the ancestors, the distance in their family tree wouldn't matter even if she and Cade could end up together. She shouldn't be interested in this trivial fact, and scolded herself for even taking the time to research the possibility. She would soon be Mrs. Trevor Callahan, and, other than learning about Rachel, the Beauregard family tree didn't matter to her. Or, it shouldn't.

On that note, the time had come to give dear Trevor a call. She reached for her cell phone in her purse but didn't feel it. Panic briefly prickled the back of her neck. She checked the nightstand thinking she may have put it there when she rushed up to her room. Nothing. What was her deal? So unlike her, she never went anywhere without her phone. This place had her all out of sorts. She must have left it in the car.

She bounded down the stairs and out the door, only to find her cell phone and a single long stemmed yellow rose wrapped with a purple ribbon lying on the hood of her car. A smile stretched across her face. Beneath the phone was a hand written note. She giggled at the stereotypical scratchy male handwriting. He was so sweet.

Sweet Caroline,

I found this in the cab of my truck. It must have fallen out of your pocket. Lucky me. Thanks again for making my day.

Your new friend,

Cade

She couldn't scrape the smile from her face as she breathed in the delicate scent of the rose. She floated up the stairs on a cloud. . .until her phone rang.

"Why haven't you called me back?"

"Hello, Trevor. It's lovely to talk to you, too."

"Sorry. I'm sorry. I've just missed you. The past twenty-four hours have been. . .stressful. Anyway, I tried calling a couple of times yesterday. It's been two days since I've talked to you and I was worried. How are things?"

"Things are going wonderfully. My dad is. . .well, he's great. I have a step mom, and a little brother and sister."

"That's good. Listen, I don't have time to chat right now, I just wanted to call and make sure you were okay. I needed to hear your beautiful voice and see how things were going with your dad. I have to go, but I'll call you later. I love you."

She paused a second too long and he hung up before she could respond. *Hmpf. How nice of him to let me share my experiences down here so far. Good to know he cares so much about me.* Probably best. She didn't really want to tell him about her research. Not yet, anyway. She also didn't want to tell him she couldn't find her ring. He'd blow a gasket.

She twirled the stem of the rose between her fingers. This was going to be a difficult summer. She walked into her room and stopped cold in her tracks. Her engagement ring was on her nightstand exactly where she'd left it.

What the heck is going on?

TWELVE

Caroline sat outside in an adirondack chair by the duck pond reading the information she had gotten from the courthouse. Eddie had spent a few hours of quality time with her this afternoon and gave her an official tour of the house where she learned his and April's room was on the second floor. Seemed appropriate that they would be in the center of the house, the heart of the structure.

Caroline was perfectly happy in Rachel's room on the third floor. She shared a connection with that room, unsure why, exactly, but she'd been drawn to it from the moment she arrived here. And, though she didn't believe in ghosts, Caroline couldn't help but feel Rachel's presence. A purpose for coming down here. She didn't believe for a second that Rachel had killed herself. Of course, she made that assessment purely based on her crazy dreams, but her gut told her there was more to the story.

Nothing she'd witnessed in those dreams could be proven, so she would certainly be committed if she tried to tell anyone about them. She needed to glean hard evidence from her dreams.

Finding Rachel's journal would help. She'd been about to hide it somewhere before Caroline woke up. Then in the next dream, after she'd overheard an argument between a man and woman and turned to leave the scene, the journal was mysteriously lying on the ground at Caroline's feet and she nearly stepped on it. Was Rachel trying to tell her it was some sort of answer to her mystery? The key to a door that had been slammed shut and locked before its time? Caroline needed to find it.

Why, after all this time, did Rachel care for people to know her story? Maybe she's haunting Caroline's dreams because she's stuck on this earth until the truth comes out. Then maybe she can finally rest in peace.

Now Caroline knew she'd boarded the crazy train. She acted as if Rachel was really a ghost that was haunting people. Haunting her.

She just didn't believe in ghosts. She believed in Demons and Angels, things she'd rather not investigate, but not stranded spirits. Maybe Google could provide some answers to the unexplainable things she'd experienced lately. After all, some of the television shows she used to watch while burning the midnight oil studying mentioned Louisiana being one of the most haunted places in the world.

Surely she wasn't the only skeptic out there. Maybe someone else had witnessed similar happenings in the area and debunked the spooky tales, proving them as myths created to scare people. That would confirm she really wasn't crazy. There had to be some reasonable explanation.

"What a pleasant surprise."

A familiar masculine scent and smooth voice interrupted her intense thoughts. She closed her eyes, ignored the flapping butterflies in her chest, and pretended not to be attracted to the source.

"I'm not used to finding such beautiful women lounging around this old place."

She'd never been a good pretender. A gigantic smile engulfed her face as she turned to see Cade's muscular arms leaning on the back of her chair. He was gorgeous.

She tried to play it as calm and cool as she could. "Well, if it isn't the Jack-of-all-trades. What's up? Not working any of your twenty-five jobs today?"

He smiled with a mischievous twinkle in his eyes, as if he knew something she didn't. "No, I decided to take the day off to prepare for a hot date I have later tonight."

"Hot date, huh? Maybe I should go inside so she won't be jealous to find you talking to me?"

His smile faded a bit. "I sure hope not, I'm not really into jealous chicks."

Caroline rolled her eyes. "Everybody has a little jealous streak in them, it's human nature. The trick is how you handle it." She added with a mumble, "Some people don't know how to control it."

"Ah. . .so the Prince is jealous." A statement more than a question.

Caroline hesitated.

He chuckled. "Hmm, I hit a nerve?"

She shook her head. "No, I'm just thinking."

"What is going through that mind of yours?"

Her eyes popped up to meet his. "I was wondering how well you control your jealousy?"

Cade laughed boisterously. "Sweetheart, I don't get jealous. If a woman doesn't want me that's up to her. I figure if somebody wants all of me, she's going to lay claim and stick to it. I don't like to play games."

"So you like to be chased then? I see, too lazy to do the chasing yourself?"

"In your case, cher, I'm up for the challenge. You are definitely worth the chase."

Caroline quietly stared at her papers, not knowing how to respond.

"You don't think you're worth chasing? Worth fighting for?"

When she didn't respond a second time, he squatted down in front of her. "You don't have a clue how amazing you are, do you?"

She scoffed and focused on her fidgeting hands, "Amazing. Hardly. You don't even know me. I have my issues, trust me."

He chuckled at her reaction. "Don't we all?" He waited for her to look at him before he stood, leaning forward, bracing his hands on the arms of her chair. She was locked in position, caged by this wall of muscled chest, biceps and broad shoulders. Mere inches from her face, Caroline held her breath as he quietly spoke.

"I wonder," he mused and his eyes flickered to her slightly parted lips, "what it would take to convince you just how incredible you are?"

His intensity had her heart doing flips and Caroline struggled to remember how to breathe, much less speak. Then he glanced at her left hand and his smile faded. He sighed and straightened back up. Caroline instantly missed his warmth. "I see you decided to put the ring on." Cade cocked his eyebrow and smirked. "So you won't forget again?"

Her brow furrowed and she spoke sternly. "I didn't forget." She narrowed her eyes, "You're the one who seems to forget."

"What, that you belong to someone else? I haven't forgotten, cher. I just don't care. When I see something I want, I go after it." His molten eyes ignited her core, and she forced herself not to squirm beneath his hypnotic focus. "If you were my girl, I'd make sure your body and soul was so in love with me, you'd never want to take my ring off your finger." He shrugged and cracked his knuckles. "You haven't said those magic little words yet, which technically means you're still on the market."

Caroline huffed, the smoldering tingles low in her belly quickly replaced by her flaring temper. "I am not on the market! Technically or otherwise! I'm not some heifer up for auction at your local sale barn. I am a grown woman quite capable of making my own decisions, and I've willingly accepted a marriage proposal which means I am officially off the market. I made the decision of my own free will. I don't belong to anyone."

"That's more like it." Amused, he moved slowly, leaning down to cage her again. His face level with hers as he stared intently into her eyes effectively causing her anger to fizzle. Slowly and deliberately, he leaned closer. Caroline froze, sure he was about to kiss her, and her heart skipped a beat. . .or three.

She couldn't believe his arrogance, his bravery, or his blatant disregard of her relationship status, but, strangely, she didn't want to stop him. She couldn't. Her defenses were weak around Cade Beauregard. She sucked in a breath and closed her eyes expectantly. His soft lips pressed against her cheek.

"Don't forget, six o'clock, my place." She heard him chuckle, and when she opened her eyes he'd already headed toward the house. Slightly disappointed, she studied his smooth, confident stride. Something about him, Caroline wasn't sure what exactly—Trevor exuded the same confident sex appeal, kindled a fire from deep within. A fire she'd only ever before felt with Trevor. Whatever power that cocky Cajun had over her, she needed to ignore it and get her feelings in check. Forbidden thoughts and images of another man bouncing around in her head would bring nothing but trouble. Unfortunately, checking those feelings proved to be extremely difficult.

Cade fascinated her, and she couldn't help but succumb to his gravitational pull whenever he was near. He invaded her personal space, her bubble, and, for some crazy reason, she didn't mind. Normally, she would step back and cross her arms to promote more space in an uncomfortable situation with strangers. However, Cade's invasion was intoxicating. Her heart flipped with a simple look, or brush of his hand as he passed, and Lord help her when he kissed her cheek just now. From only the few minutes she'd just spent with this handsome stranger, she felt her traitorous body giving in to the desire. It scared her to death.

Caroline closed her eyes and rested her head against the back of the weathered chair. She wondered where they would go or if he would get take out so they could eat in the privacy of his cabin. She smiled, giggly with excitement.

I shouldn't be doing this. Trevor would have a cow if he knew my plans for the night.

His goal in sending her down to Louisiana was to build a relationship with her father, not make a new male friend—one intent on stealing his fiancée. Maybe the simple fact she shouldn't be doing it was what had her so excited. Rebellious Caroline instead of scared-to-break-the-rules Caroline. It felt really good. And crazy. She'd only known this guy for a couple of days, yet a giggly inner-adolescent had taken over her ability to reason and act responsibly.

Completely out of character, Caroline couldn't understand where her newfound attitude had developed. It must be this whole mystical, spooky swamp town. Surrounded by the spirit of the bayou, and temptation lurking around every corner—well, from a log cabin, at least, Caroline was clueless how to handle this entire situation.

Her dad's truck pulled into the driveway and she gathered her things. Heading toward the house, Caroline glanced up at the third floor window from which Rachel had allegedly jumped. It was a long way to the ground and the statue she must have hit was no longer there. Caroline still believed someone pushed Rachel. She wished she'd paid more attention and made a stronger effort to remember the details of her dreams. She'd had no idea those crazy dreams would come into play later. Some details, however, stood out more than others, and no matter how hard she tried, she couldn't scrape them from her memory.

She met her dad at his truck and he gave her the standard hug and a kiss on the cheek. She really liked this greeting. Very welcoming and personable, it made her more comfortable.

He kept his arm around her shoulders as they walked in, and she saw something move in the second floor window. He must have seen it, too. Caroline noticed his eyes trained in the same direction. As they approached the porch, April came out to greet them. He gave her a quick kiss on the lips and then a hug. As April hugged him she glared at Caroline over his shoulder. For a second those fierce blue eyes reminded her of Trevor's. However, unlike Trevor, it was blatantly obvious April hated everything about her. Caroline quickly looked away avoiding any kind of confrontation.

Delia met them just inside the door. She wore a worried expression on her face. "Sir, there was an accident in the kitchen." Eddie's brow furrowed with concern. "No one was seriously injured," Delia quickly added. "We're all okay, it was just a scare."

"What happened?"

She smiled sheepishly. "Well, sir, as Delphine was warming the oil to fry the fish, it seemed to burst into flames, like a gas leak or something. We were able to put the fire out quickly enough, but not before Delphine burned her arm. I rushed her to the emergency room, dropped her off, and came back to clean up the mess."

"Is Delphine okay?"

"Yes, sir, she will be fine. She had a nasty second degree burn on her left arm, but she seemed in good spirits. I'm very sorry, Mr. Fontenot, the kitchen suffered some burn damage on the backsplash of the stove and some of the cabinetry. I'm afraid we won't be able to cook supper here tonight."

"That's okay, Delia. We can all go out to eat somewhere. Thank you for stopping it as quickly as you did. This could have been so much worse. You are welcome to take the rest of the day off and tomorrow as well."

Not wanting to be around April, Caroline quickly asked Delia if she could ride with her to the hospital to visit Delphine.

Eddie didn't hide his disappointment. "How long will you be at the hospital, Delia?" April sighed in frustration and turned to go back into the house.

"Oh, I don't plan to be long, Mr. Fontenot. I'm just going to check on Delphine and see if she needs a ride home. I'm sure she's stoned on pain pills right now." Delia chuckled.

"Caroline, please—" Eddie shifted his stance and glanced in the direction April went. "Please, don't feel as if you need to leave because of. . .this. I—*we* want to spend more time with you. We can all go out for dinner if you'd like?"

Caroline seriously doubted April cared to spend a millisecond longer with her, but it was sweet of him to say that. Since she'd arrived, April dominated Eddie's time and Caroline hadn't had the chance to spend much quality time with him. Thankfully, she had a few distractions to keep her busy. "No, it's okay, Dad. Really."

"Caroline, I'm not—"

"I have dinner plans already anyway, but thank you."

119

He grinned. "Dinner plans? Anyone I know?"

She blushed. "Relax, it's just dinner with Ca—um, I mean. . .Beau."

A big toothy grin erupted across Delia's face. "Oh, Miss Caroline, you need not waste your time with me! Go get ready for your date tonight."

"It's not a date. And I'm not meeting him until six."

She giggled. "Go rest up then, doll. You might just be needing all your energy with that hunk o' burnin' love." She walked off the porch and mumbled, "I know I sure would." Then she laughed aloud the rest of the way to her car.

Her dad looked pleasant. "Beau, huh? He's a great guy." He winked.

Caroline closed her eyes and shook her head. "Dad—it's just dinner. I'm engaged, remember?"

"Yep, I remember. You're not married yet."

"Gah! What is it with guys? Having an engagement ring means nothing unless there's a wedding band with it?" She stomped away shaking her head in disbelief. She'd always thought when someone accepted a proposal, he or she made a promise to marry that person. Yes, promises were easily made and easily broken, but they weren't something she took lightly.

Caroline trudged up the stairs and rounded the corner toward her room as a chill crept up her spine. A cold tingling sensation similar to her foot falling asleep. She slowed her pace and her eyes shifted around the hallway. She inspected corners, creaky floorboards, shadowy doorways, and anything else that could possibly prompt this uneasy feeling. Nothing. Her stomach rolled letting her know she hadn't eaten all day. The queasiness it induced didn't help with being spooked. She hurried her steps and slipped into her room.

It was frigid, much colder than the rest of the house. Perhaps because her room faced east, hindering the sun from warming the space. Either way, the goosebumps on her skin protested the freezing temperature so she brusquely rubbed her arms. She shivered, hoping her overactive imagination was merely working overtime.

Caroline looked around the empty room before she strolled to the window. She considered opening it to let the summer heat inside, but opted against it as she brushed her finger across the initials again and gazed out over the duck pond. She imagined Rachel standing here long ago, etching those beloved initials into the glass, and wondered what Rachel's view had been like. Caroline doubted it was quite as nice then as it is now.

Cade did a beautiful job with the landscaping. The azalea bushes were blooming and the majestic water feature to the side of the pond had tropical plants and lily pads all around it. Caroline smiled as she pictured him slaving away to create this masterpiece. He had skills. She wondered what other talents he possessed, then shook her head to erase the sinful thoughts creeping into her mind.

Trevor, Trevor, Trevor. All things Trevor.

She had to admit to herself, she was a little. . .unsure if she was ready to get married. Her frivolous, unpredictable feelings around Cade made her uneasy and caused her to doubt everything she thought was solid in her life. To be completely devoted and in love with Trevor, how could she justify the butterflies and heart palpitations, and turning every shade of red on the color wheel simply from Cade's proximity?

While Caroline admired Cade's work and forced herself to focus on her fiancé, she heard something behind her—a chair dragging across the hardwood floor.

She whirled around to see who was in her room, halfway expecting it to be Cade since she was just thinking about him, but no one was there. However, the old chair at the dressing table now sat by the bed. She hesitated while reality sank in, and a lump of terror squeezed her throat. Fighting the instant wave of nausea, Caroline rushed to the door to see if someone might have pranked her and could still be retreating down the hall, but the eerily quiet vacancy of the third floor confirmed her suspicions.

No way. It's not possible. She surveyed the hallway while rubbing her upset stomach, and solid fear crept up her spine. She zipped down the stairs and rushed outside for some fresh air before she lost it. She was thankful her lungs were busy gasping for air so she couldn't release the bloodcurdling scream that threatened to escape from her core.

Thoroughly spooked, she rocked slightly as she sat hugging her bent knees on the front steps and searched all possible explanations for how that chair moved. It certainly wasn't an earthquake. She would've felt a tremor or something, plus, she didn't know if earthquakes even existed in the marshy swamps of southern Louisiana. The floor wasn't sloped, and the closed window allowed no draft, not that a slight breeze from that solitary window could move a heavy wooden chair anyway.

So how did the chair move—rather, drag itself halfway across the freakin' room? Caroline buried her face in her arms which were now folded on top of her knees. There had to be some logical answer. She simply couldn't accept the ghost theory. Yes, she believed in the possibility that Rachel had somehow invaded her dreams. The scenery and furniture were too exact for it to be a similarity or coincidence. But Rachel's ghost physically haunting her? No. No way. Simply too unbelievable. Right?

"Ridiculous. I'm losing my mind," she mumbled and rubbed her face.

"Talking to yourself?" Standing behind her, April taunted Caroline by clicking her tongue. "People may think you're crazy if you keep that up." She sauntered down the steps and stood in front of Caroline, noticeably sizing her up from head to toe. Caroline suddenly felt very insignificant under her scrutiny. April mockingly tilted her head to one side. "Awe, what's wrong? Not feeling well? Judging by your pale, washed out appearance, you look like you've seen a ghost."

Caroline narrowed her eyes, not yet sure how to read this woman. When in doubt, politeness always took precedence. She pasted on a smile and squared her shoulders as she stood. "I'm fine. Thanks. Just getting a little fresh air." She gave April a quick nod and turned her back to the woman who probably continued to inspect her like a diseased specimen. She tried not to care. A menacing chuckle followed her inside, and she wondered if April's words were deliberate, or simply coincidental. Either way, Caroline received the crystal clear message of April's dislike for her. She just didn't understand why.

THIRTEEN

Caroline stopped at the base of the stairs, her gaze following the curved banister to the top. What had once been a welcoming, comfortable space now seemed ominous and scary. She needed to get ready for her dinner with Cade, but going in that possibly cursed room now freaked her out. What if it wasn't some silly ghost of her grandmother? What if it was something evil? Whatever existed in there clearly aimed to terrify her. At the least, unnerve her.

She didn't want another face-off with April, so she sprinted up the stairs, swooped inside her now-normal room, trying not to dwell on the bone-chilling fact the chair was back where it belonged, and quickly gathered her clothes and toiletries. Arms loaded, she bolted to the bathroom, forbidding herself to look back.

Caroline paid no attention to the scalding temperature of the water as it singed her sensitive skin. She was much too distracted to care. How had things gone completely off track and failed to make sense in a matter of hours? What was April's deal, anyway? Caroline hadn't spoken to her more than a couple of cordial greetings since April had come home from

New Orleans. She'd always been polite, even friendly to her stepmother although the woman made sure to hog every minute of Eddie's time.

Caroline had to deal with a girl her Freshman year who felt the constant need to put others down to build herself up. She was the epitome of a mean girl. Somehow, Caroline worried that April was worse than just mean. Marking her territory may not be April's only objective, but Eddie assured Caroline she would come around. Caroline needed to trust he would make a point to spend some quality time with her after he handles April's hissy fit.

She sighed and focused on each muscle group as the surprisingly powerful water pressure pounded against the knots. Trust. Not something that came easily to her regarding her father and the entire family she never knew she had. But she desperately wanted to trust them. However, considering April's role in this family, the tension between them would definitely hinder Caroline's desire for an extended stay.

Part of her wanted to surrender and escape back to Chicago with her tail tucked safely between her legs, but the other part, the moronic curious one who constantly made bad decisions, wanted to stay and further investigate this new facet of her life.

Caroline wanted to know more about Rachel and the mystery surrounding her tragic death. More importantly, she needed to understand how and why she'd dreamed of this exact place, and possibly an ancestor about whom she'd never known, all before stepping foot on the marshy soil.

No, she wasn't ready to leave yet. Her relationship with Eddie was blossoming, even with the small amount of time she'd been allowed to spend with him. She hadn't had a chance yet to bond with her new siblings, and of course she wanted to know more about the incredibly handsome Cade and his charming personality.

Caroline turned off the faucet when the water finally ran cold. Her tense shoulders hadn't seemed to loosen at all. Although, thinking about her upcoming evening with Cade had taken the edge off the scare from earlier. She dressed quickly, brushed her teeth, and left her hair loose and wavy, towel drying it as much as possible. She applied mascara and lip gloss, and after April's not-so-subtle insult, Caroline added a touch of blush to her pale cheeks. Her stomach growled furiously now, scolding her for skipping lunch. She hoped whatever Cade had planned for dinner would satisfy her monstrous appetite.

Remembering exactly where his log cabin was since the first time she'd been there would be tricky. She had cut through a few trails trying to follow a path from a silly dream, and then ran back in a tizzy, distraught about getting caught in his cabin and seeing. . .what she saw. Her dad drew a map to the cabin while grinning the whole time. Obviously not upset she wasn't spending the evening with him.

"He's having you over for dinner at his place? He must really like you."

"What? Why do you say that?"

Eddie smiled and looked in her eyes. "As long as he's lived here, I don't think Beau's ever had a girl in his cabin. Guys don't like to show a girl where they live unless they don't mind them coming back sometime. It's kind of like showing your hand in a poker game."

She didn't mention that she'd already been in the cabin—uninvited— and got way more than she'd bargained for. "Well, Cade knows that I'm engaged, so I'm sure he's just being cordial since I'm a visitor." She cringed, hoping her pathetic poker face didn't reveal her lie. She knew better.

"Cade, huh? He also doesn't tell too many people his real name. He usually goes by Beau. I only know his real name because he's on the payroll." She smiled inside knowing he'd not only told her his first name, but his middle name as well.

"You kids have a good time tonight and you be sure to tell Cade, if he messes with you he's got to deal with me."

She nodded. "Can I ask you something?"

The last time she asked him a question like that she dropped the bomb on him about why he left her. She could see he was a little more apprehensive this time. He squinted, "Sure."

"Why does April hate me so much?"

A pained expression creased his brow, clearly hoping she hadn't noticed or come to that conclusion. "She doesn't hate you, sweetheart. I think she's more jealous of you because you're in my life now. You see, I beat myself up for a long time whenever I would think about what I had done to you and your mother. You were always the missing piece in my life. She enjoyed being able to fill that void, to an extent, because it made her feel like the most important person in my world. Now that you are in my life and she knows how badly I wanted this, she's having a difficult time. . .sharing. I know it sounds really petty and immature, but I'm working on her. Just hang in there. She'll come around."

Caroline smiled and patted his face gently. "Well, aren't you just the most desirable man in town? Everybody wants a piece of Eddie Fontenot."

He grinned. "You have no idea, love. No idea."

She wasn't sure what he meant by that, but it was cool to see him blush. At least she knew where she inherited that annoying trait.

Caroline nervously twirled a lock of hair. "Can I ask you one more thing?" He nodded, concern masking his expression. "Have you ever. . .well, has anything weird ever happened around here?"

"Weird like how?"

"Like, things moving or disappearing. . ." his eyes reflected amusement and he fought back a smile. She immediately regretted mentioning it. "You know, I'm being silly. Never mind." She started to walk away but he grabbed her hand.

"No, wait. I'm sorry, I wasn't trying to discount your concern. No, I've never noticed anything strange or weird, but I'm gone a lot. When I'm here, I'm usually in my office and focused on work, so I don't pay much attention to my surroundings. Is anything wrong? Has something happened?"

Caroline shook her head. "No, it's nothing. I'm just tired is all. New place, new people, you know?"

He eyed her warily. "You're sure?"

Embarrassed for even bringing it up, she wanted out of this awkward moment so she nodded and kissed his cheek on her way out of the kitchen.

Before she headed to Cade's cabin, she gave Trevor a call. She didn't know if it was to ease her conscience or so he wouldn't call her later and interrupt her evening. She laughed at herself while dialing his number. Talk about getting in way over your head.

"Hey, baby."

"Hey! How are you doing?"

"I'm okay," she lied. She still felt uneasy and her emotions threatened to bubble over. "I just wanted to call and check in. . .you know, see how you were doing?"

"Apart from missing you terribly, I'm okay. You miss me?"

"Of course. How's business?"

"Business? You're really asking me how work is going?" He chuckled but sounded annoyed. It annoyed her in return.

"Yeah, I guess I am. Everything with your dad going well?" Suddenly his tone got defensive and sharp.

"Things are just fine. Why, what have you heard?"

What the heck is his problem? "Nothing, I haven't heard from you much, so I figured you've been busy, that's all. Geez, chill out."

"Sure, I get it. I've been fine. My dad's been riding me pretty hard, but things are fine. How are things with your dad? Has he accepted you yet?"

A shot of anger fired through Caroline and she frowned. "Accepted? Um, yeah. . .whatever that means. He hasn't added me as a beneficiary, if that's what you're implying."

"Easy, babe. I was just asking if he's treating you like a daughter now or like the kid he abandoned years ago?"

Okay, seriously, she wanted to hang up on him and flush his ring down the toilet. What was his deal? "Things are going great. Eddie never treated me like the kid he abandoned years ago. He's been nothing but accepting and hospitable since I showed up on his doorstep."

"Great. It shouldn't be long now and you'll be a part of his family."

"Trev. . .what in the world are you trying to say that you're not just spitting out? I am already a part of his family. It's like nothing ever happened. We're getting along great and I'm loving it down here. Isn't that what you wanted?" Angry now, she stomped up the stairs to her room, completely forgetting the episode from earlier.

"Oh, don't be so dramatic. I was only asking a simple question. Listen, I gotta go. I'll call you later tonight."

Oh, the nerve of him.

"Don't bother, my phone is almost dead and I can't find my charger," she lied again. "I'll call you after I find it." Her phone was fully charged and she looked straight at her charger on the dressing table as she said it. Caroline fumed. What was his problem? Why was he being such a jerk?

She'd started to really doubt her decision to accept his ring. Nearly perfect in every way, Trevor's mood swings were killing her. She still hadn't completely recovered from his twenty-five sexual partners that he could remember.

She angrily slipped the engagement ring off her finger and left her phone in her room. Already she felt somewhat better, a secret counterblow to his disregard. She put them both inside the antique wooden jewelry box so she would know where they were this time.

As Caroline was about to leave, the skies opened. Without a backward glance she grabbed her rain jacket from the closet and the map her dad had drawn and darted down the porch steps.

She sprinted to Cade's cabin, partially to stay as dry as she could, but also from anger toward Trevor. She needed to burn off some frustration.

She arrived on Cade's doorstep early because when he opened the door he didn't have on a shirt. A beautiful sight. She immediately noticed a scar on his chest. No, not just a scar, a brand. But she could not make out the design.

"Caroline! You're early!" He wore a larger-than-life smile. "Come in, come in. I didn't realize it was raining, I'm sorry. I should have come and picked you up so you wouldn't have to walk in the rain."

"It's okay." Out of breath, she panted. "I ran. . .it's good for me. . .I need the exercise."

He chuckled. "Exercise is good, but no need to run in the rain. Your mascara is running." He dabbed her face with a tissue and helped take off her rain coat. Quite suddenly, she collapsed in his arms and started bawling on his shoulder.

He hugged her tightly, soothing her. "Hey, hey. . .what's wrong? Are you okay? I know I'm ugly but you don't have to cry and make me feel worse."

She laughed and looked up at his face—just to make sure he was joking. There was no way he didn't know how hot he was, especially with that twitchy tilt in the right corner of his mouth.

She backed up and straightened her clothes, fluffing the waves in her hair. "I'm sorry. Oh, good grief, I'm so sorry. I'm such a mess. I'm just. . .well. . ." She sighed and fidgeted with her fingernails. The last thing she wanted to talk about at the moment was Trevor. She wanted to relax and enjoy her evening, and dwelling on their argument would disrupt that. "You must be thinking I'm one screwed up puppy." He didn't answer which caused her to stop and look at him. He appreciatively ran his eyes up and down her body, thoroughly checking her out and causing her pulse to race.

"I like puppies." He flashed a heart-stopping, double-meaning smile and Caroline felt her knees start to buckle.

"By the way, Mr. Beauregard, if you ever call yourself ugly again, I'm afraid I will have to punch you. Every girl we crossed in this town the other day practically had their tongues hanging out as you walked by. Therefore, since I know you are aware of your extreme hotness, any further comments like that will be assumed you are fishing for compliments."

He smiled now, but it didn't reach his eyes. He obviously still worried about her sudden break down. "Right. My bad. Thank you. . .for the compliment." She smiled and he walked down the hall to his bedroom. She flinched remembering why she knew that was his bedroom. He came back out fully clothed this time, and put on some soft jazz music. "I hope you're hungry."

"I'm starving."

The delicious smell ravaged her senses triggering hunger pangs. "Where'd you get the yummy food I smell? What is it? My mouth is watering!"

He looked offended, shocked even, but smiled. "Say what? I didn't pick this up at any restaurant. I killed it, cleaned it, cut it up, packaged it and cooked it myself. We're having deer steak. Hope you don't mind eating Bambi's daddy." She felt bad for assuming he couldn't cook and offending him.

"Are you kidding? I'm from Arkansas, I love venison!"

His head snapped up. "Wait, I thought you were from Illinois?"

She tilted her head and winked. "That's what you get for thinking."

He looked intrigued, but rolled his eyes. "Okay, my turn to bite. How long did you live in Arkansas?"

"I lived there from the time I was a baby until I went to Chicago for college."

"You don't sound like you're from Arkansas."

"I've lost most of my southern accent from living in Illinois for nearly five years."

Cade was impressed, almost relieved, to find out she was a southern girl rather than a Yankee. "So, why did you choose to go to college in Illinois?"

"My best friend Kristy decided to go there and I wanted to be there with her."

"Arkansas, huh? I'll admit, you just gained a few points in my book." He grinned.

"You're keeping score?" Caroline's never ending curiosity flared again. So much to learn about this mystifying man.

"Metaphorically, yes."

She cringed. "So how many points did I lose from sneaking into your cabin and catching you in your birthday suit?" She blushed again, so she closed her eyes and waited for his answer. He cupped her face and she kept her eyes closed for fear of what he might do. . .what she might do. His large, warm hands cradled her jaw perfectly and she instantly relaxed. She slowly opened her eyes to see him admiring her.

"Bumping into you that day was one of the coolest, strangest things I've ever experienced. Of course, after I put some clothes on, surveyed the area, and established nothing was broken or missing." He smiled, then his eyes sparkled. "But seeing your genuine reaction when you realized it was me you had bumped into. . .I will remember that for the rest of my life." Caroline swallowed hard in an attempt to hide her continued embarrassment and kindling desire.

"I realize I haven't known you very long, but I pride myself in being a great judge of character. You are the most compelling, genuine, sincere, amazing person I've ever met. I'm thankful for that raging curiosity that led you to me, even if it was one of my most embarrassing moments. I'm not easy to embarrass, so congrats." He chuckled.

"Anyway, I believe everything happens for a reason. It was no coincidence that you came to the library during the one four hour shift I work there each week."

His face only inches from hers, she couldn't help but focus on his mouth. She wanted him to kiss her. To feel if his lips were as soft as they looked. To taste the mint she faintly smelled on his breath. She found herself leaning forward slowly with her lips slightly parted. She closed her eyes, and he pressed his cheek against hers.

He whispered softly, sending shivers throughout her body. "The food is ready, cher. I hope you brought your appetite."

FOURTEEN

She exhaled slowly so not to seem too disappointed. Disappointed, but thankful for his control.

She battled feelings she'd never encountered before. How could the urge to cheat on Trevor come so easily to her around a man she just met? She had passion with Trevor, but not this yearning need for someone to touch her. It could be that Trevor wouldn't keep his hands off of her, but she didn't remember ever feeling this need. . .this hunger for raw physical contact.

He had the small table elegantly set, complete with wine glasses. *Oh goodness, if I have alcohol on a completely empty stomach, I'm gonna make a fool of myself. I'd better pass on the wine.*

He spread the food out on his small bar. As she fixed her plate, he'd already poured her a glass of wine.

"I'm sorry, I meant to tell you, I don't really like red wine. I'm more of a sweet wine kind of girl."

She thought that might save her the embarrassment of having to explain the real reason why she didn't want to drink. But he pulled a bottle of white wine from the fridge and mixed it with the dry red wine. Sangria, he called it. She stared at him, unsure what to say.

"Try it, you'll like it. Trust me." His smile was warm and mesmerizing.

She sipped the sweet, slightly citrusy liquid surprised by how good it tasted. He held his glass up for a toast. She reminded herself again that this first glass was on an empty stomach. She'd better take it slow.

"To trespassing, to bumping into strangers, to having a beautiful woman sneak up on my bare behind, and still getting her to come over for dinner. To new acquaintances and the excitement that comes with them."

"Here, here." She clinked her glass with his and, distracted by his attentiveness and the burst of flavor against her famished palate, she forgot to sip as she took a very large gulp. Her head felt a little fuzzy so she took a bite of food. Voracious hunger and this delectable food transformed her into a champion competitive eater. Cade happily watched her annihilate the dinner he'd prepared. She paused for a moment, wiped her mouth and took a sip of wine.

She shrugged. "You told me to bring my appetite."

He nodded in approval. "No, it's great! I love a woman who isn't afraid to eat. You're stroking my ego." He smiled appreciatively.

"I'm just impressed you know how to cook and are brave enough to do it for someone else. Trevor only knows how to make peanut butter and jelly sandwiches."

"Really?" Cade was appalled. "He's never cooked for you? How long have you been with him?"

Now that she thought about it, it was kind of sad. Trevor never had her over to his house, just the two of them. A few times, they ate at his parents' house, but mostly they went to restaurants, or he came to her place. She stared at her glass of wine as she gently rolled the stem between her fingers.

"We've been together a little over two years." She spoke softly, still very upset about their earlier conversation. Caroline didn't know why, but she felt like Trevor was up to no-good and that it involved her. He was keeping her in the dark about something and she didn't like it. It must've been a little obvious.

Cade reached down and gently took her left hand, tilting it, noticing her ring missing. She braced herself for a sarcastic comment. Instead, he pulled her hand to his mouth and kissed her ring finger. What a sweet gesture. Why is this guy not taken already? Though he made it no secret he was going to try to convince her she didn't need to marry Trevor, he didn't push or annoy her about it. He had completely won her over and she didn't know how to explain—or deny, her irrational feelings. But she needed to before she did something stupid.

"So, tell me about your best friend."

A smile involuntarily spread across her face. "Kristy's from Tennessee, and her dad is an auctioneer making a very good living. Because her family had plenty of money, it allowed her freedom of expression while growing up, so she was able to experiment with all kinds of fun things. As it turns out, she has a passion for fashion and a knack for the sewing machine. She's always assembling outfits for me to wear because I have zero fashion sense. If it were up to me I'd stay in my ratty old jeans, Razorback T-shirts, and bare feet all the time."

Caroline ran her index finger around the smooth rim of her wine glass. "She actually made me this incredible emerald green dress for my birthday and gave it to me early so I could wear it the night Trevor proposed." Talking about Kristy was choking her up enough, and now Trevor had popped back into her mind. Anger, insecurity, sadness, and worry pulsed through her. She had to get her emotions in check before she really embarrassed herself. "Kristy's very talented, and I know someday she'll have her own clothing line."

Caroline's eyes misted as she thought about Kristy moving so far away. "Unfortunately, she's moving to California once she graduates."

Cade chuckled and shook his head. "Razorbacks. That'll only get you in trouble around here if you represent them the day after Thanksgiving when they play LSU." He winked and took a drink before shrugging his beefy shoulders. "Alabama or Florida, on the other hand. . .well, you don't even wanna go there."

He chewed another bite while smiling at his inside joke. She knew about the tension between LSU and Florida, but hadn't followed their beef with Alabama. She didn't care exactly what was behind that particular football rivalry, Caroline enjoyed talking about the sport with someone again. Trevor hated football.

"So your bff's going to Cali, where do you plan to live once you graduate?"

The question surprised her. She hadn't thought much about it. She'd always assumed she'd move back to Arkansas with her mom, but doubted Trevor would be down with that. "Who knows? Trevor has a great job in the city, so there's a big possibility I'll have to stay in Chicago."

He let out a big laugh and then tried to recover with a cough. She glared while trying to figure out what he found so funny. She raised an eyebrow and crossed her arms.

"What?"

"Have to, huh? You don't like it up there?"

To distract him and change the subject, Caroline tried to sound innocent.

"I told you, I'm a southern girl. How old are you, Cade?"

"I'm twenty-seven, but my birthday is in a few months." He paused and tilted his head. "It's impolite to ask a lady her age, so I'm going to attempt something very risky. I'll make a bet that I can guess your age."

She grinned. Brave soul. "Well, aren't you Mr. Confident." She'd always been told she looked older than her age. Not always a compliment, but useful in harmless bets such as this. "Okay, you're on. The stakes?"

He took a drink of his wine and slowly wiped his mouth before he spoke. "You know you like it. Confidence is sexy, right?"

"Confidence, yes. Arrogance. . .not so much."

"Understood. So, the stakes. If I guess right, you let me steal a kiss."

Her heart literally skipped a couple of beats and she held her breath. This could be bad. Very bad. She slowly exhaled and took a sip of wine. "And if you guess wrong?"

"Then, hmmm. I will sing you a song."

She giggled, thrilled with the possibility of hearing him sing again, especially just for her. "You'll sing me a song?"

"Yep. Right here, right now. Those are the stakes. Take 'em or leave 'em."

"What song?"

"I'll make one up on the spot."

"Okay. I could go for some serenading tonight. You're on."

"I'm gonna guess that you are twenty-two—" She opened her mouth to say something but he interrupted. "No, wait. You mentioned a birthday. When is that, exactly?"

Caroline cleared her throat. "May thirteenth."

"Okay, I say you are twenty-three years old. That is my final answer."

She took another sip of wine. She never did have a good poker face. Her heart pounded and the room started to spin. Caroline wasn't sure if it was from the alcohol or anticipation of the kiss he was about to steal. Technically it wasn't stealing if she gave it voluntarily. He did win it, after all.

What is wrong with me? He stared at her, waiting for an answer. She tried to decide exactly how she would handle a kiss from him right now; after all, her feelings were somewhat vulnerable at the moment. Trevor's weird behavior had her all jacked up.

"Am I right?"

She licked her lips and smiled. "Indeed you are. I turned twenty-three last month."

He jumped up in triumph then he turned toward Caroline with molten, heavy-lidded eyes. His voice smooth as cream. "When can I collect my prize?"

Oh, what the heck. Live a little. She chose to give Trevor a taste of his own medicine and swallowed hard before taking another gulp of wine. "Well, I suppose there's no time like the present."

He tilted his head to one side as if he was thinking, squinted, and took a step closer. Preparing to be swept off her feet, she stood. However, she did it too quickly and stumbled. He gripped her arms to steady her, the heat from his palms searing her skin. The exaggerated rise and fall of his chest with each breath proved he was as nervous as she. That steadied her more than his grip. The soft, romantic jazz music created a perfect setting and a flush of heated anticipation swept through her body. She wanted this more than she cared to admit.

Cade curled his arm around her waist to pull her closer to him. He brushed the hair from her face and looked her over from her head down to her hips. She leaned back, a little tempted to expose her vulnerable neck for him to kiss, but she didn't. Fairly certain she had stopped breathing, Caroline wanted his mouth on hers. Now.

Cade leaned forward and brushed his lips across her forehead, down the side of her face, and across her cheek bones, before he pulled just out of reach in front of her lips. He explored her face with his mouth and it drove her wild.

Caroline blamed it on the alcohol combined with her staggered emotions, but she wanted him more than anything she ever remembered. She just knew she would spontaneously combust if he didn't kiss her already. Her eyes were closed, her lips reflexively parted in the suspense, and her breath caught in her throat. They swayed slightly to the music. . .slow dancing.

Unable to wait any longer, she instinctively leaned up on her toes and pressed her lips to his. He growled in utter satisfaction and gently kissed her back, tightening his embrace. Her soft, responsive moan set things into motion. A slight whimper escaped him as he cradled her face with both hands, handling her like fine crystal.

Then, his hands moved firmly around her back and shoulders, pulling her body even closer to him, deepening the intoxicating kiss. His passion and intensity, the way he touched her, held her, had her body thrumming with pleasure. He held her tightly, drinking her in as if she was the oasis for his desert thirst, the oxygen for his asphyxiation. Cade kissed her like a soldier back from a two-year deployment, thankful for the sense of touch and taste. The need—desperate, raw, consuming, enveloped her completely. Caroline lost herself in his atmosphere and didn't want to come back to Earth.

He slowed and finally stopped the fiery kiss. Cade reluctantly stepped back, breathing heavily. He sucked in the electrified air. His still-breathless voice a whisper. "Wow."

Wow was right. Caroline couldn't believe how much she already missed the feel of his lips on her. *What are you doing? Don't stop. Kiss me again.* The static charge surrounding them caused the hair on her arms to stand on end. The prickles consuming her scalp intensified with each breath she took, and she desperately wanted more. The passion she'd shared with Trevor, the man she regarded as a master of foreplay, never affected her quite this powerfully. Her breathless voice betrayed her false sense of composure.

"Is everything okay?"

He looked up, somewhat bewildered. "Yes, I'm just. . .shocked. That's all. Did you feel that?"

If he only knew how much she wanted to feel that again. "Yes. I certainly did." Caroline stared at her intertwined fingers and tried not to look too disappointed.

"I've kissed plenty of girls, but I've never felt like that with anyone."

She smiled. "Yeah, it was amazing." She had to change the subject, quickly before she jumped his bones. Her abstinence promise to God was quickly fading as she imagined the incredibly naughty things she wanted to do with this steamy package of rippling muscles and pheromones. Her mind raced to think of something else to talk about before she ruined everything.

The only thing she came up with was the impossible, yet undeniable presence of something in her room. She still had trouble accepting the ghost theory, but right now she desperately needed something to distract her from that panty-busting kiss. "Do you believe in ghosts?" She cringed at the awkwardness in her voice.

He coughed out a laugh. "What? Ghosts?" He cleared his throat to compose himself. "Um, yes, in fact, I do believe in ghosts. Why do you ask?" His knowing expression proved he knew she'd deliberately changed the subject, but he didn't press the issue.

With a disbelieving smile, she shook her head. "Well, I don't believe in ghosts, but weird things have been happening lately. Unexplainable things." Now she regretted bringing it up at all. This was not something she wanted to discuss with him. With anyone. "I was just curious, really, it's no big deal. Never mind, it's stupid."

"Nothing that comes from your mouth is stupid." Serious now, he seemed genuinely interested. "What kind of weird, unexplainable things?"

She was such an idiot. She should have just run out his door as quickly as she had the first time she'd been here and not looked back, but now she had to tell him something to satisfy his curiosity. "Do you know anything about the first Fontenot's that lived in that house?"

"Not much, why? Did something happen?"

"You see, you're not going to believe me when I tell you any of this so I should just. . .stop talking. I told you, it's stupid." She didn't believe it much herself. No way could she convince anyone else. He stood right in front of her and gently lifted her chin so she looked him in the face.

"Sweet Caroline, I told you. Nothing that comes from you could ever be stupid. Try me." He smiled irresistibly, breaking down her walls.

"Several months ago I had a crazy, scary dream. It was so real. When I woke I wasn't sure if I had dreamed it or if it had really happened and was like a distant memory. Apart from the first one, the other dreams were me watching from a fly on-the-wall perspective. Confusing at first, I had a few more of those types of dreams, and they seemed to almost pick up where they left off. Only, each dream was a different part of the story. . .like a soap opera."

He nodded.

"To sum up my best guess, the dream takes me back to the 1800s and the same woman is always in them. I haven't seen her picture yet, but I'm guessing the woman is Rachel Fontenot, my G3 Grandma." He smiled at her use of his acronym.

"Even crazier, when I got here and chose my room, the exact same room from my dream complete with identical furniture and bedding, I felt connected to that room. Like I was meant to be there." Caroline avoided eye contact, afraid he might be laughing at her. "I even found my initials scratched into the window pane. That's what sparked my trip to the library the day I met you." She peeked up at him from below her lashes and appreciated his focused attention. She continued quietly without a sound from her captive audience. Trevor would've already laughed her out of town by now.

"There was one specific dream of her having an argument with someone named Jackson. I think she was married to him. They argued in the woods, and, from what I could hear, she told Jackson that she'd been raped by someone. At first he didn't believe her, but she finally convinced him and mentioned a business betrayal. Once he realized she was being honest, he was ready to kill whoever it was."

"You see, allegedly, Rachel Fontenot jumped out of the window in her room and busted her head on a garden statue below, killing her instantly." Caroline subconsciously rubbed the center of her forehead. "Every time I have one of these dreams, my forehead throbs right in between my eyes. Supposedly where she hit her head on the statue." She picked up her wine glass and swirled the liquid without drinking it. "My first dream was not from a spectator's perspective. I was her in the dream and it was while she was being raped."

Caroline shifted uncomfortably. "It terrified me, and still gets to me sometimes. His voice. . ." She set her glass back down and rubbed her face in frustration. "You see, everything is way too coincidental for me to just blow it off like I want to. I don't believe in ghosts, I just don't. But all the strange things. . ."

Cade's eyebrows shot up with interest. "Go on."

"Well, the other day when I was at a pivotal point in one of those dreams, something slammed into my window really hard. I don't know what it was, but it hit hard enough to wake me up."

"It was a bird."

"What? A bird? What kind of bird flies into a window in the middle of the night?"

He shrugged. "The one I found in the garden was a Prairie Warbler. Didn't think much of it since they're common in this area. Did that bird have any significance in your dreams?"

She couldn't remember a bird significance and filed it away with the other stuff that didn't make sense. Caroline shook her head as she took a sip of wine to help prepare for the next part. "Earlier today, I stood by the window admiring the duck pond and heard a chair scraping across the floor right behind me. When I turned around, the chair from the dressing table was all the way back by the bed. I hadn't touched it."

"Has anything else strange or unusual happened to you in your room? Anything missing or moved, lights on or off that you didn't touch?"

"Yes," she sighed and nervously smoothed her hair. "When I first arrived here, I saw someone watching me from a third story window— ironically the room I wound up choosing, as I walked to the porch, but I couldn't see clearly because of the rain. Later, I learned no one lived on that side of the house, and rarely went up there except to clean or change the linens. My dad had been in his office and the only other two people in the house at the time were in the kitchen." She paced now, realizing her list of craziness was growing.

144

"After I chose my room, I admired a well-preserved antique perfume bottle and instantly smelled a fragrance as if someone stood behind me. When I walked away, the smell was gone." Caroline stopped pacing and looked up at Cade.

"You know, there was one other strange thing. I had put my engagement ring on my nightstand the other night before I went to bed and I made a point to put it next to my cell phone. That was the night the poor bird hit my window. Anyway, I had grabbed my phone to check the time when I was jarred awake but didn't touch the ring. The next morning it was gone. I looked all over the floor around the nightstand, under the bed, everywhere. I couldn't find it. Then, like magic, the next day when I walked back into my room it was there on my nightstand again, exactly where I had originally put it."

A smile stretched across Cade's face. "If this is a ghost and it's Rachel Fontenot, I'm sure she doesn't want you to marry a Yankee, either."

Caroline smacked his arm, "Oh, shut up about the whole Yankee thing. This has nothing to do with Trevor."

He laughed at his clever joke. "Well, my dear, it sounds to me like you are living in a haunted room, quite possibly a haunted house. I don't think a ghost is only bound to the room in which it died. Has anything strange happened anywhere else in the house?"

Caroline recalled aloud the almost-accident she had just before her arrival when whoever she nearly hit disappeared into thin air, then the charge in the air when she had her breakthrough with Eddie in the dining room. As she struggled to remember other strange happenings, her mouth dropped open with the memory of the kitchen fire. "Cade. . .there was an accident in the kitchen today. Delphine heated some oil to fry fish and Delia said the pan burst into flames like an explosion. She said she'd never seen anything like it. Delphine had to go to the emergency room with second degree burns on her arm."

"Oh no. Did it do any damage to the kitchen?"

"The backsplash and some of the cabinets, I think. I didn't see it. All I know is what Delia told us."

"Wow, I guess it's a good thing she only had to worry about second degree burns and not worse."

Caroline cringed. "You really think it's a ghost doing all this nonsense, or could it just be coincidences? Maybe the dreams are just a product of my overactive imagination?"

"Wait, when did you say you had your first dream?"

"Several months ago, why?"

"You were still in Chicago?"

"Yes, why? Where are you going with this?"

"Well, I'm trying to figure out if this ghost is haunting the house. . .or you." Caroline's stomach churned. "Did anything else strange happen to you in Chicago, I mean besides the dreams?"

She told him about the incident with her sweatshirt magically covering her during an afternoon nap, the picture frame falling over by itself, and the freaky episode with her cat growling at shadows. He listened enthusiastically.

"You know, animals see things we don't. Your cat could've been growling at your ghost." He was like a kid sitting around a camp fire telling ghost stories. Caroline, on the other hand, was quite freaked out.

"Do you really think Rachel Fontenot is haunting me? It just sounds so stupid when I say it out loud. Why would she come after me? I never had anything to do with her family, apart from my DNA. I'm more of an outsider to the Fontenot's than you are."

"I don't know, it could be anything. The only way I know of to see if it's a ghost, without calling The Spirit Spies, is to try to contact it yourself."

"The Spirit Spies?"

He grinned. "Yeah, you know, S.P.I.S., the Southern Paranormal Investigative Services. The ghost hunting team from that television show. They call themselves The Spirit Spies because of the initials. It's pretty cool."

She rolled her eyes. "I'm afraid they would be wasting their time and we'd look like complete idiots. I'm sure it's nothing. Probably hallucinations from the stress of this trip. I'll just wait and see if the weird things stop." She wanted to convince herself as much as him.

"You should try to do a test or something. Try doing the flashlight test where you set up a flashlight across the room that's easy to turn on and off, and ask the ghost to turn it on herself if she's really in there with you."

"Would a ghost from the 1800s even know how to work a flashlight? Maybe you could come to my room sometime and do the test for me?" Cade liked that idea a lot, though Caroline wondered, and secretly hoped, his excitement reflected more toward coming to her room rather than contacting a ghost.

"Let's do it tonight." His face gleamed with enthusiasm.

She shrugged. "Okay, fine. Don't get your hopes up too much, though. I think it's just a scary ghost story."

Cade leaned in and kissed her cheek. "We shall see, sweet Caroline. We shall see. It seems to me that Rachel Fontenot is trying to tell you something through your dreams and you're not quite getting it, so now she's moving your things to show you. I'd bet money she would be willing to turn on a simple flashlight to prove to you it's not just some scary ghost story."

"Alright then, let's do this."

The rain had stopped but darkness cloaked the woods. The trail was soft underfoot on the walk back to the house. Earthy, wet smells hung as heavy in the air as the humidity. Fog rolled through the trees, hugging the ground. Thankful Cade was with her, Caroline looped her arm through his staying very close by his side. He closed the gap by wrapping his arm around her waist instead, then leaned down and kissed the top of her head to reassure her.

They silently traveled across land that had been in her family for over a century, and Caroline imagined her ancestors walking the same path, wishing she could speak with them and get some answers. She wondered if distant members of her family fought and died in any of the wars that might have taken place in this territory. If ghosts were indeed real, was Rachel the only one sticking around?

For the first time since she'd been down in Golden Meadow, Louisiana, she was aware of her historical surroundings.

FIFTEEN

Maybe it was sneaky, but with the ambience of the spooky woods, Cade kept his arm snugly around Caroline, relishing the curve of her hip and sway in her hurried steps. As they reached the drive, Eddie pulled up.

"Hey, guys, did you have a good time?" His suggestive smile made Cade chuckle.

"Um. . .yeah, Dad," Caroline said. "It was great." She frantically tried to change the subject. "Where did you go so late?"

Cade couldn't get over how cute she was. So sweet and innocent. His ability to make her blush with a simple compliment was adorable. . .and fun.

"I ran over to the hospital for a while."

"Why did you go to the hospital? Is Delphine okay?" Caroline had switched into nurse mode. Cade wondered if her fiancé really knew what a treasure he had in her. Cade wasn't sure, and Caroline didn't offer any clue to why she'd broken down crying when she first got to his place. Could be the ghost thing, but he'd bet his truck it was the controlling bastard who put that ice on her finger.

149

Sure, the ring was huge, but did Trevor truly appreciate her? Cade seriously doubted Caroline's shallow prince was very charming. He didn't know much about Trevor, but from everything he'd heard about him, putting the pieces together wasn't difficult. A cookie cutter dick head. He'd seen plenty of the type.

"Yeah, she's fine, she's resting in her room, all doped up on pain pills." Eddie laughed. "She was talking crazy. So funny. Anyway, I went down there to pay her hospital bills. It was an accident that happened in my house, and her insurance will pay most of it, but I think it's only right that I pay the rest."

Caroline tilted her head slightly, the corners of her eyes crinkling a bit with her genuine smile. "That's very sweet and thoughtful of you." Cade fought the urge to wrap her up and run away with her. This woman had bewitched him and he was in big trouble. Falling hard for any woman, especially one he barely knew anything about, was not on his agenda, nor had it been for years. Their chemistry was undeniable, but the fiancé was a big issue. Cade needed to figure out how to remove him from the equation.

Eddie faced Cade and folded his arms across his chest. The unspoken cliché—what exactly are your intentions with my daughter—loomed in the air around them. Caroline stifled her laughter as she led them both inside the house. In the foyer, Eddie continued to stare at him expectantly.

Cade sensed the silent questioning. "Caroline asked me to walk her home."

Eddie smiled. "That was very chivalrous of you." Awkward silence followed. "She's home now. You're free to go."

Damn. I don't wanna leave yet. What should I say?

Cade noticed Caroline pucker her lips attempting to hide her amusement with his squirming under Eddie's intense scrutiny. She finally spoke up, easing the spotlight off of Cade.

"Dad, I actually asked him if he would come up to my room for a while. . .just to talk. If that's okay with you, of course?" She smiled innocently and apparently tapped his soft spot.

He hesitated for an instant then pointed his finger at Cade, his voice somewhat jovial but packing a solid warning. "Okay, but no sneaky stuff, zinger. I'll be right down the hall." He winked and chuckled as he walked up the stairs.

She whirled around, eyebrows raised. "Zinger?"

He chuckled. "He just called me a swamp rat."

She slowly nodded. "Touching. Nice to see you two have an amicable bromance. Makes for a comfortable, not-awkward-at-all working relationship." Her sarcasm wasn't convincing, but amused Cade just the same.

She started up the stairs as he followed, but then she shot off in a sprint. Cade chased her, curious to see what sparked the burst of energy. When she got to the top she spun around, putting her hand on his chest to stop him, quite shocked to find him right behind her. She obviously underestimated his abilities. There was much more about him that would surprise her, she just didn't realize it yet. Her breathless anxiety intrigued him.

"I need a minute. . .to. . .make sure my room is, um. . .tidy." She grinned, the tinge of embarrassment coloring her sculptured cheekbones. Cade smiled and nodded fully intending to break this little agreement. With four sisters, there was nothing about Caroline that could possibly shock him, and what was she embarrassed about? The woman had seen him naked, for Pete's sake. In all his glory, and he never saw it coming. A rare occurrence for him. His instincts usually took over and gave him a little warning. One thing's for certain, the next time this angel saw him naked he'd be sure he was prepared. He just needed to make sure there would be a next time.

She rushed down the hall to her room with no clue Cade followed close behind her, and scooped up the dirty clothes. Cade leaned against the door frame and smiled at her modesty as she quickly snatched a pair of pink panties from the bed and threw the clothes in the hamper. Without looking, she called for him to come in. When she noticed him already there watching her, the blood rushed to her cheeks. He grinned and shrugged not understanding why she let this trivial stuff get to her.

She gave him a dirty look and exhaled. "I should have known you wouldn't listen."

"I couldn't resist seeing the beautiful color rush to your face again."

"Ugh! You are insufferable!" She lunged and missed as he dodged her attack. "You did that on purpose. Now you're fighting dirty, zinger!"

Cade cracked up laughing as she gave him a playful shove, then he wrapped his arms around her in a bear hug, pinning her arms to her side preventing her from moving.

"Okay, so you're freakishly fast and strong. I give up."

He gave a crooked smile and playfully led Caroline backward bumping against the wall so she couldn't escape.

"You can't give up. Where's the fun in that?"

He measured her response. He didn't want to frighten her but desperately wanted to kiss her again. This woman had him acting completely out of character. He worried about moving too fast, but when her lids grew heavy and her breathing sped, his instincts took over as he placed his hands on the wall framing her face, and pressed his body against hers. Her hands stayed by her side, but she made no effort to move. She enjoyed his touch, a fact that drove him crazy with desire, but he reminded himself he was a still a gentleman.

When she looked up, her exotic eyes weakened his knees, and his lips gently brushed her forehead. He slowly dipped his head lower, pausing to silently ask permission before making his move when he heard a throat being cleared. They jumped apart like teenagers. Cade fully expected Eddie to be there with his arms crossed and a disapproving look upon his face.

It wasn't Eddie. April glared at them while communicating her displeasure without saying a single word. Her long fingernails drummed an angry beat on the tops of her arms. Even as he held his breath, he noticed her store bought tanned skin clashed with the bleached blonde hair pulled back in a tight bun. She looked every bit the regal plantation wife except there was no genteel southern hospitality written in her body language. Oh no, this was anger, borderline rage.

"Caroline, as a guest here, you need to see that you're respectful to the rest of the household and avoid the stomping. I mean, really, were you raised in a barn? It sounded like a herd of elephants trampling up the stairs. And if you're going to invite boys to your room, have a little class. Down here your last name has a reputation to uphold, and I'll not have you tainting it with senseless promiscuity." Cade could see Caroline swallow her anger, but she remained quiet.

"And this may come as a shock to you, but some of us actually have things to do." April's voice hissed and Cade wanted to ask her how the venom tasted. Disgusted, she glared at Caroline like she was a hooker before shifting her gaze to Cade and looking him up and down. Her voice raised an octave as she took a few steps toward him and asked, "Do you have something you'd like to say to me? Boy?"

Boy? She wasn't much older than him. He did not like this woman. At all. Cade refused to play her little game and simply offered his best grin, wishing he could show her exactly what this boy was capable of doing. But it wasn't his fight, so he chose the high road hoping she would just leave.

Apparently satisfied she put him in his place, she turned to blow back out of the room.

"Sorry, April, you won't hear a peep from us again," Caroline called after her. Cade wished Caroline would've fired back, but understood why she didn't. There was no telling what this psycho woman would do. Pure sugarcoated evil, she made Cruella De Vil look like a sweetheart.

April paused for a moment, and humphed before she walked out leaving the door open. Cade closed the door behind her holding his hand on it so she wouldn't open it again.

He turned back to Caroline in question and shrugged his beefy shoulders. "What's her problem? Does she think you're a child?"

"I don't know. Who cares?" Caroline sighed, "While the essence of evil is still lingering in the room, let's get this over with. How do we start?"

Cade feigned a pout. "You in a hurry to get me out of here?"

Her mouth opened, but nothing came out. He'd rendered her speechless. Cade laughed at her bravado, but sensed the fear underlying her words. He didn't know if it was Cruella De Vil she feared more or the ghost haunting her room. "Seriously, do you want to try this later? I could come back if you're not ready."

"You know I'm not trying to get rid of you. I'm very grateful you are here to do this because trying to contact a supposed ghost is definitely not something I would ever do on my own."

Excited now, Cade set his push-button flashlight on the dressing table. He angled it toward the bed, turned the ceiling light off, and sat on the bed with Caroline. He heard her slight intake of breath when he inched closely to her. He smiled, taking a few deep breaths to get himself under control. His mind kept wandering to Caroline and all the ways he could take advantage of having her on a bed in the dark if only she was his woman and not someone else's. His focus centered when a heaviness crept over his shoulders, pushing on his chest and reminding him of his goal for the evening. He had a ghost to contact.

Cade touched her hand. "I need you to try to control your laughter when I start talking to her because if she is a ghost, and if she is here, you will only piss her off by laughing at the very thought of that possibility. Okay?"

She squeezed his hand. "Yeah, okay. I'll be cool. Just don't do anything too goofy so I don't blow it."

He kept his voice calm, annunciating each word clearly. "Rachel? Rachel Beauregard Fontenot?" He could sense Caroline biting her lip to keep from laughing so he gently elbowed her. "Rachel, my name is Cade Beauregard and I'm here with your great, great, great granddaughter, Caroline. She was named after you, and you two share the same birthday. . .but you knew that already, didn't you?"

Cade leaned back on the pillow propped against the headboard. Caroline's feminine smell wafted over him fiercely reawakening a long-dormant desire in his body. That combined with their kiss from earlier had his blood rushing to the southern parts of his body. It had been a long time since he felt this way about anyone, but he pushed that thought aside for now and rubbed his back against the linen. Maybe with his scent on her pillow she would smell him after he left. He was determined to leave a lasting impression on this beautiful woman and she would think about him whether she wanted to or not.

The room eerily quiet, Cade kept talking. "If you're in here can you give us a sign? A knock or something? We'd like to talk to you." Much to his surprise, Caroline reached over and laced her chilled fingers through his. The temperature in the room had dropped to the equivalent of a meat locker, but her touch and proximity had the blood zipping through his body creating an inferno in his chest.

"Rachel, I think you've been trying to send a message to Caroline, but she doesn't believe me. She needs a little convincing. Can you help me with that?"

Just as Cade grew comfortable with the feel of Caroline's hand in his, she abruptly tensed and pulled it away. He couldn't be sure, but the bed shook a bit, and, from the slight silhouette cast from the sliver of moonlight streaming through the window, he thought she was rubbing her forehead. Cade's heart threatened to burst through his chest as he remembered what she'd told him about her head aching between her eyes in all the dreams. Rachel was here. He could feel it. With wide eyes drinking up the dim room, and pulse thrumming with excitement, Cade carried on with his communication.

"Rachel, if you're here in this room with us right now, I want you to do something for me. I placed a flashlight on your dressing table. We use these to see in the dark much like you probably used lanterns or candles. There is a push button on the end of it that turns it on. Can you press that button to show us you're here?"

Caroline leaned forward and placed her hand on his leg causing him to flinch in surprise. His focus attuned to anything that hinted of Rachel's presence. He sensed Caroline's residual skepticism, but she at least seemed curious now. That was better than her boldfaced denial. Burying your head in the sand so you don't see something won't make it disappear. It was about time Caroline realized that.

They sat in silence for a few moments staring into darkness. Nothing happened. Caroline broke the silence. "Well, I didn't think it would work. I told you this was a stupid waste of time. It's all just too impossible. This stuff isn't real. I must be hallucinating."

Cade hadn't spoken, but the bed bounced when she jerked.

"Ouch!" She smacked his leg. "What was that for?"

"What?" He had no idea what she thought he'd done, but he hadn't touched her.

"Okay fine! I'll be quiet, but you didn't have to pull my hair!"

"Caroline! I didn't touch you. I swear I did not pull your hair." He couldn't hide the subtle chuckle with his next thought. "You'd know it if I did. Trust me."

"Seriously, it's not funny. You yanked it. That really hurt."

Cade jumped up from the bed and turned on the ceiling light.

She scowled and rubbed her head while he shook his. He wanted to kiss those pouty lips again, but she kept talking. "I honestly tried, but I'm not buying into all the ghost stuff. There has to be a logical explanation for all the freaky things happening to me, so you can stop trying to scare me into believing it."

"Dammit, Caroline, listen to me! There is a ghost in your room. A ghost haunting you specifically. Believe me when I tell you, I did not touch your hair." He smiled slyly. "Trust me, if I was going to touch something of yours, in the dark on your bed, it would not have been your hair."

She jumped up off the bed and scurried to the door. "Okay, that's enough ghost hunting for me tonight. I'm craving some chocolate. Let's go see if there are any brownies in the kitchen. We can check out the damage from Delphine's accident from earlier." Cade turned off the light and shook his head in frustration. As they made their way downstairs, he racked his brain for ways to convince this stubborn girl she needed to open her mind.

Caroline hunted for some sweet treats while Cade checked out the stove to survey the damage from Delphine's accident.

This had been a very long, crazy day and she needed something to take the edge off. Finally, she found chocolate chip cookies in the cookie jar. Snagging two, she retrieved the milk from the refrigerator. Cade found two glasses, and they sat at the kitchen island sharing a midnight snack.

"I really didn't pull your hair."

She rolled her eyes. "Oh, come on. I'm not falling for that." She didn't really want to believe it was a ghost. She fidgeted with the napkin fraying the edges into tiny pieces. "So, how'd you get your arm on the other side of my head without tipping me off?"

She despised the shaky tone of her voice, but couldn't prevent it. What happened up there had freaked her out. She knew all signs pointed to paranormal activity, but she wanted to believe Cade somehow had a hand in it. That she wasn't being haunted by a tormented soul lost in between worlds.

Cade stepped up behind her to massage her shoulders. The heat from his fingers transferred to her skin telegraphing pin points of electricity lighting up all over her body. A ghost in the bedroom and a taboo attraction in the kitchen. She could barely make a coherent thought. If this man hiccuped, she'd know it, she was so aware of him. Heart palpitations, a result of the heated emotions invoked from their buzzing chemistry, reminded Caroline how little she knew of Cade. An entire year with Trevor passed before she craved his presence like this. She would have definitely known if Cade had leaned across the bed toward her. . .and she would have possibly leaned back into him.

"Caroline, I understand if you don't want to believe me. But I'm not lying to you. I did not pull your hair."

"Well. . .somebody or something did. It wasn't just a tug or snag on my shirt, it was a full-fledged yank. And it hurt."

He deepened his massage, squeezing her tense muscles thereby eliciting a moan from her. Surprisingly not embarrassed by her bold reaction, she didn't want to move for fear he'd stop melting her with his magic fingers.

"Think about it, sweet girl. It happened right after you said you were hallucinating, right?"

She tried to remember. "Yeah, I think so."

"Open your mind just a little bit. Maybe it was Rachel because she's frustrated that you won't believe it's her?"

He drew his fingers across her overheated skin and made his way to the column of her neck. His calloused thumb worked penetrating circles at the base of her skull while his hand cradled her face. Caroline's thoughts stumbled over one another. No one had ever made her feel this safe, this beautiful, this lov. . . What in the world was wrong with her? She jerked upright now desperate for an escape from his fingers, even if it meant considering the possibility of a real live ghost. A ghost that seemed intent on getting her attention.

"Yeah, I guess."

They finished their cookies and milk in silence. Her curiosity over Rachel and what she wanted got the better of her. "Cade, I'd like to try it again. You game?"

"I've grown up in Louisiana, ghosts come with the territory." He shrugged his shoulders causing the fabric of his T-shirt to bunch right along with the cluster of butterflies in her stomach. "I've never seen one before, but I know all the stories. I believe she needs you for something. You're the key." They trekked upstairs to her room, and, as always, Cade politely let her enter first. She took two steps into her room and froze. Cade ran into the back of her, not paying any attention to the fact that she'd stopped moving.

"Oh, man, I'm sorry, I didn't realize. . ." His voice trailed off as he stared at the same thing she saw.

The flashlight beamed brightly, lighting up the dark room.

"What the. . ." Cade was equally creeped out now. "Well, I guess that's our answer."

SIXTEEN

Caroline didn't know what to think. The skeptic in her immediately assumed other possibilities. "We don't know if someone else came in here and turned it on while we were downstairs."

His tone was more frustrated now. "Caroline, how would anyone else in this house know the one thing we asked the gho—uh, Rachel, to do? There's no way! We had the door closed and I was talking softly."

"April could have been listening outside the door. That's totally something her type would do."

Caroline crossed her arms punctuating the frustration in her voice. "I can tell she doesn't like me or trust me. She's just waiting until I do something she can report to my dad."

"Why are you hellbent against believing a ghost could be stuck in between worlds if they have unfinished business?" His incredulous tone revealed far more than his words did.

"Because it's ridiculous, for one thing. I believe what the Bible says about death and the afterlife. There's nothing in there that says if someone dies before they clean up loose ends then they'll be stuck wandering the earth haunting the living." Her tone came out a little harsher than she wanted it to sound, but she needed to make her point as well.

"Look, this may be easier for you living out here in the swamps, but this goes against everything I've ever believed in. You can't expect me to just throw all that out the window because a stupid flashlight turned on." She all but screeched the last few words.

Caroline worried she might have offended him when he sat on the bed and didn't respond. Not thinking, she brushed her fingers through his sun-kissed curls, absently wondering if his hair was always this long or if he needed a trim. When she noticed the intensity in his eyes studying her, the liquid gold of his irises, she sucked in a breath, quickly snatched her hand back and took a step away from him.

Shocked and a little ashamed by how perfect and natural that felt, she scolded herself. What the heck was she doing? She hardly knew this guy and had accepted a marriage proposal from someone else! She loved Trevor and shouldn't care if she offended someone who obviously held no regard for her relationship status. Caroline wiped her face and mentally formed her apology.

"I'm sorry. I'm not trying to take this out on you. I realize you are just trying to help me, and I sincerely appreciate it."

He smiled. "I'll be honest, it does intrigue me, but I'll take whatever excuse I can to spend more time with you." Cade stood and ran his own hand through the soft golden locks she had caressed only moments ago. "You're right, I may be from the swamps, and I'm not a consistent church goer, but I believe the two are entwined. She has a reason to be here. I don't know how, exactly, but she needs you."

Cade stepped closer and raised his hand to tuck a stray piece of her hair behind her ear, mimicking her previous action. "She's not the only one here who needs you."

Flattery. Caroline smiled. "Thank you. You really know how to make a girl feel good, but you don't know anything about me." She glanced around her room, nervously wringing her hands. "I probably won't be able to sleep tonight because, I have to admit, I'm a little freaked out right now."

Without missing a beat he said, "You're welcome to come sleep with me. . .I mean, sleep in my bed. . ."

She giggled. He was too cute.

"No wait, that didn't come out right. I mean you're welcome to come to my place and sleep in my bed, and I'll sleep on my couch."

"Thanks. That's a very generous offer, but I don't think my dad would like it so much." Though she wanted to, badly. Sleeping in a haunted room alone was not something people generally enjoyed doing, plus Trevor would have a coronary if he knew she even considered that. He would definitely not understand, nor would any man if he knew his fiancée shared a room with another gorgeous, virile man. He'd blow his top. She enjoyed his company, though, and he made her feel safe.

"Well, maybe I could stay here tonight. I mean, this house has plenty of rooms, I'm sure Eddie wouldn't mind letting me crash in one of them."

"That sounds great, but if you're in a different room, how is that going to help me sleep? I'm still going to be in here by myself with. . .whatever this thing is that's moving stuff and pulling my hair."

He smiled and caressed her face. "I'll stay with you until you fall asleep, and then I'll go to my own room."

Caroline liked that idea. It sounded innocent enough. "All right, I'll go talk to my dad. You can stay in here if you'd like and, I don't know, try to contact the ghost again or something."

He laughed. "Yeah, we'll have a party while you're gone. If I'm not here when you get back you'll know who did it." He laughed again.

This time she glared. "I'm not laughing. That's not funny, so don't even talk like that."

Caroline knocked gently on her dad's office door and pushed it open. Eddie peeked over the corner of the newspaper to see who had entered, and a generous smile stretched across his stubbly face.

"Hey, you busy?"

"For you, cher, I'm never too busy."

"Why do people down here keep calling me Cher? I look nothing like her!"

He snickered. "No, Caroline, it's a compliment. It's a Louisiana Creole term for sweetie, or honey, or darling. It's French. Anyway, what can I do for you?"

"Well, since it's so late and nasty outside, I was wondering. . .well, would it be okay. . ." He stared, amused with her stammering. She cleared her throat. "I would really like it if you would allow Beau to sleep in one of the extra rooms tonight."

He folded his paper, set it on the desk in front of him, and leaned back in his chair. "Can you give me a good reason why?"

She knew he would ask that. The wine she had earlier still clouded her thoughts making it difficult to find the proper words. "It's not what you think, or at least what I think you're thinking. It's nasty outside anyway, and I just haven't been sleeping well lately. You know, new room and bed and all. So I thought if maybe he stayed until I fell asleep or something. . ."

Now Eddie was concerned. "Sweetheart, if you want to change rooms or try a new bed—"

"No! It's fine. I love my room. I've just got a lot of stuff on my mind, and for some crazy reason I am more relaxed when Cade is nearby." She looked down in shame.

Eddie noticed and stood. He walked over to her and, with a fatherly touch, placed both hands on her upper arms. "Caroline, you have nothing to be ashamed of. I realize you are engaged and I'm sure what's his name is a great guy. But. . ."

He hesitated, and Caroline knew a healthy dose of fatherly advice loomed ahead, filling the unabridged expanse of years lost between them. Caroline stepped back and crossed her arms. Eddie noticed and moved back to stand behind his chair on the other side of his desk. He propped his forearms on the high-backed chair and clasped his hands.

His conflicted expression suggested he was likely weighing his options. He could say nothing and stay out of it, or offer his opinion with the risk of pushing too far. After her outburst the last time he offered advice, Caroline expected him to stay quiet. Of course, he chose the second option. At least she knew where she inherited her tenacity.

"You know, sometimes we think we're doing the right thing with someone we think is the right person, and then, if we're fortunate enough, we meet the real right person later. Lucky for you, you met him before you tied the knot."

She tilted her head, a bit annoyed by how fully—and quickly—he'd embraced the parental control part of his role as her father, freely offering his advice and approval of her behavior. Something she didn't need at twenty-three-years-old, though she was a guest in his house and would respect his authority in that regard.

She drew in a deep breath and shook her head in disbelief. "No, Dad. You've got it all wrong. I only wanted to be respectful and ask your permission for him to stay the night so you wouldn't wake up in the morning and find him in your house. Somehow you transformed that into my needing relationship guidance. Thanks for the unsolicited advice, but I am in love with Trevor. You don't know anything about him, and I've known him for over two years. I've only known Cade less than a week! He just. . .we just click, and he's easy for me to be around. We're friends. I mean, sure, I'm attracted to him, but it's not like I'm in love with him. Besides, I'm engaged."

"Yeah, you've mentioned that a time or two. You're probably right, and there is nothing wrong with clicking with someone. I have no problem with him staying the night. Just have him come in here and talk to me before you fall asleep, okay?"

"All right, but promise me you'll be nice, okay? Don't embarrass me." They shared a chuckle. When he wasn't trying to interfere with her love life, he was cool.

"You sure you don't want to change rooms?"

"Yes, I'm sure. Cade's been talking about ghosts all night and I'm just a little weirded out. That's all."

"Well, sweetheart, you are in the bayou. Ghosts are a fixture in some places down here."

She rolled her eyes and turned to leave, speaking over her shoulder, "What is the fascination with all you people and communicating with ghosts? Aren't the living interesting enough?" Smiling, she waved her thanks as she closed the door behind her.

Back in her own room, Caroline noticed Cade flipping through the pages of her small photo album. "Hey. My dad said it would be all right for you to stay, but he wants to talk to you in his office first."

Cade grinned, her heart fluttered. "Yeah? I get to deal with the dad?"

She squinted. "Oh, shut up. It's not even like that and you know it. He probably just wants to put the fear in you about not touching me. I am his princess after all."

He held up a picture from the photo album. "Okay, Princess, is this the lucky guy?"

She sat next to him. "Yes, that's Trevor."

"Nice lookin' fella. What's Trevor's last name?"

"Callahan, why?"

"No reason." He tucked the picture neatly back in the photo slip. "Just wanted to see what your last name would have been."

Standing abruptly, hands on hips and eyebrows raised, Caroline challenged him. "Would have been? You don't think I'm going to marry him?"

He gave a cocky smile. "I told you, sweet Caroline. I'm gonna sweep you off your feet and you'll be saying, 'Trevor who?'"

She snatched the picture from his hands. "You're mighty sure of yourself, aren't you? You've known me for five minutes and you think you *know* me?"

"I did well in chemistry class, and I know when something is right. And we are exactly right for each other." He brushed the hair from her forehead. "We'd be great together. And you know it."

Caroline's heart did a back flip into her stomach and she felt lightheaded as she fought back a swoon. Never in her life had a guy made her feel so completely cherished and desired. Trevor's desire was clouded with pure lust. Cade's sincerity and boldness touched her in all the right places. All of them.

"Well, unfortunately for you, Trevor beat you to the punch. You're about two years too late." The sadness and lack of conviction that seeped through Caroline's voice distressed her more than the ghost issue. Every doubt she had before now crescendoed unbearably in her heart.

Cade put his arm around her neck and pulled her closer to kiss her forehead. "You're not married yet. I've still got some time."

His hot breath tickled against her heightened skin, and residual tingles from his feather-soft lips caused flashes of what it would be like to feel them all over her body. His determined words would have sealed her gaping need for reassurance if not for the overwhelming, two-timing guilt snuffing out the burning desire deep in her belly.

"But I made a promise to Trevor. An engagement is a promise and I can't break it." She sat down on the bed beside him, her posture reflecting her resignation. "I don't *want* to break it." Trevor's face looked back at her from the now crumpled photograph in her hands. "I won't break it."

Each word sounded like a lie to her own ears. She was exactly where she wanted to be and nothing could change that. Cade grabbed her hand and threaded his fingers through hers. Her conscience rebelled. Trevor deserved better than this. Caroline looked at their hands together and then up at his face before she slowly pulled her hand from his.

Cade released a small sigh and stood.

"Look, I am not going to force you to do anything. You're a grown woman." He ran his fingers through his curls and turned away from her. They shared the silence for a moment, neither knowing what to say, until Cade spun around with urgency in his tone. "But he's not the man for you. I don't know what this is between us, but I do know he's not the guy you should marry." His voice dropped as he whispered his next words. "I see it in your eyes when you talk about him, and I can feel it here when I kiss you."

He pulled her up to stand in front of him as he placed his large hand just above her breasts in the middle of her chest. Stealing her breath and jumpstarting her heart, Caroline couldn't peel her eyes from his and cursed her body's betrayal to his touch. Cade waited a moment before continuing, never taking his eyes off their point of contact.

"I promise I'll try not to push you too fast, and I will stop if you tell me what I'm saying is wrong. Obviously, I want you to desire me as much as I do you, and, call me crazy, but I don't think I'm too far off the mark here." Cade slipped his hand up to cradle her face and smirked. "But I'm coming for you, Caroline. Make no mistake."

She couldn't breathe, couldn't think. No one had ever spoken to her like that. What was she supposed to say? Shame on her for having this strong attraction to another man, but deep down she didn't want him to stop pursuing her. No way could she let him know that, though. She chose the safest thing possible. "Thank you. I can't tell you how much I appreciate that."

He leaned down like he was going to kiss her, and then stopped short as if he changed his mind.

He sighed again, squeezed his eyes closed tightly, and rested his forehead against hers, whispering, "I'd better go see Eddie before he sends out a search party for me."

And just like that he was gone. Her body grieved at the loss of his touch. It was almost like a physical ache that she couldn't explain or ignore. Her eyes popped open, searching, and she found him opening the door to leave. Caroline had to get hold of her emotions before she did something stupid.

"I'm sure he hasn't finished setting up the firing squad yet. Don't panic."

He turned back and grinned. "Not in my nature."

SEVENTEEN

Caroline peered out the window at the duck pond. Strategically placed lights in the water casted a faded glow across the ripples from rain drops. Her focus shifted to the etching of Rachel's initials in the glass. Her initials. She wondered exactly how long those had been there, perfect as if they'd just been done.

There were just too many crazy similarities for all this to be a simple coincidence. She'd wondered if Trevor knew about Rachel before sending her down here, but he'd sounded as shocked as she was when she'd told him about sharing her full name and birthday with her G3 grandmother. Caroline hadn't told Trevor about the ghost stuff, though. He'd have laughed her right into a raging fit, and her annoyance with his defensive, abrasive attitude recently already tipped the anger scale. Enough so that she allowed herself to kiss another man. . .and it terrified her how much she enjoyed it. Caroline gently rubbed her finger across them and softly spoke. . .to her.

"If your ghost is here, and you're really stuck, you have to tell me why. I don't take hints well so try to find some way to explain it for me, or show me. I want to understand, I do. This is all new to me and goes against everything I've ever believed."

A knock rapped on the door and Caroline whirled around.

"Hey, Claire. You surprised me."

Claire timidly smiled. "I'm sorry, I wasn't trying to sneak up on you."

"No, it's okay. I just thought about you earlier this evening. I haven't seen you or Remy in a few days. What's up?"

"We've been hanging out with our friends since school got out. You know how it is, once summer break gets here, it's like a rush of slumber parties and stuff."

"Yeah, I remember those days."

"I need some advice and I don't really want to talk to April about it. I don't think she would understand."

She hid her excitement that her little sister came to her for advice. "Sure, sweetie. What's on your mind?"

"There's a guy at my school I like named Brad. He's a senior which is why I can't talk to April about this because she'd freak out. Anyway, he plays football for the high school and he's gorgeous. My friend Tracey said he heard Brad talking to some of his friends in the field house about me. He said Brad mentioned I was hot and that he planned to ask me out."

Caroline nodded, already having an idea of where this was headed. "The only thing is, Tracey said they asked him if he was going to try anything with me, you know, sexually, and he said, probably."

Caroline groaned. She'd been in this situation plenty of times.

"I've never done anything big. But I really like this guy and I'm afraid if I don't let him then he won't ask me out again. I don't know what to do. I don't want a bad reputation. If I do anything with him he might brag to his friends. But if I don't, and he starts rumors, then it's all for nothing. Not to mention I'll feel like a cheap, used whore."

"I've been exactly where you are right now. First, if you're worried about him spreading rumors he clearly doesn't deserve you. From my experience, if he really likes you for who you are and not simply for bragging rights, then he will not try anything you aren't comfortable with. Especially on the first date. If he respects you, he will appreciate you more if you stop him before he starts. Just be straightforward with him.

"You'll develop a good reputation for being a girl who values herself and doesn't give it up to the first hot guy she dates. Better to be the prude girl than the easy girl."

Claire stared down at her hands twisting her hair tie. She seemed disappointed with Caroline's answer.

Just as she looked up, Cade walked into the room. Her eyes nearly popped out of their sockets and she looked at Caroline, bewildered.

"Claire, have you met Ca—er, Beau?"

"Not officially. You're the gardener, right? I think you're always here during the day when I'm in school. I've heard about you, though." She smiled and stuck out her hand.

He grinned and shook her hand. "Hello, Claire. It's a pleasure to meet you. I didn't realize Mr. Fontenot had two beautiful daughters." She studied the baseboards, her face red as a cherry. Caroline smiled, glad she wasn't the only one he affected.

Cade's amusement beamed in the tilt of his smirk. "You two are very similar in some ways." He winked as Caroline glared playfully.

"Claire, I couldn't help but overhear a portion of your conversation. Forgive me for eavesdropping, but do you mind if I offer a guy's perspective?"

Embarrassed rather than angry, she nodded. "Um. . .sure. That would probably help." Impressed by his genuine concern, Caroline eagerly awaited his perspective as well.

"You are a beautiful girl, so any guy who gets a date with you should feel privileged. This guy may try something with you because his friends are pressuring him to do it. If you do like Caroline says and make your intentions clear before he ever gets a chance to try anything, it will save you both the embarrassment of rejection later. However, if he ever tries to force you to do something, then he's a dog who truly doesn't respect you and you should stay as far away from him as you can. He'll only hurt you in the long run." He glanced at Caroline. "A genuinely good guy doesn't mind waiting for someone he truly wants." Caroline's face blazed alongside Claire's.

"Um, thank you, Beau. You've both helped me a lot, and I appreciate it more than you know. It'll be way hard to say no to this guy. He's super hot, but I'll do my best."

Cade leaned in and kissed Claire's cheek. "You won't be sorry, cher. You'll see." Now a beautiful shade of magenta, Claire giggled the whole way down the stairs.

"You get a kick out of doing that, don't you?"

He looked hurt. "What? You don't think I helped her?"

"No, I'm talking about kissing her just to watch her blush."

He smiled and dropped his head. "Guilty."

Caroline sighed. "I hate when guys use their extreme sex appeal to their advantage."

"You think I have extreme sex appeal?"

"Oh, please. Like you don't know."

"It's always nice to hear. . .especially from you." Cade looked out the window before turning to face Caroline. He cradled her jaw in his hands just as he had earlier tonight before they kissed. "Caroline, I am not trying to push you to do something you don't want to do. I just want you to know how I feel about you. I am painfully aware of the short amount of time we've known each other, but I can also tell you with an honest heart that I've never felt with anyone the way I feel with you. Especially not this quickly. The kiss we shared earlier was. . .magical." She reached up to hold his hands, the guilt crippling her.

"Caroline, I need to ask you for something. A favor." She attempted to step back to put some space between them, but he wouldn't let her. He dropped his embrace and wrapped his arms around her small waist. "No, please don't walk away."

He pressed his forehead to hers and spoke tenderly with his eyes closed. "Would it be okay if I kissed you again?" When she didn't answer, he pulled back a bit to look at her, to study her reaction. His eyes were sincere. Genuine. "I just want to see if that magic is still there or if it was a one-time thing. You know, because we were caught up in the moment."

She really did want to kiss him again, but she worried how she'd feel afterwards. Afraid she'd want more. She shouldn't want more, but she just knew she would.

He sighed. "I mean, I don't—"

She placed one finger over his lips. "Just stop talking and kiss me."

His face exploded with happiness and then quickly darkened with sheer passion. Slowly, he ran his fingers through her hair at the temples to cradle her head again. He pressed his supple lips to hers and the forbidden excitement and naughty desire filled her with spirited emotions. Her body tingled and became buoyant with a floating sensation. Her hands grazed his smooth face before she tangled her fingers into his hair, clutching the thick waves and squeezing tightly. A satisfied rumble escaped from him as she deepened his kiss. He tasted delicious and their lips fit perfectly together. She moaned when he slipped his mouth from hers down her neck. Her head was suddenly too heavy to support.

Cade's gentleness and passion aroused all the senses in her body. Aware of every touch, sound, taste and smell, when she closed her eyes she could still see his beautiful amber-colored gaze cherishing her. He moved back to her lips, and with one hand pulled her hips closer to his revealing his desire. His other capable hand gently gripped and tugged her hair kindling a completely new, undiscovered brand of desire within her. He was a phenomenal kisser. He made Trevor look like an amateur.

His kisses culminated back to her forehead and then he hugged her, resting his chin on the top of her head. She hugged him tightly against his heaving chest, her pounding heart and heavy breathing in sync with his. He hadn't lied about his feelings for her. She could tell what she did to him. Caroline was a selfish, greedy wench doing this with Cade, leading him to believe he had a chance with her. All while knowing she would marry and spend the rest of her life with someone else. It would break his heart, and that made her very sad. She was a horrible person.

Caroline pulled away and looked up at him. His somber smile didn't reach his eyes. "What's wrong?"

"Nothing, sweet Caroline." He cringed and pulled her close again, kissing the crown of her head. "I'm lying. Don't marry him," he whispered. "Please." He tightened his hold on her, but didn't press for a response, for which she was thankful. "Just think about it. That's all I ask."

Caroline knew she should run and never look back, but she couldn't bring herself to let go of him. *Glutton. Don't be such a hypocrite. You'd kill Trevor if he did this to you.* She ignored her conscience and nuzzled deeper into the crook between his jaw and shoulder. Breathing in his heady scent, she wrapped her arms around his toned waist and changed the subject. "Still magical?"

Cade let out a breath. "Indubitably."

"Wow. I'm gonna have to look that one up later." She laughed.

He held her tightly. "Unmistakably, unequivocally, unquestionably, irrevocably, entirely, and completely magical. How's that for a definition?" He smiled, genuinely this time, and kissed the tip of her nose.

She embraced him again, unable, or unwilling, to disengage from his delectable body. "Yeah, it was pretty magical for me, too."

He exhaled a sigh of relief and held her tighter as they swayed back and forth. "Thank you. For saying that. Now maybe I'll be able to get some sleep."

She laughed. "Well, at least one of us needs to sleep well tonight."

"Sweet Caroline, my mission is to see that you sleep like a baby until the sun comes up, even if I have to camp out on the floor next to your bed."

"Oh, no way! If I wake up and find you on the hard floor I'm going to feel horrible."

He beamed. "Darlin', after that kiss I won't even touch the floor 'cause I'm on a cloud right now."

"You know, I don't get you. You met me less than a week ago, but here you are willing to do all these sweet things for me. And make sacrifices, like ghost hunting or sleeping on a hardwood floor just to make sure I sleep well. Why? Why are you being so good to me when I'm engaged to marry someone else in a completely different part of the country? You should be angry with me for leading you on. The last thing you should want to do is kiss me and go out of your way to help me. Why? How can you be so perfect? Tell me what a shameful person I am and that you can't believe how selfish I am. I'm a pitiful, trifling, shameful woman. Why won't you tell me you never want to see me again?"

I'm ranting. Why am I ranting? Shut up, Caroline!

Cade walked backwards, pulling her with him, until he got to the bed. He sat on the mattress straddling her legs in front of him. Now nearly eye to eye.

"You want to know why? It's because I believe in this life there is one person God made especially for me. . .and for you. If we're lucky, we come across that one special person, express our love for her. . .or him in your case. Then, we vow before God to spend the rest of our lives together. I believe I found my one special someone. You."

The traitor tears involuntarily streamed down her cheeks and her stomach twisted with split feelings. How could she let this happen? Was it possible to be in love with two guys at the same time? How could she be in love with someone she's only known a week? It all happened so fast and now, on top of being torn between two amazing guys, she apparently had the ghost of her G3 grandmother desperately trying to tell her something so she can rest in peace.

"Please don't cry. I wasn't trying to make you sad. Like we both advised Claire, I just want to be open and honest with you so there's no confusion. I mean, of course I want you to give the ring back and admit your feelings for me so I can spoil you for the rest of our lives, but, come on. I'm a typical guy, and it breaks my heart to see you cry."

His infectious charm and sincerity baffled her and she doubted her once stable semi-charmed life. She didn't know what would happen between them, but she knew she never wanted to lose him. Even if he only remained her friend.

"Cade, you are anything but a typical guy. You are completely the opposite of typical. You're very infinitely unique, and I'm lucky enough to have met you." This time, she leaned in to kiss him. It was a soft delicate affection, more of a thank you rather than a heated passionate kiss. She ended their contact and excused herself to the bathroom. At the threshold, she paused and glanced over her shoulder. Cade flopped back on the bed, defeated.

Caroline's phone rang from inside the antique jewelry box, and she recognized Trevor's ringtone. Why in the world would he call at one in the morning? She ignored it knowing the fragility of her frame of mind. Caroline was completely exhausted, in shock about a possible ghost in her room, and excited that her new sister had come to her for advice. Never mind the sea of endorphins she drowned in caused by the amazing kiss from that beautiful man lying in her bed right now.

She hurried to wash up and dress for bed. Just outside her room she heard Cade talking softly. She tiptoed the rest of the way and stopped just short of the doorway to listen.

"I know you're trying to tell her something through her dreams about the life you led here in this house. Please, Rachel. Don't scare her off. I care a lot about Caroline, and I. . .I don't want her to leave."

Ready to go in, Caroline coughed before rounding the corner into the room to alert him of her presence.

Having been in the warm bathroom, her bedroom felt like a meat locker. "Man, the air conditioning must work overtime in this old house. Maybe because I'm the only warm body on this side."

Cade smirked and she assumed he'd thought of a witty comeback but decided not to share. "Have you decided which room you want?" Another smirk.

"No, not yet. But I'm sure I'll find one. I'll start with the one warm body and go from there." He smiled playfully. "I'll probably take the room closest to yours."

It didn't take her long to fall asleep with Cade lying beside her. Respectfully above the covers of course. It couldn't have been long before the exhausting dream began. Rachel didn't waste any time, that was for sure.

EIGHTEEN

Running. Again. Through the woods, frantic. Why must I always be running? Caroline didn't know who was chasing her or where to go, but her clothing kept tangling around her ankles. The warm temperature was proof of summertime, but a bed of leaves had begun collecting on the ground, meaning the season was nearing its end. She stopped to listen, but heard nothing. Not a sound. Strange to not be able to hear anything at all.

She closed her eyes and focused on her surroundings. She heard birds up in a tree. . .baby birds. Little squeaks rather than full-fledged chirping. Acorns bounced off branches before hitting the ground, and squirrels chattered as they ate. Oh come on, give me something!

An obvious draft wafted through her clothing. A long, thin linen night dress. Yep, definitely thin. She wore only her undergarments beneath, but. . .wait a minute. . .this wasn't her underwear. These were some serious granny panties!

Her head throbbed again in the same familiar place between her eyes. She found it difficult to focus for the shooting pain. Faint footsteps in the distance closed in. She sprinted off again. Just like in any dream, her legs didn't work as they should, and she felt like she was running through waist-deep pudding.

Caroline hid behind a moss-covered boulder surrounded by brush and broken trees. Apart from the first dream like this, she usually participated in these dreams as a spectator. This time, she was obviously in Rachel's shoes. She glanced down at her bare feet. Or lack thereof. Caroline was nervous, frightened even, about who was chasing her, or, rather, Rachel. This couldn't possibly end well. She knew the outcome, and didn't really want the first hand experience.

The loud clunky footsteps grew near. She crouched down closer to the rock, her face pressed against the cool surface, inhaling the earthy moss.

Caroline's stomach ached. Like an egg beater churned her organs to mush. She placed her hand over her mouth and looked around for some clue to where she was, to plot an escape. She slipped her hand down to her belly in an attempt to settle the roiling sickness. Most certainly Rachel's body. Rachel's pregnant body. Maybe five months along. That explained her nausea. Rachel must have tired from failing to tell her what happened, so now she wanted to show her. Terrific. Literally barefoot and pregnant, Caroline stifled her sour laugh and shook her head. What a pitiful analogy, but terribly accurate in this case.

His boots came into view not three feet away. Caroline held her breath, fearful he might discover her, and prayed she wouldn't vomit. She couldn't see his face, but she did make out a bloody bandage on his left hand. He's after her again.

She immediately regretted all the times she and Kristy made fun of the victims in those cheesy scary movies. Her legs shook now, keeping time with her racing heart. The throb in her head pounded relentlessly and she desperately tried not to pass out. Stay quiet, maybe he'll go away.

He walked off, the crunch of his boots fading. Caroline counted to ten before releasing her breath in hopes he was far enough away not to hear. Her clenched throat threatened to close completely from sheer terror, but she focused on breathing for now. Disregarding her spinning head, she stood, and, without looking in his direction, ran back the way she came. Only, her legs wouldn't work. Panic was an issue now. She had to do something quickly, but what? A bloodcurdling scream tore through the woods and she realized it was her own as a strong hand grabbed her shoulder, pushing her down, her face pressed hard against the ground.

She did the only thing she could think of to do. She turned to the hand on her left shoulder and bit down as hard as she could manage. Just as she sank her teeth into his nasty, bloody bandage, a sharp pain ignited in her right shoulder. He yelped followed by laughter echoing off the trees. The same evil laugh she'd heard in her very first nightmare. Whoever he was, he was definitely the same one who had raped her in that first life-altering dream. She scrambled to her feet and took off, but her legs still wouldn't function. She stumbled around in a stupor. Had he injected her? Given her a shot of a paralytic or anesthetic. Caroline was drowsy, incapacitated. . .vulnerable. He pushed her, nudging her. She managed a whisper. "It's too late. Please. . .my baby. It's too late."

"Caroline! Open your eyes. You have to wake up. Caroline. Please, wake up." She slowly opened her eyes. Cade sat by her side shaking her, trying to wake her up.

"I'm awake. Okay, I'm awake," she slurred. "What's wrong?" She still felt drugged from her dream as she lifted a shaky hand to rub her eyes.

Cade smiled and flicked on the bedside lamp. "There's my girl. Welcome back. What the heck were you just dreaming about?"

182

Dreaming? Oh, thank goodness it was just a dream. Caroline slid her hand over her belly just to make sure. Cade searched her face waiting for an answer. Groggily, she attempted to explain. "I um, I was running. . .fast. So tired. . .and running. . .in the woods. Chased. . .by a pregnant man in a white night gown."

He made a weird face and laughed quietly. "What? You sure you weren't smoking something in that dream? You're not making any sense. Here, wake up some more so you can tell me what you dreamed about and who was chasing you." Still laughing, he propped her up against the pillows and smoothed the loose hair from her face with his hand. "Now, are ya with me? Are we all here and alert, or we still flying high?" Caroline pressed the heels of her hands to her eye sockets and breathed deeply. When she opened them again she got a good look at her bunk mate.

How is he not freezing without a shirt on? My goodness, he's beautiful. Yum. Grow up, dork. It's just a bare chest. . .and amazing abs. You've seen 'em before.

"Funny. Seriously, I'm good now. Anyway, about my dream." She averted her gaze and fidgeted with the bedspread to avoid the distraction of his smooth bare skin within an effortless reach. "I found myself in the woods wearing nothing but granny panties and a long thin night gown. Barefoot and pregnant. Rather than a spectator in this dream, I was in Rachel's body. And chased by a man wearing big black boots, and a bloody bandage on his left hand. I hid, but he found me. When I tried to run, my legs wouldn't work. I couldn't breathe. Couldn't think. I was so scared."

She realized her voice had dropped to a whisper, so she cleared her throat to break the emotion. "So, of course, he caught me. He shoved me to the ground and injected something into my right shoulder. But before he did that, I bit his wounded hand. Whatever he injected me with made me woozy. Maybe a sedative."

Cade stared hard at her, all humor gone. "You were pregnant?"

"It wasn't me. He was really chasing a pregnant Rachel, not me."

"Yeah, yeah, I get it. Why would someone want to hurt a pregnant woman? I wonder who he was and why he drugged you, er. . .her? Did hypodermic syringes even exist back then?" He scowled. Caroline giggled at how involved Cade had become in her delusional dreams. He looked up, surprised. "What's so funny?"

"You're really getting into my dream drama, aren't you? By the way, the hypodermic syringe needle was invented in 1853 by Dr. Alexander Wood. So yes, it was possible for him to drug her with a needle." She smiled triumphantly and tried not to focus on the flexing muscles beneath his smooth tanned skin.

"You know, you really had me worried. You were gasping, twitching and twisting like you were strapped to the bed. You screamed a few times, kept mumbling, 'It's too late' and 'Help me.' Then it took me forever to wake you up."

She leaned over the side of the bed, and saw a few blankets and a pillow spread on the floor. "Caden Luke! I told you not to sleep on the floor! You can't possibly be comfortable down there!"

Amused, he shrugged and grinned sheepishly as he turned the lamp off again to lie down. "I'm sorry, love, I just wanted to make sure you were okay. The only way I could do that was to be in here with you. It's a good thing I was so I could wake you from your nightmare."

"What time is it?"

Cade checked his watch and the green glow momentarily filled the dark room. "It's about 3:30." Maybe she should start wearing a watch so she wouldn't have to rely on her cell phone for the time.

184

"Cade?"

"Yeah, I'm right here. What's up?"

"Would you think me too forward if I asked you to stay up here with me until morning?"

"No, not at all. I've been in here all night, anyway."

"No, I mean. . .up here. With me. In the bed." He sat quietly for a few minutes. She desperately wished she could read his mind.

"Sure, love. No problem. You know, I'm willing to sacrifice myself at the mercy of your martial arts while sleeping. I'm a pretty big guy, I guess I can handle the beating." He kissed Caroline's forehead as he crawled under the covers next to her. His skin was as soft as it looked and she couldn't resist touching his chest with her ice cold hands. He flinched.

She giggled and before she rolled over she mumbled, "Maybe you should have worn a cup."

He chuckled and lay completely still next to her. . .in the bed. . .beneath the covers. A first for Caroline.

What would Trevor think if he saw this?

She forced herself to stop feeling guilty, her mind at war with part wishing he'd scoot closer and the other thankful he left a little space between them, and attempted to fall back to sleep.

Guess technically now I can say I've slept with a man. She snickered at that very thought, knowing it was nowhere even close to the same thing. She couldn't get enough of Cade's warmth and his titillating smell. The man should have to wear a warning label. He was extremely habit-forming.

In the haze of pheromones as she found herself wishing even more things she should not be wishing, Caroline drifted into a new dream. She thought she heard the bedroom door open slowly, but that could've been the dream.

As usual, the sun poured in her window at daybreak. Remembering what happened last night, she jumped up quickly to see if Cade was still in the bed with her. He'd already gone. Caroline frowned. Disappointed, she leaned over the bed checking, hoping, to see him crashed on the floor. Nothing. He must've woken up before her and decided to get in the clear before Eddie walked in and caught him in bed with his daughter.

She laughed quietly and ran her fingers through her shaggy hair. She hadn't brushed her hair or her teeth, so she hurried to get her things, glanced quickly around the room for any sign of disorder, and rushed to the bathroom. When she came back Cade was sitting on her bed. Where'd he come from?

"So, beautiful, what's your plan for today?"

"Well, it's Saturday." She walked to the window to see the morning haze blanketing the duck pond and she sensed Cade behind her. "I'm sure my dad will want to hang out with me. We haven't had a chance to hang out much since I got here. I have no idea what he will want to do, but I'm excited about spending time with him." She turned to face him. "What are you doing today?"

"My band is playing at Dupree's tonight."

"Dupree's? Oh, yeah. I remember him asking you that. Wow, that's tonight?"

He smiled and wrapped his arms around her neck. "Yes, it's tonight. Will you be able to come by?"

"It depends on what all my dad has planned, but I promise I'll try. I love live music and I'd love to hear your band play."

"Great! It's a date then!" He clasped his hands and eagerly rubbed his palms together. "Well, tentatively. . .depending on Mr. Fontenot." His eyes practically sparkled with excitement. She didn't think she'd ever known anyone so content just sitting in the same room with her.

"So, thank you for, um, sleeping with me last night." A sandblaster couldn't remove the grin from his face.

"Whoa, cher. You have no idea what those words coming from your mouth just did to me. I think I'm blushing this time," he teased and playfully brushed her chin with his knuckle. "Seriously though, it was all my pleasure, I assure you." He winked and kissed her cheek.

She wrapped her arms around his neck and gave him a tight hug. The feeling of security this man instilled overpowered every wall or façade she tried to obtain. His arms gripped her soundly, encasing her in strength, comfort, and desire. It was incredible. In the midst of their embrace a man cleared his throat. She closed her eyes, her view of the door blocked by Cade's broad shoulders. "My father's standing in the doorway isn't he?"

Cade turned to look. "Yep."

She responded without looking. "Hey, Dad." When she peeked around Cade's body to greet him, he smiled brightly.

"Good morning, darling. Did you have a good evening?" His tone surprisingly not suggestive.

"Yes, I did. Thank you for letting Cade crash here. It was helpful knowing he was. . .nearby."

"You bet. Beau, what do you have going on today?"

"Nothing during the day today, sir. Only this evening." Cade stood next to Caroline commanding her attention with his consistent respect to whomever he spoke. She couldn't remember ever hearing Trevor properly address anyone.

Eddie's forehead creased. "You have plans for this evening?"

By now Caroline's curiosity was piqued. "What's going on, Dad?" She'd only known him just under a week but she sensed his hesitancy to spit out whatever he had to say.

"Well, April wants to spend the night in New Orleans, just the two of us, and I wanted to see if Beau could. . .entertain you for the weekend." He smiled and Cade literally cheesed back at him. This annoyed Caroline.

"Seriously? I don't need a babysitter. I can take care of myself just fine. Thank you for the thoughtful gesture, but I will find something interesting to occupy my time." Eddie's pained expression reflected his realization that he'd indirectly offended her. He probably meant it as a genuine favor, but it backfired on him. "Besides, what are Claire and Remy going to do while you're gone?"

"They are both staying with friends this weekend. I gave Delia and Delphine the weekend off, and I feel awful expecting you stay in this big house all by yourself." A chill crept up her spine thinking about staying in this house alone. Cade noticed and wrapped his arm around her shoulders.

"Sir, if Caroline isn't comfortable staying at my place, I could stay here in the same room I slept in last night." He glanced down at her and winked.

Eddie looked more apprehensive now and seemed to be reconsidering his trip to New Orleans. That's all she needed, another reason for April to hate her. Caroline had to think of something before he changed his mind. "Dad, really, it's okay. Cade already invited me to Dupree's tonight to listen to his band play. Tomorrow is Sunday, so I'll probably go to church and then come home and relax. Go have fun and treat April the way she wants you to. Maybe she'll like me better if you do."

He grinned vaguely. "Are you sure about this, sweetheart? I can take April to New Orleans anytime. It doesn't have to be the first weekend you're here. She just went there last weekend. She's probably doing this—" He stopped before he said something he'd regret. Caroline finished his sentence for him.

"To get you away from me to show me how much more important she is to you than I am. Yeah, I gathered that myself. As much fun as it would be to see her not get her way, it's okay. I get it. I'm your estranged daughter, and she's your wife. Take her out, wine and dine her, and treat her the way she longs to be treated. I'll be here when you get back, and we can spend next weekend together. I promise. Please, go have fun."

He shook his head. "You must get your intuition from your mother because I never would've seen through—well, seen any of this coming."

"You're not a woman. Women are catty and can be very manipulative and conniving." Especially that one, Caroline thought. April was good, she had to give her that much. "I'll be okay, don't worry about me."

He turned to Cade. "I assume you'll see that she's taken care of while you're busy playing in your band tonight?"

"Yes, sir. I promise I will take good care of her."

"Good. I'm still gonna keep an eye on you, zinger. Even if it's a borrowed eye, so watch yourself, got it?"

Cade approvingly smiled. "Understood, sir. No offense, but I have a feeling Caroline can take care of herself." He winked at her causing her to blush—again. Punk.

Eddie noticed her blush and smiled. "Sorry, sweetheart. You get that trait from me. It doesn't happen much anymore, but in my younger days, I frequently transformed into a wide spectrum of rosy shades."

"It's all good. Apparently some guys dig it." Her eyes cut to a very amused Cade. "We'll be fine, Dad. Go have a great time."

"All right, che—uh, darling. You have a great time this weekend. Give me a call if you need me."

Before he turned to walk out, he gestured the I'm watching you sign to Cade.

Cade went back to his cabin to get cleaned up and dressed for the day while Caroline did the same at the house. Thanks to the unexplainable security vibe he emitted, her unease had fizzled some and at least she wasn't so spooked anymore. They'd agreed to meet for lunch at his place. She pulled her hair up in a ponytail to deal with the June humidity in southern Louisiana. She was not used to it.

She opened the antique jewelry box to retrieve her cell phone and engagement ring and nearly screamed. The ring was in there but her phone was not. She knew she'd left them both in there, especially the phone. Trevor's ringtone reminded her of its location around one o' clock that morning.

She slipped the ring on her finger and slammed the jewelry box closed before storming out of the room.

Something freaky was going on in this house.

NINETEEN

She arrived at the cabin forty-five minutes early and knocked on the door. Cade didn't answer so she knocked again. When he didn't answer the second time she walked to the side and saw his truck parked under the portable carport. Caroline knocked one last time and finally checked the door to see if it was locked. When the knob turned and the door opened, she closed her eyes, remembering the last time she'd entered unwelcomely. After a deep cleansing breath, she stepped into the cozy log cabin.

"Hello? Cade? You in here?" Against her better judgment, she walked toward the hallway. At the bathroom, she paused to listen before going any farther. No running water. Music drifted from his bedroom. She tiptoed to the door and held her ear close to the crack. He was playing the guitar. She assumed that's why he hadn't heard the knock. She knocked loudly on his bedroom door and the music stopped. Cade opened it wearing only a pair of cargo shorts and headphones taking her breath away. She noticed the unusual scar on his chest again, but resisted the urge to ask how it got there.

"Hey!" He plucked the buds from his ears. "You're early! You just can't stay away from me, huh?" His body was a sight to behold, and his playfulness adorable, but unfortunately, she wasn't in much of a frisky mood.

"Ha. Ha. Hey, have you seen my cell phone?" She watched, a little disappointed as he dug through his chest-of-drawers, pulled out a snug black T-shirt and slipped it over his head.

"No. I heard it ring late last night when you went to the bathroom to get ready for bed, but I never saw it. Did you check all over your room? Can you hand me that, please?"

She reached for the white dress shirt he pointed to and brushed her fingertips across the embroidered Fleur de lis pattern on the back. "Yes. I knew where I left it and where it was when it rang. I had the phone and my ring in the jewelry box on the dressing table. This morning the ring was there but the phone was gone."

Cade glanced at her left hand. "Well, that's strange. Why would someone take your phone but leave the rock behind?"

She felt awkward. Ashamed. Guilty for wearing her engagement ring in front of Cade, rubbing it in. She seriously needed to get her act together and stop playing both sides of the fence. She made a promise to someone and she needed to keep it. She quickly handed his shirt to him and tucked her hands tightly under her armpits as she paced the room. "Who knows? I'm about tired of it, though. So what do you want to eat for lunch?"

She honestly tried not to think about it. The current situation had her freaked out in every way possible, not to mention ticked off, so she tried with all her power to pretend to be calm and in control.

"What would you like to do? We could go grab some Popeye's chicken and have a picnic by the lake?"

Her last picnic with Trevor when they discussed wedding plans, sexual partners and what he was going to teach her after they were married flashed through her mind. She nixed the picnic idea and shrugged her shoulders. "No, I don't think I'm up for a picnic in this humidity. Any other ideas?"

"Well, I could take you into town to eat somewhere you haven't been, and you could meet some of my friends."

That wasn't a bad idea. Meeting his friends could be fun, get her mind off the pocket-picking ghost, and would allow her to avoid being alone with Cade all the time. "That sounds like fun."

He smiled. "Fun indeed. I have to warn you, though, some of the guys you'll meet today really are zingers." He laughed.

"Yeah? I've never hung out with a bunch of swamp rats before. This will be a very educational experience for me. Any advice you wanna hit me up with before you feed me to the gators?" She put on a good front, but beneath the smirk, she honestly wished for a tip on how to act around them. Of course, he saw through her façade.

He approached her, gently tipped her chin up and invaded her soul. "Just be your beautiful self. They'll adore you as much as I do. Don't take anything they say too seriously, and don't stress too much about their accent. Sometimes I can't even understand what they're saying." He kissed her forehead and continued getting dressed as he threaded a woven belt through the loops.

"I'll shoot you a glance if I get too lost." Excitement pumped through her, but the stress from the past few days had started to wear her down. She looked forward to hanging out and listening to some live music tonight. To unwind a little. Caroline wished Kristy could fly down for the weekend. She always knew just what Caroline needed to de-stress. Whether it's dancing, chocolate covered strawberries, rum runners or karaoke night. Plus, the extrovert Kristy is, she'd do away with some of the introductory awkwardness sure to accompany the jitters gouging holes through her entire body.

Now she really fumed that she couldn't find her cell phone. She couldn't call Kristy to beg even if she wanted to. Caroline wondered how many times Trevor had called. He's probably having his fourth conniption fit because she wasn't answering. It wouldn't surprise her if he contacted the local police department to put out a search party. She chuckled and then cringed when she accepted the truth to that possibility. *Nah, surely he won't go that far.* Cade asked her something and snapped her back to reality.

She shook her head as if to clear the cobwebs. "I'm sorry, what'd you say?"

His face crumpled with concern. "Are you okay? You seem distracted. If you don't want to go out anywhere for lunch I can fix something here for us. It's no problem."

"No, please. It's nothing. Really, I'm okay. I just have a lot on my mind. I want to go. I need to. . .get out, you know, a change of scenery. I gotta get out of that house for a while."

"Yeah, I totally get it. I can't imagine why you'd be stressed. Meeting your father for the first time in twenty-one years, your stepmother despises you, you learned you have siblings," he smiled. "You literally ran into a strange naked man who later revealed his intentions to steal you away from the man who put that beautiful ring on your finger. And to top it all off, you discovered a family ghost in your room who seems intent on contacting you about her past through your dreams. Yeah, I can't imagine why you don't want to just lock yourself up in the house alone. What kind of nut-job are you, anyway?" He smiled, but his incredibly accurate summary unnerved her.

"Well, when you put it like that. . ." she sighed, her shoulders slumped. "Let's go eat. I'm starving." Caroline tired of always being the good girl and never taking any chances. Maybe meeting some new people who knew nothing about her would help relax her, even if they were crazy Cajuns. Maybe that would be even more fun. They got into Cade's truck and headed for the Bayou. Caroline's attitude perked up with the thought and she now bounced with enthusiasm, eager to witness the true Cajun culture and see how much it differed from the stereotypical Hollywood depiction.

As they drove down a two lane back road, she stared out the window and lost herself in the beautiful oak trees. The Spanish moss draped mystically from the branches of the desolate cypress trees. She studied the picturesque green swampy marsh. Barren trees and the sharp tattered stumps arose from the water, pikes of what used to be trees before Hurricane Katrina unleashed hell. She imagined how peaceful it must be to live in the small, one-room shacks along the bayou. To have everything you need to get by, how simple life would be with no drama.

Suddenly Cade pushed hard on the brakes. She braced herself against the dash and yelped. A huge alligator lumbered across the road. It had to have been at least seven feet long, maybe even eight feet. Though difficult to tell because he waddled quickly to the other side with his mouth open in warning. He took long enough for her to get a good look at him before he disappeared safely in the swamp.

"Holy Cow! That's a real live alligator!" Caroline couldn't believe her eyes as she plastered herself to the dash. "Holy Cow! An alligator just crossed the road!" She turned to Cade whose shoulders quaked with laughter. "For real, does this happen often?"

He laughed aloud, but didn't answer her question. His amused face repetitively swiveled from her to the road and back. She didn't wait for a response.

"In Arkansas we have deer, rabbits, or raccoons that cross the road, skunks, opossums, and even the occasional armadillo, but never alligators!" Caroline was truly amazed. One thing she could cross off her list of things she'd hoped to see while down here this summer. Coolest thing ever!

After he calmed his laughter, Cade smiled and gently squeezed her leg just above her knee resting his hand there. "You are so cute."

"I've just never seen anything like that before. So stinkin' awesome! An alligator. . .seriously."

"Sweet Caroline, I can promise you one thing. You will see more alligators during your summer here than you've seen in your entire life."

"What do you mean? How can you promise that? I mean, I realize we just saw one cross the road, but how do you know I'll see more than just that one?"

He studied her for a minute and pulled his hand back to the steering wheel. "You don't know what your dad does, do you?" His seriousness sobered her excitement.

"What do you mean? Like, his profession?"

"Yes, his. . .profession. You don't have a clue what he does for a living, do you? What kind of business he runs?"

She thought for a moment and realized she'd never asked her dad anything about his life, only about why he left them so long ago. He hadn't really volunteered the information, either. "No, I don't guess so. What kind of business is it?"

Cade shook his head. "Uh-uh."

Caroline smacked his arm. "Oh, come on! You have to tell me now. You can't just leave it like that. What does my dad do?" Cade continued to shake his head with that ridiculous smirk. "Tell me."

He smiled. "No, boo, I think I'd rather show you."

Oh boy. Caroline didn't know what she'd just gotten herself into, but she was dying to know what the big secret was. Her imagination ran wild. She couldn't wait to see what Cade had in store for her, though she hoped her dad wasn't involved in anything illegal, like drug smuggling or something. A touch of anxiety crept into her thoughts.

"Awesome. Should I be worried?"

He answered with a smile and drove the rest of the way with a smug, knowing, grin on his face. He had something planned for her that she would never forget.

With no idea what to expect, a mixture of nervous energy and excitement rolled in her stomach. It could have been extreme hunger, but the look on Cade's face had her impossibly curious. For the moment, Caroline was content absorbing the ambience of the Bayou and sitting in sweet, beautiful silence.

They pulled into an oyster shell lot and Caroline spied a cute baby blue cabin with a wraparound front porch badly in need of repainting. The wooden structure appeared weathered with years of wear and tear, but the tantalizing smells radiating from the place had Caroline's stomach growling with acceptance. Her mouth watered in anticipation.

Cade helped her out of the truck. "This place is known for its crab bisque." He winked with a lopsided smile and placed his hand on Caroline's lower back to walk her inside.

"Sounds delicious. Can't wait, I'm starving." A group of men sat at a table on the front porch. They all wore white rubber boots, looked filthy, and smelled of the briny ocean mixed with the sweat from a hard day's work. One of the guys nodded, and Caroline waved back, acknowledging his subtle greeting and tried not to cough from the stream of cigarette smoke trailing from the hands of his shipmates at the table.

"They're shrimpers. Probably just delivered a fresh load of Gulf shrimp to this restaurant."

Caroline couldn't hide her surprise. "Wow, I can see why this place is well liked, then. Fresh seafood delivered straight from the Gulf is hard to come by in Illinois. And Arkansas, too, for that matter."

Cade chuckled and held the door open for her. "Yeah, it doesn't get much fresher than this. That's why I love it here so much."

At the bar, Caroline hopped up on a heavy stool as Cade greeted the balding man drying a glass beer stein. The bartender gave her a full once-over and shifted his attention to Cade with a suggestive grin. It almost made her uncomfortable until the man spoke to Cade with familiarity. His heavy Cajun accent confounded Caroline and she understood nothing he said. She nearly fell off her stool when Cade spoke just like him. The bartender changed his tone and scurried to the computer to punch in the order as he called it aloud to the kitchen. He said something else to Cade before greeting a new customer.

When Cade finished talking he turned back to Caroline. She had been staring at him with big eyes, slightly embarrassing him.

"I ordered you the crab bisque. Is that okay?"

"Sure, that's fine. I'm eager to try it. Um, how did you do that?"

"Do what?" He opened a package of crackers trying to avoid eye contact.

"Speak like that. . .to him. I couldn't understand a word you two said. What did you say to him? Was that even English?"

He smiled. "Not exactly. You're in Cajun country. It's how most people talk down here. Natives, you know?"

"I get that, but how can you sound so normal when you talk to me and have no trace of an accent, but then talking to him you sounded like that was your everyday language?" She was truly baffled. . .and somewhat turned on.

"Practice." He kept his attention on his crackers, toying with the crinkly package. "In one of my former jobs I had to work really hard to learn how to talk without an accent in case I ever needed to, but it's like riding a bicycle. It comes back to me pretty easily, especially when I'm surrounded by it. The same goes with any other language, like French or Spanish."

Intrigued, impressed, fascinated and just a little more smitten with the extremely unique new language she'd just heard, she wanted more. "So, do you speak any other languages?"

He still wouldn't make eye contact and seemed very hesitant to talk about it. "Um, I know a few. I'm not as fluent as I used to be, but I can usually keep up with a conversation."

"A few? Like which ones?"

"Why is this interesting?"

"Because I only memorized what I needed to pass my Spanish finals and get the necessary credits, that's why. I'm fascinated by the many talents of Cade Beauregard. What other languages do you speak?"

He shook his head, and, though he hadn't blushed, Caroline would swear he was embarrassed. Still refusing to make eye contact, he nodded a greeting to another patron who entered the restaurant. "I don't know, obviously Cajun, but I am pretty good with French and Spanish. I'm familiar with a few others like Thai, German, and such." He shrugged his broad shoulders. "It's really no big deal. I probably can't remember much of them anymore. I mostly just speak English and Cajun now." His face was flushed now and serious. He seemed really eager to change the subject.

Caroline smiled shyly, feeling the burn creep up her neck. "That's hot."

He burst out laughing, his smile bewitching Caroline. "What? You think that's hot?"

In full blush mode—again, she said, "Yes. I have never heard anything like that. I have to be honest, I find it very, um. . .appealing."

He wrapped his arm around her neck like a big brother would do to his little sister and kissed her temple. "Believe me, cher, you will get both ears full of it today."

After lunch they met up with Cade's friends at a daiquiri shop. She couldn't help but laugh at the drive-thru. Cade looked at her curiously. "Nothing like promoting the 'don't drink and drive' law with a drive-thru at a daiquiri shop."

He chuckled. "Relax. If you get pulled over, you only get in trouble if the straw is in it. That's when it's considered an open container."

"Yeah, that's if you get pulled over. If you don't get pulled over, chances are you're drinking and driving. It doesn't make much sense."

As they approached the covered patio, three beefy guys jumped the railing and trotted over to them. The men glanced between Cade and Caroline with big, obnoxious grins. They all spoke in Cajun. Cade laughed and answered them in the same dialect she had grown to adore. Cade looked at her indecisively, and then said something to the biggest of the three. She didn't want to stare at him, but at a glance he looked Native American with his copper skin and straight, jet black hair pulled back into a ponytail at the nape of his neck. She quit trying to understand their conversation and gave him an annoyed look before looking at the other two guys. Caroline knew Cade was talking about her and that she couldn't understand what he said.

Before she could assess his friends, Cade placed his hand at the middle of her back and began the introductions. "Caroline, this is Henry, Chris, and Ty." She smiled and gave a little wave. She would never admit this to anyone, but they made her uncomfortable with the way they were staring.

"Guys, this is Caroline Fontenot." Their eyes widened and they straightened up a bit. Cade continued, "Yes, she is the daughter of Eddie Fontenot. . .your boss."

TWENTY

Now it was her eyes that widened. "Wait, what? Their boss?" She looked up to the sky and dropped her shoulders in surrender. "Okay, I give up. Please explain."

The largest one she'd observed before, Ty, stepped forward and she got a better look at him. He was huge, and with his high cheekbones, sharp nose, and almond shaped eyes, Caroline decided he had to be of Native American descent. Ty was certainly handsome, but it was the scar on his chest that Caroline caught a glimpse of under his tank shirt that drew her attention. A brand, just like Cade's. And in the same place. She attempted not to stare as he took her hand in his, engulfing it. He had a deep voice and spoke with a strong but understandable accent.

"Hello, Miss Caroline. It's a pleasure to meet you. Welcome to Au Bayou. I had no idea Mr. Fontenot had two lovely daughters." He raised her hand to his lips and kissed it as she cut her eyes to Cade. That was the same line he'd said to Claire. She wondered if that was a common reply or if he had told him to say that. Her bet was on the latter. The annoying blush crept across her skin.

"Thank you. You're very sweet." Ty released her hand and smiled, noticing her crimson shade and looked at Cade holding back his laughter.

She turned and punched Cade's shoulder as hard as she could. "You're such a punk! You told him to do that."

"Relax, beautiful, no need to be shy in front of these blockheads. They're just like me, only not as handsome or smooth." The two other guys started talking smack, and one of them, Chris, assured her he would embarrass Cade in retaliation.

She looked at Cade slyly. "I'd be careful, then, if I were you. I may just ask one of these *blockheads* to entertain me while my dad is gone."

His smile quickly faded. "It would be over my dead body before I let one of these goons be alone in the same zip code with you."

They laughed. Chris said, "That could be arranged, you know."

Cade replied in Cajun, and Ty yelled "Hooyah." They wrestled playfully with each other until Caroline decided it was time for an intervention.

"So, are you guys gonna show me what this whole daiquiri thing is all about or are we going to stand out here and play?" They called a truce and walked inside. The air was clogged with cigarette smoke. *Ugh. I hate smokers.* Just as that thought crossed her mind, she saw the quiet one, Henry, light up. He was smaller, more wiry, but still big. His eyes met hers, and she must have made a face because he quickly snuffed it out.

When she asked Cade what drink he recommended, she apparently snapped him out of a daydream.

"What do you like?"

"Huh? Oh, yeah. Um, me personally? I like the Ignitor, but it's strong. I don't know if you need that one."

"Why? You don't think I can handle it?" she challenged.

"I don't know, boo. You seem like you might be a bit of a lightweight. You can't get enough of me when you're sober, I'd hate to think of what you might do to me after drinking an Ignitor. You might try to take advantage of me."

Of course, she should have seen this coming. He provoked her, and she completely missed it. She squared her stubborn jaw and called the waitress over. With the most mocking and sarcastic tone she could manage, she motioned to Cade. "I'll take the same thing this irresistible hunk of a man is having."

He stared at her for a minute, a playful twinkle in his mischievous eyes, and without looking away ordered. "I'll take a large Ignitor for myself and one for the lady, please." His mouth curved up on one side and he licked his lips seductively. "You sure about this, sweet Caroline? I cannot be responsible for my hands—or my lips—if my brain and good senses are inebriated. And you, my dear, are intoxicating all on your own."

She leaned in closely, enough to feel the heat from his body, and whispered, "Well, Mr. Beauregard, it would be in your best interest to persuade your good senses to overcome their temptations, since I am promised to someone else." She held up her left hand to remind him, though sure he hadn't forgotten.

His eyes fell to his wristwatch and his brow raised. "Yes, I remember that you are promised to someone else. Unfortunately, that lucky man has run into a bit of misfortune by sending his lovely bride-to-be down south to convene with a bunch of rough swamp rats who care nothing about his promises. The best I can tell, you have not said the magic words yet. So I still have a little time left on the clock. The game's not over, and lucky for me, the Yankee prince is currently. . .absent."

Laughter and high-fives didn't blot the flutter she felt deep in her belly with his confidence and no-nonsense approach. He clearly intended to fight for her. She'd never been fought over before and didn't know exactly how to handle it.

Cade's friends were interesting. The mouthy, obnoxious one, Chris slapped his hand on Cade's sturdy shoulder. "Yeah, beb, your man should be more worried about this cat and his mad skills rather than a bunch of harmless swamp rats! Beau here's a—"

"Right, Chris. I don't know many things worse than a group of Cajuns up to no good." Cade's eyes warned him to say no more and he nodded in receipt of the silent message.

Wildly curious to hear what Chris was about to say, what mad skills he was talking about, the look Cade gave him was not something Caroline wanted to approach. She would ask him later what all that was about if the opportunity presented itself.

She had to admit, she liked his persistence. His attention and desire for her made her feel beautiful and treasured. Part of her, a big part, didn't want him to give up. But the other part, the part that loved Trevor, wished Cade would stop tempting her.

Cade's buddies had started a game of pool and wanted him to play. He said no at first, but Caroline didn't want to keep him from enjoying himself, and encouraged him play. The waitress brought their daiquiris, Cade tipping generously.

She sipped her drink while watching the four guys play pool and ruffle each other's feathers. Cade hadn't lied. This very strong drink could probably take the chrome off a bumper. Luckily, her lunch could soak up the alcohol. If only she had her cell phone to at least text Trevor and tell him she was okay.

After the first few potent sips, her drink tasted more like a smoothie than an alcoholic beverage, and she eventually forgot to sip it. She sucked it down too fast through her straw, and before she knew it she was tipsy. A killer buzz before she'd even made a dent in the daiquiri. Caroline's inhibitions vanished. Her walls down, and terribly vulnerable, but, strangely enough, she didn't care. She felt safe. Well, safe enough, with Cade.

She discreetly observed Cade and his friends as they gracefully moved around the pool table. Chris seemed clumsier than the others, bumping into one of the bar tables and knocking over an empty beer bottle, but he had skills with a pool stick. He trash talked the most and had a very loud, but infectious laugh. Probably the class clown or life of the party.

Henry stayed quietly in the corner awaiting his turn, speaking only when spoken to, and smoked like a chimney. He moved smoothly around to a corner, smiled as he sank one of the striped balls, and said something in Cajun before he gave Chris a high-five.

Ty and Cade, however, moved around the table like panthers stalking their prey. They were large and muscular, but lithe and graceful. Caroline noticed a camaraderie between the two that made them more like brothers than friends. They seemed to know each other's moves before they were made, like they communicated on a wavelength unavailable to anyone else.

Strange, yet admirable, and Caroline compared their friendship to the one she shared with Kristy. Kristy knew her like no one else, which reminded her that she probably needed to have a look in the mirror. Awareness is key. That was Kristy's philosophy. One would never be caught with spinach in her teeth if she checked them frequently enough.

In the bar's bathroom, Caroline took one look at herself and cringed. Kristy's scolding voice echoed in her thoughts. She removed her ponytail, fluffed her wavy locks, dabbed tinted lip gloss on her colorless lips, and powdered the shine from her nose and forehead. She straightened her outfit and adjusted her cleavage so the girls wouldn't look droopy. One last glance and her liquid courage decided the reflection this time looked much better.

She pranced back to her table much happier about her appearance and felt four sets of eyes, and maybe a few more from the bar, following her. She suddenly felt very sexy. A goddess. That nagging voice in her head ordered her to throw the rest of the daiquiri away, but her stubborn inner diva demanded she keep drinking it. Caroline doubted she could finish the enormous cup anyway. Cade sank the eight ball and he and the other guys came back to the table. His eyes widened when he saw how much of her drink she had finished during his short pool game. He smiled and gave her a long once-over.

"How ya feelin', boo?"

"Pretty good. How 'bout you, *Beau*?"

Clearly well enough for sarcasm, she must have convinced him she wasn't drunk yet because he flipped a chair backwards and straddled it facing the table. He seemed overconfident that she would be by the time they left. She decided to slow down with the frozen deliciousness, but worried she was a tad late. Her mouth moved faster than her brain.

She desperately wanted to know more about Cade's buddies and their relationship with Eddie. "So, what exactly is it you guys do for my dad?"

They chuckled and looked at each other to see who would talk first.

"We hunt alligators for him," Ty said.

Aware her mouth had dropped open, she snapped it closed. "You. . .hunt alligators? For my dad? Seriously? How? Why?" How had she missed this fascinating little morsel of information? They seemed to enjoy her animated reaction and slid into their heavy accents again. Caroline waited for someone to speak understandably. The tennis match of looking back and forth between them made her head spin. Finally, Chris spoke plain English and included her in their little conversation.

"We hunt the gators by setting baited traps and then shoot 'em once they're caught on the trap. You know, like the show on T.V., 'cept we don't gotta worry about ratings or cursing."

"Then what? What does my dad do with them?"

Ty answered in a steady informative salesman-like tone. "He sells different parts to different people. The tail is good for meat, the head and feet are good for souvenirs, and the skin is good for clothing, shoes or purses. It's a very profitable industry down here."

She took another swig of her drink, forgetting altogether about slowing down, and continued with her interrogation. "What about the rest of it? Who gets all the extras. . .you know, like the guts?" She laughed at her weak attempt at humor, but the answer quickly shut her up.

Henry answered with a very serious expression and the rest of the guys grew quiet as well. "Voodoo. The rest of the parts, like the innards and tongue, go to the voodoo priests and priestesses."

Her eyes burned from lack of blinking. Not a terribly superstitious person, Caroline had always heard to avoid, at all costs, anything having to do with voodoo. But the whole idea and being surrounded by the mystique of it all fascinated her.

"Voodoo? Like. . .stick a little doll with pins and needles, black magic kind of voodoo?" she snickered. No smiles or laughs from them this time, they simply nodded their heads. She waved her hand dismissing the tension and seriousness, "I don't know about all that. Is that stuff actually for real? I always thought it was just made up stories to scare people. I never thought it was true! Isn't it some kind of religion or something?" Her mouth had now completely detached from her brain and she was about to embarrass herself, but she didn't care. The chills and goose bumps the topic provided were exhilarating.

Henry looked at Cade. "Go ahead, Beau, tell her what you know about it." All eyes were on Cade now.

His body language like a coiled snake ready to strike, Cade glared at Henry and spoke, more like yelled, again in the accent so Caroline couldn't understand him. She quickly put a stop to that. "Cade! Stop it! You know I can't understand you, and I want to hear what you have to say!"

He sat quietly for a minute, brooding. "It's nothing. Henry's just trying to spook you."

She didn't believe him. "Okay, if it's nothing, then go ahead and tell me." Henry chuckled now as did the other two.

"Yeah, *Cade*, if it's nothing just tell her." Henry blew a kiss before taking a long draw from his beer bottle.

Cade wasn't laughing. His jaw ticked and his angry frown deepened.

"Great job, Henry. Next time keep your big-ass mouth shut." Cade let out a few stronger curse words before he finally looked into her eyes. "Voodoo is real. It's not a myth or a made up scary story. It's real. Yes, it's a type of religion, but the darkness that exists within is real."

"How do you know this, exactly?" A little afraid to ask this question, she had to know. Cade shot Henry another hateful look and hesitantly continued.

"It can get a little confusing, but the story goes. . ." Cade let out a frustrated sigh. "My great grandfather's brother, my G2 uncle, dealt with a voodoo priestess, and it came back to haunt him. It not only haunted him, it haunted his brother, who was my great-grandfather, and my G2's son, my great uncle. I'm not exactly sure what they had dealings about, but I do know it was regarding a debt my great uncle owed someone. Anyway, things didn't end well, and my G2 uncle, who was in perfectly good health, wound up dying of a sudden massive heart attack while simply walking down Canal Street in New Orleans."

"What happened to the other two, your great grandfather and great uncle?"

Cade's frown sagged into sorrow. "My great grandfather went missing and was never found. . .not even his body. The son, my great uncle, was the one who had acquired the debt and couldn't repay it. He had a stroke at a very young age, but it didn't kill him. It just paralyzed one side of his body so he couldn't use his hand, and he always walked with a limp. Five years after the stroke, on the very same day, he suffered a heart attack. That didn't kill him either, but he had to have open heart surgery and a few stents. Two years later, on exactly the same day, he was walking through the parking lot at a grocery store and got struck by lightning." Henry snickered and Cade fired a peanut that pegged him in the center of his forehead. That shut him up.

"Anyway, that didn't even kill him, he was just a little slower mentally and walked all hunched over with a limp. His wife had left with their three children, one of which was a boy, because she was worried the curse would eventually find her son. She thought getting him as far away as she could from my great uncle and the voodoo priestess might save him, so she moved to Texas leaving her family and everything she knew. Three years later he refused to go anywhere on that specific day, so he stayed in his house, watching the news. . .alone. He had a sudden seizure and choked to death on his own tongue. There was no valid explanation for the cause of his seizure."

Caroline could not believe what she heard. First, she's forced to believe in a ghost, and now voodoo? Unreal. "Was this on the Beauregard side?"

"No, my momma's side."

"Cade, I don't want to be the disbelieving skeptic here, but, though it's not impossible to choke on your tongue, it is highly unlikely. I'm in nursing school, and one of the things we've learned in first aid is what to do when someone is having a seizure. If they're on their backs, the tongue relaxes and falls against the soft pallet at the back of the throat blocking the airway. However, they don't literally choke on it. He probably had a seizure lying on his back sleeping, and no one was there to roll him onto his side. Surely there are logical explanations for the other two deaths. I can imagine that the people who knew of their dealings with the voodoo priestess were probably watching closely for some coincidence or something."

He vehemently shook his head. "No, Caroline, it's real, and you have to promise me you will never let your ridiculously insane curiosity ever get you mixed up with it. Like you said, it's actually a type of religion and there are plenty of people down here who believe in it and the curses that can go along with it."

She had no intention of researching it, because she didn't believe in it. For now at least.

TWENTY-ONE

"I promise, you won't have to worry about me getting involved in any kind of voodoo. I don't believe it's real. I may be starting to accept this whole ghost, haunted house thing, but voodoo curses. . .ha! It's just stupid." Yeah, she was starting to act a little belligerent, talking too much, and too loud. In her stupor of thoughts, she hadn't realized she was being shushed. All four guys shushed her for talking too loudly about voodoo. Rather humorous for a nonbeliever to see. She giggled and whispered, "Geez, y'all are like a bunch of superstitious pirates. Did anything happen to your uncle? Does he still live in Texas?"

"No, his mom eventually moved back here after his father's death so she could be near family. So far, nothing has happened to him, but he's married and has three sons. My aunt is terrified something will eventually happen to her husband and/or her sons."

She shook her head in disbelief. This was all just too much to accept at one time. She didn't know much about voodoo, and believing the spooky coincidental superstitions was nearly impossible. She took another long sip of her drink.

Ty asked about the ghost. Cade blew it off as no big deal so he wouldn't pry for more information. The guys were intrigued by Caroline's sudden boldness. They asked questions she normally wouldn't answer, but in her current state of mind was more than willing to freely discuss. Chris led the charge.

"So, Caroline, tell me about that rock on your finger and who put it there." He shot a nervous yet implicating look at Cade. She wondered about the meaning behind that but decided not to go there.

"What do you wanna know about it? I don't know much about diamonds, so I can't help you there. You looking to buy a ring for someone or are you engaged already?" They all laughed when she hardly paused between sentences.

"No, I'm not engaged or married, but that's a helluva ring. Beau's not the one who put it there, huh?"

"Nope, unfortunately not. But it doesn't stop me from gettin' all hot and bothered when I'm around him. Whoo!" Caroline's southern accent more pronounced while intoxicated, she fanned herself dramatically and laughter burst out in the room. Cade's face blushed a bright red. "Wait, what is this? Am I hallucinating? Cade, sweetheart, are you blushing?"

He smiled and slipped his hand through his hair. "No, beb, your eyes are playing tricks on you. It's that large Ignitor you're drinking, it'll get you every time." The guys laughed in unison.

"I am engaged to Trevor Callahan from Chicago. He is a very handsome and successful architect."

Chris spoke again. "You don't sound like you're from Chicago."

"'Cause I'm not. I'm from Arkansas. My best friend was accepted to the University of Chicago, so I applied for a scholarship there and got it. My mom couldn't afford to send me anywhere else, so I jumped on the opportunity." Sweating now, Caroline leaned her head back to gather her hair and twisted it up into one hand as she fanned herself with the other. She didn't miss Henry's eyes trained on her exposed neck as he tipped his bottle up for another drink. It should've creeped her out, but with effects of the alcohol, it only intensified her sensuality. She closed her eyes and moaned lightly as she massaged the back of her neck. She didn't need to open them to know they were all watching her intently.

"You said you're a nursing major?" Chris asked.

"Yep." Caroline popped her eyes open and let her hair down as she reached for her cup.

"Awesome. So you gonna stay in Chicago after you're married?"

Parched, she shrugged and took another pull on her straw. "Don't know. Trevor has a great job there, so probably, but I'm hoping we can eventually move back to the South. I don't want to be too far from my mom, especially when I have a baby."

Cade flinched, catching Caroline's attention. His buddies must have seen it too, because they changed their course of questioning.

Henry surprised her with the next question. "That man of yours must be pretty good in bed to choose him over a sexy tiger like Beau." They all laughed again except Cade who kept his eyes on his drink.

"I wouldn't know. I've never slept with him." That shut them up, Cade's head tilting slightly. She'd clearly surprised him with that tidbit. Caroline should have stopped talking right then, but of course she didn't. "Honestly, I've never slept with anyone. Well, technically I've slept with Cade, er. . .*Beau*, but we didn't have sex."

The guys looked at one another confused. Cade quickly jumped in to clarify. "We shared a bed, but no clothes were removed and we kept our hands to ourselves. Now, y'all mind your own damn business." The noise level in the place intensified and the heavy accents were flying again. They were clearly teasing Cade for not taking the chance when he had it.

He really blushed now. She leaned back in her chair, exposing her slender figure from the hips up, and laced her fingers together confidently behind her head in a leisurely, yet enticing position. With her arms raised, and her body angled in such an inviting manner, her breasts were accentuated and her shirt stretched tightly across the center of her chest drawing their eyes to one location.

Cade eyed her cautiously. "I think you need to be cut off, cher. You're gonna embarrass yourself if you keep going."

She leaned forward across the small table, inches from his chair and braced her elbows on the table in front of him and winked. "Looks like you're the one I'm embarrassing, cher."

Chris boisterously cut in with no intentions of letting anything rest. "Wait, hold up, how old are you?"

She slowly leaned back in her chair and casually crossed her legs. "Twenty-three. Why?"

He shook his head in disbelief. "You're twenty-three years old, and you've never had sex before? With anyone? Ever?"

Caroline laughed. "Nope. Why is that so hard to believe? You make it sound like it's a bad thing." Another sip.

She had successfully shocked all of them. Mostly Chris. He just couldn't believe it. Cade and Ty gave each other a strange look across the table, communicating somehow. Chris took over the conversation, unable to hide his fascination.

"No, beb, definitely not a bad thing, it's just. . .wow. It's hard to find a chick nowadays who hasn't been with multiple partners by the time she's nineteen or twenty. A good girl. It's no surprise Beau found you, dude's got all the damn luck," Chris grumbled.

Caroline noticed the tendons strained in Cade's hand as he mutilated a straw, but couldn't look at his face. She knew his teeth were clenched and that her transparent resolve would fail to hide her weakness for him. Something she couldn't afford to risk.

"You dumb ass, she's engaged to another man." Henry chuckled. "For once Beau didn't get the girl." Caroline was afraid Cade would knock Henry's lights out; Trevor sure would have if one of his friends had made a jab like that at him. But Cade didn't flinch.

Instead, he said, "She ain't married yet." Laughter erupted and bottles clinked as high-fives, fist bumps, back slaps, and every other bro celebration was given. Cade smiled at Caroline and commanded her attention as he took a long pull from the straw of his equally strong daiquiri. For a moment Caroline was lost in a mesmerizing hazel fog.

She noticed Cade's eyes seemed greener while relaxed around his friends. Or it could've been because he was drinking. Or it could've been the simple fact that she knew every color speckle in his beautiful irises. Sometimes golden, sometimes olive, but always alluring.

Unspoken admiration, maybe desire, some otherworldly emotion that hadn't breached their friendship until now, penetrated her soul as Cade didn't so much as blink to break their connection. A prisoner to his charm, Caroline worried she'd never escape his forcefield of determination. She needed to escape his hold quickly if she wanted to remain loyal to Trevor because Cade's magnetism overpowered her good senses.

Chris paid her that favor with a bold confession. "Man, I think I lost my virginity when I was fourteen in the bed of my brother's old truck." More laughter filled the room and she finally broke eye contact with Cade to observe more male camaraderie. Caroline couldn't remember ever being around this many guys in a relaxed setting, walls down, raw and exposed. She also couldn't remember the last time she'd laughed this much. Her cheeks ached from smiling.

Ty spoke with a proud smile. "I lost mine at fifteen in the shed behind my daddy's house."

Henry had a quiet raspy voice. "I was sixteen and lost it to my best friend's momma. Man was she smokin' hot!" The room erupted with loud praises and hi-fives.

Then, the moment Caroline had been waiting for, all eyes turned to Cade. His turn to confess.

"What are y'all lookin' at?"

Chris prodded. "Come on, bro. It's your turn."

Cade grinned. "I don't kiss and tell, dude. That's my business." He peeked at Caroline for her reaction. She knew her face reflected her disappointment. She hoped to hear at least the age he was when he lost his virginity. After learning of Trevor's extensive experience, Caroline was anxious to learn Cade's. But she admired his philosophy. A guy who didn't brag about his intimate moments was admirable. It showed respect for others as well as himself.

Cade spoke playfully now. "Sweet Caroline, you may want to close the line of questioning before you end up getting asked something you don't want to answer. I told ya, you can't take these guys too seriously."

"Oh, come on, we're having fun, right? It's just talk. Go ahead, you ask one. There's got to be something about me you've been wanting to know. You may not get another chance like this," she said.

He hesitated and then smiled. "Okay, what is it about Trevor that you *don't* like?"

Caroline always thought there was nothing bad about Trevor, that he had no flaws, but he'd changed dramatically since they got engaged. He had a few major flaws, she just never wanted to admit them to herself. Now a bit tipsy with no inhibitions, she answered honestly.

"Well, sometimes he's jealous. Really jealous. Lately he's had a quick temper, and occasionally he drinks too much. That, of course, is usually followed by him trying to force himself on me." She ran her fingers around the rim of her drink. "Also, he likes to always be in control, and I think he's keeping something from me, but I'm not sure what it is. Apart from those negative qualities, he's perfect."

Cade's buddies quietly focused on him, who now aggressively flicked his straw. He was tense, almost angry.

"What's the matter? Did I say something wrong?"

Cade commanded her attention, speaking slowly and quietly through clenched teeth without looking directly at her. "Caroline, how many times has he forced himself on you. . .physically?" He struggled to spit out the words.

"Whoa, chill out. It's not that big of a deal. He always backs off when I tell him to. I told you, I've never been with anyone, and Trevor respects that." She looked to the other guys for some clue. "Why does that bother you so much?"

Cade pushed away from the table and stalked over to the jukebox. Caroline froze, her heart on the floor and mind swimming in confusion. She didn't know what just happened, but she'd somehow pissed him off. Her eyes searched for answers from her new friends, but their gazes were all averted. They weren't spilling it, whatever it was.

"Guys, please. What did I say?"

"A few years ago, Beau's sister was raped by her fiancé," Ty said quietly. "Bastard nearly killed her."

Caroline's stomach dropped and she instantly regretted her nonchalant attitude. "Oh, hell."

Without acknowledging the others, she immediately followed him. "Cade, I'm so sorry. I didn't know. Is your sister okay?"

"She's fine," he mumbled without looking away from the lighted buttons of the jukebox. "This isn't about her."

"Please talk to me." Like magic, her buzz was gone. "I apologize if I upset you. That wasn't my intention at all. I had no idea about your sister. Come to think of it, I didn't even know you had a sister. This is why I try to never drink too much. I've got a big mouth."

He turned with a solemn expression. "If he honestly respected you, he would never try to force himself on you. Has he ever hit you?"

"No! No, he's never been physically abusive. What I meant was that sometimes when we. . .well, when we start. . .sometimes things get intense. He tends to get a little carried away." She did *not* want to explain to Cade the details of her intimacy with Trevor. She nervously fingered a strand of her hair. "Occasionally he gets too worked up, and I'm constantly stopping him so he won't go any further. That frustrates him and it causes him to become resentful. He's never tried to hurt me. He's really very sweet to me. He just has his moments. Don't we all?"

Cade expelled a relieved sigh and pulled her into him wrapping his arms around her tightly, his strong embrace a security blanket of comfort. There was still so much about him she didn't know, but she felt in tune with him, like they'd known each other their whole lives.

He buried his face in her hair, his compassionate whisper a plea, a soothing ointment for her wayward thoughts. "I would never raise my hand to you or any other woman. I don't think I could stand it if anyone ever hurt you. I know we just met, but I already feel protective of you and I can't imagine ever not having you in my life."

Music began playing as if on cue. Cade had purposefully picked a slow song. They danced, swaying slowly. His hand caressed the curve of her back while the other one cradled her head. It was obvious to anyone with eyes that he wanted her. That he cherished her. Caroline closed her eyes and rested her head on his warm chest with her arms wrapped around his waist. Lost in the moment, she nearly forgot where she was when the song ended. His hands gently pulled her away and his soft warm lips touched her forehead in a lingering kiss.

"You about ready to go?"

She had completely lost track of time. "What time is it?"

He looked at his watch. "It's almost four-thirty."

"Wow, already?" She didn't want this moment to end. "What time do you need to be back to get ready for your show?" Honestly, she wasn't ready to leave yet, but didn't want to make him late for his gig.

"We should probably get going now."

"Okay. Thanks for bringing me here. I really had a great time today meeting your bayou boys." She didn't have to force her genuine smile. She looked forward to the next time she saw his buddies.

They said their goodbyes, and the guys told Caroline next time they would take her out on the boat while they hunted. She thanked them for the offer, but that she'd much rather see the gators when they brought them back already dead. They laughed and spoke to Cade in Cajun again. Very curious, Caroline didn't want to pry. She figured he would tell her when he was ready. She could wait. Maybe.

On the way home, Cade sat quietly. She ached to hear his thoughts. Unable to stand it anymore, she finally broke the silence. "Your friends are a trip to be around."

He smiled with a reminiscent look. "Yeah, we've all known each other since we were little kids. Our parents used to get together all the time and have big parties, so we were always close. They're like brothers to me. Especially Ty. He and I have been through a lot together. A lot."

That may partially give reason to the matching scar. She would have to ask about that soon. But not now.

"How many siblings do you have?"

"I have four sisters. One older and three younger."

Jealousy nibbled at Caroline. "That's awesome. That explains a lot then."

"Explains a lot about what?"

"Well, why you are so good about understanding the needs of women."

He let out a bellowing laugh. "Yeah, right. I don't think any man on the planet has *that* one conquered yet. Thanks for the vote of confidence, though."

"Not just the physical needs, you perv, but the other needs as well. The need for comfort and compassion, and listening. You know, the mental and emotional needs that women have. Most men are only worried about catering to the physical needs. It also explains your protectiveness toward women."

"Thank you."

"Why are you thanking me? I didn't do anything but embarrass you, tick you off, and make a fool of myself today."

"No, love, you didn't tick me off. I'm thanking you for noticing that I'm not only interested in you physically. Don't get me wrong, I am very much interested in you physically, but it's more than that. I care about you. A lot." He sighed, and his grip on the steering wheel tightened. "I just can't stand the thought of a man, even if he is your fiancé, forcing himself on you or getting angry with you for not wanting to have sex with him. It infuriates me."

She needed to change the subject. "I can't believe I said some of the things I said. I'm so embarrassed."

"Why? I don't think you said anything too bad. If anything, you made yourself look even better, if that's possible."

"Are you kidding me? I blurted out details of my lack of a sex life to three, well, four guys I hardly know. That's humiliating. Not to mention the garish confession of my uncontrollable feelings when I'm around you. No more daiquiris for me. I'm cutting myself off completely."

He laughed, clearly entertained by the memory of it all. "I quite enjoyed your talkative nature. It's definitely a side of you I hadn't seen before. What can I do to make you feel better about it?"

"Hmmm. . .you can answer a question for me."

"Okay. What's your question?"

"I know you said you don't kiss and tell, but it would make me feel a lot better if I knew just how experienced you are."

She didn't look at his face, but couldn't resist a peek from her peripheral vision. His smug expression didn't give her much comfort. She could only imagine what his number was. Gorgeous and buff, living in a small town with a good family name, he had to be desired by every female who ever crossed his path. Furthermore, having already experienced his phenomenal kisses, Caroline wasn't sure she wanted a number. "No comment?"

"Just tell me why you want to know?" He didn't seem angry, just pleasantly curious.

Ugh! Why can't he just tell me and get it over with?

"I'm just curious. You are an extremely good kisser and, well. . .I, um. . .I am just a little curious how good. . ." she sighed in frustration. "I'm curious about how much. . .practice you've had with. . .other. . .people, er—activities."

He quietly chuckled to himself at her stumbling and stammering to spit out the right words. She knew her crimson face reflected her embarrassment. Always.

"Caroline, I love how sweet and innocent you are. It makes me smile. I will be honest with you. I have been with someone before. I dated my girlfriend from high school for a very long time and we did get intimate. I was planning to propose to her when I came back to stay with my parents and finish school, but, through unfortunate circumstances, that never happened. She was the only woman I've ever made love to. There. Now you know. I'm not much more experienced than you are."

"Oh, I beg to differ! You may have only had one woman, but I'm sure you were with her more than once or twice if you were planning to propose?" If Caroline ever had a taste of him, she would be a nymphomaniac for sure. She stared at him awaiting an answer.

He nodded. "Yes, we were very. . .active. That's true. I've never been extremely promiscuous. I prefer to keep things more personal. I don't like to go that far unless I'm. . .well, I believe sex is an act of love between two people, and. . .you know, you share a part of yourself with that person mentally and emotionally, as well as physically. So, well. . .I am not all about finding random women to just. . . You know what I'm trying to say, right?"

Caroline was glad she wasn't the only one stammering over her words now.

"Yes, I understand exactly what you're trying to say. I completely agree." Unfortunately, she found it harder and harder to not fall in love with this man. How I wish Trevor felt the same way about sex. To him it was a fun game and just physical. You meet someone, do it, and go your separate ways like it's no big deal. That's not how she felt about it at all.

"So, how long were you with her? How come you guys never got married? Did she not feel the same way about it as you?"

He sat silently for a few long moments. "We were together for six years. She died in a car accident five years ago."

Yet again, Caroline felt the ground crumble beneath her feet. How many times must she stick her foot in her mouth around this angel? "I'm so sorry. I understand if you don't want to talk about it."

"Thanks. I'd rather not, if it's okay."

The rest of the trip home was quiet. She looked forward to a whole summer of hanging out with the tenderhearted soul sitting next to her. Her thoughts drifted to Trevor, the gnawing guilt slowly fading with the fact he hadn't contacted her much since she'd been here. She wondered about the true purpose for her spending the summer down here. Either way, she wasn't complaining as long as she could spend time with Cade.

Still, she couldn't understand why Trevor didn't call more. He'd called nearly every day while she lived in Chicago. Even chewed her out for not answering one day when she'd forgotten to turn her phone back on after church. Although, her phone was missing, so she couldn't know if he'd tried or not. Caroline's head spun with the passing landscape, so she surrendered to the overwhelming urge to close her eyes.

She envisioned her phone carelessly balancing on the ledge of her window sill and reached to save it. Trevor's name flashed across the screen as it bounced from the vibration of the ring. Just before she could grasp it, her phone slipped over the edge and crashed to the ground splintering into a thousand pieces.

Her eyes popped open in shock, but Cade's expression hadn't changed. He hadn't noticed her flinch, or if he had he didn't comment. She drew in a relieving breath. Just a dream. . .or was it.

TWENTY-TWO

Caroline checked the jewelry box again to see if her cell phone had magically reappeared. It hadn't. The velvet-lined box remained empty. She had no idea where her phone was, but she never realized how much she truly relied on it until she didn't have it. Especially after her crazy dream on the way home.

Once she was ready for the evening, she went to her dad's office to check the time. His desk clock read 5:45. She had a little time to kill. She stretched out on the bed with her laptop and checked her email. A ton to sort through, she skimmed the names to see if any were from Trevor. Surprisingly, none were from him, but there were a few from her mom and one from Kristy.

Caroline wrote a short and sweet email explaining to Trevor, her mom and Kristy why she hadn't answered if they'd called. She told them she had misplaced her phone and hadn't found it yet, though she wasn't sure when, or if, she would ever get it back. Trevor may not believe her because she always had it with her.

Caroline surfed the internet for a while reading headlines until she got bored. Unsure why, curiosity perhaps, she searched for fatal car accidents in the area five years ago. She didn't expect to find much. Caroline didn't know the girl's name, age, or even the city where the accident took place. Not surprisingly, she came up empty. She broadened the area to include New Orleans, finding many links to choose from.

She clicked on a random link and thought she might have hit the jackpot. The article reported the woman, Jenny Richardson, was twenty-three years old. Her parents currently lived in Mississippi but were originally from Metairie, Louisiana. She had recently graduated from LSU with a degree in elementary education. She was to be a Kindergarten teacher for the Golden Meadow lower elementary school in the fall, but she never made it. She died in June, the summer before she was to start her new job. If this was the woman Cade had been with, the picture of her included in the article was beautiful. She seemed like such a sweet person, and Caroline's heart ached for his loss.

She closed her laptop. Why, after six years and with intentions to marry her, had Cade not asked Jenny. What was he waiting for? Caroline walked to the window to peer out toward the duck pond deep in thought. A beautiful blue butterfly landed on the window sill just in front of her face. It sat calmly with its wings slowly fanning up and down allowing Caroline to admire the beauty of its ombre wings.

Suddenly, it flitted away and Caroline followed its path until it landed on the shoulder of the garden statue in the duck pond. Such beauty and grace, a symbol of new life and transition. Oh, to be able to fly with the carefree spirit of a butterfly. Feeling peaceful now, Caroline gathered her things and headed to the restaurant for an entertaining evening with her new friend.

Caroline found the restaurant with ease, glad she hadn't needed to call Cade for directions. Not that she could call because she didn't know his number and couldn't find her stupid cell phone. She ground her teeth still peeved about that.

It was cooler, but still humid outside, and dusk was just around the corner. Caroline planned it just right, she wouldn't be too early or seem overly eager. Although she shouldn't be worried about that, it wasn't like she was playing hard to get with a diamond on her finger. Men shied away when they knew a woman was claimed. Except for Cade. She wiped the smile from her face and reminded herself of her happiness with Trevor by repeating the mantra aloud.

The place was packed. Glad to have a Jeep to jump the curb and drive up on the grass, she had to park in a field for the lack of available spots. She hated walking into a place like this by herself. She heard the music blasting from the speakers and it sounded great. Smiling contently and feeling like a VIP since she knew the leader of the band, she squared her shoulders and opened the heavy glass door.

The bar was slammed. She waited patiently for two guys getting enough bottles of beer for a small army to move away. She bellied up to the bar and shouted over the music to the bartender, a short, balding man missing a few teeth. He wasn't the owner she'd met earlier in the week, but he resembled him. Caroline guessed he was the owner's brother.

"I'd like some water, please." He paused for a moment and smiled though she had no idea what about.

"He said you'd order water." Before she could reply, he turned around to fix a drink. *What the*—? He placed a glass in front of a perplexed Caroline and then rang a hand bell. The drink he gave her was not water, and for a moment, she thought he had her confused with someone else. She started to correct him, but then the band began playing a song. She recognized Neil Diamond's familiar tune, the classic she'd heard her whole life because of her name. Caroline started again to address the bartender until she heard Cade's smooth voice streaming through the microphone.

She looked to the stage and made eye contact with him as he played the guitar and sang into the microphone, seducing her with his intense gaze. The lyrics she had memorized years ago were fresh and new, as if she was hearing them for the first time, written just for her. In that moment she and Cade could have been the only two in the bar, everyone else faded away.

He didn't take his eyes off her through the whole chorus. Her face scarlet, the smile embellished was worth a thousand words. He smiled back, lighting up his handsome face, and winked.

It was perfect. Caroline got lost in the moment as Cade continued through the rest of the song. Once they broke eye contact and she snapped herself back to reality, she realized everyone in the bar stared at her. She swallowed hard and turned back to the bartender to correct him about her drink. But mostly to pretend she wasn't being sized up by a whole restaurant full of people.

He smiled. "Can I help ya, ma'am?"

"I think you must have given me someone else's drink. I ordered water."

His snaggletooth smile got bigger. "Beau tol' me ya'd order water, so he tol' me to give ya dis instead."

She tried to keep her face from reflecting exactly what she thought, so she graciously smiled and asked, "What exactly did he tell you to give me?"

"Dat's a Rum Runner, Miss Caroline. He said ya liked 'em. He right?"

Caroline was impressed and unsure how Cade knew she liked Rum Runners. Had I mentioned that to him this afternoon when I was a little tipsy? "Great! He was correct. How much is it?"

"He also tol' me to put whatever you want on his tab. I think he's kinda sweet on ya." He winked. "Can I getcha anything else?"

"No, no thank you. I'm good." That scoundrel. She hadn't planned to drink tonight since she indulged so freely this afternoon. Cade must be determined to keep her as uninhibited as possible in her dad's absence. She laughed and shook her head as she pondered his intentions. While talking to the bartender, she hadn't noticed the band take a break. The moment she realized the stereo was playing, warm hands covered her eyes. Before she could say his name, a sultry voice said, "Guess who?"

She smiled. "Hmmm. . .let me think. Stephen Tyler?"

She heard his beautiful laughter. "Noooo, guess again."

"Really? Those sexy pipes? Bon Jovi?"

"Hmph, don't I wish. You only get one more practical guess before I make you get up on stage and sing."

"Well, I'm assuming you don't want people running out screaming and holding their bleeding ears, so I will say the super hot and sexy gardener I heard outside my window my very first morning in Louisiana. Final answer."

He spun her around with a big cheesy grin. "Aww, what gave it away?"

"Lucky guess. Thanks for the drink. How'd you know I liked Rum Runners?"

He slowly smiled and winked. "Lucky guess."

About to insist that he tell her how he knew, she remembered he had looked through her photo albums. She assumed he'd seen a picture of her and Kristy drinking and started to ask when she recognized a member of his band walking over to them.

"Ty? I didn't know you played, too! I didn't expect to know anyone else here. It's great to see you again." Caroline couldn't help but feel embarrassed and shy around him after her ridiculous afternoon display. He knew more about her than she would've ever allowed someone she'd just met to know. Still, a perfect gentleman, Ty acted no differently toward her as he kissed her cheek then spoke to the bartender in Cajun.

Cade talked in her ear so she could hear him. "Order whatever you like, it's my treat. I promised your dad I'd take care of you, so please, help yourself. I gotta get back up there to play. Enjoy yourself, sweet Caroline. I'm really glad you came tonight." He kissed her cheek and ran back up to the stage. She felt like a groupie, only it was her first time hearing him perform, and things were kind of backwards with him giving her special treatment. She liked it. . .a lot.

TWENTY-THREE

The early morning sun was a much better alarm clock than that annoying one Caroline had at her apartment in Chicago. Warm and subtle rays silently crept into the room through the parts in the curtains. She felt the toasty warmth tickle her feet as it seemed to effortlessly spread its buttery glow across her bedspread. She stretched and froze in place the second she realized what lay beside her. She slowly turned her head to observe the thick locks of golden-brown hair she'd rested her hand upon. Her heart smiled when she realized Cade had stayed with her last night.

She'd stayed at the bar until the band finished packing up, exhausted by the time they left. She barely remembered walking into the house or up to her room. Come to think of it, she didn't remember that at all. She glanced down to see she was wearing her pajamas from the night before. *How in the world. . .*

As Caroline tried to figure out how she miraculously changed clothes without personally recalling the act, she caught movement from the corner of her eye. She turned to Cade smiling at her.

"How did. . .why am. . .my pajamas are. . .wait a second. Did you. . .?"

He placed a finger over her mouth. "You were dead on your feet, so I drove you home, carried you from the car up to your room and yes, I changed your clothes for you. But. . .before you freak out, let me explain. I was very respectful, and please believe me when I tell you, I had my eyes closed and didn't touch you. I merely helped you keep your balance and held the clothes for you as you stepped into them." His smile stretched across his face as he made one last little comment. "I promise, I only peeked a little."

He anticipated her reaction to his sneaky little comment and vaulted himself out of the bed just as she jumped to attack him. Quick and agile like a cat who always landed on his feet. Embarrassed he'd seen her in her underwear, she supposed it was only fair since she had already seen him naked.

Caroline threw her pillow at him, but he caught it and bounded back onto the bed. He sat on top of her and stretched her arms above her head. Holding them both at her wrists with only one of his hands, the other tickled her ribs until she cackled like a toddler. She begged him to stop before she peed in her pants. Cade finally gave in and released her arms.

Tired from laughing, Caroline laid there, arms spread, chest heaving, trying to catch her breath. He quietly sat, admiration glinted in his eyes. Once she caught her breath he leaned forward and gently kissed her forehead. He lingered above her face for a moment and then slowly, tenderly kissed her lips. Caroline responded and the tender kiss developed into a deeper kiss. Before long, their lips were locked in passion. She shouldn't be kissing him, but it felt so good. So right. She ran her fingers through his hair and wrapped her legs around his waist.

Abruptly, Cade stopped kissing her, pressed his face into the crook of her neck, took a deep breath, and slowly pulled himself away. She realized, for once, she wasn't the one stopping the lust-filled moment.

Frustrated with herself for not wanting him to stop, she was glad he did. He stood, and stepped away before they both lost control. Caroline sat up in the bed and smoothed her hair.

She got a good look at his navy blue boxers, and heat immediately singed her cheeks. With his back to her, she studied him while she had the chance. She couldn't resist studying the contours of his delectable body. Positively delicious. His bronzed skin only emphasized the rippling muscles in his back. He turned around to face her, and Caroline briefly lost herself in the definition of his chest and those amazing abs. Her eyes lingered on the unusual scar above his heart.

She squeezed her eyes closed before she spoke the words running through her mind. She had only been here a week and already Trevor's body had started to become a distant memory. *Stop it, Caroline! You are engaged to an amazing man who is just as beautiful. What are you doing?*

Worry creased his brow and he immediately shrugged back into his jeans. "I'm so sorry. I don't know what got into me. I shouldn't have kissed you like that, and I apologize. I know you're engaged, and I will respect that. I don't like it, but I'll respect it. Just tell me, honestly, that you don't see and feel how perfect we are."

Caroline wanted to answer, but couldn't find the words. She kept her eyes trained on an empty space in the corner and shook her head searching for the right thing to say, unable to respond completely before his shoulders fell.

"I see. I don't believe you, but I won't force you into anything. I promise I'll try to stop putting you in such awkward situations that cause you to do things you don't want to do."

"No, Cade, I do want—" she pursed her lips, unsure how to explain without sounding hypocritical, "Really, it's okay. I kissed you just as

233

much as you kissed me." She smirked. "I'm the one who wrapped my legs around you."

Caroline ran both hands through her hair and spoke her thoughts out loud. "I really like you. . .a lot. You do things to me that—" She huffed a frustrated breath. What a train wreck. "I love Trevor, but the two of you make me feel good in. . .different ways. It's hard to explain. With Trevor, I feel desired and beautiful, but sometimes he makes me feel dumb, like I can't think or do things for myself. When I'm with you I feel. . .sexy and appreciated. . .alive. I worry, because with you, sometimes I find myself wanting to be rebellious and daring."

He flashed a wicked grin.

"I have a difficult time controlling my thoughts and actions around you, and, because I'm engaged, it worries me. It confuses me. I don't want to stop hanging out with you because you give me a love for life, for living and experiencing new and exciting things. I made a promise. I just have a lot to think about and consider, about myself, and what I want."

Hope lit his eyes. Caroline needed to reevaluate her life decisions, but she couldn't help but be a little upset with Cade for causing her confusion and pain.

"I don't want to be a home wrecker, but you can't deny our chemistry, Caroline. We fit perfectly together, I know you've felt it. That zing, the static current whenever we touch, my heart tries to bust out of my chest whenever you smile at me. I haven't had someone like you in—well, it's been a very long time since I've been this happy around anyone."

Cade sat next to her on the bed, dipping the mattress and causing her to lean his way. She didn't resist and rested her head on his shoulder. "When. . .my girlfriend. . .died, I buried myself into my work and music. I fell into a dark place and wasn't sure how else to cope with the grief. I felt lost, like everything of value in my life had been stripped away from me against my will. I had just come home. . ." He looked down at her and paused, hesitant to continue, so she sat up again encouraging him to go on. She sensed his difficulty as his Adam's apple bobbed with every swallow.

"I had missed out on a lot of time with her and then I blinked and she was gone. A horrible, very gloomy depressing time in my life. I wouldn't wish that on anyone." His jaw tensed. "If I put myself in Trevor's shoes, I would annihilate any man who tried to take you away from me. I can't be that guy."

A war raged within him, evident as he forced his mouth to speak the next few sentences.

"I'll back off. Step away. Concede. As difficult as it'll be for me, I will refrain from kissing or touching you inappropriately. I'll do everything in my power to resist you." He stood and paced to the door, before turning to meet her gaze. "Caroline, I do appreciate you. I promise to be nothing but respectful for the remainder of your time here." He'd made his decision.

A terrible sadness washed over her. She'd just been dumped, but she hadn't. Why was she so upset? She should be happy he would stop tempting her to cheat on Trevor. Why was she not elated and thankful? She didn't want to admit it, the sheer possibility was insane, but she was falling in love with Cade. How was that even possible?

Caroline dropped her head and grumbled like a pouting toddler. "I don't want you to stay away from me. I know we should chill out and stop flirting so much, but I don't want to. Is that terrible of me?"

His face emotionless, Caroline thought, hoped, she detected a glint of desire in his eyes.

"Sweet girl, you won't have to stay away from me," he said. "I will stay away from you as much as I can force myself to."

Sudden anger fueled her into a tirade. "You don't have to stay away from me and stop being my friend just because you can't kiss me or be with me! That's ridiculous. We can still hang out and be friends. It's possible. It just takes self control."

He smiled with fascination at her acute burst of anger. "You've got a short little fuse there, don't ya, Fireball?"

Fireball? "Whatever. I just don't like for someone else to make my decisions for me." Caroline felt like he'd grounded her from being near him. Whatever it was, she didn't like it one bit.

Suddenly, a noise crashed downstairs and Cade immediately crouched in a protective stance.

"We're the only ones here, right?" Caroline nodded, too afraid to say anything.

His face dead serious, he made a hand signal that she didn't understand, and whispered, "Wait right here, I'll go check it out."

"You're crazy if you think I'm gonna stay up here all by myself in a haunted house. I'm coming with you. I'll be right behind you."

He shook his head and smiled. "A short fuse and stubborn. You do have some Cajun in you, don't ya."

"Guess I take after my dad. Now, stop judging me and let's go see what made that noise."

They tiptoed down the stairs. The noises were louder in the kitchen. Whoever, or whatever, pilfering in there was not trying to be quiet or inconspicuous. Cade held her behind him with one hand and he walked first, very slowly, into the kitchen.

Caroline grabbed him with her cold hands. "Wait!" she whispered. "What if it's a ghost?" He flinched, and she tried to hold her laughter in.

His whisper barely audible, Cade moved without making a sound. "I'm gonna buy you some gloves for those freezing hands. I seriously doubt it's a ghost making all that noise. Now stop talking and stay close."

If she'd gotten any closer, she would have been wearing his jeans with him, which, on second thought, wouldn't have been too bad. Caroline slid her arms around his bare waist over the luscious ridges of sheer muscle and used his body like a shield, peeking around to see if she could spot anything unusual. He stiffened at her touch and she quickly removed her hands. She stepped up beside him when she realized there was nothing in there. Completely freaked out with goose bumps and all, Caroline looped her arm through his and clung to him for courage.

They took a step farther into the kitchen. Someone popped up from behind the lower cabinets right in front of them. Cade moved like lightening, jumping back, and tucking her protectively behind him in one fluid move. Caroline screamed and the mystery guest screamed even louder. Delia smacked her hand over her chest feigning a heart attack, her pale skin blanched from her fright.

"Delia, what are you doing here? You have the day off, remember? I thought you and Delphine went out of town for the weekend?"

Delia's gaze focused intensely on Cade's bare chest. She blinked and swallowed hard as she prepared to speak, but didn't take her eyes off Cade. "I got back early and was just tryin' to get the kitchen ready for the week. Beau, honey, you can't sneak up on an ole lady like that. . .wit ya shirt off. . .and them muscles poppin' out all over the place, lookin' all. . .like you look. Ya nearly stopped my poor heart."

Caroline glanced at Cade who was intrigued by Delia's inability to control her bold stare. He looked at the wall behind her with a huge grin on his face. *Oh, he's loving this!*

"Yes, Ma'am, I apologize for startling you. And thank you." The irresistible smile Caroline had grown to love followed his apology. Delia blushed and fluffed her hair. Caroline laughed so hard, she snorted.

Her hand fluttered to her mouth and she apologetically shrugged. "Yes, but it's only seven in the morning on Sunday," Caroline said. "You don't have to be here until tomorrow. Why are you here so early?"

"I wasn't sure what all needed repairs, so I came to assess the damage. I been up since five this morning, Miss Caroline. This ain't early for me." She eagerly looked back at Cade, this time with a smile. Caroline didn't know why Delia was so enamored with his bare chest. She saw him all the time without a shirt when he was landscaping. Maybe Delia just hadn't seen him this closely, half-naked before. A smirk flooded across Caroline's face as she remembered she'd seen him more than half-naked.

Man, I'm pathetic. What, am I proud of that now? I should really be ashamed of myself. But I'm not.

Cade spoke, puzzled. "Ms. Delia, surely you're not responsible for repairing the damage? At least not all by yourself?"

She shook her head. "No, honey. I merely wanted to come see what all needed to be done so I'd know who to call for the repair work. Sorry if I disturbed y'all." Her wide smile and suggestive tone hung in the air.

"No, you didn't disturb us. We were just talking about what we're going to do today. That's all." Caroline's feeble attempt to explain proved useless.

Delia inspected both of them, their tousled hair, Caroline's skimpy pajamas and Cade's bare chest. "Uh-huh, just talking. Okay, whatever you say, Miss Caroline. Whatever you say." She smiled and called over her shoulder as she walked off. "I'll be back later today after lunch. You two have fun, ya hear?"

Caroline bit her lip and Cade stifled a crooked smirk, but no matter. They cracked up laughing until tears pricked her eyes. She could only imagine what they must have looked like to someone else. Caroline was just glad it was Delia who saw them and not April, or worse, Trevor. She really needed to try to get in touch with Trevor. She wished her phone would magically reappear. If Rachel's ghost had it, Caroline was about to lose her patience. How do you demand a ghost to do something?

She checked the clock again. "I guess I need to get ready for church." He stopped at the base of the stairs.

"You're welcome to come with me," she said. She hadn't expected him to go with her, she just figured she'd throw the offer out there. She'd invited Trevor many times, and he always had some reason why he couldn't, or wouldn't, go with her. Cade, as usual, surprised her.

"Sure, I'd love to."

Caroline's eyes nearly popped out of their sockets. "Seriously? You want to come to church with me?"

Cade chuckled. "If that's okay with you? You did offer. Change your mind?"

"Oh, I would love for you to come with me. I just wasn't expecting. . .I'm not used to. . ." she sighed. "It's just, I usually go either by myself or with Kristy."

"Well, I'd like to come if you don't have a problem with it."

"Certainly. Meet me back here at 8:45?"

"I'll be here."

After church, they went to Cade's place to have turkey sandwiches for lunch. Cade had obviously been to church before. His comfort and knowledge with the songs was impressive. As if she needed to be any more impressed with him.

While they ate, she decided to ask Cade more questions. "So what is it like having four sisters?"

He took a drink of his water. "Dramatic." He chuckled and took another bite.

Caroline smiled. "I can see how it would be."

"What about you? Other than the two you just met, do you have any other siblings?"

She shook her head as she swallowed her bite. "Nope, I'm an only child. My mom never remarried."

"Really? How come?"

"It's a long story. I always wondered what it would be like to have a big family."

He smiled big. "It's a blast. Christmas is the best, but every time we are all able to get together for a meal or any occasion, it's always fun."

More envy. She wished she could have had the same types of experiences he'd had making memories with his sisters.

"So I take it you want a big family, too?" Before she finished the sentence he nodded his head. An involuntary smile spread across her face as she studied a potato chip on her plate. The locally made chips were delicious. Crunchy and spicy. A nice addition to a bland turkey sandwich.

"From your smile, I suppose you want a big family as well?" He'd stopped eating for a moment to wait for her answer. "Caroline?"

Caroline absently glanced up and concern creased his brow. "What? Oh. . .yeah, I'd love to have a big family. I've always wanted to get married and have three or four kids running around the house. You know, big dinners, big holidays and festive, noisy Christmases. It's always been a dream of mine." She avoided eye contact.

"Well, you're on the road to making your dream a reality. You've met the guy and set a date, all that's left is saying the words and doing the deed." He laughed again at his choice of words, but this time she didn't laugh. "Have you guys set a date yet?"

Unwilling to address the sore subject, she figured he sensed her unease. "Sort of. Trevor chose January fourteenth of next year."

"Trevor chose that day? Uh-huh. And what about you?"

"I would much rather wait until late spring or early summer. I don't see a need to rush into anything. I told him I wanted to wait until after I graduate so I won't have anything distracting me from my school work. I'm so close to graduating, and I can't let anything mess me up now, or I'm afraid I won't finish."

"When do you graduate?"

"December seventeenth. Trevor initially wanted a Christmas wedding."

Cade nearly spewed water all over her. "Christmas? Man, he didn't want to waste any time, did he?"

"I know. I told him no way because then I wouldn't be able to go home for Christmas to spend the holiday with my mom. I told him I wanted to plan the wedding after graduation, not during it."

"I see. You told him that, so he graciously decides on January fourteenth? How thoughtful of him."

"He said he's worried that if we don't hurry and book the place now we won't be able to get in anywhere. I don't know. I just feel like he's rushing me into a wedding for some reason. He assured me it didn't matter to him, that he'd be willing to elope if I wanted to, but he knows I want a wedding. I don't think he's trying to control me. It's just. . .I don't know. I don't like deadlines. They stress me out."

"Well, how does he feel about children? Do you two agree on that aspect of your relationship?" Again, she didn't answer him. "Does he have a big family?"

"No, he's an only child, too."

"Okay, I think I'm getting it now. He wants to hurry up and get married, but you would rather wait. You want lots of kids and a big family, and I'm guessing he doesn't. Does he want any kids at all?"

"Yes, he said he would like to have one, but he only wants one because. . .well, it's stupid. I'm not gonna say."

"Oh, come on, you can tell me. I promise I won't laugh."

"You'd better not laugh or say anything bad about him."

He held three fingers up. "Scout's honor."

"He only wants one child so there won't be any fighting, favoritism, or questions about who gets our inheritance."

Cade sat silent and still, wearing no expression. He picked up his sandwich and took a bite. She stared, waiting for something. "Nothing? No comment or opinion? No sarcasm? Snide remark?"

"Nope. I said I'd be nice."

"Well, I wasn't so nice. I started a big fight about that little difference of opinion. I told him I would rather have a house full of rowdy, happy squealing kids than worry about who our inheritance goes to. That's extremely selfish."

"I have to agree with you there. So, tell me why you are marrying him?"

Because he asked me? Come on Caroline, think!

"I love him. He is very caring and affectionate. He surprises me all the time with special dates and thoughtful little gifts. He's witty and handsome, and he loves me. Sure there are things I don't like, but, for the most part, the good things outnumber the bad ones." Only, the bad things are BIG things. "He really is a good guy. His dad pushes him around too much. He lets his dad get to him, and it stresses him out."

"What does his dad do?"

242

"He's a real estate developer or something. I'm not sure exactly what he does. I think he buys land and creates subdivisions or housing areas. Something like that."

"What's his dad's name?"

"I doubt you'd know of him. I think he primarily deals in the Midwest. His name is Kenneth Callahan. He's had his own firm for the past seven or eight years, but I'm not sure of the name. Trevor mentioned once that his dad got into it with his previous company, and he and his partners had a big falling out. I don't know much about him because I've only met him a couple of times. He's not the friendliest person in the world." Caroline desperately wanted to change the subject. "So what are your parents like?"

When Cade talked about his family, his face lit up. He thought very highly of his parents. "Well, my dad is a hardworking man. He's spent most of his life working to support his family and raise us the way he believed we should be raised. My mom is beautiful and good at everything she does. . .which is pretty much everything. She cooks, sews, knits, sings, takes care of the house, takes care of us kids, plays the banjo and the piano, and in her spare time she's a doula. My parents are amazing people."

"What exactly is a doula?"

Cade smiled. "Someone who is trained to assist women during childbirth."

"What about your sisters?"

"My older sister, Catherine, is twenty-nine. She's a first grade teacher. My middle sister, Caitlyn, is twenty-four. She's an air traffic controller in the U. S. Navy. My next youngest sister, Carly, is twenty-one and in college to be a veterinarian. And last is my baby sister, Cameron. She's eighteen and wants to be a doctor."

"Wow! Catherine, Caden, Caitlyn, Carly and Cameron. That's a lot of C's." Stupidly and without thinking, Caroline added, "I'd fit right in with your family."

Cade stared at his bottle of water and quietly replied, "Yes. . .you would."

She quickly tried to think of something else to talk about, but thankfully, Cade's phone rang. He jumped up to answer it while she beat herself up for the slip. *Rub some salt in the wound, Caroline, go ahead. Ugh! Stupid, stupid, stupid!*

"That was your dad. He called to let me know they are back and asked if we wanted to come see the souvenirs he brought you. Shall we?" He held his arm out to escort her.

"We shall." She loved the way he made her feel special. "I wonder if he tried to call my phone?" Not that she would hear it.

"Yeah, he mentioned that. He said he tried to call yours and he heard it ringing up in your room. It must be in there somewhere."

There was no way. She turned that room upside down looking for it. If it was in there, it was because someone, ghost or not, just put it back where it belonged.

"Yeah, I guess we'll see, won't we?"

TWENTY-FOUR

Eddie stood on the porch waiting for them with a huge smile and his arms out wide to hug Caroline. He kissed her cheek followed by a tight hug. "Great to see you, love. Did Beau take good care of you while we were gone?"

"Yes, he kept me busy and fed, just like he promised. Did y'all have a good time?"

April walked out onto the porch. "Caroline! Nice to see you again. I trust you had a good weekend and didn't get too lonely here by yourself." She turned her focus to Cade, lancing him with an icy glare.

"Hello, April. I was just fine while y'all were gone. Did you have a nice time?"

"Yes, it was lovely, thank you. We spent quality time together and got a lot accomplished." April slinked her arm around Eddie's waist and nibbled his ear. Caroline's stomach roiled at the forced display of affection while Eddie looked uncomfortable and slightly embarrassed.

And what did she mean by accomplished? Odd choice of wording. What could she possibly have had to accomplish? Caroline was under the impression it was just a romantic weekend. So weird.

Caroline forced a smile. "Great. I'm glad for you."

Even though April was smiling, her eyes still pierced daggers through Caroline's heart. This woman hated her, and it was no secret to anyone. Why, all of a sudden, had April put on this front, pretending to care about her. She also didn't get why April hated Cade so much. Jealousy that he wasn't interested in her? Caroline, a woman herself, couldn't figure this woman out. No wonder men were so clueless.

Eddie quickly cut in and placed his arm around Caroline's shoulders to lead her into the house. "Come in and see what I—we bought you on our trip. I think you're going to love it."

In the living room were two packages sitting on the sofa. Naturally, Caroline started with the larger one. She pulled out a beautiful Mardi Gras mask, complete with feathers and glitter painted around the eyes. The smaller package was even better. A heavily lacquered baby alligator head. She looked up at her dad and April with a big smile. "Thank you! It's awesome. I love it. More than you know."

"I suggested getting you a voodoo doll." Caroline's skin crawled with April's peculiar tone. "But your father said you would think it was ridiculous." She laughed. Caroline looked at Cade who glared at April. He didn't think her little joke was funny at all.

"He was right." Caroline tried to make her tone as dry as possible, for Cade's sake if nothing else. April quickly stopped laughing and glared. Caroline gave Eddie a hug and a kiss to say thanks. She turned to April, who stood in preparation for the affection, but Caroline stopped short. "Thanks, April. They're great." She retreated with the gifts upstairs, and felt cold blue eyes stabbing her in the back.

She walked directly to the jewelry box and cursed under her breath when she opened it. Her phone rested inside, no doubt with a plethora of missed calls. Probably all from Trevor. If Caroline knew anyone in law enforcement, she would take it straight in for fingerprinting. Though the person she guessed who had taken it wouldn't leave any fingerprints. *Ugh! So frustrating!*

Caroline checked to see just how many calls she'd missed, and there were plenty. Her dad's most recent call, of course. Her mom had called six times, Kristy called three times, Jamie called once, and Trevor a whopping eleven times. The strange thing about his calls, though, is they were all made within a sixteen hour period. Each call approximately an hour-and-a-half to two hours apart, and then they stopped abruptly. She guessed that must have been when he received her email explaining she'd lost her phone. She quickly dialed his number and prepared herself for a good chewing.

Trevor didn't answer his phone, and she smiled when she heard his sexy voice on the recording. She let him know she had her phone again if he wanted to call back.

She turned in time to find Cade standing in the doorway knocking on the frame. She perked up. "Hey! You're not going to believe this. I came in here and my phone was right where I had left it in the jewelry box. I looked all over this place, including in this very jewelry box, and it was nowhere to be found. I come back and it's sitting here like I never lost it to begin with. I'm not crazy, so someone's screwing with me, or there really is a ghost in here messing with my things."

He grinned, but she could tell he wasn't convinced the ghost did it. He'd helped look for it, too, and neither one of them found it. "Were there any calls made from it?"

"I don't know, I didn't check that. I only looked at missed calls." Caroline scrolled through the sent calls and the last one had been made before it went missing. "Nope, not since the last time I used it."

The little crease between Cade's eyebrows deepened as he searched for a possible solution. "That's really strange. Something isn't right about this, and I'm gonna get to the bottom of it."

"Maybe we can try the flashlight test again, or we could just ask her if she took it and try to figure out why. I can't see why a ghost would need a cell phone, or even know what one is, but I suppose stranger things have happened." Happy to have it back, Caroline didn't even care where it had been.

"So, April seems to have warmed up to you a little," Cade said.

"Huh! Is that what you call it? I see right through her little act. I know she doesn't like me and the feeling is mutual. Only I'm not willing to be fake."

"Yeah, she doesn't appear to care much for me, either."

She gave him a crooked smile. "You're not used to that are you? People. . .particularly women, not liking you?"

He smiled bashfully. "Oh, come on. You know as well as I do she can't stand me. I just don't know why. I've never spoken a word to her."

"Maybe that's why she doesn't like you. Because you never paid her any attention. Maybe she's jealous because she's lived here for so long, and you've never given her the time of day, but then I come along and you and her husband both want to spend time with me. Did you think of that?"

"Nope, that's why I've got you to give me a little insight into the delusional female mind."

"Glad to help." Caroline's phone rang, and she knew from the ringtone it was Trevor. She gave Cade an apologetic look, and he nodded as he leaned in to kiss her cheek.

"See ya later, sweet girl." He walked out without looking back.

Caroline eagerly answered the phone. Glad to be excited to talk to Trevor. The past couple of days had her worried, but the butterflies in her stomach proved her true joy to hear from him.

"Hey. Sorry I missed your call, I was in a meeting. What's up?"

"Nothing. I haven't talked to you much since I've been here and wanted to call you. Did you get my message?"

"No, I didn't get a chance to listen to it. I just saw that you had called, so I wanted to give you a call back while I had a minute."

"Oh. Well, I couldn't find my phone all weekend and I thought you may be worried about me."

"Yeah. . .I got your email."

"Oh, good. I should have emailed you sooner. I'm sorry, I guess I didn't think about it."

"Yeah, I'm sure you're keeping yourself busy down there."

She ignored his snarky tone. "Not too busy, there's not a lot to do down here. I met some of the people that work for my dad. That was pretty cool. Oh, yeah! Guess what I saw cross the road?"

"What?"

"Guess!"

"Oh, come on, Caroline, I don't have time for this. I don't know. . .a chicken?"

"An alligator! It was the coolest thing I've ever seen. It was huge. You should have seen it!"

"Okay, well that's kind of cool. Where were you when you saw it?"

"We were driving down some back road. I'm not sure exactly where we were."

"We?"

"Cade and me. He's one of the guys who works for my dad. He's cool, you'd like him." She lied through her teeth. Trevor and Cade had

249

absolutely nothing in common except their interest in her, which she had no doubt they would not enjoy discussing with each other.

"Ahhh. . .I see. Good to know you're not bored. Anything else going on?"

"No, not really." Tingles prickled her neck as she lied.

"Don't let your extracurricular activities get in the way of your agenda."

"My agenda?"

"With Eddie."

"Trev—"

"Listen, I gotta run for now. My dad's waiting for me. I'll call you later. Try to keep your phone with you this time."

"Sure. I miss you."

"You, too. Bye."

Something was wrong. She couldn't pinpoint it, but something was definitely strange about that conversation. Not the Trevor she knew. He seemed quiet, distracted. . .distant. Usually he was very focused and playful when they talked on the phone, but the last few times they'd argued. Or one was defensive about something. But at least there was emotion of some sort. This call was very unemotional and it left her depressed, sad. Something was definitely wrong.

That evening turned out to be quite uneventful. Cade at his place, and Caroline in her room. He had fulfilled his duty for the weekend, so she supposed he didn't want to overstay his welcome. The internet had nearly put her to sleep when a knock on her door filled her with hope. She scolded herself for wishing Cade had come calling.

"Come in." Claire walked in, her bloodshot eyes were swollen and her cheeks splotchy. "Oh no, honey, what's wrong?"

Claire sank down on the bed, indecision creased her brow. She sniffled. "You got a minute?"

"Sure, what's up?"

"Well, I saw Brad, that guy I told you about, at a party this weekend. We flirted and he seemed really into me all night. He came out of the bathroom one time with white powder around his nose. I think he was doing blow. You know, cocaine."

"Oh no! Claire, you do *not* want to get mixed up with that."

"Well, it gets worse. When he saw me, he grabbed my hand and dragged me into one of the bedrooms. He tried to force me to have sex with him." She started crying again.

"What did you do?"

"I told him no and fought him. He's strong. . .so strong. He ripped my shirt." She twisted the tissue Caroline had given her until it nearly shredded. "I remembered what you and Beau told me, so I screamed for help and Lindsey came busting through the door. He stopped, but not before threatening both of us. I called the police and he got busted."

"Wow, Claire. You definitely did the right thing." Caroline shook her head in disbelief. "That's intense. I'm so glad you're okay."

More relaxed and animated now, she stood and paced the room. "I know! I was so scared! I have to say, it felt really good to slap him across the face."

Brad had shattered Claire's confidence. Caroline needed to give her reassurance. "I'm glad you did what you did. And I'm sure Lindsey is thankful, too. Rape is a serious violation both physically and mentally. Things could've been so much worse." Caroline smiled and gave her a hug.

"I'm glad you're here. I've always wanted a sister. I wish you could stay and not have to go back to Chicago at the end of the summer.

"I know. Me, too. We have cell phones, so I'll always be just a text or phone call away."

"So. . .does Beau have any brothers or cousins he wouldn't mind introducing me to?"

Caroline giggled. "He *is* pretty hot, isn't he? I know he doesn't have any brothers, but I'm pretty sure he has cousins. I'll see what I can find out and let you know."

Claire bowed her head and fidgeted with her fingernails. "Thanks for listening to me and helping me with my drama. I really do appreciate it."

"You are welcome. I love this. I never had any siblings, and, well this is like a dream come true for me. I do have one question. Have you ever tried to talk to your mom about stuff like this?"

"Well, April isn't my real mom. She's my stepmom, and we've never really gotten along like a mother and daughter should. She tries, but it's obvious it's difficult for her, so I'd rather not bother. You know? We're kind of like oil and water, we don't mix."

"Wait a minute. April is your stepmom? How? Since when? Who was your biological mother?"

"My mother's name, at least the woman I considered my mother, was Elizabeth. She was Dad's second wife, but not my biological mom. Elizabeth couldn't get pregnant, so they adopted."

Caroline was seriously confused. "So, is April Remy's mom?"

She shook her head. "Nope, he's adopted, too. Elizabeth died a couple of years after he was born. We don't have the same biological mom, but she and Eddie adopted us both as babies."

Caroline vaguely remembered her dad mentioning Elizabeth, but she didn't know what to say. "Wow. So Remy's never really known any mother besides April?"

"Yep, that's why they're closer than she and I are. I was five when Mom—er, Elizabeth died, so I still kind of remember her."

Things were becoming a little clearer now. "How old were you when April and Eddie got married?"

"Nine." Claire didn't seem too thrilled about April, but Caroline chose not to touch that subject. April had only been married to Eddie for seven years. No wonder she's so jealous. That still didn't give her the right to be hateful to everyone else.

"I will always be here for you. I promise. Now that I have you and Remy in my life, I'm not going to let anything come between us." She gave Claire a long, tight hug. Eager to bond with her more, Caroline would make it a point to spend some girl time with Claire this week. She had a great feeling they would be really close.

After Claire left, Caroline gave her mom a call. Excited to talk to her and tell her about all the new stuff she'd learned. She didn't think her mom knew about Elizabeth. If she did, she probably didn't know Eddie remarried the snake he's with now. Caroline was relieved to hear her mom's voice. She missed her terribly.

Delphine was recovering, but still on pain medicine and her arm in bandages. The kitchen, however, had not recovered. It had been a couple of weeks since the accident, and there were repairs still needing to be made before Delphine could use the appliances, so Eddie had gone into town to buy some live crawfish for a July fourth celebration. Caroline's first crawfish boil ever and she was excited to soak in as much of the Louisiana culture as she could.

Eddie had invited Cade and his family over for crawfish, as well. She didn't ask, and he didn't explain, but she figured Eddie did it to persuade her to reconsider her engagement. No doubt he would love for her to be down here close to him.

Caroline stared deep in thought at the blaze beneath the huge pot of boiling crawfish, mesmerized by the dancing blue and orange flames licking the metal to heat it. She didn't know what to think anymore. She loved Trevor. She was in love with him. She agreed to spend the rest of her life with him. She'd only known Cade for a short time. Less than it could've been if he hadn't backed off. They hadn't been hanging out as much, so there was no possible way the doubts running through her mind had any merit. Right?

Just a silly crush reflecting her love for southern culture. She needed to convince herself that rather than 'absence makes the heart grow fonder,' it was more 'out of sight, out of mind.' She remembered the burning passion she and Trevor shared before she came down here when he declared his intimate promises. Caroline reassured herself about her decision to make a stronger effort to keep in touch with him. She'd talked to Trevor every day, not spent so much time with Cade, and most importantly, absolutely no more kissing him. Definitely a bad idea if she planned to immerse herself in all things Trevor. She told herself this responsible strategy had helped curb her forbidden desires for their powerful connection. Though it hadn't, really.

Cade was her friend and she loved being around him. His interest in her was more than just physical, and that was difficult to ignore. She must continue to make the effort, though.

Cade showed up with two of his sisters and his parents. He looked a lot like his dad, but Cade had his mom's smile. He hadn't lied, she was beautiful. Blonde hair, blue eyes and gleaming white, perfectly straight teeth. She stood tall and elegant, alongside her two daughters. The oldest,

Catherine, and the youngest, Cameron, were the two that joined them. Caitlyn was stationed on a ship with the Navy, and Carly in Baton Rouge for summer school.

Catherine was amazing. Tall, around five-foot-ten and curvy, she definitely could have been a model. She had long, reddish brown curly hair and her mom's blue eyes. Her infectious smile made her very easy to talk to and admire. Very welcoming and sweet, it was obvious she loved children and working as a teacher. Caroline couldn't help but think about what Ty had told her. She wondered if Catherine was the sister whose fiancé had raped her. Caroline didn't want to assume anything.

Cameron, with straight, medium brown hair, was quiet. Not quite as tall as her older sister, but still taller than Caroline. Not curvy like her sister either. In fact, just the opposite. Cameron appeared very thin and built like a preteen boy. It didn't seem to bother her as it was obvious her confidence was healthy. She hoped to be a doctor someday. When Caroline discussed nursing school with her, she lightened up a little and asked a few questions regarding the medical field. Very sweet, and shy, Caroline gathered Cameron to be introverted, unlike her older siblings.

Cade's dad was a very reserved and quiet man. With the same golden tan and hazel eyes as Cade, as well as the thick wavy hair, he stood shorter than Cade, but not by much. Slim and fit, but beneath his shirt she detected muscle definition. Cade's family was very physically fit. She wondered if they all worked out together.

Caroline hadn't worn her engagement ring. Remy warned her how messy eating crawfish could be. The subject never came up, but she prepared herself this time in case anyone asked why she wasn't wearing her ring. Cade kept his word about stepping back and not tempting her anymore. This saddened Caroline. She missed having his attention, but she appreciated it just the same. Still, it did nothing to hinder the desire she felt for him just by being in his vicinity.

Eddie dumped the large pot of red steaming crawfish onto a newspaper-covered table, and everyone ate like a pack of wolves on a feeding frenzy. Unsure how to eat them, she stood back and watched for a few minutes. Her dad came to her side after he set another batch on the burner to boil. He showed her how to hold them, twist the head off, pinch the meat from the tail and pull it out with her teeth.

"What is that black strip along the back of the meat?"

Everyone laughed.

Cade's dad spoke up, which surprised her. "That's the protein, the good stuff."

Everyone burst into laughter again except for Caroline. She didn't get the joke.

"The good stuff? No, seriously, what is it?"

Claire finally let her off the hook. "It's poop. I don't eat it, I peel it off with the shell."

Ugh. If she could manage to get past the whole mudbug, poop-filled, open circulatory system thing, the meat from the tail really did taste good. One thing she refused to do was suck the juice from the head once she pinched it off. So gross.

She noticed a few times, when she glanced at Cade, he was already looking at her. He would smile and then look away. Caroline knew she shouldn't, but she felt really depressed. She sensed a sadness in him as well. He was still friendly and didn't avoid her, and it wasn't awkward, but the flirting had stopped. He wasn't quite as playful and attentive, and she missed that. She was bummed he wouldn't be pursuing her anymore, and she didn't understand why. She had no right to want his affections.

After dinner they sat on the back patio around the fire pit and Cade sang a few songs for them with his guitar. He had such an amazing voice, and Caroline had become completely enamored with his talent. Though he stared at his guitar while he sang, there may as well not have been anyone else around. In her mind, he sang only to her. While lost in his music, her phone vibrated in her pocket. Trevor. She excused herself to the bathroom to answer it.

"Hey. What's going on?"

"Not much, we had a crawfish boil tonight with some friends."

"Cool, a crawfish boil, huh? I've never had crawfish before. What's it like?"

"Dirty, but delicious. I wouldn't suck the head or eat the poop, though."

Trevor let out a hefty laugh. "O-kay. That just sounds gross. I'm glad you enjoyed it though. So what's on your agenda for this week?"

"Nothing that I know of. I'm going to try to hang out with my sister some and get to know her better, but other than that, not much. Why?"

"Just curious how you'll be spending your time away from me. Have you bonded anymore with your dad?"

"Not as much as I would like. He goes out of town a lot, and his wife is a little stingy with him. I haven't gotten to talk to him much."

"Well, when you do, let me know what he says and how everything goes."

"Okay. . .am I supposed to be asking him something that I'm not remembering? You sound like you know something I don't know?"

"No, no, no. I'm just eager. . .to see what you guys, um, you know. . .to see how you guys grow closer. You know, father and daughter bonding and all that."

"No, I don't know much about that since I never had a father figure in my life, but I suppose I follow you. I'll, um. . .keep you posted, I guess."

"Okay. I'll give you a call later."

"Okay. I love you."

"Love you, too."

That was strange. Trevor was acting weird again. Why must everything be so freakin' confusing? For this to have been such a fantastic summer, Caroline now had a terrible case of the blues. She hoped the next few weeks would get better.

She'd slipped back out on the patio hoping to listen to more of Cade's singing, but disappointment flooded when he wasn't even present. Everyone stood in the yard chatting while Eddie prepared to light some fireworks. Caroline wandered up behind the crowd, thankful the dusk could hide her sulk as she absently searched the faces of the crowd.

"He's not a fan of fireworks."

Caroline jumped in surprise, mildly annoyed with herself for being in such a bad mood, and Catherine giggled.

"Sorry, didn't mean to startle you. You know, you shouldn't frown like that, it'll give you premature wrinkles."

"Sorry, I'm not trying to frown. Just a little moody."

"No, I get it. Trouble in paradise?"

"No, no trouble. Cade and I are fine, just friends."

A knowing grin slowly stretched across Catherine's face. "I was talking about your fiancé, but it's interesting how you associate paradise with my brother. Something you should probably think long and hard about before you say those two life-changing little words." With that Catherine squeezed her in a side hug and walked away leaving Caroline to wonder what the heck just happened. Had she lost her mind?

Caroline huddled beneath a tree in the shadows and watched the explosion of colorful lights in the sky. The popping and booming of celebration echoed through the trees sounding like a battlefield. A perfect representation of the war raging within herself. What was up with Trevor? Cade? Herself?

Maybe it was her overactive imagination again, but her gut told her there was trouble on the horizon. She had a bad feeling that her horrible observation skills would allow her to get punched right in the face and not see who did it. It was a shame Rachel couldn't give her a heads up about her own life.

TWENTY-FIVE

A couple more weeks passed with no unusual occurrences or significant changes. Caroline had grown very close with Claire and Remy, as well as her dad, but she still regretted not being able to spend as much time with Cade. Completely ridiculous. A grown woman and a grown man should be able to spend as much time together as they wanted. No reason why they couldn't act civilized around each other. He wasn't avoiding her; she avoided him, and she missed him terribly.

After the crawfish boil, and the boneheaded comment she'd made to Catherine, Caroline made a point to talk to Trevor nearly every day, but even those conversations were melancholy and boring. More like standard news updates rather than exhilarating conversations between two people in love. And he constantly sounded aggravated or annoyed. Caroline had to do something before she went crazy.

Friday morning she woke up with the sun, just like she did every morning. She showered and dressed with the intention of visiting Cade and reigniting the friendship they had so easily established within hours of meeting. She planned to apologize for being rude and unsociable the last few weeks. With only a short time left in Louisiana, she wanted to spend as much of it with him as she could.

Caroline twisted her hair up in a messy bun in preparation for the sticky July Louisiana heat. Afraid to leave it in the room for fear it might disappear again, she put her ring in her pocket telling herself it was so it wouldn't slip off her sweaty finger. Then she slid her cell phone in her other pocket and zipped down the stairs and out the door.

The quaint little cabin came into view. Excitement bubbled within her and Caroline quickened her last few steps. The nerves had her breathless and shaky as she approached his doorstep. She knocked and waited anxiously to see his handsome, smiling face, but he didn't answer. I guess he's not home.

Now really depressed, Caroline stood there for a few minutes without moving, halfway expecting him to surprise her and open the door. Nothing happened. She nervously rubbed her bald ring finger with her other hand, and chose not to check the knob this time. Disappointment consumed her, but sulking on his porch in hopes he'd magically appear wouldn't accomplish much. She would head back to the house instead.

She turned and stopped cold at the unmistakable sound of a rattle. The beady-eyed snake was only two feet away to her left, plenty close enough to strike. Her heart pounded hard enough to burst from her chest. She tried to yell for help, but her voice came out a muffled gurgle. Probably because her heart had jumped up into her throat.

What do I do? Think!

A gunshot echoed through the trees. She leaped backwards and screamed covering her heart with her hands. Numb from fear and not knowing if she'd been bitten or shot, her shaky legs gave out. She dropped and curled up into a ball, her hands clamped over her ears and her eyes squeezed shut.

Someone nudged her with his boot. The large backlit figure was unrecognizable, but she was relieved to see an actual person rather than a six-foot rattlesnake attached to her leg steadily pumping venom into her bloodstream. She glanced around for the serpent. It lay, or what was left of it, splattered on the ground.

Caroline sat up and recognized her would-be savior. "Henry! Oh, thank goodness!"

"That rattler looked like he had your number. You a'ight?"

"Yes. Yes, I'm okay. Thanks to you."

A sly grin stretched across his stubbly face, studying her. Suddenly, something about him made her uneasy. "No. No, cher, I'm not the one who killed your snake. I wish I had. I'da saved the skin to mount on my wall and ate the meat for a week or two. No, doll face, I didn't kill your snake." His bleary eyes glistened strangely and he smiled again, but it wasn't comforting. Like he knew something she didn't know, and had no intention of disclosure. The hairs on her neck stood up.

"Then, who did? If you didn't save me, why are you here?" Truly confused and now agitated with Henry for not just telling her what happened, Caroline stood and protectively crossed her arms.

"I don't know what to tell you, sexy. I can help you calm down, if you'd like." He stepped closer and reached for her face. She instinctively stepped away. Something wasn't right. His breath reeked of alcohol, and it seeped from his pores. Her gut was uneasy for a good reason.

"Where's Beau?" She hoped his name would remind Henry they were standing in front of Cade's cabin. She didn't like the distant, crazy look in his eyes, nor did she appreciate his creepy innuendo.

"I bet he's somewhere out in these woods huntin' down a wild animal. You know, you can't never be too careful out in nature. There's predators all around." He took a step closer, and she finally put her hand out to stop him.

"Look, Henry, I'm sorry. I'm only here to find Cade. I can see that he's not here, so I'm leaving now. If you see him, please tell him I stopped by."

He grabbed her upper arm. "What's your hurry, doll face? I'm sure his door's open." He suggestively stroked his calloused fingers down the length of her arm. "I'll be happy to keep you company while you wait. You know, to keep snakes or other wild animals from sneakin' up on ya."

Caroline tried unsuccessfully to pull her arm from his grip. She rushed to think of anything to escape this uncomfortable situation. Trying to appear in control of her emotions, her shaky voice betrayed her. "Thank you, I appreciate your offer, but my dad is waiting for me."

Still smiling, Henry backed her up to the outside wall of the cabin and cornered her, pressing his heavy body against her, effectively blocking any escape. He brushed a loose strand of hair from her eyes as he studied her face. His focus centered on her mouth.

"I'm sure your daddy won't mind you bein' a few minutes late. You know, I never met anyone as sweet and innocent as you. Fresh and untainted." His eyes roamed her curves. "I wonder what it is that you been waitin' for all these years? I bet it'd feel pretty damn amazin' to see what's hidden under this delicate skin. To unleash that wild cat in you." He whispered, "Just a sweet little taste." Henry licked his lips and focused on her mouth again as his hand came up to cup her breast. "Might bring out the wild animal in me. You know, make me feel alive."

She closed her eyes turning her face away from his. The bile rose in her throat and she focused on not barfing from the putrid smell of his filthy, alcohol and sweat soaked clothes. He chuckled, clearly amused by her disinterest. Flashbacks of the first dream she had when Rachel was raped rocked her memory, only this wasn't a dream. *This can't be happening. Cade, where are you?*

His face only inches from hers, Caroline gagged at the disgusting smell of his nasty beer and nicotine breath. His hand massaged her sensitive breast, plucking it attempting to arouse her. She choked back the bile and squeezed her eyes closed, focusing on everything but this invasion so she wouldn't lose all sense of reality. Rather than resist, she took a deep, shaky breath to prepare for whatever else he was about to try. Someone who hunted alligators for a living could certainly handle her attempts to fight him off.

"Please, Henry. Don't," she whispered, pleading.

"Oh, now I like the way that sounds. Say my name again, cher. Beg me to stop. I want to remember the sound of that in my dreams tonight."

It took everything she had to control the waves of fear convulsing through her body as she attempted to find her happy place. Then the most beautiful sound in the world caressed her ears.

"Henry!"

Words she didn't understand slipped from Cade's mouth, but from the tone she could guess what he said. Henry's grip on her breast loosened and he slowly lowered his hand. For her benefit, Cade repeated himself in English, clearly a censored version.

"Henry, you wanna step away from her before I blow your damned head off?"

Henry sighed and stepped back with his hands up. A sinister smile wafted over his face as he turned around. "Aw, come on, Beau. I was just messin' with her. You know, to ruffle her feathers a little."

"You can go ruffle the feathers of some other girl, but you leave this one alone. Got that, slick? She's not some two-bit whore you met on Bourbon Street. She's my friend, and your boss's daughter, for cryin' out loud! What the hell are you thinking? Have you lost your mind? Why you here, anyway?"

"I tol' ya, bro. Just messin' with her. I brought you the twenty bucks I owed you."

"Later. You know the way out, so I suggest you take it now, while your balls are still attached."

"Yeah. Sure thing, boss. You don't gotta go all Rambo on me. I'm out. Caroline, no hard feelings?"

She didn't answer or look at him. Instead, she turned toward the cabin with her face in her palms. An emotional basket case, completely shaken up, she was immensely relieved for Cade. But she didn't want either of the men to see her as she closed her eyes against the tears streaming down her cheeks. Her shoulders shook, and the uncontrollable sobs rattled her bones. Cade scooped her up and carried her inside.

"Caroline, it's okay. It's just me. Calm down. . .you're safe." He laid her on the couch and knelt beside her. "I don't know what got in to Henry. I've never seen him act like that. I'm so sorry."

He handed her a handkerchief from his pocket, and it smelled good. Like him. She sat up, a little calmer now. "What just happened? What was that all about? I thought Henry was your friend? I met him that day, and he was fine."

Cade stared at the floor thinking. "I'm not sure, love. But I promise you I will find out and make sure nothing like that ever happens again. Henry's always been quiet and distant, but I never expected him to do something like this. It's beyond anything I ever thought he was capable of. I just need to know if you're okay. Are you? Okay?"

She nodded, but the tears flowed freely again. He wrapped his arms around her cradling her head on his shoulder. "Oh, sweet girl. I'm so sorry." He kissed her temple. "I'm sorry I wasn't here fifteen minutes earlier." She pulled her head back to look at him.

"Were you the one who shot the snake?" She had almost forgotten about the terrifying rattler. She'd never had two horrible experiences within a fifteen minute timeframe before.

Cade's lips curved into a grin. "Yeah, I killed it. It was a timber rattlesnake."

"H-how. . .how did you see it? How d-did you know? Where were you?" Caroline was baffled.

"Well, I was up in a tree hunting. Well, mostly thinking, but I had all my hunting gear. Anyway, I was messing around with my scope and saw movement near my house, so I looked through it in this direction. I saw you knock on my door. I didn't know why you had come, but when I realized you were upset that I hadn't answered it made me happy. I watched you for a few minutes through my scope, and that's when I saw the snake behind you. I'd never forgive myself if something happened to you, especially something I could prevent, so I set my cross hairs on the snake's head and pulled the trigger without thinking twice about it."

He could have missed the snake and accidentally shot her. Normally, the simple fact he had a gun pointed at her would have infuriated her, but for the moment she didn't care.

Cade moved onto his knees in front of Caroline and cradled her face in his hands as he spoke, looking directly in her eyes. "Caroline, I know he's my friend, but if Henry had gotten any closer to you. . .I might have blown his brains out. I saw his body language towards you after I killed the snake. At first, I was relieved he had shown up, but I couldn't hear what he said. When I saw the look on your face as you put your hand out to stop him, alarms blared in my head. I immediately climbed down the tree and ran as fast as I could to get here. That's when I saw his hand on you and I nearly lost it. Looked like I stopped him just in time. What did he say to you?"

She fidgeted with her fingernails. Unsure why, she didn't want to tell him everything Henry said. "You know, I don't even remember. I'm just shaken up a little. I guess he succeeded in ruffling my feathers, huh?" She laughed nervously. "It's over now, so let's just not worry about it, okay? I'm really glad you showed up when you did. Thank you for saving me— twice."

Cade softly kissed her forehead. "It was my pleasure, sweet Caroline."

It made her deliriously happy to hear him call her sweet Caroline again.

"I'm sorry I let it get as far as it did. If he had hurt you, I swear I would've. . . Well, it wouldn't have been pretty."

"Well, he didn't, so we're good. Both of us." She reached out to hold his hands. "Look, I need to talk to you. I don't like the way things are with us right now. I've missed you the last few weeks. Terribly. I know it's my fault that we haven't been hanging out, and I want to apologize. I know I jumped your case for this, and then went and did it myself, but just because I'm engaged doesn't mean I can't be your friend."

His smile prompted her to continue, and, like the coward she was, she kept picking her nails to avoid eye contact. "You've been nothing but respectful, helpful, and friendly to me since I came here, and the past few weeks I've treated you like dirt. I've avoided you. And for what? Because I'm attracted to you? Because I don't trust myself with you? None of that is fair to you." His grin transformed into a full-fledged smile. She looked up at him through her lashes. "Will you forgive me? Please?"

"Whatever it is you think you've done wrong, I promise it's totally forgiven. I've missed you like crazy. After hanging out with you the first week you were here, and then only seeing you in passing over the last few weeks, I'll be honest, it's killing me. Yes, I forgive you as long as you can forgive me for not stopping Henry sooner."

Caroline was so happy she could kiss him. However, considering the reason she had avoided him to begin with, she decided against that, but it still didn't stop her desire. Instead, she launched off the couch and gave him a bear hug, knocking him off balance. They both ended up lying on the floor with her on top of him. It should have been awkward, but it wasn't. She lifted her head to look at him, and he gave her a big cheesy smile.

"Man, you've been here for all of ten minutes and you're already jumping my bones."

She couldn't hold back her laughter as she playfully smacked his chest.

"Oh well, at least I get to hang out with you again. I'll pretend I don't know how bad you really want me."

Caroline shook her head at his tireless efforts. "You are really something, you know that? You make me happy, Caden Luke. Thank you for that." She knew she shouldn't, but she gave in to her weakness and softly kissed his lips. He kissed her back briefly, but then gently pushed her off of him and sat up.

Afraid she'd already ruined the short moment of normalcy, Caroline studied him. As if nothing had happened he asked in a chipper voice, "Hey, you wanna go to a movie tonight?"

"That sounds fun, but I have a better idea. How about we try to do another ghost experiment? Let's see if Rachel's still hanging around. You up for that?"

A wide smile transformed his face and his eyes lit up. "Yeah, buddy! Let's do it!"

"Do you have lunch plans?"

"Well, I was hunting for my lunch, and I killed me a rattlesnake."

If Cade's laughter was any indication, her face must have turned green. "I'm sorry, snake isn't really on my diet. How 'bout a burger?"

"Sounds great. Let me clean up and I'll meet you back at the house."

Things were looking up for the rest of her summer now that she and Cade would be together more. Caroline enjoyed his company, more than she should, but her loyalty to Trevor limited the extent of that, so she'd take what she could get. She was mostly just thankful they worked everything out and their friendship wasn't compromised. She skipped back to the house, frolicking like a little girl. She hardly noticed the white rental SUV parked in the driveway. She bounded up the porch and the front door swung open before she touched it.

"Trevor!"

TWENTY-SIX

Genuinely happy to see him, Caroline jumped into Trevor's arms. He hugged her back and seemed happy at first, but then he let his arms fall. She backed up to see his handsome, but solemn face. "What's wrong? Is everything okay? Why are you here?"

He walked out to the front porch, his back to her, and she followed. What prompted his surprise visit and why didn't he tell her he was coming? Even more, why wasn't he happier to see her?

"Where have you been, C?"

"Down the trail in the woods. Why?"

"By yourself?"

"No, I went to visit a friend who lives in one of the outbuildings. What's this about, Trevor? Why do I feel like you're interrogating me?"

"Would this friend be male?" He still had his back to her and she didn't like his tone. Her heartbeat pounded in her head from her rising temper.

"Yes. The guy I told you about before, Cade. He works for my dad and has been the only friend I've made down here besides Claire and Remy."

"Uh-huh. Why do you suppose that is, Caroline?"

"Oh, for cryin' out loud, Trevor! Just spit it out. What are you implying here?"

He whirled around with anger emanating from his body. "I'm implying that maybe the reason you haven't made any other friends is because you have been spending all of your time with Cade!"

"What do you want me to say, Trev? Huh? You are the one who wanted me to spend the summer down here. You are the one who wanted me to come meet my dad and clear the air. This was all your idea! What. . .now you suddenly don't trust me?"

Fury swirled in Trevor's eyes. What was he angry about? Her blood chilled when his glare focused on her left hand.

What she expected next was not what she got. She expected a lecture, shame for not wearing his ring, a guilt trip. As she prepared in her mind what she could possibly say that wouldn't sound like a pathetic excuse, he shocked her.

"Caroline, have you. . .been intimate. . .with this guy?" He spat out the words with bitterness.

"Intimate? Is that what this is about? You're down here because you think I've slept with him?"

"Have you?"

She laughed in disbelief. She assumed this was about their engagement and her commitment issues, jealousy for paying attention to everyone but him. But this was Trevor. Everything was about sex. She should've stopped there and apologized for any misunderstanding, but of course. . .she didn't. She would antagonize him to the breaking point.

"Why, Trevor? Are you worried somebody else dipped their spoon in the honeypot before you could? Is that what this is really about?"

In two strides he immediately glowered over her. His fingers dug into her shoulders as he pushed his words through clenched teeth.

"You are mine! This is about you sleeping in the same bed doing God-knows-what with another man while wearing my ring on your finger!" He yanked her left hand up to her face. "Or not! Where the hell is your ring, Caroline? Are you too ashamed to wear it after your behavior?"

How did he know about sleeping in the same bed with Cade? Who could have told him? Realization came crashing down. April. She took Caroline's cell phone that weekend, which explained why it miraculously reappeared the same time they returned. That conniving hussy. April had it out for Caroline. No wonder Trevor was livid. She glanced up at the second floor window that belonged to her wicked stepmother. The curtains rustled. April was watching.

"Your silence is deafening, Caroline." He dropped her hand with a slight shove in disgust. "So it's true?"

"You don't know what happened. I can explain if you'll calm down and just listen."

"Calm down? You want me to calm down? Seriously, Caroline, how could I possibly do that, knowing all the times you stopped me dead in my tracks? All those times I had to take cold showers to calm down because you weren't ready to make love to me. All those frustrating times I apologized for pushing you too far. Then you come down here and sleep with some guy you only knew for what. . .a week? Then you lie to me about it! How is that supposed to calm me down?"

"Trevor, I did not have sex with him! And I did not lie to you!"

Their shouts echoed across the courtyard.

"Sure, Caroline. I'm just supposed to believe what you say now? If I had known you were going to come down here and whore around I would never have encouraged you to do this!"

She slapped his face. Trevor shoved her back against the house where Caroline tripped over a potted plant and hit her head on the porch beside the rocking chair. Normally, Trevor would come rushing up to apologize for hurting her, for not knowing his own strength, but this time, he simply walked to his rental car. Caroline jumped up, ignoring the blood dripping down her temple, and ran after him.

"Trevor, please! Please stop! I need to talk to you!" He stopped but didn't turn around. She stood right behind him and spoke again. "You have to believe me when I tell you I didn't have sex with anyone. I am engaged to you, and I do love you. My ring—it's hot and I knew I'd be sweating. . ." This wasn't coming out right. "I didn't want to mess it up or lose it. About Cade, he only helped me. I couldn't sleep and he—"

Trevor swung around, a storm of sheer rage. "I'm sure he was happy to help you sleep, you lying, cheating slut! I can't believe you would do this to me! You have disgraced me and my family."

She tried to put her arms around his neck to kiss him and prove she wanted to be with him, but he stopped her by gripping her forearms and squeezing them very tightly.

"No, Caroline, don't! Do not try to distract and manipulate me with your meaningless attempts of affection. It's not going to work."

Unsure if it was from his words or because he squeezed her forearms too tightly, tears sprang from Caroline's eyes. Her voice only a whisper. "You're hurting me." He didn't loosen his grip. "Trevor, please! You're hurting me! Stop! You're going to break my arms."

He let go in a shove, causing her to fly back and skid across the gravel driveway.

From out of nowhere, Cade appeared and the men erupted into a nasty brawl.

Caroline stood and yelled for them to stop. She couldn't have them beating each other to a bloody pulp over a simple misunderstanding that April instigated. But they didn't stop. They fought with equal measure of ire to the point of frightening her. Caroline had to do something, quick. She got her chance as they stumbled briefly apart.

Caroline stretched her arms out with one guy at the palm of each hand and gasped for air between sobs. They both sported bloody lips and noses. But honestly, Trevor looked worse than Cade.

"Will you two please just stop for a minute and shut up so I can explain?"

Furious and breathing heavily, they nodded in agreement. "Okay. Now then. . .Trevor, this is Cade. Cade, this is Trevor. Trevor, I have *not* had sex with Cade. He is just a friend, and I have to say he's been a respectable gentleman the entire time I've known him. I had experienced some very strange things in my room, and I asked him to stay in there with me until I fell asleep. That is all. Cade, Trevor did not hit me. Yes, he shoved me, but I lost my balance and hit my head on the rocking chair. My clumsiness made it look much worse than it was, that's all. I'm okay. Can you two please not fight with each other, especially over me? I hardly think any of this is worth a broken nose or a knocked-out tooth."

Trevor shook his head. "Caroline, can I please speak to you? In private."

She looked at Cade, who cautiously eyed her to see if that was what she wanted.

Cade vehemently shook his head while shifting his eyes back to Trevor. "I'm not leaving you alone with him, Caroline. I don't care if he's your fiancé or not.

"Cade, trust me. He won't—"

"Caroline, please don't ask me to leave you in such a vulnerable position. You know how I feel about this. I saw him shove you and I assure you it was no accident."

"I know. I know how you feel about it and I promise you he won't hurt me. We just got caught up in the moment and I tripped. Right, Trev?" She looked at Trevor who regarded Cade like he was a prowling tiger. Caroline couldn't tell if Trevor was more angry or worried. "Trevor, tell him." His silence made Caroline want to scream. She was tempted to step back and let Cade finish what he started. If Trevor hadn't gotten physical with her in the first place, they wouldn't be in this position. "I think you owe me that much."

His glare pierced a hole in her heart. "*I* owe *you*? I don't think—"

"Trevor! Just tell him you won't hurt me." She silently begged him with her eyes to understand, and his shoulders sagged slightly. He reached for her hand and pulled her close.

"Of course I'm not going to hurt you." He glanced at Cade as he leaned in close and whispered. "You can call off the dogs now."

Caroline turned to Cade and gave a shy but reassuring smile, though she didn't think it did much good.

"Promise you'll call me if you need anything?" His serious gaze shifted to Trevor, but he still spoke to her. "I'll be around."

"Promise. Thank you."

Trevor didn't say anything. He simply glared back at Cade. Caroline grabbed Trevor's hand and led him into the house. In her room, she explained everything about what had been happening. She told him about her crazy dreams and how things mysteriously went missing only to reappear a few days later. She even showed him the initials scratched in the window. She couldn't tell if he believed her because she thought she saw an eye roll when she mentioned a ghost, but he did apologize for overreacting and calling her such horrible names.

He kissed her head where she had hit the rocking chair, and kissed the scratches on her palms from pushing her onto the gravel and shell riddled driveway. Then he passionately kissed her lips. All the love she had for him flooded back as she lost herself in his familiar embrace.

He whispered in her ear as he held her tightly. "I've missed you, baby. It makes me crazy to think some other guy has been close to you the way I am. I get jealous thinking about you depending on another man for anything."

Caroline pulled her ring from her pocket and held it up. "Like you said. It's your ring on my finger. That has not changed."

He smiled her favorite crooked smile that she'd fallen in love with and slipped the ring back on her finger just as he had when he proposed. Then he asked her to take him to the place with the delicious gumbo.

"Dupree's? You got it. When do you have to go back?" She wanted him to meet her dad before he left.

"I go back tomorrow. Quick trip. I had to see for myself if you were cheating on me." He shook his head. "I didn't believe it."

"You must have believed in the possibility since you're here. I'm guessing you talked to April?" She rolled her eyes. It disgusted her to even say the tramp's name out loud.

"Yeah, she called me. She sounded genuinely concerned."

Caroline's eyebrows raised. "Genuine? Right. There's nothing genuine about that woman. She hates my guts, and it's obvious she's trying to ruin my life." Caroline stepped away from him and brushed her hand across the smooth wood of the antique dressing table, admiring the preservation of the fine furniture. She stared at it for a moment. Something was different, but what?

He chuckled. "Well, don't be too hard on her. When she spoke to me, she seemed to have your best interests in mind."

Caroline inspected the table and the ornate mirror trying to figure out what was different about it. "Trevor, you can't believe anything that woman says. She's a fake and has malice written all over her face. She's jealous and hateful and. . .just don't trust her—with anything. She's a horrible, heartless person, inside and out."

"Oh, come on, Caroline, don't hold back." The unpleasant, yet familiar voice coming from the doorway immediately cursed Caroline with a sinking, queasy feeling. "Why don't you tell him how you really feel about me? After all, I *am* the wicked stepmother." April stood in the doorway to her room, dressed for a red carpet event. All decked out as if she needed to impress someone. Caroline didn't appreciate her snarky little comment.

"April. What a surprise. Headed to a funeral?"

April ignored her, slithered closer to Trevor and smiled as she stretched out her bony hand to shake his.

"Hello, Trevor. I'm April Fontenot. It's a pleasure to meet you in person and put your handsome face with that amazing voice."

Trevor shook her hand. "Hello, April. Thanks for the heads up, but it seems it was all a misunderstanding."

April smiled like she'd won a bet.

"However, the next time you decide to intrude in someone else's life, you should first make sure you have all your facts straight. Though, I do appreciate you giving me an excuse to see my lovely bride-to-be."

April's smile quickly faded. Caroline flashed her a huge grin, and inserted a little snark in her own voice. "Thanks for your help, *Mom*, but everything's under control. You may go screw with someone else's life now."

277

Her eyes narrowed briefly before she turned back to Trevor with a smile. "Please, don't feel the need to rush out. You're welcome to stay for a few days or weeks, whatever you'd like. Anything you need, I'm sure I can accommodate." She gave him a sultry grin. April flirted with him. In front of Caroline. Bitch!

"Thanks for the invitation, but I'm flying out tomorrow. I have work to do."

"Suit yourself. You should take Caroline back with you so she doesn't cause anymore. . .misunderstandings." She referred to Caroline as his property. Like she wasn't standing in the room with them. Caroline fumed. April left and Trevor curiously looked at her.

"I can see why you think so highly of her."

"You have no idea. Let's go eat."

They were already outside when it dawned on Caroline she didn't remember seeing the antique jewelry box on the dresser. Someone had taken it.

TWENTY-SEVEN

I shouldn't have let her go off with him alone. No respectable man is physically abusive with the woman he loves. Cade couldn't get the image out of his head. Trevor shoved Caroline and she flew back nearly four feet. This guy was a first class prick. There had to be some kind of dirt on him that Cade could find to show Caroline and prove this theory.

Cade had to cool his temper and burn the adrenaline pumping through his veins. After the quick five mile run, he showered and walked back to the plantation house to wait for Eddie to get home from work. Cade wanted to be the first person to inform Eddie of the details, certain Caroline would sugar coat it to keep Trevor from looking like the bad guy. Eddie needed to know exactly how this maniacal bastard treated his daughter.

Cade sat quietly in the rocking chair on the front porch stewing. He glanced down and noticed a red spot on the leg of the rocking chair. Is that blood? Caroline's blood? Vehemence vibrated his bones. What happened before he got there just in time to step between them? Why would she make excuses for what Trevor had done to her? Sure, she may have tripped, but if he hadn't pushed her so hard, she wouldn't have lost her balance.

Any man who resorted to physical anger toward a woman was a spineless coward. He certainly didn't deserve Caroline. An amazing person inside and out, it made no sense for her to be with someone like Trevor.

Gravel crunched under the SUV's tires and Eddie pulled into the driveway.

Cade stood and eagerly met him as he slammed the door of the Tundra. "Hey, man. What are you doing here today? You work Tuesdays, right?"

"Yes, sir. But I'm not here working today."

Eddie's smile stretched across his face. "I see. Then you're here for Caroline? Where is she?"

"She's not here." Cade clenched his fists to rein in his temper because every time he thought about Trevor, the rage boiled. "Can you take a walk with me so we can talk?"

Eddie's brow furrowed, but he didn't question. "Sure. Is Caroline okay?"

Cade led him to the back yard out of sight in case Caroline came home before he finished disclosing the afternoon's events. She would be pissed with him for ratting her out, but Eddie needed to know exactly what happened, and Cade knew Caroline wouldn't be completely honest in her details.

"Yes, sir. Her fiancé surprised her with a visit, and they're out to lunch right now." Cade shifted uncomfortably, suddenly unsure about Eddie's feelings regarding Trevor. If he liked him, it might be more difficult to convince him that Trevor was a worthless dog.

Eddie's face remained indifferent. Cade knew Eddie didn't know much about Trevor, so he probably didn't have a problem with him being here, but Cade also knew Eddie hoped Caroline would be persuaded to choose him in the end.

"He surprised her, huh? That's good, I guess. Took him long enough. She's been here over a month. Did you meet him yet?"

Cade snorted. "You could say that."

Eddie squinted in the sunlight and studied his face. He focused on the sliced lip and the bruised swelling around Cade's jaw. "I see. Didn't go so well, huh?"

Though he tried, Cade had difficulty not seeming too anxious or talking too fast. He normally didn't have this much trouble controlling his temper. He'd mastered that art years ago, but it had been equally as long since he'd been this enraged.

"Well, you see, sir, that's just it. I didn't know he was coming, either. And Caroline and I had just decided to hang out again. On my way up here to take her to lunch I heard yelling. My gut told me something was wrong so I sped up a little. When I got closer, I saw this dude shove her. She went flying back like a rag doll and skidded across the gravel. I sprinted the rest of the way and stepped in between them. He would hit me before he laid another finger on her."

Cade cracked his neck in conjunction with his knuckles and drew in a deep, calming breath. "Apparently he didn't like someone else stepping up for her as he so kindly showed me with his fists."

Eddie's eyes hardened. "He shoved her?"

"Yes, sir. And I don't think that's all he did. Before I got up here and saw them, I heard her yelling at him. She said something about breaking her arms and that he was hurting her. She told me he had shoved her and she tripped over the flower pot on the porch. I also saw a little spot of blood on the rocking chair."

Eddie expelled a string of curse words with his breath as he brusquely rubbed his face. His jaw muscles twitched with the clenching of his teeth.

"She made excuses for him, like it was her fault and she deserved it." Cade shook his head and pressed his eyes closed. "I've seen his type before and I'd bet my truck this isn't the first time he's gotten physical with her." Cade's sister had done the same thing when her fiancé smacked her around. Cade wasn't around and couldn't do anything about it then, but the bastard messed up by almost killing her when Cade was finally home.

"I don't like him, sir. Not only because I love Caroline, but I saw how rough he was with her and the way he spoke to her. He's an a—well, he's just not good for her, Mr. Fontenot."

"It's good that you were around and able to step between them in time. Could've been much worse. Thank you." Eddie cocked a crooked grin. "I'm surprised, Beau. With your highly trained skills, I can't believe he's still walking. Why'd you hold back?"

He dropped his eyes to the piece of gravel he kicked around. He didn't want to go into detail about the way he'd envisioned himself ripping the guy limb from limb. "I didn't think Caroline would appreciate me killing her fiancé with my bare hands right in front of her."

Eddie laughed boisterously. "No, I suppose not. Why don't you come in and have a glass of tea with me? We'll have some lunch and wait for my future son-in-law to get back so I can meet him."

"Thank you, sir. I'll come in for a bit, but I don't think I'll stick around once he returns. I don't think I'll be able to control myself if I see him again. I *really* don't like him."

"Fair enough. Come on in. I could use some company right now, anyhow."

They got their tea and went to Eddie's office to chat. Eddie checked his messages and slammed the phone down, cursing under his breath.

"Something wrong?"

"These stupid real estate development companies. They won't leave me alone. Apparently my family's property is worth a considerable amount of money, and it's right smack in the middle of a fast growing area. They're trying to ruin the beauty of Golden Meadow with shopping malls, master planned communities, and other types of commercial properties—all around me. I've had a couple of different companies bugging the piss out of me to sell."

"That sucks. What companies?"

"Well, they're mostly local, but there's one company in particular that doesn't make any sense to me. I'm not worried about the local ones. The one that doesn't fit is a place up in Illinois. Why the hell would a company based in the Midwest be interested in property down in southeast Louisiana? Don't worry though. As long as I'm alive there's no chance in hell anyone's gonna buy this land. It's been in my family for nearly two centuries."

"Illinois? What's the company name? Do you know where in Illinois?"

"Not sure. It's like, KT, or KP Real Estate something or other. I don't know, I didn't exactly chat them up. I told them to go to hell. Why? You heard of 'em?"

Cade's mind spun at warp speed. That rang a bell. Why?

"I don't think so, but it sure sounds familiar. It seems like I should know who that is, but I can't figure out why." The relentless gnawing at his gut was nauseating. Why couldn't he remember the significance of that?

Cade heard the gravel crunching again as a car was driving up. "If it's all right with you, Mr. Fontenot, I'll let myself out the back door. I'd rather not be here when they walk in. Caroline's gonna be angry enough with me for scratching up his pretty face, but when she finds out I told you, I'd rather not be here."

"Sure thing, Beau. Thanks for coming in and giving me a heads up. I appreciate it. Oh, yeah. . .next time, if there is a next time, don't hold back. Ya hear?"

"Roger that, sir. I hope you get a better first impression of him than I did. Have a good afternoon."

Cade slipped out the back way and tried hard to figure out why a Real Estate company in Illinois should be significant. On the way back to his cabin in deep thought, he pondered what Eddie had told him. KT. . .KP. . .or maybe KC? It hit him like a ton of bricks. Could it be? KC—Kenneth Callahan! Caroline said Trevor's dad was a real estate developer in Chicago. That had to be his company. Too much of a coincidence for it not to be. Why else would someone from Illinois be interested in this property in southeastern Louisiana? That couldn't be why Trevor was with Caroline. . .could it? Surely the prick's not that heartless. Adrenaline flowing, Cade sprinted the rest of the way to his cabin to do some research. This may be exactly the break he needed to prove to Caroline she shouldn't marry this punk.

Trevor enjoyed the gumbo as much as Caroline had, so she was happy he wanted to try Dupree's. She couldn't understand why she cared whether he liked this area. It wasn't like he would ever consider living this far south.

Nothing happened during their lunch. Well, except the owner and his look-alike brother stared at Caroline the whole time while speaking Cajun to each other. She had no doubt they gossiped about her, and why she'd come with anyone but Cade. Words like, "Bonne a rienne" and "Canaille," stood out in their speech, and she didn't know what they meant, but she didn't care. She was with the man she loved, her fiancé, the man who proposed to her and gave her this beautiful ring.

However, she did plan to ask Cade later what those words meant. If she still remembered them. She pulled out her phone to Google it, but didn't know how to spell the words. The ones that popped up from her botched attempt weren't very nice.

Though he said he had forgiven her, Trevor still seemed strangely silent and uninterested in conversation. She had forced him.

"So, other than thinking I was fooling around with someone else, is there any other reason you came down here?"

His head snapped in her direction and he answered quickly. Almost too quickly. Very suspicious. "No. Why would you think there would be any other reason for my trip down here? Did someone say something about it?"

"No. Good grief, Trev. It was just a question. I hoped for something like, 'Well, C, I missed you like crazy and wanted to touch you and hold you in my arms'. Instead, you act like I've accused you of something."

He smiled nervously and chuckled. "No, I'm sorry, I've just been really stressed lately. I did want to see you and physically hold you in my arms. But when that chick, April, called and told me what you did, I was afraid I would lose you. With that in my head, the journey down here was definitely not a joy trip."

"What exactly did she tell you? When did she call you?"

"Don't worry about it. It's over and done with. Dredging up the details will do nothing but cause pain and suffering for all parties involved."

"I'm not trying to dredge anything up. I did nothing wrong and simply want to know what that demon told you about me."

"She wasn't very specific, so I really didn't know what to expect. When I got here and you weren't at the house, I started worrying." He stared straight forward with a distant look, probably replaying in his mind what happened. "Then when I saw you coming from the woods with a big smile. . .and you were so surprised to see me. I figured I wasn't the one who had put that beautiful smile on your face. It was almost as if I caught you doing something you shouldn't have been doing. It just. . .it wasn't a good feeling."

Guilt reared its ugly head. She'd been smiling coming from the woods from excitement that she and Cade would be spending more time together. She had kissed him, for goodness sakes! Caroline *was* surprised to see Trevor.

No wonder he's upset with me. I would have been upset with me, too.

Caroline wasn't a terribly jealous person—well, at least she didn't think so. But just thinking about some other chick with her paws all over Trevor. . . It made the country girl in her ready to beat the pink right out of any woman's panties.

She reached across the console of the car and held his hand. "I'm so sorry, Trev. I didn't want to cause you any more stress than you already have. I promise I'll try to be more supportive of you. Why are you so stressed at work anyway? What's going on?"

"It's nothing, really. I'm working on something with my dad's firm, and he's just riding me really hard. Honestly, he's driving me crazy. I can't tell him that or he'll flip out, so I'm forced to just sit back and take it like a dog with his tail between his legs. It's humiliating."

"What kind of project is it that allows him to have so much control over you?"

He sat quietly for a few minutes. "It's nothing. I don't want you to worry about it. It's my problem, not yours. I want you to focus on building a strong, solid relationship with your dad so you can be a major part of his life."

This greatly confused her. Trevor had initially said he wanted her to make amends with Eddie to clear the air, then he made that comment about being accepted as a daughter, and now he wanted her to be a major part of Eddie's life? Each time he mentioned it, he made it even more personal.

"Trevor, I'm already a part of my dad's life. He told me there wasn't a day that went by when he didn't regret not keeping in touch with me. He recognized me the minute he saw me on his doorstep. We're cool now. There's no hard feelings, and I feel completely accepted. There are no skeletons in the closet and the air is officially cleared. My mission is accomplished."

He hesitantly smiled. "That's great, babe. I'm glad you guys hit it off. So what will you do the rest of the summer? Just hang out with each other and bond some more? Has he mentioned anything about you being included in his inheritance? I mean, that house has been in his family for a very long time. I'm sure he would like to have someone to leave it to."

"Is that what all this is about? My inheritance from him? Don't forget he has a wife, Trevor! A wife who hates me with a passion. Also, I have two siblings who have been with him since birth, so I'm sure if something were to happen to my dad I wouldn't get much of anything, if at all. He's only known me for a month, so I'm quite sure he hasn't rushed out to make things legal."

She turned in her seat to face him. "Technically, I've done what you wanted me to do, so I could come back to Chicago with you if you wanted. I've told my dad we're getting married and that he's invited. I think he will come if he can get off work, and, since he's his own boss, that shouldn't be a problem."

Trevor gripped the steering wheel tighter, his eyes darted about erratically—out the window, at his mirrors, at the car's gauges. "Well, Caroline, I can't. . .I don't see any necessary. . . You don't have to. . .well, are you ready. . .well, there's no reason for you to come back now. . .so early. I mean, don't you want to hang out with your dad more and learn more about him. . .his family? I mean, you. . .you could learn more about that chick who scratched her initials in the window or something. You should definitely stay and bond with your dad more. You've only been here for a month. That's not enough time—I mean, it's not very long to reconnect with someone you haven't seen in twenty-something years. You know?"

Her sinking suspicion that he didn't want her to come back yet unsettled her. "Actually, I've been here almost two months." Annoyance ate at her that he didn't even know how long she'd been gone. "What's up with you? You're very distracted. Is there something you're not telling me? Have *you* been with someone else?"

"What? No! Of course not! Why would—what makes you think that?"

"That! That right there! You are stammering. You never do that. You're acting weird. I just have a bad feeling that I'm missing something, and I can't figure out what it is. You would tell me, wouldn't you? If something was going on? Something that involved me? You'd tell me, right?"

He didn't look at her as he answered. "Sure. You know I would. I'm fine, I'm just. . .still shaken up about the whole reason I had to come down here."

Caroline flinched. Would her guilt ever subside? Maybe it would go away once they were married and, by man's law as well as God's law, she was legally bound to be faithful. Surely she could control her thoughts and emotions better around Cade when held accountable for her actions legally, physically and spiritually. She caused this whole mess.

Caroline smiled when she saw her dad's truck in the driveway. Trevor noticed and smiled. "So, I finally get to meet your dad. Should I be nervous? Is he going to be cleaning his guns or sharpening his knives when I walk in?"

She laughed. She'd never had to worry about bringing home a guy to meet her dad. The whole experience was new to her. "Oh, don't be silly. I'm sure he's doing something simple and harmless, like extracting the venom from his rattlesnakes."

Trevor's eyes grew huge, and his voice raised an octave. "Come again? Did you say rattlesnakes?" Caroline laughed so hard, she realized she had to pee. Then she remembered her frightening experience with a rattlesnake that morning. She seriously doubted Trevor would've acted as gallantly as Cade had, nor be as good a shot. Come to think of it, she didn't know if Trevor even owned a gun, much less knew how to use one.

Caroline led the way and couldn't help but notice Trevor's hesitation as they entered the foyer. Eddie came barreling around the corner with an indignant look on his face. She instinctively stepped between him and Trevor, red flags popping up everywhere. She assumed he had already spoken to Cade, and anger bit through her pleasant mood. Though not surprised after what happened to his sister, she still wished Cade had at least given her the opportunity to explain to Eddie before tattling like a preschooler. Eddie looked her over while she introduced them.

"Dad, I'd like you to meet Trevor. My fiancé."

He had the same fierce green eyes she had when angry. He fixed his sights on Trevor who held his hand out to shake Eddie's hand. "Hello, Mr. Fontenot, I've heard a lot about you. I'm happy to finally meet you."

Eddie didn't extend his hand, nor did he remove his eyes from Trevor's. "Forgive me for not reciprocating those feelings. I heard about what happened earlier today, and I can't say I'm thrilled to see the bruises on my daughter's arms." Caroline inherently folded her arms across her stomach and hugged herself trying to hide the now colorful bruises.

Trevor dropped his eyes to the floor. "Yes, sir, I apologized to her already for that, and I'll apologize to you, as well. I briefly lost my temper, and what I did was inexcusable. I'm sorry the results of my actions today are your first impression of me. I love your daughter very much and would never do anything to hurt her."

Eddie snapped. "Well, it looks like you already broke that promise today. What's to say you won't lose your temper again sometime? What will you do to her then? Today you nearly broke her arms and threw her across the driveway. What's it gonna be next time?" Caroline seethed and wanted to punch Cade right in his big mouth. "I just got my daughter back in my life, and I refuse to allow anyone, especially the man she's choosing to spend the rest of her life with, to mistreat her because of a temper tantrum."

Trevor stiffened. Caroline could see this would not end well and stepped closer to Eddie. "Dad, please. It was all a big misunderstanding, and everything is okay now. I'm sure Cade made it out to be much worse than it really was." Eddie's tender, saddened eyes studied her.

"Caroline, no man—no respectable man," his eyes flashed to Trevor and back, "Would ever physically harm you for any reason. Misunderstanding or not, he bruised you." Her dad touched the bloody spot on her head where she'd hit the rocking chair. She winced in pain. She had forgotten about that one.

"Dad, that was my fault. I tripped over the plant on the front porch and lost my balance. It's no big deal."

He glared at Trevor again. "Tripping over it and being pushed over it are two totally different things, sweetheart."

Caroline started to interject again and explain how she tripped, but a scalding hand wrapped around her arm and pulled her back a step.

Trevor shifted, obviously needing a significant amount of control to speak calmly. "Mr. Fontenot, may I call you Eddie?"

"No."

"Okay. . .Mr. Fontenot. As I already told you, I have apologized to Caroline for my inexcusable actions, and she has forgiven me. I can assure you nothing like this will happen again. You have my word."

"Your word? What's that to me? I don't know you from Adam. How is that supposed to make me feel better? I'm a realist, Mr. Callahan. I believe what I see, and what I see is my daughter looking like a battered woman, by your hand. Tell me, why did you come down here, and what caused you to be so angry?"

Trevor's piercing blue eyes were cold as ice now. He was livid. "Mr. Fontenot, I do not have to explain myself to you or anyone. Caroline is my fiancée and this is between her and me. With all due respect, it's none of your business."

"Right. Well, her well-being is my business, and, from what I can see, you aren't proving to be very good for her."

"That's rich coming from someone who ran out on her when she was just a baby. I hardly think your opinion is relevant in this case."

Eddie's glare turned murderous. "You self-righteous, spoiled little—"

"Dad, please stop. Trevor and I are together. I love him, and he loves me. You have obviously only heard one side of the story. You should go talk to April. She's the reason all this happened, the reason Trevor is down here. She stole my phone and got his number so she could call him and stir the pot. She told him I slept with Cade and caused him to come down here thinking I cheated on him."

"What? April did this?" Eddie looked confused. Shocked. This surprised Caroline because he had to know know exactly what kind of woman he married. Or maybe she was an Oscar-worthy actress and had him duped.

"Yes. I told you, she hates me. It's no secret, everyone in this house knows it."

"I'll take care of April. Right now, I'm concerned about your safety. If he'll hurt you like this once, he will do it again. It's only a matter of time." Eddie held her hands in his before cupping her cheek. "I love you, cher. I've waited a long time to be able to say those words to you, and I'll be damned if I'm gonna let some pompous, hot-tempered, control freak slap you around. It's just not right."

Caroline hugged him, emotion bubbling over. "Thank you, Daddy. I appreciate your concern, but I'm quite capable of taking care of myself. I've been with Trevor for over two years now, and this was the first time he's ever completely lost his temper with me. Frankly, he had good reason. He thought I had cheated on him. I would be out of my mind, too, if I thought he was cheating on me. It's all good. Please, don't worry about me." She kissed his cheek and held Trevor's hand as they walked up the stairs. She pretended not to notice the lingering glare between the two of them as she led the way.

TWENTY-EIGHT

Caroline sat beside the duck pond mulling over everything that had recently happened. Trevor caught a flight home that morning, and their memorable goodbye kiss still seared fresh in her mind.

She stared at the garden statue she always admired from her window. She finally realized what it was. An angelic statue, a lovely, moss-covered, and ancient stone sculpture of the Virgin Mary offset in the water near the edge of the pond. Mary sat majestically in a group of fragrant blooming lily pads that surrounded her. A gathering of loyal and loving followers. Mary's mournful empty eyes creeped her out, as if the virgin stared right through her soul. Caroline sighed and her thoughts drifted through the past two months of her crazy life.

Her engagement, meeting her long-lost father, learning about her siblings, and of course the wicked stepmother. She encountered the ghost of her G3 grandmother, the mysterious dreams, and the wonderful guy who she hoped and believed would be in her life forever. Never mind he and her fiancé couldn't stand each other.

Why would April do something so conniving? What did she ever do to April except show up in her life? She also wondered what Trevor's obsession was with her inclusion in her dad's inheritance? Money couldn't be an issue—his family rolled in it. Caroline couldn't imagine him wanting to live down here in the Bayou. She laughed aloud just thinking about Trevor living in the country. He'd be scared out of his loafers if he came across a wild animal.

She couldn't forget about the horrible things he'd said when they argued. The entire time they were together, before the engagement, he never so much as raised his voice. Now, all of a sudden, he was aggressive and defensive. . .violent, even. She thought about what her dad had said. Would it get worse after they're married? Why was he in such a hurry to get married, anyway?

He'd called her a slut, a lying, cheating whore, and the strangest thing about disgracing him and his family. What did his family have to do with this? Even if she'd slept with Cade, it wasn't like she and Trevor were already married. Of all people to judge her for allegedly sleeping with someone, Trevor had no room to talk.

It angered him a complete stranger told him something sexual had taken place between her and another man. He didn't know of any truth to the rumor, but still Trevor attacked her character with nasty accusations. It scared her how easily the hurtful and disrespectful words slipped from his tongue. His anger reminded her of the man from her first dream, the guy who raped Rachel and claimed someone had double-crossed him.

She didn't think Trevor's problem had so much to do with her sleeping with someone else, but more that a stranger had called him with this information. He was furious with the thought of her giving in to another man after he had waited so long and tried so hard. His public embarrassment had hurt his pride.

Her mind slipped effortlessly to Cade. Such a good man stuck in a horrible cliché. Nice guys finish last. Respectful, understanding, talented, and incredibly handsome. He could cook, he was tidy and clean, built like Hercules, and from a great family. Independent and self-sufficient, intelligent, funny, multi-lingual, he could shoot a gun with impressive accuracy, thank goodness, and possessed an adorable protectiveness toward all females. A little overconfident at times, but not annoyingly so. He was the perfect man.

Still, he was mysterious. Caroline wished she knew more about his past—his burn scar, his staggering fighting ability, his ex-girlfriend, and what's with the flighty jobs? He's smart and talented, so why not have a more stable career? However, all these factors have affected his character and made him perfect. If she'd met him two years ago she would probably be married to him already. Caroline smiled. And working on that big family they both wanted.

Completely relaxed with visions of happy children, she drifted off to sleep.

Alas, the familiar pain between her eyes throbbed, piercing her brain with intense stabs. Her stomach roiled, but not with the usual nausea. Caroline forced herself to ignore the discomfort. She opened her eyes to the blinding sunlight. No wonder she felt sick. Someone, a man, carried her and she bounced with each determined step.

The nausea stronger now, she couldn't stop it. She vomited all over him, and his loud cursing proved his repulsion. He dropped her in her own vomit. She continued heaving emphasizing the pounding in her head. With his back to her, she couldn't see him. He dressed in the same period clothing from her previous dreams, and his greasy hair hung to his earlobes. His left hand sloppily bandaged with bloody gauze.

So this was him. She would finally see his face. She wanted to say something, make him turn around, but then again, she didn't want to call any more attention to herself than necessary. Caroline didn't know her place on his agenda. She glanced down at her hands, a wedding band. She touched her belly, a baby bump. Occupied with studying her clothes, he grabbed her hair at the back of her neck.

"Come on, doll face. We have a little ways left to go, and, since you decided to get sick all over me, I'm gonna make you walk the rest of the way."

"Where are you taking me?"

"Well, now, that's for me to know, isn't it? Don't worry, you'll find out soon enough. I want to make sure everything is perfect so he doesn't miss anything." He laughed. The same evil laugh from before. Reminiscent and familiar. This dream must have started just after her last. Weak and still very queasy, she couldn't determine how her legs were able to work. She hardly felt them.

Close behind and pushing her along in the direction he wanted her to go, she saw the plantation house in the distance. Though the trees on the property were much smaller than she remembered, the house presented a beautiful majestic picture.

"Here we go. Home sweet home. Fortunately for us, everyone is at worship so we shouldn't be disturbed."

"Won't they wonder why I'm not there, too?"

He chuckled. "Don't you wish they would? The way you've been acting of late has everyone convinced you've gone mad, sha. They all believe you are too depressed to drag yourself out of bed. People have decided you're hopeless, and they've stopped trying to help. Of course, I had a lot to do with that, thanks to my precious little serum here." He patted his pocket.

"What kind of serum would that be? If everyone thinks I'm mad anyway, don't you think you at least owe me the luxury of knowing what drug you're poisoning me with?"

He walked quietly for a few moments still tucked behind her. "Yes, I suppose there's no harm in you knowing. You won't be around much longer to tell anybody, anyway."

Caroline's heart leapt into her throat. I knew it. She didn't commit suicide, she was murdered! Who was this lunatic and why did he kill Rachel?

The house and the grounds looked very much the same on the inside as it did in Caroline's present day. Same azalea bushes lining the porch, same buffet table and bench seat in the foyer, same chandelier hanging from the ceiling. But she was not Caroline, she was Rachel, and she didn't want to go upstairs.

She hesitated, but he got more forceful and shoved her. She tried to distract him with questions. "So tell me. What exactly is in your serum?"

"I crafted it myself after a long discussion with a drunken apothecary in New Orleans one night. A mixture of a few of my favorite ingredients. A bit of opium, a touch of ether, a tad of belladonna and a drop or two of some other little special ingredients. Just enough to make people think you're deranged."

"Why are you doing this?"

"You don't know? Perhaps you should ask your dear sweet husband. But, oh. You won't have a chance, sha. The end is near for you."

That ruled out Jackson as a murder suspect.

They crested the top of the stairs, and he prodded her step-for-step into her room. Every time she tried to turn and get a look at him, he would grip the back of her head to keep it forward.

"Face forward, sha. I don't need those pretty eyes distracting me from my purpose. You had your chance to be with me, and you chose to throw it all away for that double-crossing traitor. Now you'll both see what it's like to lose what you wanted most."

She knew what happened next, though she didn't wish to experience it for herself.

"Now's the time to whisper your final prayers. I'll leave you alone with your thoughts for a moment, but I'll be just outside this door so don't get any ideas." With one final shove into the room, she stumbled against the bed as the door slammed behind her.

Caroline recognized something about this particular scene. She looked out the window trying to remember. It was the opening to one of her past dreams where Rachel cried while writing in her journal. The journal! She had hidden it somewhere by the bed. Caroline knelt down, and spotted a slightly loose floorboard. She reached for it to pry it up.

A sharp, shooting pain stabbed the side of her neck. The room quickly blurred. He must have been mixing his death concoction while allowing Rachel to pray for help, only she wrote a note instead. . .the suicide note.

Caroline had to find that journal! The fuzzy room went completely dark.

Caroline's eyes fluttered open. She wondered how long she'd been asleep next to the pond. The journal! She jumped up with the intention of finding that floorboard, but she stood too quickly after just waking from such a deep sleep. Dizzy, she stumbled. Her heel caught on a large garden stone and she flew backwards into the duck pond with incredible force, landing with a big splash. A stinging, burning pain enveloped the back of her head just before everything faded to black.

Caroline woke up in a room she didn't recognize. Her head throbbed badly, the beep of a heart monitor radiated through her brain. Only this time, the hurt bloomed from the back of her head. Her hospital gown scratched against her skin and the odors of disinfectant filled her nose. Wires and tubes protruded from her head and arms. An IV dripped into a needle sticking into a vein. This wasn't good. Not at all.

Eddie and Cade walked into the room.

"Dad! What's going on? Why am I in a hospital?"

She attempted to sit up, but they rushed to her side and pushed her back to the pillow. She started to protest, but Eddie explained.

"Sweetheart, you had quite an accident."

"An accident? What happened?"

Cade's melodic voice soothed her weariness. "You lost your balance and fell in the pond. While that would normally have been very funny, and I would love to tease you mercilessly about it, it wasn't. You slammed your head against the base of the Virgin Mary statue, and now you have a concussion. You scared the crap out of me—" Eddie cleared his throat and Cade added, "Us."

A concussion. In nursing school, she proudly gloated about never having a broken a bone, but a concussion? Wow. "I guess I won't be winning any medals for grace, huh?"

They chuckled, but her head hurt too much to join. Cade on one side and Eddie on the other, both admired her with genuine worry. "Guys, I'm okay. Stop looking at me like I just woke up from the dead or something. How long am I gonna be stuck in this room?" Neither one answered, they shared a glance and focused on her again. "Seriously? Dad, when can I come home?"

"The doctor said he wanted to keep you in here for a little while to observe you. He wants to make sure your concussion wasn't worse than he thought, and that you're healing the way you need to be."

"What? How long is a little while? Wait a minute, I learned about concussions in school and those are usually just an overnight stay. Why is he keeping me here? I can't be cooped up that long, I'll go nuts! I don't know anyone here, and you guys both work. Where's my phone? I'm calling Mom."

"I already did. She couldn't come because they are doing some kind of new training at her work this week, and she's the trainer."

"How long have I been in here?"

"You checked in two days ago. The doctor said you cracked your skull and you lost a lot of blood. You'll have to stay in here for a while so he can monitor you. He's afraid if you are up and around too much you may faint and cause even more damage."

"I cracked my skull? So it was worse than just a concussion."

Cade leaned in close and spoke softly. "Sweet girl, I will be in here every day to stay with you. I promise."

"I can't ask you to do that. You have a life. You have more than one job. I'll call Kristy, she'll come down to stay with me."

Eddie handed Caroline her phone. After a quick call, Kristy promised to book the first flight out in the morning. Caroline didn't want to be a burden, and having her best friend come visit made her feel better about the fuss she caused.

"Did they at least give an estimated amount of time I would be stuck in here?" she asked.

"I'll go talk to the doctor," Eddie said, "and see if I can persuade him to let us bring you home if we promise to make you stay in bed."

"Thank you. That would be awesome. Tell him I promise not to get up unless I have to pee."

Cade smiled and pulled up a chair, "You don't even have to do that. You have a catheter."

Ugh. Caroline hated catheters. "Who's gonna dump it for me? You? I don't think so."

He smiled playfully. "Well, it's either that or I could help you to the bathroom and watch you pee. You decide."

There was absolutely no way she would have him watch her pee. She finally nodded. He smiled victoriously. The silence began to turn awkward and she remembered the last time she'd seen Cade. The look on his face when she left him, though only slightly bruised and bloody, in the driveway to walk away with Trevor. She wasn't mad at him for telling. After learning what happened to his sister, she understood his concern.

"I'm so sorry about what happened. I promise, Trevor has never laid a hand on me like that before. I honestly don't know what got into him. I guess Friday just wasn't my day. First, the stupid snake, then Henry, then Trevor. . .now this. I should have locked myself in my room for the weekend. Anyway, I'm really sorry."

"You don't need to apologize for anything that happened." He gazed down at her hands encased in his. "I lost it when I saw him throw you down. I'd heard you yelling at him for hurting you, so I ran as fast as I could until I could see you. When I saw him push you like that, well, I had to be there before he had a chance to touch you again."

"Thank you. I guess I owe you for three saves now."

Cade's eyes sparkled. "Four. I'm the one who pulled you out of the pond and got you to the hospital."

Dang it! "I guess it's a good thing you are around. How'd you know I fell in?"

"I was headed in the direction of the plantation house when I saw you napping by the pond. I wasn't going to bother you at first, but you woke up, so I walked your way. I thought you saw me coming, but somehow you lost your balance and fell in. I swear it looked like someone threw you in the pond the way you flew up in the air. I dove into the pond to get you and didn't realize you'd hit your head until I got you out and saw all the blood."

He kissed her hand, his lips lingering on her skin for a moment. "My heart stopped," he whispered. "So, I used my shirt to wrap around your head and applied pressure to the wound to slow the bleeding. Then I brought you straight to the Emergency Room." Cade pressed his forehead to her forearm and whispered. "I was so scared, Caroline." When he looked up, his eyes glistened. "I've seen plenty of head wounds, but I thought you were going to die when I saw the amount of blood gushing from your head."

"Wait, how have you seen plenty of head wounds working as a landscaper, musician, and part-time librarian? I didn't realize first aid was essential in those fields."

Cade briefly looked away. "I've had other jobs before those, Caroline. That's beside the point, though. Seeing you in that condition scared me to death. I thought I was going to lose you."

She blinked away the tears and changed the focus of their topic. "This may sound paranoid, but I'm not sure all these crazy accidents are simple coincidences. I've never had this much bad luck in such a concentrated amount of time before, and I'm not clumsy. What if Rachel isn't the only ghost lingering around the Fontenot plantation?"

Cade frowned. "You think you have a ghost trying to hurt you?"

Caroline shrugged. "I don't know. I don't think Rachel would try to hurt me since she's been trying to tell me something through my dreams, but I don't think my brushes with death are just dumb luck. I feel cursed!"

"You're not cursed, sweet Caroline. You're too sweet."

"That's great and all, thanks, but there's something going on. If Rachel is hanging around, what's to say some other evil spirit isn't sticking around, too?"

Cade pondered the thought. "You're right. We shouldn't rule out the possibility. Guess I'll just have to keep a closer watch over you." He winked.

Caroline huffed. "After my summer here, I'm gonna have more scars than a prison guard."

Cade squeezed her hand. "Scars are sexy, right? I have my fair share of them, too. Don't worry about all that. They add character."

"Yeah, right. What scars? I've seen you—all of you before, and I never noticed any scars. . .except the one on your chest. What is that from, anyway?"

He avoided eye contact as well as her question. "You only saw all of me for a split second, but believe me, they're there. I have plenty of scars and each one has its own painful memory."

"Well, I think you look perfect, so there." She tried to feel the back of her head, but the bandage wrapped around it prevented much touching of anything. "Did they. . ." she gasped, patting her head, feeling for her hair. "Did they have to. . .cut. . .my hair? Shave my head?" Terror enveloped her. Cade's eyes dropped a little, answering her question.

He smiled sweetly and kissed her forehead. "Caroline, honey, you would be beautiful if you were bald. They only shaved the little section around the wound so they could clean it and stitch it up. They left the top half of your hair long so it would cover the short part. You just won't be wearing any ponytails for a while."

Caroline's tears fell down her cheeks. "Oh, well. At least I'm alive, thanks to you. Now I'm just ugly." She squeezed his hand as he kissed the tears from her cheeks.

"That's not possible. Don't cry, sweet Caroline. Believe me when I tell you, it's not your hair that makes you beautiful. It's your soul. Like I said, you'd be beautiful with no hair at all."

Lightheaded, she closed her eyes. Cade kissed her forehead again, pushed the call button for the nurse, and tenderly whispered in her ear.

"Get some rest, sweet girl. Let the medicine work for you. Sweet dreams."

She heard scurrying footsteps and whispers as her consciousness swirled with impending darkness. A heavy fog clouded her senses pressuring her to give in, but she fought it. Finally, a reassuring squeeze from Cade's hand and Caroline allowed herself to drift away in a haze of dancing children, auburn hair, and snakes.

When Caroline woke up, her foggy head struggled to focus on the faces staring at her. She blinked a few times, but closing her eyes felt too good and she nodded off again. *Wake up! You can sleep when you're dead. There are people here to see you. Wake up!* Against her own will, she let her subconscious win and opened her eyes again. This time a male voice said something unrecognizable, but familiar and pleasant.

She blinked a few more times and heard the voice again. Finally she was able to make out some faces. The first one, her dad's handsome, smiling face. She shifted her gaze to a smiling Claire, then to Remy beside her playing his hand-held video game. Caroline glanced around the rest of the room looking for one more face, but didn't see it.

"Beau's on his way. He got stuck by a draw bridge on his way here from work." Eddie must have read her mind. She managed a crooked grin and he chuckled. "Don't worry, sweetheart, we are taking you home. You've been asleep for eighteen hours."

What the. . .

TWENTY-NINE

Caroline nearly exploded. "What! Eighteen hours? I've been asl—what? How have I. . .why didn't you wake me up?"

"Easy, tiger," her dad chuckled. "You needed the rest. The doctor is giving you oral pain medicine to bring home, and you can relax in the comfort of your own room."

Cade bounded through the door like a college student late for class, eager to see Caroline. Elation swelled in her heart. So adorable.

"Well, hello, beautiful," he said, panting out of breath. "I've missed that dazzling smile of yours."

Caroline's heart quivered, as the butterfly flutters her wings. "Hey there, handsome. It's great to see you. So hot for me that I take your breath away, huh?"

The room filled with laughter and Cade grinned. "Ma Chérie, you have absolutely no idea. No idea."

They gazed at each other for a long, quiet moment until Eddie cleared his throat to remind them of their audience.

Caroline flinched. "So, what are we waiting for? Let's roll! I'm ready to get home." It was easy to call the plantation house home. She was comfortable there, apart from the whole ghost issue and her impossible run of bad luck.

Eddie held his hand up. "Wait just a minute, love, we have to wait for the doctor to see you first. We've all been anxiously waiting for you to wake up. You had us very worried."

Caroline gasped. "Did Kristy make it in? Did someone go get her from the airport? She was supposed to catch the first flight out before I had my mini-coma."

Cade smiled. "Relax, I picked her up from the airport."

"How did you know who she was?"

"Well, I had seen her picture in your photo album, but I also had a sign with her name on it." He smiled very cryptically. Like the cat that ate the canary.

"The photo album. So I was right and that was how you knew about the rum runners. How very observant of you." He was still smirking and she couldn't take it anymore. "What's that smile about? What happened?" Caroline was completely intrigued now and a bit peeved. What had Kristy thought of him? Had Cade found Kristy attractive? A jealous twinge pulsed through her. She's your best friend, and you're engaged to someone else, so get over it. You can't have the best of both worlds.

"Kristy is quite charming, isn't she?" Cade looked directly at her. He knew something he wasn't sharing.

Now she was utterly confused, somewhat disappointed, and a bit territorial. "Yes, she is. She's beautiful and she's single, too. Maybe I could hook you guys up or something." Her tone came out a little harsher than she intended it to be. She blamed it on the jealousy. Their audience shifted uncomfortably and Cade's smile faded. That must not have been what he hoped to hear. Caroline flashed him a crooked grin. "She's high maintenance, though. I don't think you could handle her."

308

DEADLINE

His smile stretched across his handsome face. "Yeah, I gathered that."

"So. . .where is she?"

"She asked me to drop her off at the house so she could get ready for your homecoming. I don't know what exactly she's planning to do because all you really need is your bed, but she said she had some preparations to make."

Caroline smiled. That sounded like Kristy. Who knew what she had planned?

Caroline couldn't stop thinking about Cade's cryptic smile when he spoke about their meeting. *Why is this bothering me so much? He's not even her type.*

Dr. Breaux was not the stereotypical doctor, by far. The proverbial tall, dark, and handsome, he wore his hair longer than normal and a large dimple crowned his smile of perfect white teeth. She blushed. She glanced at Claire whose face also glowed red. At least she wasn't alone this time.

"Well, hello, Miss Fontenot. It's nice to see you with your eyes open. I was beginning to wonder if you were under a spell, waiting for your handsome prince to give you the long-awaited kiss."

Cade shifted his weight, uncomfortable with that analogy. She opened her mouth to speak, but nothing came out. The doctor spoke before she could further embarrass herself with jumbled words.

"I am not entirely comfortable with your discharge, but your father assures me he will make you stay in bed." He glanced at Eddie who nodded in response. "I have a prescription for some pain medicine you can take home with you. I need you to take it easy. Now is your chance to have people catering to you."

His beautiful smile left her speechless. He didn't sound like he was from this area, and she wondered if, like Cade, he'd had to work to lose his accent for professional reasons.

"Now, if you start feeling worse I want you to call me at once. Okay?" She silently nodded like a bashful child afraid to speak. He grinned and gave her one last check up, examining the bandages around her head, before he allowed her to leave.

Back home, Cade carried her up the stairs. Before he turned the corner into her room, she smelled Kristy's designer perfume. Excitement to see her best friend overwhelmed her. Kristy stood next to the beautiful canopy bed, noticeably excited, too. They squealed, and as soon as Cade laid Caroline on the bed, hugged and cried.

"Oh, C. You scared me so bad! I couldn't believe my ears when I heard what happened. I'm so glad you are okay! Even with all the bandages, you still look fabulous, you know." Kristy smiled and smoothed Caroline's hair. "You make a concussion look good."

"I have to agree with her." Cade's smooth voice broke through the air like a knife slicing through soft butter. Kristy beamed before she turned to look at him.

"Hello, again. I'm sorry, I was on the phone the whole way here and didn't get a chance to thank you for picking me up from the airport, and for saving my best friend's life. I promise to find some way to repay you."

He smiled the same peculiar smile. "No need, cher. Caroline being alive is payment enough. Thank you for coming to stay with her. I know she's very happy you are here." His eyes moved to back to her. "Caroline, I'm really glad you're back home now, where you belong. If you're comfortable, I'm gonna go down to the kitchen for something to drink. Can I bring you anything?"

"I'm fine, thank you, Cade. Really. . .thank you so much. I don't know how I'll ever be able to repay you for rescuing me four times in one weekend. I'm grateful you were there for me when I needed you."

"Always, cher. Always." He winked and walked out.

Kristy turned to Caroline with big eyes. "He is the hot-naked-wet guy you ran into, isn't he? Why didn't you tell me he was perfect in every way possible? He's amazing! I can see now why you wanted to stay here all summer." She laughed quietly but stopped when she saw the look on Caroline's face. "Uh-oh, what's wrong. I know that look. Did something happen?"

"No. Well, kind of." Caroline fought an oncoming headache and didn't want to go into detail about everything, plus she still battled the unwelcome jealousy. "I'll tell you all about it later. What kind of preparations did you have to make for my homecoming?"

"Well, it's not much, but now I'm not sure I want to give it to you. I may need to make a few modifications to it first."

Caroline stared, clueless. "Okay, I give up. What is it?"

Kristy stared at her for a minute before she sighed deeply and stood. She pulled a cart full of fresh flowers from the closet. Roses, lilies and orchids of every color imaginable filled the top of the restaurant-style dish cart. An unbelievable fragrance engulfed the room filling it with the amazing sweetness of the bouquet. In the middle of all the flowers was a beautiful 8x10 framed photo of Trevor and Caroline from Kristy's red carpet birthday party. Caroline loved everything about it and couldn't understand what Kristy meant about needing to make modifications.

"I figured you'd be stuck in bed for a while and nothing would please you more than your favorite flowers surrounding this beautiful picture of you and your sweetie. I had no idea you had a great view already."

Caroline ignored her innuendo. "It's wonderful, Kristy! What modifications would you need to make? It's perfect!"

"Right. Perfect." Sarcasm dripped from Kristy's words.

"What? Go on. . .tell me. What exactly was that supposed to mean?"

"Nothing that we need to discuss right now. Why don't you lie down and let me pamper you for a while? You should rest up so you can tell me all about what has been happening with you over the past six weeks." She fluffed Caroline's pillow and covered her up. "Man, there's nothing wrong with the air conditioning in this old house, it's freezing in here! Are you cold or is it just me?"

If she only knew why it was so cold. She'd hit the door running. "I'm always cold in here. That's why I have so many blankets on this bed."

"Good, I'm glad it's not just me. I've been nippin' since I walked in here, geez." Kristy rubbed her arms to warm them before tucking her hands in her armpits. "So, I'll go get some water for you to keep by your bed while you relax and take a nap. I'm going to get better acquainted with Mr. Sexy-naked-wet-guy downstairs." She giggled as she kissed Caroline's forehead and bounced out the door.

Exhausted, Caroline sank into her pillow. Her head hurt too badly to be jealous. A nap sounded good, so she closed her eyes and found her happy place. She must have fallen asleep immediately, because she barely remembered touching the pillow.

"Mmmmm. . .coffee. May I join you for a cup?" Cade looked up from his newspaper, surprised to see Kristy in the kitchen. Something about her reminded him of Caroline. He noticed a similarity in poise and mannerisms confirming their close relationship. He imagined she was quite a handful, though. Caroline had her pegged when she called her high maintenance.

"Sure, Miss Kristy," Delia chimed as she walked around the corner with a cheerful smile. "How ya like your coffee?"

"Black is fine, thank you."

Cade cocked an eyebrow. "Black? Interesting."

She confidently glided over to the table and sat across from him. "Interesting? Does that surprise you?"

"I don't know too many women who drink their coffee black. It's. . .interesting. That's all."

"I used to wake up early to have coffee with my dad before he left for work in the mornings, so I learned from him." She leaned across the table toward him. "Can I ask you something?"

"Sure." Cade leaned back in his chair and crossed his arms over his chest. She amused him with her no-nonsense approach. Not one to reveal his hand this early in the game, he was eager to see what she had on her mind.

"What's up with you and Caroline?"

He chuckled. "What do you mean?"

"Okay, a good sign that there is definitely something going on is when a person answers a question with a question. It's obvious you two have feelings for each other. How'd you meet?"

She already knew the answer, he'd bet on it. A sly smile stretched across his face. "We, um, just happened to bump into each other one day."

She studied his circumscription and slowly smiled back at him. "Mmmm-hmmm."

Cade leaned forward, more serious. Not kidding anymore. "Caroline is like no other woman I have ever met in my entire life. Yes, I have feelings for her. Stronger than I wish they were. How did you two become such close friends?"

"Best friends," she corrected him as Delia placed her coffee on the table. "Caroline is from Arkansas, and I am from Tennessee, but we have known each other since we were thirteen years old."

"If you're from different states, how did you become best friends?"

"Well, we met when we were placed as roommates at a summer church camp. We got along so well, we kept in touch. I'm from Nashville, Tennessee, and Caroline is from Beebe, Arkansas, which is about twenty miles from the camp. About a six-hour drive to get from my house to hers, but we kept in touch through calls and emails, and managed to visit each other every summer."

"Can I ask you something else?" Cade said.

His intensity noticeably made Kristy uncomfortable, but she recovered quickly. Gracefully, she smiled and leaned back in her chair, just as he had, and crossed her arms.

He smiled. "What all can you tell me about Trevor?"

"Wow, that one came from left field. I expected a question about Caroline, or myself, but not Trevor, of all people. Why in the world do you want to know about him? Sizing up the competition?" She winked.

"Curiosity." Cade stayed serious and focused so she would know he wasn't joking.

"Well, Caroline's probably already told you he's an architect for a firm in Chicago. He's a workaholic, but somehow manages to make some free time for Caroline." He comes from a rich family, so needless to say he's spoiled and doesn't like not getting his way." She shrugged uncomfortably, and brought her steaming coffee mug to her lips. "Um, what all do you want to know?"

"Do you like him?"

Kristy frowned and he had a feeling it wasn't from the coffee. She had an opinion of Trevor, alright. If she bit her tongue any harder, Cade was sure she'd draw blood.

"Man this coffee's good. What kind is it?"

"Do you like him?" Cade refused to allow her to avoid the question which she clearly wanted to do. She carefully leaned back in her chair with her mug and crossed her legs as she let out a sigh.

"I like him all right, I suppose. Why?"

He lowered his voice and leaned forward, resting his elbows on the table. "Bull." She paused, mug halfway to her mouth, and challenged him with her eyes. He'd get it out of her. "I don't believe you." She looked up to the ceiling and grunted as she took another sip. "Please, Kristy. Be honest with me. I promise Caroline won't know you told me anything. No one will. You have my word."

Cade didn't waiver as she studied him for several long moments. He wished he could know what was zipping through her sharp mind. She didn't seem the type to miss anything. He observed her glossy manicured fingernails, sleek shiny hair, and flawless complexion. A perfect complement to her designer clothing. Caroline mentioned Kristy was a master seamstress and fashion guru. Attention to detail was this woman's thing. The type to be in the know at all times.

"Mmm-hmm. Okay, first you have to tell me why you want to know all this stuff. I don't like talking about Caroline behind her back, but I have a few questions of my own. How about we take turns?"

Cade appreciated her loyalty and nodded. "Okay, that sounds fair. Ladies first."

Kristy laughed. "You're good." She shook her head, conceding. "Okay, fine. No, I don't particularly like him. He's the kind of guy I would like to buy for what he's worth and sell for what he *thinks* he's worth, if you know what I mean." She smoothed her hand through her hair. "I don't like the way he talks to Caroline, treats her, pushes her around, belittles her opinion. He's very manipulative and controlling. Sometimes he acts more like her father than her boyfriend. . .well, fiancé, now."

Cade noticed her jaw clenching. "I pretend to like him because Caroline's crazy about him, though I can't understand why. He's hot, but, frankly, he's a prick. I love her and want her to be happy, but sometimes I just want to throttle her for not seeing him the way I do. If he'd ever tried to talk to me, I would've told him to take a hike. There, now it's your turn to answer one."

Cade raised his eyebrows and thoughtfully puckered his lips. Pretty much how he'd sized Trevor up. That deserved a return answer, he supposed.

"What was Caroline talking about when she thanked you for saving her life?"

Cade smiled. "Which time?"

Kristy's jaw dropped. "You mean there was more than once?"

He nodded. "Yeah, it definitely wasn't her lucky day, or weekend for that matter. We had. . .well, we didn't really talk or interact for about three or four weeks because of circumstances being what they are. She had apparently had enough of our time apart and came to my cabin to talk."

Kristy listened intently to his heroics, hanging on every part of the story. After hearing about the rattlesnake and Henry, her eyes glimmered with a dreamy haze. Cade had seen this hero worshipping look before and prepared himself for some follow-up questions.

"Wow," she said. "I probably would have tackled you right on the front porch and showed you my undying appreciation."

Taken aback, Cade raised his brow at her bold statement. Not what he was expecting.

"Ah. Yes, you will see there aren't too many of us out there who are quite as innocent as sweet Caroline. She's definitely one of a kind. I apologize for my bluntness. I'm really not a slut, just a little more experienced than my BFF. Please, go on."

Cade smiled, tucking away that tidbit of information for later, and told her about his fight with Trevor. "It felt really good to mark up his arrogant, pretty-boy face." He mumbled under his breath. "Though I would have liked to do more."

"That bastard." Kristy lacked any surprise which worried Cade. "It is typical of controlling guys to get physical. But Caroline has always insisted Trevor was different. Why did he even come down here?"

"I'm not sure how, but I think he got the idea that Caroline and I had slept together. I didn't get to talk to her much while he was here, so I don't know everything that happened."

Kristy studied his expression, probably searching for any indication he and Caroline had indeed been intimate. But Cade had a great poker face. She took a sip of her coffee and, without removing her eyes from his, finally just asked him. "So. . .have you? Been intimate? With Caroline?"

Cade stared back and smiled. "She's your best friend. I figure you already know the answer to that question."

"I can respect that. She'll tell me if she wants me to know. It's no biggie. If I know Caroline, you two have probably had some incredibly intense kisses, but that's it." Cade was impressed. She knew her best friend well, but he didn't need to let her know anything just yet, so he kept his face expressionless. She chuckled. "You're pretty good at keeping secrets, aren't you?"

"It's what I do."

"Hmmm. Interesting. Okay, carry on."

He could tell he stirred her curiosity, but he'd give her no more. Cade described the accident that hospitalized her best friend.

"If you hadn't been there, Caroline would most likely have died," Kristy said.

He refused to let his mind wander there and cracked his neck. Strangely uncomfortable with her praises. Normally it wouldn't bother him, but with Caroline it was different. Everything was different with her.

"You are quite the proverbial knight in shining armor," she added.

"It's my turn to ask now." Cade smirked, pondering what to ask next. "Has Caroline ever mentioned anything about Trevor's dad or his business?"

"Hmmm. I don't think so. She only met his dad a time or two. I'm not sure they have ever spoken anything more than cordial hellos. But I had heard of his family before she and Trevor ever began dating. My dad works up in Illinois sometimes, and the Callahan family is frequently in the news." Kristy drummed her fingernails on the table.

"I know he's a quiet man and had been partners with some other company in New York before they did him wrong. The story I heard is that his three other partners formed a sort of mutiny against him and bought out his shares without him knowing anything about it. Supposedly he was left with nothing."

Kristy took another sip of coffee while he let that soak in. Mutiny. Callahan was broke. Very interesting.

"I think all this happened when Trevor was very young," she said. "Anyway, Kenneth Callahan hit rock bottom. They moved to Chicago, and, out of nowhere, he started his own real estate development firm and built it from the ground up. He's quite successful now. Everyone always wondered where he got all the money to start his own company. They used to say he stalked the obituaries and preyed on innocent widows and widowers," she shrugged. "I think his firm is called KC Real Estate Investors, or something like that."

A shot of adrenaline surged through Cade's veins. He jumped up from his chair and bolted around the table nearly causing Kristy to spill her coffee. He smiled triumphantly as he leaned down to kiss her cheek. "Thank you so much, cher. You just confirmed what I was suspecting. I have to go make a phone call. We can continue our questions later." He kissed her cheek again and dashed out the door. Suspicions confirmed, Cade had more digging to do.

THIRTY

Without opening her eyes, Caroline heard Kristy return to the room, mumbling about the icy temperature. She checked the vents, but they were already closed.

"Why is it still so cold in here?" Kristy complained in a whisper. She tucked a blanket to Caroline's chin to ensure she kept warm.

"What in the world? Did she get out of bed to do this? I'm gonna rip that girl apart if she did."

Caroline finally greeted the light, prying open her heavy lids and yawned. "What'd I do this time?"

Kristy spun around in surprise. "Nothing." Kristy looked back at the dressing table before facing Caroline again with a frown. "Did you get up for anything?"

"No, why? What's wrong?"

"It's no big deal, just something. . .strange. That's all. The flowers. . . Don't worry about it."

Caroline zeroed in on Kristy's confusion.

"What? What about the flowers? What is it? What'd you see?"

Kristy stared at the peculiar flowers, seemingly waiting for an answer to the riddle to instantly pop up. "Well, when I came in just now I found three orchids lying in the shape of an F on this dressing table. I hadn't removed them from the cart, and I'm certain nobody else has been in here during the short time I was downstairs. It's just very odd, that's all. No big de—Caroline, what the hell? You're white as a sheet! Are you okay?"

All the blood had drained from Caroline's face. "No way," she whispered. "It's impossible."

"What? What's impossible, honey? What are you talking about? Do I need to call your doctor?"

Her heart pounded so fiercely, Caroline felt she could pass out at any moment. If proof was what she needed, she got it.

"Caroline Fontenot, you better tell me right now. Nursing is your thing, not mine. Do I need to call your doc—"

"Rachel," she whispered.

"What?"

"It's Rachel. She's here. Now."

THIRTY-ONE

"Honey, what are you talking about? Am I supposed to know who Rachel is? Whoever she is, why would she sneak in here to rearrange your orchids? And nearly give you a heart attack!"

Still dreaming, or maybe hallucinating, Caroline was going crazy. It was becoming difficult to distinguish the difference between her dreams and real life.

Kristy was fussing over her dabbing her face with a cloth and attempting to check her pulse rate. "I swear, Caroline, if you do that to me again I'll kick your butt. I don't care if you are bedridden. You had me freaking out. I've never seen anyone so white, not even in the horror movies. You seriously looked like a vampire."

Caroline grabbed Kristy's hand and held it until she calmed down. "Okay, Kris, this is going to sound crazy, so just hear me out. Rachel is my great, great, great grandmother. Murdered in this room, but everyone thought she killed herself. Apparently her ghost is determined to clear her reputation by haunting me."

Kristy sat on the bed, silent, staring at Caroline. She touched Caroline's forehead with the back of her fingertips. Caroline knew Kristy wouldn't believe her. She knocked her hand away. "I don't have fever. I'm completely sane and didn't believe it at first either, but those flowers just proved everything I doubted." Caroline pointed to the arranged orchids. "Rachel did that. I just saw it in my dream. . .the three orchids for the shape of an F. It's her. She's here. . .now."

"Rachel? The. . .uh, ghost. . .of your great, great, great grandmother?"

While Kristy was trying to digest what she just told her, Caroline noticed it missing. "Where's the jewelry box?" She'd been so busy she forgot to look for it earlier.

Kristy let out a frustrated sigh. "Caroline, what jewelry box? You're talking crazy. What is going on? I'm so confused. You're not gonna go all creepy-puking-exorcist-chick on me are you?"

"The antique jewelry box that was on the dressing table. Have you seen it?"

"Sweetheart, I have no idea what you are talking about. There was nothing on this dresser when I got here. I believe I would have noticed an antique jewelry box if there was one there."

Caroline pushed herself up. Her head lolled, like a bowling ball balanced on a toothpick and Kristy adjusted the pillows to support the heavy weight. Caroline closed her eyes to the spinning room, and, when she finally opened them, the clarity was like looking through someone else's eyes. She asked Kristy to look under the bed, up against the wall.

"Honey, I think you need to rest a little more. You're not making much sense right now. Whatever you dreamed about must have been pretty intense, because you're acting crazy. Here, why don't you lie back down."

Caroline held her hand up to stop Kristy from going any further. "Kristy, please. Humor me. Just look under the bed against the wall to see if the jewelry box is there."

She rolled her eyes and knelt down on the floor as she peeked beneath the bed. "Oh. My. Gosh. How the heck did you know this thing was under here?"

Caroline went numb. In her most recent dream, Rachel hid the jewelry box under the bed. Rachel's ghost was trying to tell her something. But what?

"Can you reach it?"

Kristy scoffed. "Not without crawling under the bed on my belly, and you really are crazy if you think I'm about to do that because of a dream. We'll get your Cajun cupcake up here for that."

This was so frustrating! What was Rachel trying to tell her? It didn't help that Caroline's head throbbed. "Can you get me some of that pain medicine? My head is pounding."

She stood slowly. "S-sure, C. Of course. So, these dreams you're having. . .are they, like, premonitions or something?"

She swallowed the pills and took a deep breath. "I don't think so. Aren't premonitions something you see that hasn't happened yet? The stuff I'm seeing is what happened to her back when she was alive in the 1800s. It's like watching a movie that someone keeps pausing. Confusing at first, then it was fascinating, now it's just frustrating. I'm ready for the dreams to end. She's wearing me out. Anyway, I had asked Cade to stay up here with me one time because strange things were happening in this room and I was a little freaked out."

Kristy nodded exaggeratedly. "Well, yeah. I can totally see why. He's a hottie. But a ghost? Really? I just don't know, C. I mean, do we need to call someone or something? The Ghostbusters? A medium? A Ouija board?"

"Kristy, don't patronize me. I'm serious." Caroline recounted all the odd happenings, and Kristy, thankfully, kept her sarcasm to a minimum.

"Now the orchids. In my dream, her husband, Jackson, my great, great, great Grandpa Fontenot, had strategically placed these orchids in her room with a love note attached to each one. They had just gotten married and he had placed them in the shape of an 'F' for Fontenot. It was very sweet."

Caroline's cell phone rang. Kristy looked at her without moving. They both recognized Trevor's ringtone.

"Do you want me to answer it for you? Do you feel like talking?"

"Yes, I can talk. Will you get it for me? Did anyone call him to tell him what happened?"

"Nope. We left that honor exclusively to you."

"Great. Well, I'm not gonna tell him, either. He doesn't need to worry."

Kristy handed Caroline the phone and walked out, mumbling under her breath. "Yeah, I'm sure he would just be worried sick."

"Hey, baby," Trevor said. "I've been calling you. How's it going?"

"Great! Everything is great. How are you?"

"I'm doing well. Are you sure? I'm really sorry about everything that happened this past weekend. I thought about it, and I acted like a complete jerk. Can you ever forgive me?"

"Yes, I forgave you already. It's okay. I'm sure that's just a touch of the many fights we'll have in our marriage. I just wish you would have let me explain before you flew off the handle. I still love you, so we're cool."

"Good. That's music to my ears. Listen, I can't talk long, I just wanted to call and apologize. I love you, and I can't wait for you to come home." Caroline's gut twinged as she hung up. Chicago didn't feel like home. . .not like Louisiana did. Not like this house.

Cade rounded the corner into her room and immediately brightened her mood. "Hey, gorgeous. How are you feeling?"

"Oh, you know, I'm hangin' in there. Keeping the head-banging to a minimum, but I'm still rockin' out." Her pathetic attempt at humor was funny in itself.

Cade sat on the bed next to her and chuckled, shaking his head.

How am I going to leave this guy? I'm gonna miss him so much.

He held her hand, playing with her fingers as he intwined them with his own. "You're pretty amazing, you know that?"

She snorted. "Amazingly clumsy, and obviously the most helpless person in the world."

"Nah. Not helpless. Everything happens for a reason, right? Maybe God knew I needed you in my life as much as you needed me." He smiled and kissed her cheek. "There is a reason I just happened to be there each time you've had an. . .unfortunate experience." He shook his head. "You definitely have an angel watching out for you, that's for sure."

"Yeah, and his name is Caden Luke Beauregard." A few beats passed in silence. "Hey, can you do something for me?"

"Sure, love, whatever you want."

"Can you get the jewelry box out from under the bed and hand it to me, please?"

"Why is the jewelry box under the bed?"

"I don't know. I have a guess about why it's there, but I'm still having a difficult time accepting it. "

He flashed a crooked grin. "Rachel? How did you know it was under the bed?"

"It was in my last dream. I saw her slide it under there, but I don't know why she did it. Kristy was too freaked out to grab it and refused to get her clothes dirty."

He chuckled and crawled on the floor as far under the bed as he could fit. He came back up with the large, antique jewelry box. Caroline opened it and found it empty. She searched all around the blue satin lining to see if there were any loose corners or torn material. . .something, anything, that could be hiding a clue. Nothing.

"Now why on earth would she hide this under the bed if she wasn't trying to tell me something? This makes no sense." Caroline sighed, frustrated. Cade flattened on his stomach and shimmied on the floor under the bed. He knocked on the floorboards where the jewelry box had been sitting. The last one he rapped sounded hollow.

"This one's loose. One end of it bounced up when I hit it."

"Really?" She remembered the dream before she fell into the pond. "Of course! The journal! Pull it up and see what's under it!"

"I'm gonna have to move your bed to get to it. It's pretty far under there."

She prepared to stand up, but Cade quickly stopped her. "Just where do you think you're going? I can move this bed with you in it. You stay right there."

"It's heavy."

"I think I can handle it, thanks." Cade winked and, with little effort, pushed on the side of the bed to scoot it toward the window. He had squatted down to push on the bottom part of the bed, so his muscular shoulders were eye-level. Caroline admired the definition in them as they flexed while moving the bed and imagined kissing on those shoulders. When she snapped out of her little fantasy, he was smiling at her.

Busted. . .again! Ugh!

He stopped pushing and sat on his knees. He stared deep into her eyes, melting what little restraint she had toward him. Even if she'd wanted to look away, she couldn't. With her two-timing feelings, the conversation she'd overheard while at Dupree's with Trevor flashed through her mind, and she remembered the phrase she wanted to ask Cade.

"What does Bonne A Rienne mean?"

He frowned. "Why? Where did you hear that? Did someone say that to you?"

"Just tell me. What's it mean?"

"Who said it?"

"Tell me."

"It's not nice."

"Cade. . ."

"It's Cajun for a woman who sleeps around. The *opposite* of you. Where did you hear it?"

"Nowhere. Forget it."

"Tell me."

"No. It's no big deal." She squirmed uncomfortably with the reputation she'd obtained in her short time in the bayou.

"I need you to know something." He held her hand and gently stroked her skin with his thumb. "When you fell in the pond, I was. . .well, it scared the hell out of me. I really thought I had lost you. When I pulled you out and saw all the blood, your blood, I nearly panicked." He kissed her hand and stood, turning his back to her with his hands on his head and spoke to the wall. "I realize you are going to marry someone else and that you love him, but I just need you to know how I feel about you." He turned back to face her and knelt down again.

"I have never cared more for a woman in my entire life than I do for you. I love you, sweet Caroline, and I always will. I don't care what your last name is or who you're with, I will love you until the day I die. Even after that, I'll be the ghost haunting your dreams." He smiled. A sweet, playful smile that captured a piece of her heart she would never get back.

"Look, I love Trevor, but the feelings I have when I'm around you are. . .different." Cade's eyes dropped in a calm, rejected manner. He looked hurt, so she continued. "They're stronger than the feelings I have when I'm with Trevor. I don't know what to think about it. It's confusing. I have no idea how I'm going to leave you and this place." Immediately perking up, his eyes were beacons on a foggy night. She slowly continued.

"I am usually very cautious with expressing my love. I have a hard time believing it's possible to fall in love with someone I just met, but what I feel for you. . .I have no words for. I don't know how to express it. I love everything about you. I love being with you, I love talking to you, I love eating and walking and laughing with you. I love kissing you. I love it a lot, and that scares me."

"Why does that scare you?"

"Because I shouldn't love being with anyone more than I love being with my fiancé. I shouldn't love kissing anyone as much as I love kissing the man I'm going to marry."

"Then you're marrying the wrong guy. Don't marry him," Cade pleaded. His eyes begged her to reconsider.

"I shouldn't. . .I can't—" Cade placed one finger over her lips and slowly leaned in.

"Just shut up, would ya?" He kissed her, his warm lips melting her into a puddle. His scent swirled through her senses, urging her to return his kiss. She caressed his cheek and slipped her hand to the back of his head, keeping him firmly in place. His heart beat rapidly beneath her other palm splayed across his chest.

Cade trailed his lips to her neck and gently continued from her throat to her collarbone as if she would crumble with the slightest touch. His fingers laced through hers on each hand and he softly whispered, "Let's see what's under this floor, shall we?"

Much to her disappointment, he pulled away and knelt down. Caroline sighed. "Why can't this whole mess just be easy?"

"The only easy day was yesterday, sweetheart."

He picked up the loose floorboard and swept his hand all around the inside of the hollow floor. His eyes brightened, he pulled out something wrapped in some kind of cured animal skin. Caroline held her breath as he unwrapped it—a brown leather journal, exactly like the one she had seen in her dream. Rachel's sacred journal. The one she had been trying to show Caroline. Finally!

Happy, she squealed until a sharp pain shot through her head. Tears streamed down her face. Cade quickly set the journal on the bed and gingerly stroked her face with concern.

"Hey, are you okay?"

"I'm fine, just a sharp pain. I'm so happy!" She picked up the journal and brought it to her nose to take a deep, sensory breath. She immediately traveled back in time through her dreams. It smelled of musty paper and leather, like a new baseball glove that had been wrapped in yellowed, aged newspaper for years.

"I can't believe we finally found it! This may have all the answers I've been looking for! Thanks to you, Rachel will have closure so she can finally rest in peace. Thank you. Thank you for everything."

Tears involuntarily sprang from Caroline's eyes. She could finally get to the bottom of this and have some peace again. She couldn't have done this without Cade.

"Thank you for understanding me when I told you about my crazy, psychotic dreams. Thank you for saving my life time and again and for always being there for me. You truly are amazing."

He smiled and kissed her again. She eagerly accepted the sweet, gentle kiss that quickly accelerated, burning with passion. Her hands tangled in his wavy hair when he pulled his lips away and hugged her. He buried his face into the crook of her neck and turned to whisper in her ear again.

"Thank you, sweet Caroline. For saving me."

THIRTY-TWO

Sipping coffee while looking over the final set of blueprints to approve for a local contracting firm, Trevor leaned back in his chair and spun around to look out the windows of his posh corner office. He liked this job, but sometimes he wondered what it would be like to have his own company like his dad.

His Dad. He'd be a hell of a lot happier if Dad stopped riding his case about Caroline so much. Why did he care when they got married? Nothing in it for him.

Each time Trevor thought of his trip to Louisiana, his stomach churned. When that chick, April, called him, he thought it was a wrong number. But when she mentioned who she was married to and physically described Caroline, she had his full attention. Her words echoed in his head.

"You may want to make a special trip down here to check on your little blushing bride before she ruins everything. She's making nice with the gardener, and I saw them in bed together the other night."

Like a tuning fork, sheer rage vibrated through him, and he couldn't concentrate on anything but confronting her and pounding the gardener.

Trevor touched his busted lip, wincing at the still-present sting. The nightmare he had right after Caroline left for that godforsaken state still haunted him. He'd regretted sending her down there ever since. Now this. . .

All the times they'd gotten hot and heavy with just kissing and petting, he could only fantasize what it would be like to go even further with her. Every time, every single time, she stopped him. It was getting old, and he was tired of taking cold showers. But Caroline was worth waiting for. Something about her was different. Special. Just one glimpse of her could drive him wild.

He smiled imagining their wedding night. The things he had planned for her were sure to unleash the freak hidden within her. Caroline was feisty out of the bed, he couldn't wait to see how she would be in the bed. He'd already had a little taste, albeit it was tiny because that's all she'd allow, but he'd seen a glimpse of her passionate reactions to his touch. That's why he couldn't stand the mere thought of her even sitting on the same bed with another man, much less having sex with him. Just thinking about it sent fits of burning fury shooting through Trevor's heart.

Jealousy was one thing, but his inability to physically control his temper with Caroline worried him. He'd never in his life raised a hand or used his strength against a woman. Yet, while in Louisiana with her, it was like someone else controlled his arms, his thoughts. He felt terrible about hurting her, and, just as he was about to rush to her side to apologize for throwing her on the ground, that home-wrecking redneck jumped in front of him. The dude's surprising capability to fight shocked Trevor. Of course, he was a gardener, and physical labor and heavy lifting were a daily routine for him. Still, the boy had skills that were learned, not inherited.

Either way, it didn't sit well with Trevor to have another man, especially an attractive one, rushing to Caroline's defense. Who did he think he was? The dude tried convincing him that they were just friends. Trevor had been in a fraternity, he knew the type. They didn't generally put themselves in the line of fire unless there was something in it for them. Guys like him don't fight for valor, they fight because they're getting laid. It's raw male nature. Had Caroline not turned him down so many times sexually, Trevor would never have believed she and the gardener hadn't been intimate. If she could resist him, Trevor knew the gardner didn't get anywhere.

Trevor recalled a peculiar conversation he'd had with his dad two-and-a-half years ago after successfully completing a large job with a Fortune 500 company in Chicago.

"Son, I want you to introduce yourself to Caroline Fontenot. She's going to be a junior next semester, and I need you to make her fall in love with you. Do you think you can handle that?"

Trevor had quite a reputation for being a ladies' man, and loved a good challenge, but when he questioned why, Kenneth wouldn't explain. He just insisted it would be worth it for Trevor in the long run for him to sweep her off her feet. The thought of that had not excited Trevor, considering he had no idea what she looked like. For all he knew, she was an ugly chick who couldn't get a date to save her life. He certainly didn't need his dad's assistance in finding a woman. But curiosity prevailed, and he decided to see what all the fuss was about.

Trevor's friend in campus administration got Caroline's information so he could just happen to run into her. He finally saw her at the grocery store, frustrated because she couldn't fit all of her groceries into her car with the furniture and other supplies she had already purchased for her apartment. Irritated and angry, and breathtakingly beautiful, he took one look at her and instantly became smitten. Amused by her red-hot temper, Trevor helped her fit everything in the vehicle, and used that opportunity to make his move. Unsure why his dad wanted him to meet her, for once he was thankful for the nosy, unsolicited request.

Trevor chuckled at how cute Caroline was when angry. The past two years with his beautiful little spitfire had been amazing. He would do whatever it took to make sure he didn't lose her. Whatever it took.

Trevor's office phone rang, jerking him away from his thoughts. He rubbed his face and cleared his throat to answer the phone.

"Trevor Callahan."

"Hello, Son."

"Hello, Dad. How are you?"

"Fine, thanks. Did you have a pleasant weekend?"

"Pleasant enough, yes. You?"

"How's Caroline making out in Louisiana?"

He snorted a laugh at the irony of his choice of words. "She's making out fine, I suppose. She and her dad seem to have hit it off okay. Better than I expected them to."

"Is this going to be a problem for you?"

Trevor seethed. "No, Dad, I think I can handle it."

"Good. See that you do. We don't want that sweet little girl to change her mind about marrying you, do we?"

"What exactly is that supposed to mean, Dad? Why are you so concerned about my marriage to Caroline, and why do you care about her relationship with her dad?"

"Nothing you need to worry about yet, son. I just don't want you to miss out on getting a piece of the pie, that's all."

Trevor grew annoyed with his dad speaking in riddles. "What pie would that be? What is it about Eddie Fontenot that has you so driven? Do you even know him?"

"No, I don't personally know him, I only know of him and his family's business."

"Okay, well I met him personally, and he was extremely unpleasant. He didn't seem like a typical friendly Southerner to me."

"Meet me for lunch today at the sandwich shop around the corner from your building and I'll explain everything to you. I don't want to talk about it over the phone."

What could possibly be so secret that he couldn't talk about it over the phone? This should be interesting.

The sandwich shop bustled with people, most getting their orders to go. Trevor chose a table in the back corner and waited for his dad to arrive.

Kenneth Callahan was a moderately tall, husky man who wore his jet black hair shaggy to compensate for a receding hairline. His pale skin, which contrasted greatly with his dark locks, was heavily lined with stress and age. His father was probably quite handsome in his youth, but the years had not been kind to him. Despite the weather, his dad usually wore a long, dark coat and a matching hat, very noir gangster, Al Capone.

Kenneth walked in and casually glanced around the room. When he spotted Trevor in the back corner, he grinned and made his way to the table.

"Good choice in seating, son. I almost didn't see you way back here."

"Well, it sounded like our lunch conversation wasn't necessarily going to be public record, so I figured it was best to remain inconspicuous."

Kenneth smiled as he waved over a waitress. "Order what you want, son, my treat."

This was unusual behavior. His dad rarely wanted to meet him for lunch, and, when he did, he never paid for anyone other than himself.

"Thanks. You don't have to do that. I can get my own lunch."

"Don't be ridiculous. It's my pleasure. We have much to discuss, so order anything you'd like. We may be here for a while."

That wasn't what he expected to hear. "Sure, no problem. I don't have any appointments until later this afternoon, anyway."

They ordered their food and waited until the waitress walked away before continuing their conversation.

"Listen," Kenneth kept his voice low. "It's time I fill you in on our family's history. After all, it's impossible to know where you're going unless you know where you've been, right?"

Trevor's guard flew up, but he was curious to hear what his dad wanted to disclose.

Kenneth leaned across the table, speaking just above a whisper. "Okay, I'm just going to cut to the chase here. Our family hasn't always been wealthy. In fact, just the opposite. We've all had to work very hard for what we have. We also haven't always been from New York. Your great, great, great, great grandfather, Peter Callahan, was raised in Southeast Louisiana."

Trevor's eyes nearly popped out of his head. *Why haven't I heard of this before now?* He stared at his dad, waiting for him to continue with the story, when the waitress brought their food to the table.

"This may get somewhat confusing so try to keep up. Peter was in business with a man named Jefferson. They were partners in a business called Gulf Coast Import and Trading Company. They had huge success during that time and it was beginning to become more than they could handle, just the two of them. Each of them had a son approximately the same age, so they agreed to allow their sons to be the primary owners

337

whenever they were of age to accept responsibility and take over the company. This way the old guys could be there to help if needed, but they could enjoy the benefits from the company without the work."

Trevor nodded. "I'm following you, but I don't understand where Caroline or her father fits into this story."

"Just shut up and listen, would ya? I'm getting there." Trevor bit his tongue in anger. He hated the way his father spoke down to him.

Kenneth Callahan was well known for his explosive, violent temper. Too many times growing up, Trevor would hear his parents in the other room arguing and suddenly his mom would scream and start bawling. The next day he would see a purple bruise across her cheek or a black eye. As he got older there were times his mom would disappear for a few days only to show up wearing a long sleeve shirt on a hot summer day. She became quite good at masquerading as the quiet, supportive wife, but Trevor knew better. That's why his loss of control with Caroline in Louisiana scared him so badly. He didn't want to be an abusive husband like his dad.

"So, when Peter's son, George, was only a teenager, Peter became very sick with pneumonia. Back then, medicine was nowhere near what it is today. Even with the best medical care money could buy, he ended up dying from the disease before George was of age to officially take over his share of the company. Things went as planned with Jefferson keeping to his word. Jackson and George were still intended to run the company once they reached the age and learned the trade. However, Jefferson's son, Jackson, became engaged to a lovely young lady named Rachel, to whom George had a serious attraction." Kenneth snorted. "Hmpf, leave it to a woman to ruin things."

Trevor rolled his eyes at his dad's chauvinistic view of women and took a large bite of his sandwich. Ken noticed and disregarded it as he continued. "As an engagement present, Jefferson and his wife built this huge mansion on their enormous plot of land for his son and his soon-to-be wife. Jackson and Rachel got married and she immediately got pregnant. By immediately, I mean on the honeymoon."

Trevor shrugged. "So, what's the problem with that? Happens all the time."

"George had the Callahan temper, which I'm sure you are familiar with." Trevor shifted uncomfortably. "He was already insanely jealous of Jackson because he married the woman George wanted, and she had his baby—a boy named Joseph. Once Jefferson had a grandson to carry on the family name, he backed out on his longstanding agreement with Peter and made it strictly a family owned company. Instead of leaving the rightful share of his company to George, as he had promised, he changed the legal paperwork to state the rightful heirs to the company would be his son, Jackson, and grandson, Joseph."

"How could he do that?"

"George wasn't of age yet, but Jackson was. He was a year older, and once he had legal ability to take over, Jefferson threw the verbal agreement out the window. There wasn't a damn thing George could do. . .not legally anyway."

Trevor leaned back in his chair, his eyes narrowed. "So George, who was my great, great, great grandfather, got double-crossed by his father's partner and his partner's son?"

"Precisely. Like I said, there was nothing George could do about it because in lieu of Peter's death, Jefferson became the sole owner of the company, therefore inheriting all legal rights to change anything he wanted. This launched a huge war between these two families. If only Peter had been there to defend his son, Jefferson and Jackson wouldn't have been successful with their conniving double-cross. Things would have worked out entirely different and much better for our family." Kenneth slurped the last bit of soda from his glass and obnoxiously waved it to catch the waitress's eye.

"George lost it. He snapped. He moved to New York to start his life over and get as far away from Jefferson, Jackson, and Joseph as he could. That's where he met his wife and started his family in their new life. He vowed to teach every male in his family how to run a business, and, rather than imports or trading, he took a vested interest in contract construction and real estate. This knowledge has been handed down throughout the generations, and here we sit. I own a real estate investment company and you are a successful architect."

"So what happened to Rachel? You didn't mention him wanting to get away from her."

"Apparently after she had the baby, she suffered from postpartum depression or psychosis, or something. They didn't even know what that was back then, much less how to treat it. Everyone just thought she'd gone crazy. She wound up killing herself by jumping off a building."

"That's a very interesting story, Dad, but you still didn't tell me what that has to do with Caroline."

Kenneth leaned even further into the table, momentarily interrupted by the waitress bringing his drink back, and stared at his son with serious, focused eyes. "Peter Callahan's business partner who ruined everything we stood to inherit was Jefferson Fontenot, Caroline's great, great, great, great grandfather. Her dear old dad, Edward Fontenot, still owns the Gulf Coast Import and Trading Company and lives in the plantation house Jefferson built for his son."

Trevor choked on the gulp of water he'd taken. He carefully placed his glass back on the table and swallowed.

"I need you to clarify exactly what this has to do with me. . .just so I'm not confused."

"Once you and Caroline are married, you will legally inherit what she does if her father dies, as long as she is included in his legal last will and testament. If she is included in his inheritance and something happens to him before you're married, you get nothing. If something happens to him after you're married, but she's not in his will, then you get nothing. Now do you see why I've been pushing you to marry her and get her to make nice with her pops?"

"Excuse me? This war you just spoke of between two families was between the Callahan's and the Fontenot's? My future in-laws? You are the reason I even met her." The gross realization of the truth swept over Trevor and he suddenly felt sick to his stomach. "That was planned from the very beginning, wasn't it? You needed me to make her fall in love with me so we would get married and I would 'get a piece of the pie.' Am I right?"

Kenneth smiled, obviously proud of Trevor's ability to put the pieces together, and took another bite of his sandwich. He spoke while chewing, smacking in between sentences. "Absolutely. It's fool proof. Assuming you don't go and screw it up."

"That's why you insisted I send her to Louisiana to make amends with her estranged father." Trevor couldn't believe what he was saying. The pieces were falling into place of a puzzle he didn't want to be a part of and couldn't see a way out of without hurting himself or Caroline. *I'm such a fool.*

Still smiling, Kenneth replied, "And from what I heard this morning, it's working out beautifully. Right?"

Rather than being amused, Trevor was furious. He'd been betrayed by his own father. "Does it not matter to you that I actually love the woman I marry? How could you just assume I would fall for and propose to the one person whose family, from over a century ago I might add, you wanted to get revenge upon?"

"Of course it matters to me, that's why I let you be with her so long and decide to propose on your own before I told you the whole story. It's the patient snake that gets the mouse, you know. If she had dumped you or something, I would have found a way to intervene, but I had no doubt in your skills. You are quite talented with the ladies, I've noticed." He winked at Trevor as he called the waitress over for yet another a drink refill.

Disgusted, Trevor shook his head. Knowing the whole story, it seemed underhanded and sneaky to marry Caroline. "You didn't even know these people, these ancestors you're declaring revenge upon, why do you care what happens to their business or fortune?"

"Because it was our inheritance that their family stole. We deserve to have what the Fontenot's have enjoyed for so long, and only now we are in the position to acquire it. What did you think I was talking about when I mentioned your piece of the pie?"

"I thought. . .I assumed it had something to do with my inheritance from you. A gift you'd give me early as a wedding gift, not some. . .ridiculous revenge plot!" Trevor thrust his hand through his now-unruly hair. "Besides, I'm sure the story has been distorted over time. And this has nothing to do with Caroline or her father." He shook his head in disgust. "I can't believe you've forced me to put her in this position."

"Trevor, you are doing nothing wrong here. You love her, she loves you, you're getting married. The only thing I did was help you two cross paths."

He had a good point. "I just wish you had told me all this sooner."

"Would you have participated then? Probably not."

Trevor thought about it, and his dad was right. If he had known of any possibility that Caroline would get hurt, he would have backed out before things had gone too far. But now he really was in love with and engaged to her. Trevor desperately wanted to spend the rest of his life with her. To wake up next to her every morning. Even more, to go to bed with her every night.

"So what exactly is it you want me to do now?"

"Just make sure that girl marries you. The sooner, the better."

"Dad, I can't just present her with a deadline and say be there or else. Caroline would never go for that."

"Well, you're the man, make her do it."

Once again, Trevor rolled his eyes at his pig of a father. "Dad, it doesn't quite work like that. Caroline is a very intelligent, strong-willed, independent woman. If I tried to make her do something like that, she'd throw my ring back in my face and tell me to get lost. I'll take care of it. I just need some time to digest this new. . .enlightening information."

"Good. That's what I like to hear."

"There's only one major thing I don't understand. For one thing, Edward Fontenot is in perfect health, so I don't see him dying any time soon. Anyway, he has two other children and a much younger wife. I'm sure they are also included in his will. How do you plan to get past them?"

Kenneth stared into his cup and shook the ice around. "Yeah, when I learned about them, it created a few speed bumps in my plan. The kids aren't biological, so it shouldn't be too much of a problem. Don't worry about the minor details, I'll handle that part. I'll take care of them and Edward Fontenot. I've already spoken to his wife and she's ready."

Trevor nearly jumped out of his seat. "What! *You* are the reason she called me and stirred up so much trouble? Do you know what you almost caused me to do?"

Kenneth glared, speaking slowly and quietly. A warning. "Easy, boy. Don't you raise your voice to me. I did what I had to do to handle the situation. I knew you wouldn't go down there and handle things if you didn't have a good reason."

"I almost ruined everything! If Caroline wasn't so understanding and forgiving, I very well could have."

"What in Pete's name did she have to forgive you for? She's the one who can't keep her legs closed! If anything, she should be begging you for forgiveness!"

That was all Trevor could stand. He stood and tossed a twenty dollar bill on the table. "I watched you physically and verbally abuse Mom my entire life. I will not stand around and allow you to talk about my fiancée in that manner. This lunch is over."

"Trevor. . .sit down. Don't you dare walk away from me, boy. I'm not finished talking to you," Kenneth warned.

"No, Dad. I'm done taking orders. You're on your own for revenge. Leave Caroline and me out of this."

Trevor walked out and didn't look back. Even if she had done something wrong while in Louisiana, it didn't give his dad the right to insult her—his future wife, the mother of his future child. . .or children, if she had her way. Regardless, his underhanded father tampered with Trevor's family. He had to find a way to protect his own investment from Kenneth Callahan.

THIRTY-THREE

Caroline clung tightly to the journal Cade found beneath the floorboard. She hadn't looked in it yet. She couldn't help but feel she was invading someone's privacy. However, Rachel had invaded her dreams, so it seemed only fair. The click of heels neared just outside the door. She quickly tucked the journal under the covers. April peeked around the door, and Caroline moaned in dread.

"Hello, daughter."

Caroline scoffed. "One would first have to be a mother to have a daughter."

April's indigo eyes narrowed, and for an instant she looked positively evil. "If you knew what was good for you, you'd watch how you spoke to me."

"What do you want, April?"

"Don't mind me, I was just checking to make sure you didn't have any other guys hidden in your bed again."

Eddie silently walked up behind April, but Caroline did not shift her focus from her stepmother. "Sorry to disappoint you. If I see any I'll be sure to send them to your room so you can accommodate them like you so willingly offered Trevor. Do you need to steal my phone again or do you have his number memorized?"

"It's too bad he didn't take me up on that offer. I could show him how a real woman treats her man."

"Really, April? Perhaps you could use those skills on your husband. I wouldn't mind experiencing that myself."

April winced and glared, knowing Caroline had provoked her nasty confession.

"Hey, Daddy," Caroline grinned wide. "Great to see you. Your timing is impeccable. April was just leaving."

April huffed, spun on her heel, and bumped into Eddie on her way out hardly fazing him.

"Hey, kiddo, how ya feelin'?"

"I'm okay."

"I'm glad to see you still have your wits about you." He nodded his head toward the direction April had retreated.

"What is her problem? Why does she hate me so much?"

"Don't let it bother you. She's upset with me because I added you as a beneficiary in my will. She'll get over it."

Caroline's eyebrows shot up. "Wow, you added me to your will? That's kind of a big deal, huh?"

"Sweetheart, *you* are kind of a big deal." His smile reached his bright eyes. "You are my daughter, my only biological child, my baby. I've missed out on the first quarter of your life, and that is something that will haunt me until the day I die. I love you. You deserve it as much as Claire and Remy. April's just mad because she signed a prenuptial agreement. If anything happens to me, then you, Claire, and Remy will get more of my inheritance than she will."

Caroline failed to hold back her amusement. She burst out in laughter and covered her mouth. Eddie laughed aloud and leaned down to kiss her cheek. "I did have a reason for coming to visit you. I thought you may be bored, so I brought you some of the old Fontenot photo albums to look through. I can go over them with you and point people out if you'd like. I don't know every bit of our family history, but I know most of it."

Caroline perked up. "You must have been reading my mind. That is exactly what I would love to do. I can't wait to see pictures."

"This is the oldest of the albums." He settled in the bed next to her and opened the ancient album. "I figured we would start with the oldest of the ancestors we have pictures of and work our way to the current ones. Is that okay?"

"That's perfect."

The first yellowed, sepia-toned photograph was of three people. "This is Jefferson and Madeline Fontenot with Jackson when he was about ten years old. Jefferson was my great, great, great grandfather."

"Cade would call him your G3 grandfather." Caroline said.

"Hmm. That's much easier to say. I'll keep that in mind." Eddie turned the page and her heart leapt into her throat with the next picture—a wedding portrait, and the woman in it looked just like Caroline, only a fuller, curvier model. "This is my G2 grandfather, Jackson, and his wife, Rachel." Eddie ran his finger along the edge of the photo, lost in thought, before he spoke again. "Rachel's story is a very interesting, very sad story. I never knew her personally, and I'm not sure why, but she holds a special place in my heart."

"I look just like her."

Eddie grinned. "Yes, you certainly do. I used to think I looked like her. . .until I saw you." On the opposite page was a single portrait of Rachel. "I think she may have been pregnant with my great grandfather,

Joseph, in this picture. The story goes, she got pregnant on their honeymoon."

"She's so young." She knew the answer to the question she was about to ask, but wanted to hear what he had to say about it. "Why was her story sad?"

His eyes fell to the picture as he spoke. "All I know is what I was told, but she was a beautiful, vibrant and caring woman. She went out of her way to help anyone in need, and she was very smart. Apart from Rachel and my dad, longevity was prevalent in the Fontenot family. I was fortunate to know my great grandparents well into my adolescence. My great grandpa used to say his father would tell him she was a spitfire and anyone who crossed her had to deal with her wrath. Her story is sad because it's believed she developed severe depression after the birth of Joseph and couldn't deal with it."

"Postpartum depression is no joke, for sure."

Eddie pursed his lips together and focused on the picture. "Yeah, but they didn't even know what that was back then. They'd put people in the asylum for any random thing, so I guess she was lucky in a sense. She could've been locked away."

"What did she do instead?" Caroline knew the story from her dreams but wanted to hear what everyone else thought had happened to Rachel.

"Supposedly she closed herself up in her room and slowly began to go crazy. She became paranoid and harmful to herself. She eventually jumped out of the window of this very room and hit her head on a statue." He tilted his head thoughtfully. "Ironically, it's the same statue you hit your head on in the duck pond." Eddie lovingly caressed the side of her face and smoothed her hair. "Thank goodness it wasn't the same outcome."

Caroline's jaw dropped. "Wait, it was the same statue? Why was it in the duck pond?"

"After Rachel's death, Jackson couldn't stand the sight of it, but he also didn't feel comfortable throwing away a statue of the Virgin Mary, so he had it stored in one of the outbuildings. A few years ago when I had the duck pond remodeled, Beau had found the statue in the shed behind his cabin. He was doing the landscaping and asked if I wanted him to use it in the design. I didn't see any reason not to, so I told him to go ahead." He looked at the bandages wrapped around her head. "Now I wish I'd told him otherwise."

"Oh, Dad, you can't blame yourself for this. I tripped and fell backwards over a rock. It was my own clumsy fault, nobody else's." She studied his face, his worried scowl, and changed the focus.

"So do you believe Rachel killed herself?"

"I wouldn't know. I wish I could have known her. From the descriptions I heard growing up, she didn't sound like the type to do such a thing. I want to believe she didn't, but there's no way to be sure. Why else would she go flying out the window?" He chuckled, "You might have inherited your clumsiness from her. She could have accidentally leaned too far to look at something and fallen rather than jumped."

"Ha, ha. Very funny. I wasn't clumsy until I came down here." She turned the page and saw a group of men, two young and two old. "Who are these guys?"

"This is Jefferson and Jackson Fontenot with their business partners Peter and George Callahan."

"Huh! Callahan! That's Trevor's last name. What a strange coincidence." By now the crazy parallelism of everything no longer surprised her. It seemed to surround her family.

Eddie's brow furrowed. "Yeah. . .strange."

Something seemed familiar about the one he called George, but she couldn't figure it out. He looked like a decent, handsome man in the picture. It could have been the coincidence in the name, or the square jaw, but Caroline could swear George slightly resembled Trevor.

The next page bore a picture of a very pregnant Rachel. Beautiful with hair a lot like Caroline's. The picture was black and white, but her long, thick hair seemed lighter, more red than auburn, and wavy. Caroline knew exactly what shade Rachel's hair was from seeing her in the dreams, which meant she must dream in color. That's pretty cool.

Rachel had the same features Caroline shared with her dad. She and Eddie both looked like her. Maybe that's why Rachel held a special place in his heart. Eddie turned the page to a portrait of Jackson, Rachel and baby Joseph. Though in those days nobody smiled for pictures, Rachel wore a smirk, and they really seemed happy. The next few pages were pictures of Jefferson and Madeline with their grandchild, the whole family, just Joseph and other random photographs. But there was one picture. . .chills flurried from her head to her toes.

The candid shot of three men in an office setting shouldn't have shocked her. Jefferson behind the desk, Jackson on one side and she guessed George stood on the other side. But George's left hand was heavily wrapped with gauze.

"Caroline, what's wrong? You've been staring at that picture forever. I think you may have even stopped breathing. Are you okay?"

"Yeah, I'm fine. I was just wondering what happened to this guy's hand. What was his name again?"

"George Callahan. I'm not sure exactly what happened. I never heard the story behind that."

"What's the story with George? He was a business partner?"

"Well, the way I heard it was, he and Jackson were supposed to take over the business Jefferson and Peter owned as partners. Peter died fairly young of pneumonia, leaving the entire company to Jefferson. He intended to let Jackson and George take over the company, but supposedly George was very jealous of Jackson's relationship with Rachel. When the two of them got married and had a baby, George couldn't handle seeing them together as a family, so he moved up north. The company stayed here in Louisiana and was kept within the Fontenot family."

Caroline knew better, but now wasn't the time to try and explain. "Do you own the company now? What's it called?"

"Gulf Coast Import and Trading Company. I own it, but I have other people that manage it for me. I mostly handle the paperwork and legal matters of the company. You know, the fun stuff."

"That's awesome. To still be successfully owning and operating a company that has been handed down for so many generations. Wow, that's just. . .awesome."

"I don't think I had much of a choice in the matter. My dad didn't ask me what I wanted to be when I grew up. He just told me what I needed to do and taught me everything he knew about it. Luckily for me, I enjoyed it."

They looked through all the rest of the albums, and Caroline learned everything she could about each of her ancestors, including her grandparents who had passed away from a freak accident six years ago. He didn't disclose how they died and she didn't want to pry. Otherwise, Eddie was a wealth of information. Caroline felt more connected to him and this place than ever before. Now very tired, and her head aching from holding it up for so long, Eddie recognized her need for rest and closed up the family history lesson for the evening. He gave her some pain medicine, and she instantly drifted into a dizzy, exhausted stupor.

From the corner of the room, Caroline watched Rachel try on several different dresses. She had difficulty fastening each of them around her waist. Rachel cinched the latest dress and turned sideways to look at her belly in the dressing table mirror. She ran her hands down around the barely noticeable bump. Rachel's shoulders slumped and she began crying.

A baby's cries echoed from down the hall. Swiping her tears Rachel rushed to her closet and put on another dress. The dress resembling a nightgown fit loosely and hid her belly well. Caroline guessed that was the idea.

Just as she spun to the door, a small dark-haired woman with her hair high in a severe bun appeared with a baby cradled in her arms.

"He just woke up from a nap, and I believe he is hungry, Mrs. Fontenot."

"Thank you, Ms. Marianne. I'll take him now."

"Yes, ma'am. I'll be downstairs if you need assistance with anything."

Rachel held the baby up to look at him, and she smiled. "Well, hello there, Mr. Joseph. My beautiful boy. Momma's so happy you woke up from your nap. Are you hungry? Are you ready to nurse?" She sat in a rocking chair by the window and she fed baby Joseph, cooing with a content, satisfied grin. She genuinely seemed happy.

Caroline learned about postpartum depression in school, and this woman did not have the symptoms. She softly hummed a lullaby to Joseph while he nursed. Much like the baby, Rachel's soothing voice relaxed Caroline. "It was him, you know?" Rachel said.

Caroline had an eery feeling Rachel wasn't just talking to her infant, but to her.

"He violated me and caused me to be with this child growing in my womb. How could I possibly hate something so innocent and precious growing within me?" Tears flowed in streams down her cheeks. "I will love it as if it was Jackson's own blood and I will never tell anyone who the baby's father really is."

Her gaze brimmed with love over baby Joseph. "It will be your baby brother or sister, and we will love you both." She looked out the window. "Someday that horrible man will have to stand before judgment for the crimes he's committed. Someday he will pay for what he's done, but I'll be damned before I let an innocent child suffer the consequences of his jealous rage. I will love this baby with all my heart. I will. That evil mongrel will never know."

Joseph finished eating, and she cuddled him up on her shoulder to burp him. She hummed the same soothing lullaby as she rocked him to sleep.

Caroline awoke to Cade caressing her face with the back of his hand.

"Hey, sweet girl. How are you feeling?"

Her mouth was incredibly dry, Caroline's tongue stuck to her palate. She managed to form a single word. "Parched." She licked her lips, but, with her tongue so dry, she may as well have rubbed cotton on them.

Cade smiled and handed her a glass of ice cold water. She gulped it down and handed it back to him. He went to the dressing table and refilled the glass from a pitcher. "Man, you came prepared. Was I catching flies or something?"

He chuckled. "No, your mouth was closed."

He sat back on the bed beside her. "You were dreaming again, weren't you?"

"Yes, how'd you know that?"

"You were talking in your sleep. You said Rachel's name a few times and 'Baby Joseph' once or twice. Just before you woke up you hummed what sounded like a lullaby."

Caroline was embarrassed. Singing had never been her strong suit. The only way anyone would ever hear her sing is if they overheard her in the shower. "Me. . .singing. I hope you listened carefully 'cause that's the last time you'll ever hear that again."

He smiled. "You have a lovely voice. I don't know why you don't realize that. So what was your dream about this time?"

"Oh, Cade, it was so sad. I was in Rachel's room as a spectator this time, watching her stress over something to wear. I saw her rubbing her pregnant belly, and assumed it was Joseph, the baby she had with Jackson, my G3 grandfather. Then I heard a baby crying, and a lady brought him to her so she could feed him. I heard her talking to herself about being pregnant while she nursed him. She'd been raped, and the baby was the result. Cade, she was pregnant when she died and nobody knew."

"Who raped her? Whose baby was it?"

"I'm not certain, but I have a good idea. I saw a picture of a man in the old albums my dad showed me. He had his left hand bandaged just like the creep that's been chasing Rachel in all my dreams. I think it was a man named George Callahan."

Cade abruptly stood up. "Callahan? Like. . .Trevor Callahan?"

"Yeah, I thought the same thing at first. But it's just a coincidence. Trevor's family is from New York, not Louisiana."

Unconvinced, Cade didn't press the issue. "Are you hungry? Do you want me to bring you something to eat?"

"You know, I feel like I've been in this bed forever. I would really love to get up and walk. Would you help me walk downstairs so I can sit at a real table and eat?" She was glad her doctor had sent a nurse this morning to remove that disgusting catheter, or there was no way she'd be able to do this. How embarrassing.

"I think that's a great idea. Let's get you up and moving."

They took the stairs with caution, Cade holding on to her tightly. Despite her shaky legs, it felt good to walk around and get the blood flowing. And she didn't get dizzy once. They ate lunch while Delia and Delphine entertained them with their quick wit and humor.

Cade helped her back up to her room and settled comfortably in bed. "If you're feeling up to it," he said, "I would like to take you out this weekend. Are you interested?"

"Out? You mean, out of this house? Into civilization? Are you kidding me? I'm very interested. Let's do it! Do you think the doctor will allow it?"

"Well, he said to keep you in bed for at least a week and then slowly get you up and moving. It's only Tuesday, so you have all week. I think as long as you felt up to it, he probably wouldn't mind. I want to take you up to New Orleans and show you around the French Quarter."

Caroline hardly contained her excitement. "New Orleans! I've never been there. Do we have to wait until the weekend?"

Cade laughed. "Yes, ma'am. I don't want to rush your recovery and cause you to have another accident. This will just give you something to look forward to." Cade leaned in and kissed her cheek. "I've gotta run. I'll see you later, beautiful."

When he closed the door, Caroline eagerly pulled the journal out from under the covers. What did Rachel have to say from the grave? She gently traced her finger along the scroll design on the front of the leather journal and carefully opened it to the first page to Rachel's perfect script.

These are the personal thoughts

of

Rachel Caroline Fontenot

Beginning in June of the year 1885

Caroline's hands shook as she carefully turned the page, stepping back in time. The first page must have been written when Rachel and Jackson had gotten home from their honeymoon. She began this journal right after she got married, and there were several entries from different days, or possibly weeks, on one page.

Today was a glorious day. My dashing new husband and I enjoyed our honeymoon cavorting around the French Quarter in New Orleans. It is a dreadfully grand city. I shall greatly enjoy hearing my new name.

I had an encounter with Jackson's business partner, George Callahan, today. He is a considerably rugged fellow. He fancies me even as a married woman.

His temper is quick, and often he appears to be terribly angry. He is quite mysterious and dark. It concerns me, but I will not speak of this to Jackson as they are friends.

Mr. Callahan approached me today. He is appallingly jealous of my relationship with Jackson. I'm afraid he is capable of more than I realized. I shall strongly attempt to avoid him from this time further.

Clearly, George made no attempt of keeping his feelings secret from Rachel. Had Jackson known how George felt about his wife? In one of her dreams Caroline had overheard an argument between Rachel and Jackson after her assault. He seemed to know who she spoke about and Jackson wanted to kill him. Had Jackson ever confronted George about raping his wife? If that had been Trevor, he would have already committed murder in the first. Caroline turned the page and continued reading.

Today was a blessed day. I cannot be certain, but I believe I am with child. I have been ill and quite dragged out. My clothing is snug, and, at times, I instinctively touch my abdomen as if to comfort my unborn child. God has truly smiled upon us.

I felt beautiful today at church as several people congratulated Jackson and me on our upcoming child. I happily allowed the children in my class to feel the baby move. I am eager to meet the little angel within me.

Mr. Callahan came to the house today. I assumed he was meeting with Jackson. As I walked past them, I could feel his eyes on me. It made me feel frightfully uncomfortable. I spoke to him regarding his ill father, Peter. He seemed distraught and told me his father's health is dwindling because of the pneumonia. I felt sad for him and requested he send my well-wishes to his father.

I finally met the perfectly handsome little boy that occupied my womb for so long. Joseph Beauregard Fontenot was born on the 9th day of February in the year of 1886. He is perfect in every way imaginable. I never knew love until I gazed into the precious eyes of my son.

Caroline smiled as the desire to have a family fluttered in her chest. She hated that Trevor only wanted one child but still hoped he would someday change his mind. Maybe after he held their first child in his arms and looked into the baby's eyes, he'd decide it was worth having more children.

It's been some time since I've written last. Joseph has been keeping me busy, and I have enjoyed watching him grow and develop. He is three months old now and eats frequently. I greatly appreciate the help I receive from Ms. Marianne. She has allowed me to rest and has taught me a great deal about babies. She is truly a blessing.

Today was a horrible, wretched day. I decided to take a walk and breathe the fresh springtime air. I was unexpectedly approached by Mr. Callahan. He tried to kiss me, so I struck his face and ran away from him. This angered him, and he chased me into the woods. He violated me beyond words. He ripped the garments from my body, and I experienced the worst pain of my life as he forced himself upon me against my will.

He did to me what only a husband should do to his wife. I am severely distraught and afraid for my life and that of my family. I'm not certain what he was talking about, but he mentioned something of Jackson and Jefferson double-crossing him. I pray for the safety of my loved ones.

Caroline tried to imagine what that must have been like for Rachel. Having such a traumatic thing happen and not being able to tell anyone about it, then finding out she was pregnant as a result. Caroline's first dream only led her through the prelude of the crime, she never saw the climax. What she did see was intense, and to truly understand was to experience the trauma herself. That, Caroline prayed, would never happen.

She flipped to the back of the journal to see if Rachel had been able to scribble anything in her rush to hide it before she died. The last written page was in the middle of the journal, signifying a precious life cut short—too short. Caroline's eyes filled with tears as she read the emotional last words of her great, great, great grandmother.

This will be my last entry. George Callahan has drugged and captured me and informed me of his immediate intentions to end my life. He said people will believe my death was by my own hands. But this is my final testament. I love my husband, son, and unborn child too much to take my own life. He doesn't realize it, but he will be taking the life of his own flesh and blood that has yet to walk upon this Earth. I pray that God protect my family and have mercy on his soul.

George Callahan is a cold-blooded murderer.

THIRTY-FOUR

Caroline's suspicions had been right. George Callahan, the man with the bloody bandage in all of her dreams, had been the one who raped and impregnated Rachel, and eventually the one who drugged and killed her. Caroline wished she knew more about this horrible man. Whatever became of him? Everyone thought her death a suicide because nobody ever found the journal that held the truth. That's why Rachel was so intent on haunting Caroline's dreams to help her find it.

Why would it matter now? Why, after all these years, does she care that anyone knows the truth, and why choose Caroline?

She hated to think anyone with the same last name as Trevor could be a cold-blooded killer. The Callahan name had become special to her. Now that she'd read Rachel's journal and learned the truth about George Callahan, she had difficulty saying the name out loud without thinking about what happened to Rachel.

What had he meant about being double-crossed? Rachel hadn't known anything about it either. But Jackson knew. In the dream, after she told him about George and what he had said, Jackson's tone immediately became apologetic for not protecting her.

Eddie said George left Louisiana because his insane jealousy couldn't allow him to see Jackson, Rachel and Joseph together as a happy family. What if there was more? If he'd known Rachel carried his child, would he have stayed? And not killed her? What if Eddie was wrong about why George left everything and everyone he knew and loved? What if George really was double-crossed by Jackson? George didn't leave town because of his jealousy. He left because he didn't want anyone to discover he'd killed Rachel Fontenot. Caroline resolved to research his death. For all she knew, he could be haunting her, too.

That would have to wait. Caroline needed to prepare for her outing to New Orleans.

She and Cade were planning to spend the night in a hotel on Canal Street. To avoid any more unpleasant face-offs with Trevor, Cade was a gentleman and reserved two separate, but adjoining rooms. She didn't plan to tell Trevor about her weekend in the city, but at least this way, if he found out, he couldn't accuse her of anything. Caroline was sure April would do her very best to fill him in on the details.

As she packed the last of her toiletries in her overnight bag, Cade knocked on the door. He held a beautiful bouquet of purple daisies. "Oh, Cade! I love daisies! They're my favorite color, too! Thank you so much, they're breathtaking."

"You're welcome, sweet girl. They pale in comparison to you, but I suppose they'll do." The blood rushed to her face. It was amazing how she could still blush around him even after all they'd been through.

"How are you feeling? Good enough to go on some tours?"

"Oh, yeah. I've been looking forward to this trip all week. I can't wait."

In two hours, they'd arrived, checked in to the hotel, and caught a trolley car for sight-seeing. The majestic homes in the Garden District and the beauty and history of this city fascinated her. All the while, Cade watched her more than the sights. After the streetcar ride, they strolled along the Riverfront to the ferry and the paddleboat.

They meandered through the French Market, and Cade pointed out the Port where Naval ships dock. It had been a while since he'd seen his sister who was stationed on a ship. From the look on his face as he stared at the large Naval ship, he really missed her. Caroline admired Cade's love for his family.

"I almost forgot something," she said. "I promised Claire I would ask you if you have any cousins we could set her up with?"

Cade smiled. "Hmmm. Shouldn't be a problem. My family's huge and I have a ton of cousins. She's beautiful, so I'm sure just about any of them would be interested."

"Well, she wants him to be like you. So, whichever cousin it is, he must be tall, dark, handsome, respectful, thoughtful, sweet, and protective."

He laughed. "She doesn't ask for much, does she?"

"Let me tell you something, Caden Luke, guys like you are hard to come by. If you can find someone like you for Claire, I'd bet money she will end up marrying him."

The hurt flashed in his eyes that she was not choosing to marry him. "I'll see what I can do. She's about to turn seventeen, right? My cousin, Josh, is a lot like me and he's only twenty years old. I think Claire would really like him."

Cade led her to a line of mule-drawn carriages, approaching a beautiful white carriage with a red velvet seat. He held out his hand. "Shall we?"

They stepped up into the carriage as the driver snapped his reins to get the mule moving. She'd never been on a romantic carriage ride and Cade was just the man to show her the beauty of the city. She snuggled in to his arm wrapped around her shoulder and awed at the colorful myriad of street vendors and tourists. Twilight slipped in on a gentle breeze, twinkling lights wrapped in trees and draped on historic buildings blinked on, and distant jazz music mingled with the clopping of the horse's hooves.

Cade twirled his finger in a lock of her hair. She'd never been with anyone who focused on the little things she loved so much. "Thank you," she whispered.

"No, cher. Thank you for allowing me to share this experience with you. I've been happier in the last two months than I've been in the last five years, and it's all because of you. Thank you for saving me from myself." He gently kissed her forehead. She didn't want the romantic moment to ever end. She rested her head on his shoulder and enjoyed the rest of the ride with Cade. . .alone. Too bad they hadn't booked one hotel room. But it was probably a really good thing they hadn't.

The driver dropped them in the heart of the French Quarter near Bourbon Street. Cade, very protective as they navigated through the crowd, was a walking shield of solid muscle as he encased her in his sheltering arms. He blocked, shoved, and averted obstacles with precision, his reflexes unprecedented. Finally, they entered a hoppin' Cajun restaurant. The stage inside rocked Zydeco music, complete with spoons, washboards, and an accordion player. They enjoyed the food and entertainment until Caroline's fatigue finally showed through her façade and they returned to their historic hotel.

Cade joined her in her room as she plopped down in one of the cushy accent chairs. He put on soft jazz music and poured water in two wine glasses.

"Cade, you don't have to drink water just because I have to with my pain meds."

"I don't mind," he said, sitting in the chair beside her. "Spending time like this with you is intoxicating enough."

Unable to resist him any longer, she rose, straddled his legs, and sat in his lap. His eyes grew big and followed her every move. She set her glass on the desk behind him and cradled his face in her hands. Leaning forward, she pressed her lips to his forehead, trailing down to his cheek. His hair was soft under her fingers and she breathed in his musky scent. He shivered under her kiss on his earlobes and she smiled, gently tasting his neck and back up to his cheek where she finally rested her eager mouth on his soft moist lips.

He drew in ragged breaths and his heady response in his return kiss revealed his struggle to hold back. They kissed like lovers, desperate and urgent. His hands grasped her hips and he ran them up her back. Her skin tingled alive under his palms skimming across her breasts until finally clasping her face. He sat up straighter, deepening his kiss as one hand dropped down to her lower back pulling her closer to him. She rocked her hips a little and he released a deep throaty moan. He abruptly pulled away, dropping his head and rested his forehead on her chest.

"Caroline, I. . .can't. I don't want to force you to—"

"You're not forcing me to do anything. I came to you, remember? I'm tired of pretending." She breathed a frustrated sigh. "I thought you would be. . .happy about this."

He raised his eyebrows. "Girl, if you had any idea how much I've been waiting for a moment like this—it's just. . .what I want from you goes deeper than just the physical need. I want you. Believe me, I do. But I want *all* of you. Unfortunately, you're still engaged. I can't allow you to do something that will ruin what you have with Trevor. You obviously love him or you wouldn't still be with him, especially after—well, you just wouldn't still be with him if you didn't want to be."

He brushed the hair from her face and stared deeply into her eyes. "Please, don't be angry with me. I want you. . .every little delicious morsel of you. I want you more than I've ever wanted anyone in my entire life. Please believe me. I want to learn everything about you, every freckle, birthmark, all your ticklish spots. . ." he raised an eyebrow, "your hot spots." She smiled, exhilaration coursing through her with the thought.

"Plus, I want to explore that amazing mind of yours. I want to search your beautiful green eyes until I can see your soul. I love everything about you, Caroline, but I cannot allow myself to do anything else with you until you are with me." Caroline stiffened, embarrassed, and started to climb off of him. He quickly recovered and gripped her hips to stop her.

"Wait, don't get up yet. I'm so sorry, sweet girl. I'm not trying to hurt you, I swear. But I don't want to be the other guy, you know? As long as you're promised to someone else, out of respect for you, myself, and even him, I cannot be the one thing you regret doing in your life."

Her eyes closed. "How embarrassing." She snickered, "So this is what it feels like. I'm usually the one who always has to stop in the heat of the moment and be responsible. Now I understand how disappointing and frustrating it is."

"Oh, believe me, cher, I am definitely hot in the moment. I just can't do this to you right now. I'm sure you are confused enough with everything that's going on with your dad and April, Trevor coming down to surprise you, then falling and cracking your skull. The last thing you need is me complicating things even more."

"I'm not angry with you. If anything, it makes me adore you that much more. If it had been Trevor in your shoes tonight, we'd be making love right now. He would have completely taken advantage of the opportunity without holding back or thinking of anyone but himself."

She slipped off his lap and sat on the side of the bed. "Thank you for respecting me, and yourself, enough to say no. And for keeping me from hating myself in the morning. Thank you for taking care of me and for valuing everything I stand for by being responsible in my moment of weakness." She shook her head in wonderment. "You are, without a doubt, my guardian angel."

"No, love, you're mine."

The next morning they ate breakfast at a cafe that had been in the French Quarter for over a century and enjoyed delicious beignets and cafe au lait. They browsed gift shops along Decatur Street and Jackson Square. Caroline spotted a voodoo shop, but Cade was very adamant about keeping her away from it. She joked about only wanting to find an April doll to stick pins in from time to time. He didn't have much of a sense of humor when it came to voodoo. Strangely enough, that only made Caroline even more curious about the mysterious culture. She dropped the issue—for now.

After a couple of tours they landed back on Decatur Street to have muffuletta sandwiches for lunch. Caroline decided she was officially in love with New Orleans. The overall magic of the city had cast a spell on her, and she was head-over-heels.

"Have you noticed your dad being stressed out?" Cade asked on the drive home. "I mean, any more than usual?"

"Not really, why? I haven't exactly been around him long enough to know what he's like on a regular basis, though. What's up?"

"Has he mentioned anything to you about people harassing him to sell his property?"

Her heart sank. "No! Why? Is he going to sell?" She'd just discovered the beautiful wonderland that belonged to her family and looked forward to visiting on a regular basis, if not living there someday. Assuming, of course, she could talk Trevor into it.

"I don't think he's going to sell if he can help it, but he's had a couple of different companies questioning him about it. Apparently, all the land around his property has been bought up by someone who has plans to build commercial properties and master planned communities. The Fontenot plantation is the only thing stopping the entire area from being a continuous flow of the same type of atmosphere."

Awful news. Terrible. Caroline's mood darkened. "You don't think he'll sell, do you? I mean, you've known him longer than I have, but my impression of him is that he loves that house more than anything."

"He told me, as long as he was alive, nobody would own that property but his family."

That made her feel a little better. Eddie still had youth and good health on his side, as well as the family longevity he'd mentioned. She had no worries of him kicking the bucket anytime soon. "Whoever it is that's pressuring him to sell needs to be kicked in the pocketbook! This is historical property we're talking about here. It has extreme sentimental value. Does that not mean anything to people anymore?" She frowned.

Cade smiled a crooked grin and looked at her from the corner of his eye. "You're cute, you know that?"

"I'm serious. It makes me very angry to think that someone is trying to bully him into selling something that is sacred to him. What kind of selfish, inconsiderate, greedy punk would do such a thing? It's horrible."

"I agree, sweet girl. I totally agree."

Cade didn't speak for the remainder of the drive.

Caroline drifted off to sleep and instantly began dreaming.

Rachel walked, more like floated, toward Caroline from a distance, and she wore the same long white night dress she had on when she died. Caroline couldn't tell where they were. Rachel glowed very brightly, almost backlit, only Caroline could see her face rather than just a silhouette. Her long red hair gently flowed, but there was no breeze. She came closer, and her lips were moving, but Caroline couldn't hear what she was saying. She couldn't hear anything but complete silence.

As she got even closer, Caroline tried to read her lips, and a whispering moan replaced the silence. She made out a few words. Rachel was distraught and seemed to be trying to warn her about something. . .or someone. She could only decipher, "Don't stay," "him," and maybe the word "hurt" in there somewhere, but what she said after that, Caroline had no idea. The background noises, and the haunting, overlapping whispers, didn't help.

"Rachel, I can't understand you." Caroline shook her head. "What are you trying to tell me? I can't hear you." Rachel frowned and looked very sad. She stretched her left arm out reaching for Caroline, but her hand suddenly disappeared and Rachel became frightened. Then, as if someone yanked a rope wrapped around her waist, she flew backward, reaching out for Caroline with both arms now and disappeared into the light.

Caroline gasped as she woke from the strange dream. Cade chuckled. "Welcome back. Did you have a nice nap?"

As she caught her breath, she whispered, "No, not really. Where are we?"

"We are about twenty miles from home. Are you okay? Rough dream? No snakes, I hope." He smiled at his little joke.

"No, no snakes. Just a creepy ghost dream. It was really strange. I don't really even know how to describe it."

"Do you want to try?"

"No, not particularly." The dream was a warning, a red flag, a flashing buoy in a foggy harbor. The image of Rachel snatched backwards and disappearing completely unsettled Caroline. What was that supposed to mean? She hated cryptic dreams. Don't stay. Don't stay where, here in Louisiana? Don't stay in Chicago? Him. Him who? Trevor, Cade, Eddie? What if she meant George's ghost? What was the whole hand thing about, anyway? Caroline let out a frustrated sigh.

Rachel's dreams all had a meaning, eventually leading Caroline to the journal. This dream had to have some significance, too. But what?

When they pulled up in the drive Caroline hopped out of the car and up to the porch before Cade had completely gotten out of his seat. She had gone straight into the kitchen to get a glass of ice water. Cade brought in her bag and carried it up to her room.

"Caroline," he called. "You need to come upstairs. Now."

She rushed as quickly as she could manage up the stairs to the third floor bedroom. When she walked into her room, all the air vanished from her lungs."

On her bed sat a rigid Trevor. . .glaring at Cade.

THIRTY-FIVE

"Surprise. Again." Trevor looked less than thrilled.

"Trevor, hi." Caroline clutched her chest, out of breath from running up the stairs.

He nodded toward her overnight bag in Cade's hands. "Am I interrupting?"

Cade's stone-cold, guarded expression didn't fool her. He was wound tight and ready to snap.

She leaned against the door frame to catch another deep breath. "No, we were just getting back."

"From?" Trevor was surprisingly calm.

"Cade took me to New Orleans to show me around. You know, before I have to come back to Chicago."

Trevor forced a smile. "I see. Before you have to come back."

Cade set the bag down and stepped closer to Caroline. "Trevor, nothing ha—"

"Stop!" Trevor commanded as he shot to his feet. Fire blazed in his ice blue eyes and he held his hand up to Cade. "I don't want to hear a single word from you," he sneered. "I want Caroline to tell me why she feels she *has* to come back to Chicago instead of wanting to come back. I want to hear it from her mouth."

Caroline swallowed hard. *Why did I say that? I do want to go back to be with Trevor, right?*

"Trevor, I didn't mean it like it sounded. I do want to come back with you, but Cade knew I was tired of being stuck in the house for so long, and he knew I'd never been to New Orleans."

Trevor's frown deepened with confusion. "Why were you stuck in the house?"

Crap! Way to open your big fat mouth. "Well, you see, I fell and hit my head. . .hard. I had a concussion, and the doctor didn't want me up and about too much."

"You had a concussion?" Trevor's brow crinkled with genuine concern, his tone softened. "You didn't think that would be something I would want to know about?"

"I didn't see any reason to worry you."

"Sweetheart, I could have come down here to be with you. I could've helped take care of you." He cut his eyes accusingly at Cade.

"I knew you were working and I didn't want to be a burden."

Trevor hugged her tightly. "Baby, you are anything but a burden. We're getting married. In sickness and in health. I want to take care of you."

Trevor's shoulders stiffened just as Kristy entered the room. She stopped cold in her tracks. "O-kay. I've obviously interrupted you guys. I'll be leaving now."

Hurt and angry, Trevor stepped back and looked at Caroline. "You called Kristy? Nice, Caroline. You called your best friend for help before you called your fiancé. What does that say about me?"

Kristy couldn't escape from that room fast enough.

Cade shifted uncomfortably. "I'm gonna go. . .do something. I'll let you guys talk."

"Trev, don't be like that. It wasn't a big deal. I just needed someone who could come down here for a few weeks and not have to take off work."

"Caroline, for something as serious as a concussion, I would take off work. I especially want to know about it at least!" Trevor pulled her to the bed and sat down beside her. "I miss you like crazy. I can't stand not being able to see you every day, or at least several times a week. I miss getting to talk to you on a regular basis and kissing you whenever I want." He kissed the side of her face trailing his lips down to her jaw. "I'm ready to be married to you so we can be together all the time," he whispered. "I'm ready to be the one who takes care of you, Caroline."

She grabbed his hand and looked down at their entwined fingers. "I miss you, too."

He lifted her chin to kiss her. He smelled so good, and his mouth tasted of cinnamon. His kiss reminded her how much she loved him. Trevor rested his forehead against hers and spoke with his eyes closed. "Caroline, come back with me. Come back to Chicago with me. You don't have to stay here any longer since you and your dad are cool now. I want you back home with me where you belong."

Where you belong. She flinched. Those were the same words Cade had used when she arrived home from the hospital. She wasn't sure exactly where she belonged anymore. "Trevor, I'm not. . .I can't just leave. I have to say goodbye to everyone."

"That's okay. I'm not due to fly out until tomorrow evening anyway. You'll have some time to say your goodbyes."

The ground crumbled from beneath her. "I just don't know. I'm already settled here. Kristy's still here, my car is here. . .it's so quick."

"It's not a difficult decision, C. I want you back with me. I should've brought you back with me last time when you offered. I love you, and it's killing me to be away from you this much. When I asked you to come down here for the summer, I wasn't expecting you to reconnect with your dad so quickly. I didn't realize the difficulty I would have being away from you. Let's go back and get married now."

Caroline's eyes nearly popped out of her head. "What? Now? What are you talking about? That's. . .that's insane! I don't have a dress, we don't have a church reserved, I'm not finished with school. This is all too rushed. You know I can't deal with deadlines, Trevor."

"It'll be easy, C. We don't need a church, we can have a small intimate ceremony next to the scenic lake where we had our picnic. We could have a Justice of the Peace perform the ceremony, and it'll all be done before school starts. That way you won't have anything to worry about during your last semester because you'll already be married. No wedding plans to worry about. No stress over our wedding night."

His eyes flamed with passion and he softly brushed her hair behind her shoulder to kiss her neck. She hoped with all her might he wouldn't notice the small stitched area where her head had been shaved. He whispered in her ear, his hot breath kicking her heart rate into high speed. "The virginity issue will be solved, the sex will be great, and you'll be able to completely focus on your studies. It makes perfect sense." He stole her breath in a vigorous kiss. He pulled back, excitement lit his face. She felt guilty for not reciprocating his enthusiasm.

It did make sense. But she didn't like that her virginity was an issue. Still, he did have a point about having it all over with, she only wished she had a little more time before she had to leave.

"Why tomorrow? Give me a week to say my goodbyes."

"Why do you need a week? You have more than twenty-four hours. That should be plenty of time to give your hugs, exchange emails and phone numbers, and say your goodbyes. Everyone important to you lives right here in this house, right?"

Caroline's stomach fell. All but one, but she couldn't say that or Trevor would fly off the handle. No way would Trevor understand her need to say goodbye to Cade. At least not without making her seem like an unfaithful whore again.

He kissed along her jaw and neck, brushing his lips across her thrumming pulse. "Let me take care of you." Good grief, the man was a master at seduction.

"Please, baby. I need you," he whispered.

She smiled. "Okay. Let's do this. . .before I change my mind. I'll say my goodbyes, and we can fly home tomorrow."

Trevor jumped up, scooped her into his arms, and spun her around. It made her smile to see him so happy. It could be her agreement to marry him soon and he saw an end to his continuous sexual frustration, but she preferred to tell herself his happiness stemmed from her coming home with him now rather than waiting six more weeks. Now she had to figure out what to tell everyone.

Kristy was going to have a cow. She'd already told Caroline she wanted to make her wedding dress. Could Kristy come up with something in such a short amount of time? Eddie was going to be disappointed in Caroline leaving sooner than planned. He didn't have a high opinion of Trevor, either. But maybe in time, he would. And Cade. Her heart ached with the very thought of the sadness in his eyes. Ugh. Her head throbbed.

"I'm going downstairs and get another glass of water." She grabbed her pain pills from her bag. "Do you want anything?"

"I'll come with you." He held her hand as she led the way. "I could go for some of this incredible sweet tea I've heard so much about."

Caroline tried to convince herself that she had made the right decision. It really didn't matter if they married in August rather than January, right? She planned to marry him anyway, so what's a few months?

Delia greeted them with a big smile. "Hey, Miss Caroline! I'm so glad you're feelin' better. Your color has come back and you look lovely as always. Me and Delphine was so worried about you."

Caroline rounded her eyes and gave a near-imperceptible shake of her head, stopping Delia before she said too much. She didn't want Trevor to know it was much worse than she'd led him to believe.

Without taking a breath in between, Delia glanced at Trevor and switched the subject with fluid skill. "What can I get y'all?"

Trevor looked at Caroline curiously. Nervous now, she glanced from him to Delia. "Delia. This is my fiancé, Trevor Callahan, and he would like a glass of your delicious sweet tea. I'll just have a glass of water, please."

"Certainly." Delia eyed her suspiciously. "Mr. Callahan and I met briefly the last time he visited, but never officially. Pleasure to see you again, sir. You two can have a seat and I'll bring it right out to you."

"So that's the famous Delia you told me about? She's um. . .nice."

"Yeah, she's the first person I met when I got here. I really like her, and we've become quite good friends. I'm going to miss her."

He squeezed her shoulder. "Don't worry, we'll be back here. I promise."

Caroline was glad to hear it. She assumed he hated this place because the only experiences he'd had here were extremely unpleasant. And since Trevor was waiting for her when she returned from New Orleans, Rachel must have meant for her not to stay in Louisiana or Caroline would hurt him through her undeniable feelings for Cade. She felt better about her decision.

She only hoped Cade would understand. He was the main reason she doubted her decision. Once she married Trevor, she would never again be able to kiss Cade. Truthfully, Trevor would probably do everything in his power to keep her as far away from Cade as possible. And that made her very sad. She didn't want to admit it, but she had fallen in love with Cade. She was in love with two men, and couldn't allow herself to do this to Trevor any longer. After all, she'd loved him first and for longer. It was good that she was leaving early. This way she wouldn't be tempted to make any more reckless decisions, like trying to seduce Cade in a romantic hotel room.

She couldn't ignore the ball of fire in her gut. She was getting married in six weeks. Holy Cow.

"You did what? Caroline! Have you lost your mind?" Kristy took the news just as Caroline expected. "You know, I've heard of people doing crazy things in desperation, but this is low. Even for Trevor."

A twinge of anger stung Caroline. "What is that supposed to mean? Trevor only suggested this. I'm the one who agreed to it. This way I can get the whole wedding thing out of the way so I don't have to worry about it during the semester."

Kristy's tone changed. "Uh-huh. The whole wedding thing, huh? Who are you? Where is my friend who used to dream up lavish wedding details with me? You remember her? The girl I used to look through bridal magazines with and dog ear pages of dresses we liked, the spontaneous girl who despises being pinned down with any sort of deadline. I want that girl back."

Turning her back to Caroline, Kristy peered through the window and quietly asked, "What about Cade?"

"What about him? He's just a friend."

Kristy whirled around. "Oh, whatever! I've known you for a long time. I've seen you around different guys before. When you're with Cade, you are the Caroline I know. When you're with Trevor, you're. . .different. You're quieter, not your bubbly, quirky, sarcastic self. It's like you're afraid to say something that Trevor may not like. You seem happier and comfortable around Cade. You can be yourself around him instead of having to put on some kind of act. It's obvious you and Cade have serious chemistry. Are you going to just turn your back on that and pretend it never existed?"

"I've only known Cade for six weeks, Kristy. That's hardly long enough to learn anything. How could I possibly be in love with someone I barely know? We're just good friends, that's all. I love Trevor and we will be very happy together. It's his ring I have on my finger and him I'm going to marry. Everything will be perfectly fine."

"Who are you trying to convince, Caroline?" Kristy scoffed and stared out the window again. "Me or yourself?"

"How about my dress?" Caroline suggested hopefully.

Kristy whirled around with her arms crossed. "Are you serious? You still want me to make your dress. . .in six weeks?" Her body language rejected the whole prospect.

"Well, if it'll be too much trouble, I'm sure I could buy one off the rack. I don't want to be a pain." Caroline hoped her reverse psychology would work, but Kristy's stoic expression and angry stance made Caroline nervous.

Finally she grinned and shook her head. "You're always a pain. But I love you, anyway. Of course I will make your dress for you. It won't be easy, but I will somehow manage to make you a fabulous gown. I just think you're making a mistake by rushing into this."

Caroline hugged her and squealed. "Thank you so much! I love you, too. You will be my maid of honor, right?"

"I'd better be! Who else can put up with your kind of crazy?" She hugged Caroline and backed up to look at her. "You're my best friend and I am here for you. . .for whatever you need. That includes smacking some sense into you."

"Good. I hoped you would say that." Caroline hesitated before asking another favor. "Since my accident, I don't think I can handle being in a car for that long, so I'm flying back with Trevor tomorrow. However, I still need to get my car back up to Illinois. Is there any way I can get you to drive it up there for me?"

Kristy forged a smile, clearly not excited about driving either. "Sure, C. I will get your car back to Chicago. Where are you staying when you go back? Not with Trevor, I hope?"

Caroline hadn't thought about that. She'd given up her apartment assuming she'd be here all summer. "I don't know. I didn't think about that part."

Kristy rolled her eyes and sighed. "It seems you didn't think about much at all before agreeing to this craziness. Here, take my key, you can stay at my place until you get hitched. Or maybe until you come to your senses. I'll be up in a few days to start on your dress."

"Thanks, girl. I don't know what I would do without you." Caroline hugged her again. "Now I guess I need to go break the news to everyone else."

Delia and Delphine were the only ones home and when Caroline walked in, Delia's eyes shifted behind her to see if anyone followed. "Is your fiancé with you?"

"No, he's getting my car checked out and an oil change. Why?"

"Honey, he is definitely a looker! He's beautiful! Sorry if I almost blew the whistle on you earlier, boo. I didn't know he wasn't in the loop."

"He's in the loop now, I just didn't fill him in on all the graphic details."

She raised her eyebrows. "Uh-huh. You can get away with that now, but once he's got his meat hooks in you, there will be no more hidin' from him. Men like him don't allow secrets."

"What do you mean, men like him? What kind of man is that, exactly?"

Delia sensed her defensive tone and back pedaled. "Oh, nothing, Miss Caroline. He just seems like the type that likes to know what's going on around him, that's all."

"What is it that everyone else sees in Trevor that I don't see?"

"Aww, Miss Caroline. Don't worry about everyone else." Delia patted Caroline's hand. "Maybe what you should be asking yourself is, what it is that you see in him that no one else *can* see. That's what matters."

Caroline relaxed. That made her feel a little better. "Thanks, D. I appreciate it."

She set a glass of tea in front of Caroline. "Anytime, boo. Anytime."

Caroline stared at the ice and she wiped the dripping condensation from the glass, stalling. "I came down here to tell y'all something."

Both women looked at her with concern. "I'm heading back to Chicago tomorrow with Trevor. We're getting married at the end of August."

Delphine's mouth dropped open. Delia nudged her, and she closed it. Delia spoke up first. "Congratulations. That's great news. We'll miss you, but we're glad to have gotten to know you this summer." Her expression turned serious. "Have you, uh. . .have you told Beau yet?"

"No. Not yet. Not something I'm looking forward to. He's not going to be happy about it, I'm sure."

"Oh, he's a big boy. I'm sure he'll be okay. Just make sure you tell him goodbye before you go. I imagine if you didn't, he *would* be upset about that." Delia went back to cleaning.

"Right, I'm headed over there now."

Caroline had never dreaded anything so much in her life.

Please, God, give me some strength.

THIRTY-SIX

Torn between running and crawling to the cabin, Caroline dreaded the confrontation. Part of her wanted to hurry up and get there to spend as much time with Cade as possible. But the other part wanted to put off telling him goodbye. He was going to be very upset with her for leaving early. She knocked three times. She waited, remembering the last time she stood at his doorstep when the snake slithered up behind her, then Henry slithered up shortly after. She shuddered and knocked again. No answer.

Just in case he hadn't heard the first two times, she knocked one more time and checked the knob to find it locked. Her eyes welled up with tears. She patted her pockets for a pen to leave a note and came up empty. She didn't know when or if she would ever see him again. With tears streaming down her face, she headed back to the house. Why was she so upset about leaving? She should be excited. She dreaded coming down here, and now she dreaded leaving.

Maybe once she returned to Chicago surrounded by familiarity, things would fall back into place. Once she was exclusively with Trevor again, perhaps her memories from the bayou would be distant. Only, she didn't really want them to be.

She stepped from the trail out on to the lawn. Her dad's truck was in the driveway. She drew in a deep breath. "Here's goes nothing. Time to put your big girl panties on, Caroline." She found him at the table reading the paper. "Hey, Dad, can I talk to you for a second?"

He looked up with a big smile. "Sure, sweetheart. What's on your mind? Did you and Beau have fun in New Orleans this weekend?"

"Well, yes, we had a great time. I love the city."

"That's great. I thought you would."

"Okay, I'm just gonna spit this out. Trevor came in to surprise me, and I'm flying back to Chicago with him tomorrow."

He didn't hide his disappointment. "Oh, Caroline, is everything okay? Are you not enjoying your time here?"

"No, it's not that. Trevor misses me, and, well, I miss him, too. So I'm going back early. Also, he—we have decided to go ahead and get married before school starts." He sat expressionless without uttering a word. Caroline nervously shifted her weight. "Say something."

He held her gaze for a few quiet moments before his focus returned to the newspaper still in his hands. His emotionless reply hurt as he spoke without looking at her. "Congratulations. When's the big day?"

"August twenty-seventh. It's in Chicago, will you be able to come?"

He folded the paper and stood placing both hands on her shoulders. "I wouldn't miss the opportunity to walk with you at your wedding and give you away. Of course, I would much rather be giving you away to marry someone from down here. . .say, a handsome young gardener I know who is crazy about you. But I will do my very best to support whatever decision you make."

Her gaze dropped to her fidgeting hands. "Well, that's good. Because I've already made my decision. I'll see you in Chicago in six weeks then. I'll email you the details and directions when I have them."

She sprinted up the stairs before she started crying again. He made her sound uncertain and indecisive, but she was engaged to Trevor before ever coming down here. She loved him and keeping her promise to marry him was the right thing to do. In her room, she feverishly packed her things, uselessly fighting back tears when Kristy walked in.

"Caroline, what's wrong?"

She wiped her eyes and faced Kristy. "Cade wasn't home. I need you to do me a favor and tell him why I had to leave."

Kristy held her hands up in protest. "Oh, no you don't! I'm not gonna be the one who breaks his heart. You're gonna have to do that all on your own. Haven't you heard of people killing the messenger? And he seems very capable of doing just that."

Caroline couldn't stop the flow of tears. "Please, Kristy, I can't just leave without letting him know something. I don't want to leave a cheesy 'Dear John' letter. Can you just relay a message for me, please? Just tell him I had an amazing time this weekend, and I appreciate everything he's done for me. Tell him I care deeply for him, and that's why I'm leaving."

Kristy stared at her long and hard. "You want me to tell him you left because you love him?"

Caroline nodded, unable to speak from the sobs racking her body.

"Caroline, that doesn't make any sense," Kristy yelled.

"It'll make sense to him. Just tell him, would you?"

Kristy waited for an explanation. Frustrated, Caroline sputtered, "It's not fair for me to stay here leading him to believe he and I have a chance, while I'm engaged to be married to someone else."

"As your best friend and maid of honor, it's my duty to tell you that you're being stupid! You don't marry one guy when you're in love with another. Especially when the other is as incredible as Cade."

"I love *two* incredible guys who both want to be with me. I have to choose the one I made a promise to. Can you please just tell Cade what I said?"

"Or you can choose the one you're more compatible with," Kristy argued.

"Promise me!"

Kristy didn't look away as she answered. "Sure. I promise, I'll take care of it."

Caroline sighed in relief and, between sobs, thanked her.

"C. . .if you're so sad, why are you leaving? It's obvious you're not ready to go yet. I'm sure Trevor will understand if you want to stay longer."

"Trevor will not understand if I want to stay longer. He will assume the only reason I want to stay is so I can be with Cade."

"Is it? Is that the only reason you would want to stay?"

"N-no. I would love to spend more time with my dad, Claire, and Remy, too. I love it here, and I'm going to miss this place, that's all. I'm ready to go back and get this over with."

"Caroline." Kristy's tone dropped. "Marriage isn't something to take so lightly. This is the rest of your life we're talking about here. It's not just something you hurry up and do to get it over with. It's one of the biggest, most important decisions you'll ever make in your entire life. You're still young. There's no reason for you to rush into this. Just wait. Wait until you're sure. Certain about which guy is right for you. Follow your heart and everything will fall into place."

Caroline hastily threw her things in her suitcase, paying no attention to her sloppy packing job. "I know, and you're exactly right. I am sure everything will work out. I *am* following my heart. I love Trevor, and I'm going to marry him. It's just going to be a little sooner than I had originally intended, that's all. Things will work out, you'll see. I'll stay with you at your place until the wedding, and I will proudly wear the stunning bridal gown you make especially for me."

Kristy shook her head, but Caroline ignored her and continued. "My hair and make-up will be perfect, my close friends and family will be in attendance, and my no-longer-estranged father will walk me down the aisle to give my hand in marriage. I will finally have my happily ever-after, and you will be by my side looking ravishing in your self-designed bridesmaid dress. I'll even let you pick the color."

Lacking the enthusiasm Caroline hoped for, Kristy responded dryly, "Sounds perfect."

Trevor walked in the room and acknowledged them both. "Hello, Kristy."

"Trevor." Kristy gathered her things. "Congratulations. I understand you'll be getting married. Very soon."

Trevor smiled at her disapproval. "Yes, isn't it wonderful? Caroline has finally overcome her fear of long term commitment and agreed to set a date."

Kristy smiled cynically. "Yes. Wonderful." She brushed past him. "Take care, Trevor."

"Well, she's just a ray of sunshine and rainbows today, isn't she?"

"She's not too happy about my decision to get married so quickly. She wants to make my wedding dress, and now she only has six weeks to design and create a masterpiece."

"Caroline, we're getting married outside by a lake. It doesn't have to be a masterpiece. It's not that big of a deal."

"It's a big deal to me."

He pulled her in for a hug and slowly leaned in for a kiss. "So, we're only six weeks away from our wedding night. Are you as excited as I am? I'm getting aroused just thinking about it."

Glad he couldn't see her face, she rolled her eyes. "Seriously, Trevor? Is that the only thing you can think about right now? Sex?"

"What?" He shrugged and held palms up. "I'm a guy, of course that's what I'm thinking about. What else am I supposed to think about?"

"Um, how about committing our complete body and soul to each other, vowing before God to love, honor, and cherish one another for the rest of our lives, together as one. You know, those kinds of sentimental, important things."

He smirked. "The wedding night kind of counts as us coming together as one."

"Good grief, Trevor! You're such a horn-dog. Go take another cold shower. I have stuff to do before I can leave." He laughed and tackled her on the bed. His speed and strength startled her at first, but she relaxed when she realized he was just messing around. Unfortunately, her physical and mental bodies were distracted and in two different worlds.

That evening, Caroline had a rough night of fitful sleep. Tossing and turning, she couldn't forget about that last creepy dream of Rachel trying to tell her something. What did she desperately want Caroline to know?

The sun danced through the curtains at daybreak, and Caroline woke to the aroma of coffee. She would miss the delicious New Orleans java Delia brewed and the homemade waffles, bacon and pancakes Delphine had waiting every morning."

She sighed. Caroline didn't want to leave yet. She needed to talk to Cade. She resolved to try his cabin one more time before she left. Trevor had bought her a ticket on his flight scheduled to depart at three and it's a two hour drive to the airport. She had until noon at the latest. Caroline needed to get up and get dressed, but first—coffee.

While in the kitchen having coffee with Delia and Delphine, she heard the front door open. She quickly ran around the counter and through the heavy kitchen door hoping to see Cade. Instead, Claire and Remy walked into the house, arguing like a typical brother and sister. She loved having siblings. It was a great feeling. Claire's face lit up when she saw Caroline.

"Hey! What are you doing today?"

Caroline searched for the right words from the thousands swimming through her mind. "Well, my fiancé surprised me with a visit this weekend, and, well, um. . .I'm going back to Chicago with him. Today."

Claire's mood shifted like the weather. "What? Why? You just got here! We haven't had enough time together."

"Oh, back off, Claire. If the girl wants to go back with her guy, let her go. You wouldn't care what anyone else said if you were in her place."

"Shut up, pea brain!" Claire hissed at Remy. "What about Beau?" She challenged. "Are you just gonna leave him, too?"

"I was engaged when I came here. I wasn't expecting to meet anyone, much less fall—" she swallowed hard.

"Go ahead, finish your sentence. We all know what you were about to say, but do you?"

"I can't stay here when my life is in Chicago. Trevor and I are getting married at the end of August. I have a lot to do; besides, I would have to leave in six weeks anyway to go back for school."

"It's not fair." Claire practically pouted. "You walk into our lives and make things so much happier around here for everyone. . .for me. Now you're leaving just like that? It sucks! Don't leave yet. Please."

"I know, and I'm so sorry." Caroline waved her cell phone in the air. "I always have it with me. . .well, except in rare cases when my wicked stepmother decides to steal it to cause trouble."

Claire smiled and hugged Caroline. "I'm really going to miss you."

"I already miss you." Caroline pulled Remy over for a hug. "I'll miss you, too!"

"Man, I was just gettin' used to havin' two sisters around here."

Caroline glanced at the time on her phone. Five minutes till ten. She needed to head out before Trevor left his hotel to come pick her up. She sighed. Only two hours before she had to leave. "I'll be in touch, I promise. I love you guys."

"We love you, too." Claire blinked back her emotion.

"Well, I have to go see one more person before I leave."

Claire's tears now flowed freely. "Good luck with that. He's gonna go nuts."

"Yeah, that's what I'm afraid of." She ran up the stairs to get ready.

Caroline didn't see Cade's truck in the driveway. She had a horrible feeling she missed her chance to say goodbye. She knocked loudly and checked the doorknob. It was still locked. Where is he? She hadn't seen him since he retreated from her room while she and Trevor argued. Where could he have gone? She was almost out of time and tempted to wait on his doorstep. She trudged slowly back to the house, dragging her feet in case he happened to drive by. If leaving with Trevor was the right thing to do, why did it feel so wrong?

She had to stop overanalyzing her feelings. At the house, Trevor loaded his rental car with their bags. *Time to go already?* Trevor smiled. Unaccustomed to the Gulf Coast humidity, he sweated profusely.

"You about ready, beautiful?"

She tried not to look and sound as pitiful as she felt. "I guess so. I didn't get to say goodbye to Cade. Is that everything?"

"That's everything." Trevor pettily replied, "He's a big boy, I'm sure he'll live." He encircled his arms around her neck and kissed the tip her nose. "Now, are you ready to run away with your handsome prince and live happily ever after?"

"It's what I've always dreamed of," she mumbled.

THIRTY-SEVEN

Cade walked into the plantation house kitchen in the middle of a conversation between Eddie, Delia, Delphine, and Kristy. "Which daughter left a hole in your heart?" he asked, overhearing Eddie's last sentence.

The shock spread on their faces, except one. Kristy lowered her head, avoiding eye contact. He sent out a cautionary plea. "What's going on?" The silence concerned him. "Where's Caroline? Somebody better tell me what's going on. Right now."

"She didn't tell you, Beau?"

Kristy stood quickly, interrupting Eddie. "Cade, please come outside with me. I need to talk to you. . .where there are no knives or anything breakable within reach."

"She didn't tell me what? What the hell? Come on! What didn't she tell me?"

"Shhh. Just come with me. Please."

She dragged him from the kitchen by his hand.

Confused, Eddie whispered, "I thought Caroline talked to Beau yesterday?"

Delia quietly answered, "So did I."

Cade impatiently followed Kristy onto the front porch. "Seriously, Kristy. Where is Caroline?"

"Sit down."

"Oh please, come on! Is she okay?"

"She's fine. Please. Sit."

Against his better judgment, Cade sat in the rocking chair. "There. I'm sitting. Now tell me what the hell is going on."

"Okay. Caroline is fine. She has a message she wanted me to give you. I didn't want to be the one who told you, but she made me promise." Cade frowned. "She went back to Chicago yesterday with Trevor." He abruptly stood, his fighting instincts ignited.

Kristy flinched. "Sit down, please. You are huge and intimidating, and if I'm gonna get this out I need you on my level." Cade stiffly perched on a rocking chair, his movements slow and calculated. "She came by your cabin twice and was very upset when she couldn't tell you goodbye." Kristy sighed and rubbed her face in frustration as she paced in front of him. "I woke up dreading this talk I would have with you today. I can't tell you why she left. I *can* tell you what she told me to tell you, but I didn't believe a word of it, and neither will you."

"Well, what did she tell you to tell me?"

Shaking her head, she closed her eyes. Cade was sure she said a little prayer. "It didn't make any sense to me, but she said it would make sense to you. She said, 'Tell him I care deeply for him and that's why I'm leaving.'"

Cade didn't react. Not outwardly. But inside, he battled an onslaught of emotion, frustration, desperation, and a little anger. And something else. Something like victory.

"You see, that's what doesn't make sense to me. She loves you, so she's leaving to get married to another man." Kristy looked braced, like she waited for Cade to blow up and start yelling, but he didn't. "Aren't you going to say anything? Yell at me? Kill the messenger?"

"She loves me?" Cade smirked.

"Um. . .yeah! Hel-lo? Any idiot can see that. Where have you been? Did you hear that last part, though? About her leaving to marry someone else?"

"Yeah, I heard you. But if she loves me I've got some time to change her mind."

Kristy cringed. She clearly had more to say. "Oh yeah. There's one more thing I forgot to tell you. Trevor is a first-class manipulator, you see, and he, uh. . .he somehow managed to talk her into marrying him in, um, six weeks."

Cade flew out of the chair and towered over Kristy, gently gripping her shoulders.

"Damn. You're fast and strong, yet gentle. You have freakish control over your temper. You're beautiful and you smell great. Caroline is an idiot."

"She's marrying that bast—she's getting married in six weeks?" A string of profanities escaped him.

"Believe me, hot stuff, I tried very hard to talk her out of it. It's painfully obvious she loves you more than him, but for some crazy reason she is stuck on the fact that she just met you and that she's already agreed to marry Trevor. It's like she's convinced she can't give the ring back. Or worse, she's afraid of Trevor. Who knows what's going through that crazy girl's head? I've known her for ten years, and she still manages to surprise me."

"This is not good. She can't marry him. Do you understand that? We cannot let this wedding happen."

"Well, what do you propose we do? I'm open to suggestions. She's staying at my place until the wedding, and I'm supposed to drive her car back to Chicago."

Cade lit up. "I have some things I need to do first, but I have an idea. You go ahead and fly back up there, tell Caroline something was wrong and the car wouldn't start. Tell her I wouldn't let you drive it all that way until I had the opportunity to check it out."

Kristy pursed her lips. "Nope. Won't work. Trevor took it into town before they left and had everything checked already. She won't believe anything is wrong with it."

"I don't care if she believes it or not, either way you'll be there and her car won't be. I will drive it up there myself. I just need to check on some things and get my facts straight first."

"Wait, what are you talking about? What facts?"

"It's a long story, but I'll try to sum it up for you. He sat her in the rocking chair and paced. Eddie has been contacted by several companies lately trying to coerce him into selling his property. He's turned them down flat because he has no intention of selling. One particular company has been trying to bully him—KC Real Estate Investors."

Kristy sucked in a breath.

"Yes, you heard me right. That day in the kitchen when you told me about Trevor's dad, I nearly flipped. I had just spoken to Eddie about the harassment. I did some checking and Kenneth Callahan also owns all the surrounding properties around the Fontenot plantation. I'm going to see if I can learn more about our friends, the Callahan's."

"What in the world would Trevor's dad want with property down here when he lives in Chicago?"

"I'm not sure, but I'm going to find out. I need to do the research. Kristy, you don't think Trevor is only marrying Caroline to get his hands on the Fontenot property, do you? I mean, clearly his dad wants it, otherwise he wouldn't be trying to force Eddie's hand."

"Yeah, but if it's his dad who wants it, what good would it do for Trevor to marry Caroline?"

Cade looked at her sternly and lifted his chin. "Think about it. If Trevor marries Caroline, and Eddie makes her a beneficiary, and then something happens to Eddie, Caroline inherits her share. A share which also belongs to Trevor through marriage. Right?"

"I don't know. Legality is not my field of expertise."

Cade smiled. "Well, darlin', I'm going to find out. I have some favors I need to call in, but I will get to the bottom of this. Hopefully, I can change her mind." Cade kissed Kristy's cheek and hugged her tightly. "Thanks for being the messenger. Sorry for intimidating you. Please don't tell Caroline anything I told you. I don't want her to know until I have all the facts."

Kristy smiled, agreeable to anything he proposed. "My lips are sealed. I promise."

Cade contacted his old college classmate, Tony, now working in New Orleans as a private investigator, and asked him to dig around for any dirt, no matter how small, on Kenneth Callahan. Cade also called a buddy about family law, specifically wills.

Cade searched the web and genealogy sites for George Callahan. Narrowing his search to the New York Callahan's involved in new construction and real estate, Cade shouted when he saw the results. "Jackpot, baby!"

His research provided some very interesting tidbits. George Callahan had moved to New York shortly after Rachel died. He married an American Indian woman named Suni, and they had a baby named John. John grew up to own a construction business that helped define some of the well-known architecture in Manhattan.

John also married a Native American woman and had a son named William who eventually took over the construction business after his father retired. William raised his son, James, to learn everything he knew about owning and operating a booming business. James married, and Kenneth Callahan was born. Raised in Manhattan where he learned about business from his father, he graduated college, and five years later, married Miranda Jones. Four years after that, they welcomed a bouncing baby boy named Trevor.

Cade closed his computer and digested the new revelation. Trevor was a direct descendant of George Callahan, the man who was in love with Caroline's G3 grandmother and eventually killed her. Now his G3 grandson would finally get a piece of the Fontenot fortune. Apparently, George was determined to hide from his past, but couldn't forget it. He taught his son everything he had learned, from watching Peter and Jefferson, about running a successful business. That knowledge was handed down generation after generation.

Cade stared blankly out the window, deep in thought.

So, if Kenneth Callahan was a partner in a New York firm, what happened that caused him to move halfway across the country to start over? Was Kristy's gossip right? Had he been hoodwinked by his New York partners and forced to move and become a bottom-feeder? If so, who helped him get back on his feet so quickly?

Maybe Tony would get some of those answers. The pieces were coming together. Cade smiled, pleased with his success. For now, he had just what he needed. Proof that Trevor was directly related to the man who killed Rachel Fontenot.

"I talked to Cade." Kristy rolled her suitcase to the corner and sat down on the couch across from Caroline. "He didn't flip out like I thought he would."

"He didn't? Really?" Disappointment ate at Caroline.

"Don't get me wrong, he was definitely not happy about you leaving early and not saying goodbye."

"What did he say?" She frowned, trying and failing to hide her eagerness to know his reaction. "Did he look upset?"

"Sure. I mean, he wanted to know why. I told him what you asked me to, word for word. He seemed to understand."

Either Kristy was being annoyingly vague on purpose, or she really didn't have anything else to report. Caroline nodded.

"Well, that's good. I guess that's it then." She couldn't mask the obvious sadness in her voice. Cade hadn't asked fifty questions like she figured he would. *I guess it wasn't as difficult for him to let me go as I thought it would be.*

Kristy noticed her disappointment, but didn't press the issue. Very unlike her. "Yeah, I guess that's it. Oh yeah, I ended up flying back anyway."

"What? Why? How am I gonna get my car back up here?"

"When I told Cade my plan to drive it back up here for you, he didn't like that idea." Kristy smiled with a reminiscent look in her eyes, alerting Caroline's curiosity. "He said he didn't feel comfortable with me making the long drive alone, and if he didn't have work he would've driven me himself and just flown back."

Kristy fanned herself with her hand and a dreamy expression. "He's very chivalrous, isn't he? Worrying about my safety, and offering to drive all that way when he didn't have to. . .so sweet." Kristy shuddered, "Mmm, probably best. All those hours in a car alone with that hot, Cajun beefcake. Whoo, I don't know if I could handle that." Caroline felt the sickening jealousy climbing her entire body. "Anyway, he wanted to make sure everything was okay with it before I left. He said something wasn't right with the transmission, that he would fix it, and your dad could drive the car when he comes up for the wedding."

"That was thoughtful of him. I guess Trevor didn't think to have the transmission checked."

"Yeah, I guess not. I tell ya, I wish Cade felt the same about me as he did for you, 'cause I'd be all over that." Kristy laughed, but all Caroline could focus on was how Kristy had used the past tense regarding Cade's feelings for her. "Well, I'm beat. I'm gonna go take a shower and wash the day away."

Caroline swallowed back her disappointment along with her tears. This was for the best. "Thanks for doing this for me, Kris. All of it. I owe you big."

Kristy hugged her. "You're welcome. I love you, and you know I'll do whatever I can to help you, but yes. . .you owe me big." She gave Caroline a quick kiss on the cheek and walked into her room, closing the door behind her.

It took nearly the entire six weeks for Cade's buddies to get him the information he needed. And Tony didn't want to discuss over the phone what he'd found. Said Callahan was low and mixed up with some nasty people. He overnighted an envelope with everything Cade needed. Tony wasn't kidding. It was big.

Cade rushed through the door and found Eddie diving into a shrimp po'boy sandwich.

"Beau, what's up? You look like you just ran a marathon. You all right?"

"Yes, sir. I'm okay, but I have something important I need to show you."

"Sure, what's going on?"

Cade slid the manila folder on the table and sat down with Eddie. "KC Real Estate Investors is owned by Kenneth Callahan. Trevor's father."

The lines on Eddie's face intensified. "Really? That's interesting. Do you have any idea why he would be interested in owning my property?"

"Yes, sir. He's the one who bought all the surrounding properties, as well. Mr. Fontenot, we can't let Caroline marry Trevor. I don't want to hurt her, but if she marries him, she will be hurt worse in the long run."

Eddie skimmed the papers Cade set in front of him. "Beau, I know you have feelings for Caroline, but crashing her wedding is not the way to win her heart."

"I understand that, sir, but winning her heart is not my intention at the moment. Protecting her is. And protecting you."

Eddie's eyes flashed up to his. "Why would I need protecting?"

Cade flipped to the last page in the folder. "Read this, sir. It's very important we stop that wedding."

Eddie read the information and his eyes enlarged when he got to the end. His serious expression confirmed his understanding.

"Where did you get this information? Is this fact or assumption?"

"One of my good friends is a private detective, and I asked him to do some digging for me about Kenneth Callahan. I received this in the mail this morning. I also got a call from him confirming the severity of this news."

"Is Trevor involved?"

"I'm not sure, but it's possible. After seeing the way he treated Caroline, I wouldn't put it past him."

"Yeah, I met the little prick, too. I wasn't impressed. But the Mafia? Really? He didn't seem that threatening to me."

"No, but his dad may be."

"What do you suggest we do?"

Cade smiled. "I was hoping you'd ask me that." He filled Eddie in on the details of his plan and Eddie left is half-eaten sandwich to immediatey go upstairs and pack. Cade's bags were already loaded in Caroline's Jeep as he jumped in and hit the road.

He headed for Chicago with his manila folder full of valuable information in the front seat beside him and a smile on his face.

THIRTY-EIGHT

Caroline stared hard at the painted face looking back at her in the mirror. Marriage. Married. Mrs. Caroline Callahan. It's happening, for real. The suffocating pressure compacting her chest knocked the wind from her lungs as she peered at her unfamiliar reflection in the full length mirror. Her heart threatened to explode in the steel cage supporting her shoulders. A panic attack was most unwelcome today.

Is this what she really wanted? She believed in the sanctity of marriage, and loved Trevor, but was marriage the answer right now? *Am I truly in love with Trevor, or am I more in love with the idea of having a wedding and the security of being married?* Trevor was a great person inside and out. Everything a girl could ask for. Well-educated, fun, athletic, successful in his career and, not to mention, undeniably gorgeous.

I'm overreacting, that has to be it. Trevor will give me a wonderful life and be a great husband and hopefully someday a wonderful father. The white chiffon blinded her in the reflection, but the beautiful flow of the material hugged her curves. She looked incredible.

Kristy interrupted Caroline's thoughts as she complimented her own work. She smiled proudly as she pinned the veil on Caroline's head full of cascading curls that effectively disguised the shaved area of her head where she'd cracked her skull.

"Are you sure you're ready for this, Mrs. Callahan? No going back once you say those magic words." She shivered and closed her eyes, allowing that to sink in. Kristy noticed and honed in on Caroline's strange behavior. "Listen to me, Caroline Fontenot. If you're not 110% sure this is what you want to do, you need to let me know right now. It's okay, you know. Trevor will be upset, but I'm sure he would appreciate you backing out before you say your vows. After all, a divorce can be a lot more expensive than a wedding."

Caroline sighed. In her white wedding dress, symbolizing her purity and innocence, she was finally about to have her happily ever-after. Right? Was this really happening?

"Caroline? Seriously, are you okay?"

"Yes. . .yes, I'm fine. It's just. . .something doesn't feel right and I can't pinpoint what it is. Nerves, I'm sure. Let's do this."

"Please hurry," Kristy mumbled under her breath. But she didn't seem to be talking to Caroline.

Kristy drove like a maniac to the park. She grumbled about the beautiful day and not getting her wish for a thunderstorm. Caroline might have complained had it not been for the nerves bundled in her stomach and fighting back the urge to puke.

They stepped out into the hot sunshine, and a huge gust of wind blew Caroline's veil into her face, swirling it around her head.

"Ugh! Stupid wind! This 'Windy City' crap is for the birds! They can have it! I can't believe I agreed to get married outside, in Chicago, in August. I swear it must be 100 degrees out here. My make-up is melting off, and my hair is falling flat. This is ridiculous."

Kristy laughed and checked her watch again. "Relax, diva, you look gorgeous. Now, stop fighting with your veil and let me fix it before you get lipstick all over it."

"That's the fifth time you've checked your watch in ten minutes! What are you waiting for?"

Kristy untangled the tulle material from Caroline's now-sticky curls. "Nothing. I just don't want to be late." She glanced over Caroline's shoulder and unsuccessfully wrestled back a smile. Caroline tried to turn around to see what Kristy had seen.

"Wait!" Kristy held Caroline's face in place. "Hold still a minute, I need to check your make-up." Kristy pulled a make-up bag from her car and powdered Caroline's nose.

"Okay, okay. I think I've got enough make up on. Now let's go before I'm late to my own wedding!"

"Oh, chill out. We are way too early anyway, and you've got forty-five minutes before you are supposed to let anyone see you. It's just over that hill and it'll take us all of three minutes to get there. You will be fine, trust me." Kristy glanced nervously over Caroline's shoulder again.

"If we're way too early, why do you keep checking the time?" Caroline realized she hadn't looked at a clock all morning with the time Nazi pulling her in one direction or another. She wondered about Kristy's strange behavior and the drive behind it.

"Caroline, as your maid of honor, I need to ask you a very important question. Can you think of any reason, anything at all, why you should *not* get married today?"

403

"What are you talking about? Come on, you're supposed to be helping me, not freaking me out."

"Exactly! If you are even the slightest bit confused or hesitant about going through with this today, especially on such short notice, please don't do it. You've only been engaged for five months. Don't give me that crap about it being your decision to do this now. You were pressured to get married this quickly. No, forget that—Trevor manipulated you into getting married this quickly. I know you, and I know this is something you would never willingly do."

"Kristy, don't do this. . .not now."

"Caroline, please. Listen to me. The only reason Trevor pushed you to do this now is because he was afraid if you waited any longer, you would change your mind. Afraid if you spent any more time with. . ." Kristy's focus moved to the space behind Caroline, causing her to turn around. Dressed in a suit and tie, a model of perfection, stood the man everyone knew she should be with.

Caroline sucked in a deep breath and tears instantly welled, threatening to break the dam of lashes. "What are you. . .I didn't think you. . .H-how did you know where. . . Why—"

"Hello, beautiful. Have you missed me as much as I've missed you?" He brushed away a rogue tear that escaped from the pool in her eyes. "Don't cry, sweet girl. I'm here because I would hate myself forever if I missed this opportunity. May I steal a few minutes with the stunning bride before you rush off? I have something important I need to tell you. It may just stop you from making the biggest mistake of your life."

Cade produced a handkerchief from his pocket and dabbed the tears before it ruined her makeup. Kristy, all smiles, willingly volunteered her new car for them to escape the wind and talk. Kristy had to be behind this somehow. Her strange behavior now replaced by smiles and spontaneous giggling.

Cade chivalrously opened the door for them to crawl into the cramped spaces of Kristy's Audi. Kristy slid into the back seat. He sat in the driver's seat and started the engine to blast the air conditioning. Holding a manila folder, he turned to Caroline, very serious, yet cautious.

"Caroline, I've been doing some research over the last few months. I believe what I've discovered will hugely impact your decision to get married today. You need to know this rushed, impromptu wedding went above Trevor's head. His dad's been playing puppet-master all along."

Caroline remembered the conversation she overheard between Trevor and his dad and her spine turned rigid.

"How do you know this?" she whispered, praying it wasn't true, and trying to ignore the piece of her heart that hoped it was.

"Just hear me out first, and then I'll explain how I got the information." His eyes implored her to understand and begged permission, so she nodded. "I called in a few favors. Kenneth Callahan, Trevor's father, has bought all the land surrounding your dad's property. He owns KC Real Estate Investors and has been the punk harassing Eddie to sell the plantation." Stunned, Caroline didn't have a chance to respond. "There's more. I researched the genealogy of the Callahan family and discovered that Trevor is a direct descendant of George Callahan."

She shook her head, confused and about to argue this claim, but no words would come out.

Cade covered her icy cold hand with his. "Caroline, George is Trevor's G3 grandfather. After he killed Rachel, he moved to New York to start a new life and escape being hanged for murder."

Caroline shook her head. She didn't believe this. The irony was all too coincidental. Impossible.

"You have to believe me, sweet girl. I know my timing stinks, but I just found out for certain myself."

Confused, shocked and growing angrier by the second, Caroline said, "How—what does this have to do with me marrying Trevor today? So what if he's a descendant of George Callahan? That doesn't mean Trevor is a murderer."

"Caroline, Eddie has put you in his will. He showed it to me before I came up here. It states that as his only blood relative, you inherit the Fontenot plantation and family business if he dies. April, Claire and Remy will only get money and vehicles. Once you and Trevor are married and you add his name to everything, he is entitled to it all."

Caroline pursed her lips and squeezed her eyes shut. "Cade—"

"It gets worse. I asked around, and learned about the legend of the feud between the Callahan's and Fontenot's. Apparently the Callahan's harbored resentment when George was not offered partnership with Jackson after Peter Callahan passed away. That resentment coupled with a thirst for revenge has been handed down through the generations."

Caroline knew this already, but let him continue.

"Kenneth tried to force your dad to sell, but Eddie told him to go to hell. This didn't sit well with Callahan, and bruised his massive ego, so he's contracted a hit man in the Louisiana Mafia to take him out once the papers are signed in both yours and Trevor's names. Don't you see, Caroline? Once Trevor has control of the property and business, he can sell it to KC Real Estate investors and it will no longer be in your family." Cade stroked his fingers down the length of her stunned face. "The Callahan's will have finally avenged their family."

Cade pulled out the last sheet of paper. "Please believe me, cher. As much as I would love to keep you from marrying Trevor, I'm not tacky enough to crash your wedding for no good reason. Once you and Trevor say, 'I do,' Callahan is going to send a message to this hit man, and Eddie will immediately be in danger."

Cade, passionate now, wiped a tear dripping from Caroline's nose and lifted her chin to look into her eyes. "Sweet Caroline, Kenneth Callahan is going to kill your dad so he can finally have what his G2 grandfather, George, did not. He's out for revenge."

Caroline tried to think through the maze of anxiety, confusion, and emotional upheaval swirling through her head. Obviously, she could stop their plan by simply not adding Trevor to the will, but she knew he, and apparently his overbearing father, would never be okay with that. "Does Trevor know about this?"

Cade stared out the windshield. "I don't know. I can't see how he wouldn't, but I am not certain."

"Okay, I need to think for a minute. This is crazy. How could. . .how could someone do this? Who sits around and plots this kind of stuff?"

"Kenneth Callahan does. His father and grandfather passed down the story of the Callahan's and the Fontenot's to him. It's like the legendary feud between the Hatfield's and McCoy's. The families have hated each other for over a century. He wants to be the one who avenges his family name and takes what he believes is rightfully his."

"Why would he want an old plantation in southern Louisiana when he lives in Chicago? It doesn't make any sense."

"He doesn't want the plantation, cher. He wants to take it from your family, tear it down and build a huge metroplex community on it. His main purpose is revenge against your family for what they allegedly did to George. He holds your family responsible for the hardships he and his ancestors have endured over the years. By tearing down everything the Fontenot family spent a century-and-a-half building, he will have his revenge. In the process, he will make millions. You see, it's the perfect plan."

Realization set in. "This is what Rachel has been trying to tell me!"

Cade leaned back, closed his eyes and sighed in relief. "Yes," he whispered. "She's been trying to warn you about the Callahan family. That's why she was so intent to show you how and why George had killed her."

"It makes sense, now," she whispered. "That's why she picked me. Because I was engaged to Trevor." The clues all came crashing together. "The dreams started right after I got engaged. The cracked picture frame, the sweatshirt, glider. . .the cat. That's why my ring kept disappearing, she led me to the journal, I saw the rape in my dream. . . That's why she even made me experience things from her perspective. Desperation to make me understand."

Reality set in and she gasped, grabbing Cade's hand. "What about Eddie? Is he okay?"

"Only if you don't marry Trevor today."

His golden eyes burned a hole through her emotions, and she turned to Kristy in the backseat. "You knew about this, didn't you?"

Kristy shook her head. "No, not all of it. I knew he was checking in to some things, but I didn't know what."

Caroline smirked. "That's why you were acting so weird, checking your watch and looking all around. At least now I know you're not possessed." They shared a laugh until the gravity of the situation and what she must do now sank in.

Fear shot through Caroline. She couldn't let anything happen to her father, to her family. "What am I going to do? Trevor will be furious with me. What do I say?"

"Sweet girl, Trevor manipulated you into rushing into something he knew you weren't ready to do. One way to find out if Trevor knows about his father's plan is to gauge his reaction when you tell him you can't go through with this today. Tell him you're not ready yet, and you need more time to think and prepare. If he loses his temper, then it's a good bet he knows something about this. A *good* man would understand if you needed more time to make a decision this important."

They stepped out of the car.

"I agree with Cade. I will be right by your side when you tell him, C," said Kristy.

"Cade, thank you for being brave enough to bring this to my attention today. I can't say I'm excited about your timing, but I am grateful for your help in protecting my family. Now, I just need to figure out how in the world I'm going to handle this. Trevor does not do well with public humiliation."

Kristy clasped her hands together. "Well, it's time he learns. Let's do it! Let's get this party started. . .or stopped as the case may be."

Kristy removed the veil and they walked hand in hand toward the wedding site. Cade stayed far enough behind that he could see if they needed help, but wouldn't be the cause of trouble. His smile a fixture on his face as he followed her. Trevor Callahan was about to receive the sucker punch of his life, and Cade was thankful he'd be there to witness it.

THIRTY-NINE

As she topped the hill, Caroline observed all one-hundred-and-fifty guests seated in their chairs awaiting her arrival. Her heart and nerves sank into her gut.

"Well, here goes nothing."

"No, here's to standing up for yourself and protecting your family," Kristy said sternly.

Caroline breathed deeply, calming the urge to faint. "Right."

Kristy grinned big. "You can do this, honey. I know you can, and I'll be with you every step of the way. I promise. Your dad and Cade will be there, too." They walked together up the aisle.

By guests' expressions, she was stunning. But Trevor looked confused by her untraditional entrance.

When she approached him, he smiled, but she didn't. Kristy took one step back to give Caroline room to face him.

Noticing Kristy's smug grin, Trevor's smile faded. "Baby, what's wrong?"

Shaking from head to toe, more like quaking, Caroline whispered, "I need to talk to you. Can we take five minutes and step away from everyone?"

Bewilderment flitted across Trevor's face. "What's going on? We can't go anywhere." He looked around at the guests. "All these people came to see us get married, so let's just go on with it. We can talk afterwards," he whispered.

She stood her ground not taking her focus off him. "No, Trevor. I need to speak with you now. It's important."

Trevor's eyes hardened, obviously embarrassed. "Sweetheart, whatever it is, it can wait until after the wedding. Do *not* embarrass me."

Caroline glanced around their audience, all the eyes watching and now whispering, and her heart dropped. Trevor's side held all the major industry professionals in Chicago, as well as some of his dad's friends. He would not take this well at all, and she wished he would just swallow his pride and step away like she asked. But, of course he didn't.

Angry now about Trevor's concern for his embarrassment with the situation rather than what she had to say, Caroline fumed. "Okay, fine. You leave me no choice. I'm sorry, but I can't marry you today. I'm not ready yet. I need more time to mentally prepare and think things through."

She flinched under the fury flashing in his eyes.

"Things have just gone way too fast," she continued "and, as I was getting ready, I realized I couldn't do this yet. Not today, anyway."

Trevor shot a fierce look at Kristy, and then plastered on a fake smile as he spoke loudly enough for the first few rows of guests to hear. "Oh, Caroline, don't be silly. You're just nervous. You don't know what you're saying. Now, stop talking, turn around, and let the nice man marry us."

He faced her and whispered through clenched teeth, "Why are you doing this to me?"

A glimpse of the Trevor she loved broke through the cracks of his hardened façade. Pain and tenderness briefly shimmered in his eyes. . .very briefly. "Sweetheart, I didn't want to—"

"Oh, save it. You knew you were gonna do this from the very beginning, didn't you? That's the only reason you agreed to move the wedding up, so you could publicly humiliate me. Am I right?"

So angry, she couldn't control her sarcasm. "Oh, sure, Trevor. That's exactly what I did. I waited until the perfect moment, got all dressed up, and made my parents drive all day across four states just to make sure I ruined your precious little image. That's what I was secretly plotting all this time. Get real." She softened her voice so only he could hear her. "I was honestly gonna go through with this until I saw myself in the mirror. I'm just not ready to get married yet. I'm sorry. I need more time."

Trevor glanced around at the guests again, and his fake smile returned. "Darling Caroline, you just have cold feet. Don't worry about anything, sweetheart. Let me do the worrying for us. Now, just follow along so we can let everyone get back to their lives."

Caroline tired quickly of being treated like an imbecile. "No."

Trevor turned and scowled. "No? I don't understand why you're doing this, but I'm sure it's just nerves. I love you and you love me, and today is the day we're—" Trevor froze mid-sentence as he glowered over her shoulder. She turned to see Cade standing at the top of the hill. She snapped her head back, Trevor's nasty glare fixed upon her. "Oh, I can see everything much more clearly now. It's all starting to make sense."

"Trevor, he has nothing to do with my decision."

"Right. I may have been born at night, sweetheart, but it wasn't last night. You filthy liar! I was right when I came down there, wasn't I? You might've had me fooled then, but not now. How long have you been sleeping with him?" His face a reflection of his complete repulsion.

"Trevor, please. Lower your voice. I haven't—"

"Why, Caroline? Don't you think everyone here deserves to know why you're backing out on the wedding? Go ahead. Tell them. Tell them it's because you've been sleeping with another man!"

Shocked gasps filled the gusty winds. Caroline wanted to die.

"That's the pot calling the kettle black coming from the Chicago man-whore," Kristy exclaimed.

"Shut the hell up, Kristy. You have no business in this."

Wrongly humiliated by a man who claimed to love her. Her temper flared. "I haven't slept with anyone, but not because you didn't try! I've remained pure up to this very minute. Can you say the same? Or can you not *remember*?"

Trevor sneered. "I'm not the one who whored around while wearing someone else's ring on my finger!"

Caroline reacted by slapping him across the face as hard as she could. The crowd of witnesses fell silent, waiting for his reaction. They didn't have to wait long as the stinging pain in her hand was quickly replaced by a blinding smack to her cheekbone. Caroline gasped, along with every member of the audience, literally seeing flashing stars as she flew back into Kristy's arms. Kristy comforted her before screaming at Trevor.

"You sorry son of a bitch! Don't you ever touch her again."

Caroline quickly recovered, squirmed out of Kristy's arms, and turned to the audience, knowing what would happen next. As she expected, Cade was furiously sprinting at warp speed up the aisle flying in like Iron Man to demolish Trevor, and Eddie scurried up from her right, but Caroline stepped between them and Trevor with her hands out.

"No, not yet. I'm okay," she lied. The tears of pain fell down her swollen cheeks and she felt like the left half of her face was the size of a hot air balloon. Lips numb, and eye rapidly swelling shut, she turned to Trevor who, strangely enough, looked distraught and sorry for what he'd just done.

Cade placed his trembling hand on her shoulder and she worried he would kill Trevor if he ever touched her again. Cade wasn't going anywhere, and she knew he would explode at any moment if it weren't for his incredible control. She chose not to push that and allowed him the contact as she stepped closer to Trevor.

Caroline dabbed her cheek and sighed, realizing what a mistake this whole affair was. "Trev, I tried to tell you we needed five minutes alone. You are the one who chose to make this a public spectacle. I can see I've made the right decision today. You are not the man I want to spend the rest of my life with. I'm sorry, Trevor."

She turned to walk away, but Kenneth Callahan blocked her path. Flanked by Eddie and Cade, she found the courage from within to lock eyes with him—emeralds clashing with sapphires. "Excuse me, Mr. Callahan. This has nothing to do with you, so please move out of my way."

"I'm afraid I can't do that. You have chosen to humiliate my family, so you will not be going anywhere but on your honeymoon with my son." Cade stepped between Kenneth and Caroline, joined by Eddie. They formed a screen blocking him from Caroline, and Cade spoke calmly.

"It's time for you to leave, Mr. Callahan."

Caroline heard him protest, and thanked Kristy for catching her as she turned to search for Trevor. She found him standing in the same place staring at her in disgust. Kenneth Callahan's threatening tone blasted over her ringing ears, weakening her knees. "I tried to tell my son you were a filthy whore, just like all the women in your family, but he wouldn't listen to me." Caroline turned toward him, but couldn't make eye contact, though she heard the sneer in his voice. "All he could say is how forgiving you were. Forgiving. HA! If you were my daughter, I'd—"

Eddie spoke. "You'd what? Tell me, Callahan. I'm curious. What exactly would you do?"

Cade crossed his arms emphasizing the bulge of his biceps.

"Mighty brave with your guard dog here, aren't you, Fontenot?"

Caroline retreated to speak to Trevor again, but this time she found him by the lake staring at the water. Genuinely saddened. Against Kristy's protests, she walked to him while her dad and Cade handled Mr. Callahan. He turned his back to her. Another more subtle slap in the face. "Trevor. I need to know something. Did you know about our family's past?"

He whirled around in shock. "Is that what this is about? Something that happened over a century ago?"

"Well, partly, yes. Did you know about your father's plans?"

"Caroline, I am *not* my father."

"Just answer the question."

"Yes, he told me about the plantation, your inheritance, and all that. But I promise I knew nothing about this until after I had already fallen in love with you and proposed."

"You see, Trevor, that's not the problem. You should have told me. The minute you found out, you should have come to me and told me everything. That's what true love is. It's about honesty, trust, and respect. Unfortunately, I now have lost all three of those qualities in my feelings for you. That's why I can't marry you." She lightly brushed her fingers across her swollen face and winced. She still couldn't believe he hit her.

415

"Just so you know, my intention today was only to postpone the wedding for a later date. I had no desire to cancel the wedding. I just needed the truth from you and your father. Now, after all this, I could never be your wife." She handed his ring back and walked away trying to ignore the pool of tears in his eyes and his wounded expression.

Caroline rejoined Kristy, Cade and Eddie just as Eddie announced his knowledge of the hit man Kenneth hired. All the wedding guests were speechless and listened intently as the drama unfolded.

Kenneth simply smiled. "You think you're clever and have it all figured out, don't you? If your family hadn't cheated George Callahan out of his share of their business, then we would own fifty percent of your fortune."

"If George had been hung for raping and murdering Jackson Fontenot's wife, Rachel, as he should have been, you wouldn't be standing here today," Caroline declared. "Your family lineage would have ended with him, thereby making the world a safer place."

"You think I'm the bad guy in all this." He laughed the same evil Callahan laugh from her dreams. "If I were you, Mr. Fontenot, I would watch my back. You have enemies all around you. Perhaps when you did your research, you missed something." Kenneth stared at Eddie's confused face and laughed sinisterly again. "Let's go, son." He turned to walk away, but Trevor didn't follow him. When he stopped to see why, Trevor stared at him angrily. "Trevor, I said come on. Let's get out of here."

"No, Dad. I'm done. You and your revenge plot have caused me to lose the one thing I treasured about my life. Seriously, Dad? The Mafia? A hit man? I will never go anywhere with you again."

"Don't be ridiculous. I didn't cause you to lose anything. You did that all on your own by allowing that little tramp to go to Louisiana by herself. If you were a real man, you could have controlled your woman like a true Callahan. You have too much of your mother in you."

"You disrespectful son of a bitch! The part of Mom that is in me is the part with a beating heart. You are a ruthless coward who can't handle rejection. You step on the people who try to help you. Respect must be earned. It's not your right or my duty. I'm finished letting you bark orders at me. Finished. And if anything happens to Eddie or Caroline I'll be with the proper authorities turning you in before you can say Godfather."

Kenneth curled his lip and spun on his heel, uttering profanity laced disparages about his son.

Trevor stepped closer and reached for Caroline's hand. She flinched away and Cade bowed up about to take over, but Trevor sadly retracted his hand, motioning to Cade with both hands that he meant no harm. Caroline's heart swelled and she grabbed Trevor's hands, confident he wouldn't hurt her again. She was angry he'd hit her, but she could see the shame within him and understood it was an irrational reaction. One she didn't care to repeat, though. He'd do well with a fraction of the control Cade had.

Trevor's sheepish grin reflected a moment of insecurity as he gazed deeply into her eyes with genuine heartache. "I'm terribly sorry things turned out this way. I think we could have had a good life together."

"I'm sorry, too. But I disagree. You hit me, Trevor. That's inexcusable. And frankly, as long as your dad is around, I don't believe we would have ever been happy together." She squeezed his hands. "This is for the best."

A single tear rolled down his cheek as he slowly leaned in to kiss the bruise he'd caused on her face. She winced with the pain. He rested his forehead against hers and whispered, "I'm sorry for hitting you. I really am." His lips brushed the place his forehead had been for one last sweet kiss. "I do love you, and I probably always will. Goodbye, Caroline."

Her heart broke a little as he walked away.

FORTY

Caroline sprinted up to her room thrilled to be there again. For the first time in four years she was finally in a place she wanted to call home. She traced her finger over Rachel's initials etched into the window glass. On the drive back to Golden Meadow with her dad, Caroline mentioned she'd like to visit Rachel's grave. She didn't know if Rachel would ever come to her in her dreams again, and thought it would be nice to say thank you and goodbye. Eddie agreed.

Caroline whispered a thank you as she lay a single red rose at the base of the regal angel-topped tombstone. Rachel had saved her life as much as Cade had, and for that Caroline would be forever in her debt. As the sun descended behind the tomb, shadows from the elevated angel's wings fanned across the ground creating a spooky pattern.

A tremor crept up her spine. All this ghost stuff still freaked her out and she wondered if she'd have anymore unexpected visits from the spirit world. A little pep in her step propelled Caroline's return to Eddie's truck so she could get away from the cemetery before dark. Just in case.

Caroline shivered again as she recalled her final visit with Rachel. She rubbed her finger across the initials once more before her gaze shifted out over the duck pond. The statue of the Virgin Mary that had been strategically placed close to the edge of the duck pond was now in dead center. She chuckled, certain Cade had been the one to move it.

The door knob jiggled behind her and she made eye contact with the piercing blue eyes she had come to loathe during the past few months. Interesting that her eyes were the same exact shade of blue as Trevor's, which Caroline had loved so much until now. April's shocked expression amused Caroline.

"What the hell are you doing here?"

Caroline forced a grin. "Nice to see you, too."

"Aren't you supposed to be on your honeymoon?"

"Nah, I changed my mind." She shrugged, nonchalantly.

April flustered over the extreme change of plans. Her face crumpled into a confused frown. "W-what do you mean you changed your mind?"

"That's exactly what I mean. I changed my mind. Now, if you don't mind, I'd like to get settled into my room, again."

"Actually, I do mind. What do you think you're doing here?"

As sarcastically as she could manage, she cheerfully answered, "I'm going to live here now. Aren't you so glad? We can be BFF's."

Daggers shot from April's eyes. "Shouldn't you be living with your husband? What does your father say about this?"

She clearly hadn't heard what happened at the wedding. "My father is the one who drove me back here. By the way. . .I missed you at the wedding."

She stumbled over her words now. "Well, I-I had—where's Trevor?"

"Tell me again why that's any of your business?"

April stepped up to her and narrowed her eyes. "Listen here, you little tart! You should mind how you talk to people." Close enough to have a good look, she scrutinized Caroline's face, zeroing in on the place Trevor had struck her. "You never know what someone could be capable of."

"Why, April, that sounded dangerously like a threat. Maybe it's you who should mind how you talk to people."

"No, sweetheart. You have no idea who you're dealing with." She turned on her heel and headed out the door.

Caroline cracked her knuckles. She'd like to show April what she was capable of. The days of shy, weak, too-afraid-of-confrontation Caroline were over. She'd turned a new leaf and things would be a lot different from now on. Better. She cradled her cheek, thankful the swelling went down quickly and the bruising minimal.

She went back downstairs to see if Eddie needed any help with her things. Outside, her heart jumped into her throat when she saw the broad shoulders and gleaming face. Cade rushed up on the porch, and swung her around in a bear hug.

"Hey, sweet girl! I'm happy to see you again!" He kissed her cheek, careful not to touch the tender area and admired her face. "You look beautiful. How are you feeling?"

Trying to keep her cool, Caroline couldn't stop smiling. "I'm feeling great. Happy to be single." She took a step back and nervously fingered a lock of her hair. "Thank you so much for doing the research and making the effort to come all the way up there and enlighten me. You were right, that would have been the biggest mistake I ever made. And if you hadn't saved me, yet again, I would probably be attending my father's funeral right about now."

Caroline fidgeted with her cuticles before stating the obvious. "I can't believe how quickly Trevor turned on me. Everyone tried to warn me, but I wouldn't listen. So, thank you for being persistent enough to finally get through just in time. I honestly don't know what I would do without you in my life."

"Sweet Caroline, it is always a pleasure to come to your rescue. He's lucky he had so many witnesses present, that's all I gotta say about that." He stroked his finger along her jaw. "I'm just grateful you were willing to listen to what I had to say on such an important day. I can't tell you how excited I was to see your car here." Cade casually leaned against a large white column and crossed his ankles. Caroline admired his relaxed pose and billboard-worthy looks. So handsome. "So how long do you get to stay this time? When do you have to be back for class?"

She smiled and looked down at her feet. Bashfully, she tucked her hair behind an ear. She hoped he hadn't caught her fantasizing about him. "Well, I was getting tired of living around a bunch of Yankees, so I thought I might stick around here for a while."

Cade's jubilation was priceless. "Yeah? A while? How long is that, exactly?"

"I was accepted to the nursing program at LSU. I don't start till the spring, so I have a little time off to take a breather and relax." She smiled sweetly. "You don't know anyone around here who could show me around, do you? Someone to teach me the dialect?"

He smirked. "I'm sure I can dig up some poor yahoo to do the job." He gently kissed her cheek again and one corner of his mouth curved into a grin. He ran his fingers through her hair and cradled her face in both hands. "If it's too soon, let me know, but I heard you weren't engaged anymore and I've been dying to kiss those lips since you walked out that door."

Caroline's cheeks burned prompting a playful grin from her real life hero. "That's the rumor. I am currently unattached and free to kiss anyone I'd like."

"Yeah?" he whispered as he leaned in slowly.

Caroline nodded, overcome with desire and unable to answer. Her eyes closed, lips parted, and all at once she was swept away with a sense of freedom and elation as Cade reminded her of his passion and feelings for her. When the kiss ended, Caroline's head buzzed with pheromones and she felt lightheaded, but Cade didn't seem affected. Disappointment struck thinking she didn't blow his mind the same way he did hers.

"You hungry? I know a place that's got some really good gumbo," he said breathlessly.

Never mind. Caroline smiled triumphantly and her mouth watered with just the thought of that savory gumbo. "Are you kidding me? I've been suffering withdrawals." She didn't mention he was part of those withdrawals.

Cade drove them to Dupree's where they slurped down the scrumptious food, engaged in nonstop conversation. He explained how he found all the information about Kenneth Callahan and the family. Caroline told him about her amusing interaction with April that afternoon.

"You know, the strange thing was her genuine shock to find me in that room. Forgive my pun, but she looked like she had seen a ghost."

Cade let out a bellowing laugh. "That's a good one. I wonder why she was so surprised."

"Well, she asked me why I wasn't on my honeymoon and didn't understand why Trevor wasn't with me. She then went on to threaten me after I got snippy with her. I told her it was none of her business, and she shot me a warning look as she said, 'You should mind how you talk to people because you never know what—" Caroline stopped mid-sentence with an epiphany. "No! I can't believe it! I can't believe I didn't see it earlier!"

"What is it? What didn't you see earlier?"

"April! She's the one! She's the one behind it all. She's got to be. She's the enemy right in front of us that Kenneth was talking about!" Excited now, Caroline asked, "Do you know anyone on the police force here in town?"

"Yeah, I have a few buddies from. . .a previous job who are on the force now. Why?"

"Can you give them a heads up that we may need them on a moment's notice?"

Cade smiled, accomplished. "I already did that, love. All I have to do is send one of them a text and they'll be on their way. You gonna tell me what's going through that crazy mind of yours, or are you gonna keep me guessing?"

She stood and asked if there was a place she could buy a tiny voice recorder.

"I have something like that. What are you up to?"

She blinked at him. "You have something like that? Really? Just lying around?"

He smiled and stared down at his drink. "I have some surveillance equipment on hand, yes. Why?"

"I am going to try to bust April and get that lying heifer to confess her sins. I need to be able to inconspicuously record it though."

Cade sounded skeptical. "Are you sure April has the intelligence it would take to pull off something that clever? Even if she contrived all this, what makes you think she's going to tell you anything? She despises you, she's certainly not going to trust you enough to confess anything."

"I am pretty good at provoking her into saying more than she should. I'm going to try to make her mad enough that she blurts something out or incriminates herself in some way."

Cade shook his head. "I don't know, cher. She just doesn't seem like the type that would be able to come up with an idea like that. She's kind of ditzy. Besides, why would she care about Eddie's inheritance? She signed a prenup."

"You're right, she did. Even if she did want to kill Eddie off, she wouldn't get anything out of it but some money. Maybe Kenneth was willing to pay her some of what he got out of it?"

"Now you're reaching for straws, love. I don't think Kenneth Callahan knows how to share money."

Caroline shrugged. "Yeah, maybe you're right. I just wish we could figure out what Kenneth meant when he said Eddie had enemies all around him. Who?"

Cade took a long gulp of water and leaned back in his chair. "Maybe he just said that to get the focus off of himself? Maybe he was simply trying to freak us out since we made a public spectacle of him and his son?"

"Yeah, you're probably right." Caroline's shoulders sagged. She was sure she'd figured it out. "April is sinister enough, but I doubt she's smart enough to be the mastermind of any operation. She's just plain mean."

Cade leaned forward and stared into her eyes. "Enough about her. Let's talk about you."

"Yeah, because I haven't been in the spotlight enough over the last few weeks."

Cade chuckled. "You've been through a lot this summer. How do you intend to spend your semester off?"

Caroline stared at different focal points on the walls as she really thought about the answer to that question. "I'm not sure. I think I would like to learn everything I can about the area. I would love to learn the language you speak sometimes with your friends, that way I'll know when you're talking about me." She winked and he playfully shook his head, smirking. "I would also love to learn how to cook some of this delicious food you guys have down here, and I'm definitely in love with the coffee."

Cade's eyes sparkled. "Sweet Caroline, I will make it my mission to see that you accomplish your goals." He smiled and kissed her cheek.

Once the word spread Caroline was staying for the long run, Eddie hosted a party in her honor. He called it a Fais dodo and said it's a southern Louisiana tradition anytime there's a celebration. The house overflowed with people she'd never met, but somehow they all seemed to know her. Cade stayed by her side the whole night. April opted not to attend Caroline's homecoming party, most likely because she was anything but excited about her return. She claimed to have not been feeling well and stayed in her room.

Claire was surprisingly the life of the party. Eddie had rented a karaoke system, and Claire quickly became the entertainer of the evening. Her beautiful voice prompted massive applause in which she relished after each song she sang. Cade stayed true to his word and brought his cousin, Josh, to meet Claire and they immediately hit it off.

Eddie kissed Caroline's cheek. A handsome man, he had a very distinguished look about him, especially when dressed nicely in this relaxed setting. He practically glowed with happiness. "How are you enjoying your party?" Cade excused himself so she and Eddie could talk.

"It's lovely. Thank you. I can't get over the lights and decorations. It's a great surprise. I am feeling very special."

His infectious smile lit up his whole face. "That's what I was hoping for. You are very special to many people around here."

She raised her glass to her lips. "Yeah," she mumbled, "except April." Listening to Claire sing a Faith Hill song, Caroline had at least four different people she didn't know approach her and ask if she and Cade were a couple. One elderly lady even asked if they'd set a date yet! Caroline wouldn't mind being his girlfriend someday, she looked forward to it, in fact, but frankly she was perfectly happy to be single and free for a while and able to do whatever she wanted. Caroline was in no rush to jump into another serious relationship.

Cade sidled up beside her and whispered in her ear. "Need some fresh air?"

"You have no idea."

The fresh air was thick with moisture, but a revitalizing breeze rustled through the trees. They strolled to the duck pond. Chirping crickets harmonized with the bullfrogs and lightening bugs blinked across the lawn.

"You okay?" Cade asked.

"Sure."

"That's convincing," he said as he kissed her hand before helping her off the path to cross the grassy area.

"Why does everyone think I have to be with someone to be happy? Why can't I just be single for a while without someone poking a nose in my business telling me about a friend or cousin they can set me up with? I've been through enough mistakes and drama lately."

Cade's eyelids flickered with disappointment.

"Present company excluded," she mumbled.

He grinned. He enclosed his comforting arms around her and gave a little squeeze, but didn't let go. "I know you've been through hell, and, believe me, I wish there had been something I could have done to make it easier for you."

With one finger he brushed a strand of hair from her forehead. "I also know that you are in no rush to jump right into another relationship." She nodded, and, when he didn't continue, she looked up into his eyes.

"What I want you to know is that I am a very patient man. I will be here for you always, for anything you may need or want. I want to be with you, together, as a couple. But I want to make sure you're ready before it happens. I'm here for the long haul, so don't worry about me. I'll be around whenever you're ready. In the meantime, I will thoroughly enjoy spending quality time with you as your friend and nothing more. Well, I may steal a few kisses every now and then if you'll let me."

She laughed, and he smiled, playfully kissing the tip of her nose. She wrapped her arms around his neck and gave him a soft slow kiss. Gradually, the kiss deepened, turning hot and passionate. She'd forgotten how good he was. He ran his fingers up through her hair, squeezing the tendrils and tenderly cradling her head in his palm.

She wanted Cade and everything he had to offer, but she needed a little time to adjust to being without Trevor. Guilt about leaving him at the altar riddled her, piercing gaping holes in her heart. She'd never intended to end her relationship with him, only postpone the wedding until she could learn more about Kenneth's plot. Although Trevor helped her feel better about that decision when he slapped her in front of a hundred and fifty people.

Cade reached into his pocket. "I have something for you."

Her heart skipped a beat as she stared at the little box in his hands. She wasn't ready for what she thought it contained. "What is it?"

"Open it. Trust me, you need it." He smirked.

She opened the package revealing a lovely wristwatch. She couldn't help but laugh aloud. "You're right. I desperately need one of these. It's beautiful!" Involuntary tears welled up in her eyes. "Thank you. I love it."

He grinned. "It's not just any watch. It has a GPS in it so you will never lose your way as long as you're wearing it. I can't have you wandering off in the woods and getting lost." He chuckled. "With your luck, you'd get eaten by an alligator."

"You're probably right. That's awesome! I didn't know they even made watches like this."

"They don't. I special ordered it." He shrugged. "I know a guy." They laughed and then his face fell serious. "Believe me, cher, you're worth it."

"Thank you. You're amazing."

"You're welcome." He helped fasten the watch onto her wrist and lavished her with another kiss. He was incredible. So thoughtful.

They should rejoin the party before she was tempted to ravish Cade.

Movement from the corner of her eye caught Caroline's attention. Two people, a man and a woman, sneaking on the fringes of the shadows of the nearby gas lamplight. Instinctively, she crouched behind the bushes.

Without a sound, Cade squatted next to her and whispered, "What are we doing?"

"I see someone, a man and woman, in the shadows. They're talking, but I can't make out what they're saying. Can you see them? Can you tell who it is?"

Cade peeked over the bush and squinted. "It looks like April, but I don't know who the guy is, his back is to us."

April. Figures. Such a hypocrite! Jealous of Eddie showing any kind of affection for her, his daughter, yet slinking around with another man while pretending to be in her room with a migraine. What a conniving, trifling, two-faced tramp. Caroline grabbed Cade's hand. "Well, that's not surprising, the hussy. Come on, let's go back to the party."

He hesitated, trying to get another look at the guy.

"We're wasting our time on her, he's probably one of her booty calls. He must like cold fish."

Cade's eyes widened and he made a disgusted face. "Ew. That's just gross."

Claire had taken a break from singing to dance with Josh. They were dancing so closely, they could've been mistaken for a couple already. Caroline was tempted to yell "Get a room," but thought better of it. Cade looked at Caroline and smiled.

"Looks like I chose the right cousin for Claire."

Caroline stroked his ego. "Yes, Mr. Beauregard. You are quite the matchmaker. What do you say we show them how it's done?" She held her hand out to dance. A circle formed around the two dancing couples and Caroline's cheeks flushed from all the smiling eyes upon them.

Cade never took his eyes off Caroline through the entire dance. Once the song ended he didn't let her go. Instead, he lowered his lips to her and reminded her again of his love for her. His kiss literally took her breath away. . .again. Like magic, they were the only two people in the room, and Caroline couldn't have cared less how many people watched them. For this moment, in her mind, they were the only two people in the world. She moaned in approval, and he reciprocated.

In an extremely sultry, incredibly sexy voice, Cade softly spoke the most romantic words Caroline had ever heard. "Mi aime Jou."

Dazzled but confused, she leaned back to question him. An enchanting smile stretched across his handsome face. "It's Cajun. It means, 'I love you.'"

"Wow. Those words have never made me feel quite like that. I'm in love with the dialect down here." He briefly looked wounded, but recovered quickly. "Caden Luke Beauregard, you are the best thing that's ever happened to me, and I am so in love with you."

He squeezed her closer. "I'm glad you broke into my house that day and caught me naked. Otherwise I may not have ever met you, and that would truly be a tragedy."

Caroline rested her head on his broad muscular chest and listened to the steady beat of his heart. Not one for tragedies, she could totally get used to Cade and his bayou paradise.

While Caroline danced with her father, Cade excused himself to go outside. He peered in the darkness, searching for April and her mystery man. Satisfied with his brief moment of privacy, he pulled out his phone and scrolled through the numbers he had saved in a special folder. He stared at the name from his past. Taking a deep breath, he pressed call. Cade spoke quietly and in short words to make it difficult for anyone listening to understand him.

"Yeah. It's Beau. I need you. When can you be here? Outstanding. See you soon."

He took a deep breath as he hung up the phone, placing it back into his pocket. He closed his eyes, realizing what he was about to do. Dredging up people from his past would surely dredge up buried memories, as well. It was worth it, though. She was worth it.

The End

Thank you for reading *Deadline*, book one in the Bayou Secrets Saga. Though a version of this book was formerly published in 2012, I appreciate your patience and understanding throughout the rewrite and rerelease, and I hope you enjoyed it.

Book 2 in the Bayou Secrets Saga, *Lifeline*, will be released in 2014.

Book 3 in the Bayou Secrets saga, *Flatline*, is in the writing phase and will soon follow. I love and appreciate my readers and apologize for the delay in the publication of this series.

Please follow my website and social media where I will frequently post updates about my progress. Also, if you would be so kind, please leave a review so others may know what to expect, and feel free to contact me through my website to let me know how you liked the first book in the Bayou Secrets Saga.

Sincerely,
Judy McDonough

www.Judy-McDonough.com
www.Facebook.com/JudyMcDonoughAuthor
www.twitter.com/JudyMcDonough
www.goodreads.com/JudyMcDonough
www.pinterest.com/Judy_McDonough

MEET JUDY MCDONOUGH

Judy McDonough is a southern author of the Paranormal Romance series titled *The Bayou Secrets Saga*. An Arkansas native and U.S. Navy veteran, she was stationed in New Orleans where she met her husband, Mike. In eleven years, they've lived in Louisiana, Tennessee, and now reside in Texas with their three young boys.

Judy is a member of the Romance Writers of America and is the publicity chair for the Northwest Houston chapter. Fascinated with the supernatural and haunting elements of the South, her writing style will always include some facet of the extraordinary whether through her characters, their settings, or the situations in which they find themselves.

Though her series is Paranormal Romance, that's not all she intends to write. She believes a vivid imagination should not be limited to only one style, so Judy plans to continue creating powerful, inspiring, thought-provoking stories no matter the genre. Brilliant ideas strike at random times in any glitter-coated form, so she wants to polish those raw gemstones to invent compelling stories.

You can follow Judy through her website and social media outlets.

www.judy-mcdonough.com

AUTHOR'S NOTE

Thank you for reading **DEADLINE,** book one in the Bayou Secrets Saga. Though a version of this book was formerly published in 2012, I appreciate your patience and understanding throughout the rewrite and rerelease, and I hope you enjoyed it.

Book 2 in the Bayou Secrets Saga, **LIFELINE**, will be released in 2014.

Book 3 in the Bayou Secrets saga, **FLATLINE**, is in the writing phase and will soon follow. I love and appreciate my readers and apologize for the delay in the publication of this series.

Please follow my website and social media where I will frequently post updates about my progress. Also, if you would be so kind, please leave a review on Goodreads and Amazon.com or Barnes and Noble.com so others may know what to expect, and feel free to contact me through my website to let me know how you liked the first book in the Bayou Secrets Saga.

Sincerely,
Judy McDonough

8057757R00238

Made in the USA
San Bernardino, CA
28 January 2014